BROKEN HEROES

EVIE JAMES

ISBN eBook 979-8-9901969-3-3
ISBN Paperback 979-8-9901969-4-0
ISBN Audiobook 979-8-9901969-5-7

Cover and Book Design: Evie James
Cover Photographer: Michelle Lancaster, @lanefotograf
Cover Model: Cooper Black, @captaincblack

THREE SIDED
PUBLISHING, INC.

Publisher Contact:
Evie.James.Author@gmail.com

Love is not about being perfect,

but about finding someone who is perfect for you.

~ Evie James

Day Shift - A medical mafia romance with suspense.

When an obedient mafia daughter trapped by a marriage contract smashes into a tree thousands of miles from home, she lands in the care of a fierce, ink-covered nurse with a scarred heart—left with no memories, no past, and no idea who she is.

Constantine, Conan to his buddies, is a happy-go-lucky playboy turned ER nurse who believes true love is just a fairytale. In a twist of fate, a beautiful woman arrives in his emergency department, unconscious and unidentified. Meeting Jane Doe in her most vulnerable moment, he is inexplicably drawn to protect her, plunging him into a perilous world he never knew existed.

Raised in the shadow of powerful organized crime, Anastasia faces an arranged marriage to a man she despises with death as the price of refusal. She agonizes over a life without affection or personal choices, all while holding dangerous secrets of her own. After a high-speed chase and a devastating crash, Anastasia wakes up in St. John's Hospital with no recollection of where she came from or the threats that surround her. As she grapples with her amnesia, the threat of her ruthless family looms ever closer, putting her and everyone around her at imminent risk.

And as if that's not bad enough, what are the odds that the mysterious woman's family wants to exact revenge on the ER nurse who helped save her life—the very man they seek to settle a score for a previous altercation?

Can they overcome the deadly forces that threaten to tear them apart, or will their budding love story be cut short by the mafia families they are trying to escape?

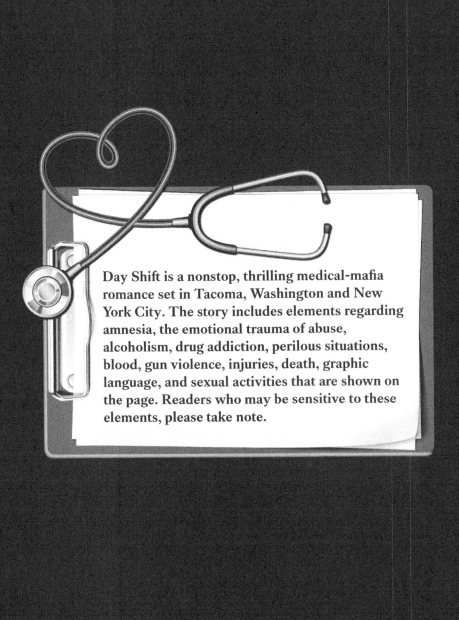

Day Shift is a nonstop, thrilling medical-mafia romance set in Tacoma, Washington and New York City. The story includes elements regarding amnesia, the emotional trauma of abuse, alcoholism, drug addiction, perilous situations, blood, gun violence, injuries, death, graphic language, and sexual activities that are shown on the page. Readers who may be sensitive to these elements, please take note.

Day Shift Official Street Team Playlist

1. "Good Thing" by Zedd, Kehlani
2. "Favorite" by Isabel LaRosa
3. "Fast Car" by Luke Combs
4. "Nothing Else Matters" by Metallica
5. "Say Something" by A Great Big World
6. "You Put a Spell on Me by Austin Giorgio
7. "Good for You" Selena Gomez, A$AP Rocky
8. "Just the Way You Are" by Bruno Mars
9. "The Tortured Poets Department" by Taylor Swift
10. "I Wanna be Yours" by Sofia Karlberg
11. "S&M" by Rihanna
12. "Let the World Burn" Chris Grey
13. "Amnesia" by 5 Seconds of Summer
14. "Battlefield" by Jordin Sparks
15. "Play with Fire" by Sam Tinnesz, feat. Yacht Money
16. "Lose Control" by Teddy Swims
17. "Don't Give Up on Me" by Andy Grammer
18. "Chasing Cars" by Snow Patrol
19. "Take Her Home" by Kenny Chesney

Playlist created by:
    @brooklynlwolves
    @readingwithdesi
    @smutcartel

Chapter One

5/24

Dropping the last of the day's paperwork on my desk, I slumped down in my chair with an exasperated huff. The late afternoon doldrums had set in, and I couldn't help but glance at the clock every other minute. Only fifteen more and I could escape this stifling cage of books and whispered conversations for a couple of days off—the weekend promised freedom.

"Anastasia," my elderly colleague, Marjorie, called out in her perpetually soft voice. "Could you reshelve these returns before you leave?"

"Of course. Happy to help," I said with a tight smile. My heart sank as I eyed the teetering stack of books on the cart she ever so slowly pushed in front of my door. Marjorie was an older woman who had taken me under her wing when I'd first started working at the library. How could I tell her no?

1

Here at the Roosevelt Library, I spent my days drowning in historical and political documents. I was the keeper of countless volumes, each one a testament to past power struggles and societal shifts. For the last six years of my life, I had protected these documents and ensured they remained in good condition so they could enlighten future generations with their tales of political intrigue and historical milestones.

Situated in Columbus Hall on the Eveningside Heights campus of Kennedy University in New York City, this library served as a veritable gold mine for those with a penchant for political science and the city's history, attracting the university's students, faculty, and researchers traveling in from other universities to consult the more unique materials. Right after graduation, the job had practically fallen into my lap, and I hadn't been able to say no. I had to maintain the pretense of being a well-bred, well-educated, well-behaved young woman of society to keep the family happy, and this job served its purpose well. Working at this prestigious university bolstered my résumé in a world where appearances were everything—a necessary evil.

The sooner I finished with my work here, the sooner I could head home and slip into my true self—the one that thrived in the darkness, unburdened by the expectations of family and society.

Methodically, I sorted through the returns, organizing them by call number, and positioned them on the cart, standing on their edges with the spines visible. My mind wandered to the club. It was where my heart was, where I longed to be. The anticipation of spending my weekends running it kept me sane during the long, monotonous hours I spent in the library stacks.

An hour and a half later, as I was finally squaring everything away, Mr. Henley, my boss, came down the aisle and cleared his throat behind me. I was stooped over, digging through the bottom drawer of an ancient-looking filing cabinet, so I slammed it shut and jerked to a standing position.

"Anastasia, locking up soon?" he asked, peeking over his glasses at me.

"Yes, just wrapping up," I said, pulling open the top drawer and slipping the last file into place. My movements were precise, practiced—exhibiting the *responsible employee* facade I had perfected.

"I'm sure you're aware it's more than an hour past closing," he said with a frown. "You need to head on out. Remember, the university frowns on paying staff overtime." With that, he continued moving down the aisle.

"Trust me, I'm more than ready to be out of here," I mumbled, heading toward my small office, where I quickly shut off my computer and gathered my things.

Crossing the library, I headed toward the exit on the north side, which was the quickest route to the 116th Street subway station. I hoped the train would be a little less crowded since it was after seven o'clock.

The moment I stepped outside, New York City's cacophony of sounds enveloped me. Horns blared and people shouted, mingling with the distant wail of a siren. The scent of hot kebabs wafted through the air, momentarily overpowering the familiar odor of diesel exhaust from a nearby food truck.

"Hey, watch it!" a man barked as he bumped into me, nearly knocking me off-balance.

"You watch it," I muttered, not bothering to glance at him.

The subway station came into view. The green light at the top of the subway steps blinked on, as a streetlight illuminated a nearby navy-blue sign displaying the university's name in crisp white Helvetica. Hurriedly, I descended the steps, the ground beneath my feet rumbling with the approach of a train. I swiped my phone across the sensor and pushed through the turnstile, joining the throng of commuters on the platform.

"Stand clear of the closing doors," a disembodied voice announced as I squeezed into the crowded car. "Downtown 1 to South Ferry, next stop one-ten," the conductor shouted over the muffled PA system. Around me, the other passengers stared blankly or tapped away at their phones. Beads of sweat formed across my forehead from the stifling heat.

Soon, the train was jostling along, the sharp screech of metal-on-metal blaring through the car. The overhead fluorescents threw a harsh light on the sea of blank faces around me. I held onto the overhead handrail, leaning against the cool glass of the train doors, my eyes stuck on my reflection—a ghostly image against the fast-moving dark tunnels outside. The rhythmic clatter of wheels became a monotonous rumble, and time seemed to stretch on as I stood there gazing at the window. The dull chatter of passengers blended with the noise of the train, creating an urban soundtrack that was both familiar and soothing.

As the train took us farther into Manhattan's core, stopping and starting to let passengers on and off, my thoughts drifted to the night ahead at my favorite place on Earth. I barely registered the stops before my own, mentally going over the millions of things that needed to be done once I got to the club. The flickering lights outside the window seemed to dance with my wandering thoughts. I anticipated the influential clients I would greet, the music that would fill the air, and the edgy familiarity of the club.

"Next stop, 18th Street," the voice called out, barely audible above the noise of the train. I was past ready for the pulsating beats of Club Xyst, the taste of a strong cocktail on my lips, and—most importantly—the freedom to be my true self, even if just for a few stolen hours.

"Eighteenth Street," the voice announced, snapping me out of my thoughts. The train screeched to a stop, its doors sliding open with a whoosh. I stepped out onto the platform and took a deep breath, the humid summer air smelling like a stinky sauna.

The moment I stepped off the stairs and onto the sidewalk, the familiar sights and sounds of my neighborhood embraced me. Brownstone buildings lined quiet side streets, their stoic facades softened by stoops adorned with potted plants and colorful window boxes. Laughter and music spilled from open windows.

"Hey, Anastasia!" called Mrs. O'Malley from her perch on a nearby stoop. She waved at me and gave me a warm smile. The elderly woman was always there, reading the Times and watching over the neighborhood like a guardian angel.

"Hi, Mrs. O'Malley," I replied, returning her wave as I passed. Home awaited me just a few doors down, its red-brick exterior and wrought-iron railings welcoming me back after a long day at work.

Six steps up, I keyed in my code, then shoved open the heavy wooden door and stepped inside the vestibule separating it from my front door.

As soon as the door clicked shut behind me, I breathed in the welcoming scents of home—waxed wood and a hint of lavender. This was a haven funded by my real father's dubious generosity, a fact I tolerated for the independence it afforded me.

I was quick to kick off my sensible shoes and shrug out of my cardigan, sighing as a cool stream of air washed over my skin. I was eager to leave behind the good little librarian and mafia daughter personas for the night.

By day, I was Anastasia Genovese, a librarian with an impeccable pedigree, trapped in a life mapped out by my family. By night, I was someone else entirely, a woman who commanded the shadows of Club Xyst with confidence and gusto.

Growing up, I had been known as Anastasia Volkov, the daughter of Viktor and Valentina Volkov. My father, a man of formidable stature and chilling brutality, was a powerful Russian businessman. Despite our shared blood, he was as much a mystery to me as the underground operations he ran. The one thing I was familiar with was his callous reputation. He was not a man to be trifled with.

My mother was beautiful yet distant, more an aloof figure than a source of maternal warmth. I struggled to remember any heartfelt exchanges or tender moments I'd ever shared with her. It was as if her capacity to connect on an emotional level was reserved for a part of her life I was not privy to. The only blood relative I had any connection to was my twin brother, Nikolai, who, unlike me, was deeply entrenched in our family's business affairs back in Russia.

My parents had ambitions that soared higher than any skyscraper in Manhattan. Their eyes were set on forming an alliance with one of the most influential American mob families—the Genoveses. The key to this ambitious plan lay with my Aunt Elena, my mother's sister, who had married into the Genovese family. She had hoped to bear an heir to maintain the line of succession since her husband's older brother's injuries prevented him from doing so. Aunt Elena had tried everything to have a baby, but not even IVF had worked for her and Uncle Luca. That's how I got dragged into this.

At twelve years old—when most girls were worrying about getting good grades and impressing their crushes—I'd been plucked from Russia to become merely a chess piece in their political games. Elena had taken me under her wing as my legal guardian and rebranded me as Anastasia Genovese—an American girl with an innocent smile and a last name that bore no trace of my Russian lineage.

I'd left behind one of Moscow's cold, utilitarian public schools to be enrolled in one of the most elite boarding schools in America, the Austen Elmhurst Preparatory Academy for Girls in Upstate New York. It was a place where affluent families sent their daughters off to learn etiquette and social graces alongside algebra and English literature.

After being sent away to boarding school, any semblance of closeness with my mother had evaporated. Our interactions had become sporadic, each conversation feeling more like a formal assessment of my performance rather than a chat between mother and daughter.

Yet despite this new identity and the many miles separating me from Russia, I'd never been able to fully shake off my ties to the Volkovs. My knowledge of my family's illicit dealings was vague and shadowy. For many years, I'd known my father was a powerful businessman, but had no idea he was part of the mafia. That, I had learned more about well after I'd finished college when my aunt had laid out what it meant for my future.

But for now, I just wanted to be like any other American girl. My dreams were big, and I wanted to live life on my own terms. I wanted to be more than just a pawn on the chessboard of mafia politics, more than just Viktor Volkov's daughter or the Morettis' future daughter-in-law. Dammit, I wanted control over my life!

The thought of marrying Frankie Moretti, a man from deep Brooklyn whose personality was as dry and tedious as the financial ledgers he so meticulously managed, loomed over me like an impending life sentence. His role as CFO for the Moretti family had him accounting for the dark money flowing into their coffers, which was buried deep within offshore accounts in the Caymans. To me, spending time with him was about as exciting as watching paint dry.

Elena and my parents had secured an arranged marriage between me and the pretentiously named Francis Aloysius Moretti. It was all an element of their strategy to unite two of the most powerful American mob families in New York.

I dragged my tired feet down the hallway and into the kitchen, tossing my cardigan onto a table between the kitchen and the living room. My stomach grumbled, reminding me I'd skipped lunch in favor of work. Craving something warm and comforting, I pulled out my phone and ordered delivery from my favorite little Italian place just around the corner. A steaming bowl of spaghetti carbonara would hit the spot.

While I waited for my food, I thumbed through the day's mail. Among the usual bills and junk, a thick *Bridal Guide* magazine caught my eye, an unsolicited reminder of the future I was dreading. My fingers clenched around its glossy cover as my skin prickled with irritation. With an indignant huff, I flung it onto the kitchen counter. Just because I was entering into an arranged marriage, it didn't mean I had any interest in planning a wedding.

Sure, I'd resigned myself to marrying Frankie, but I was not about to embrace it with open arms. The thought of planning a wedding, of picking out floral arrangements and choosing color schemes, felt like a mockery of my freedom. It was as if they were asking me to plan my own funeral instead.

I despised this patriarchal tradition my family held dear—this system that treated women like commodities rather than human beings. It wasn't just about not being able to choose the man I would marry; it was about losing control over my life. My future husband had been carefully selected for me based on alliances and power struggles, not love or compatibility.

The whole thing left an acidic taste in my mouth—much like swallowing vomit. The notion that, in this modern age, where women were CEOs and world leaders, I was being bartered off like some medieval maiden for political gain was sickening.

My resentment toward this impending union ran far deeper than mere personal aversion to my fiancé. The arrangement symbolized everything wrong with our family and its dynamics— the criminality we perpetuated and the lives we ruined under the guise of preserving our lineage and power.

I longed for freedom from these invisible chains—freedom from being dictated to by men who saw me as nothing more than a tool in their quest for power. But for now, playing along seemed to be my only means of survival. My mother had made it clear that, if I wanted to remain breathing, I would marry Frankie and give them no trouble about it.

I opened my phone and scrolled through my planner, forming a mental checklist of everything I needed to do at the club tonight. As the business manager, I had several tasks to complete: reviewing the night's VIP guest list, checking inventory levels, ensuring proper staffing, and confirming security protocols. The last thing we needed was unwanted attention from the police or the IRS.

Although there was a lot for me to get done, tonight also held the promise of pleasure. I hoped Lucian would be interested in more than just working. Our no-strings-attached arrangement allowed us to let off steam in the most delightful ways and was exactly the kind of release I needed after the week I'd had.

There was just enough time before my food arrived for me to take a quick shower. Setting my phone on the counter, I headed upstairs to my bedroom. Here in the privacy of my apartment, I could drop this whole Goody Two-shoes act and relax. This was my sanctuary, a place where I allowed myself to indulge in all the creature comforts I usually avoided. Every piece in this room felt like a well-deserved splurge, making it my little world of comfort.

I began to shed the day's pretense, quickly unbuttoning my blouse. The garment slipped from my shoulders and fluttered to my feet. I shimmied out of my skirt and panties, letting them drop to the growing pile on the floor.

With a sigh, I stepped into the shower, where the warm water washed away any remaining traces of my day job. Steam filled the bathroom, blurring the edges of reality as the water drummed against my skin. A little shot of adrenaline coursed through me at the thought of who might show up at the club tonight. We often hosted actors, artists, and political elites who enjoyed a night out in an exclusive venue where cameras couldn't follow.

Lucian would be there tonight too, which usually meant the night would be more entertaining. His smoky gaze had a way of sending fire through my veins, and his touch never failed to deliver exactly what I needed.

Club Xyst wasn't just a business venture for me; it was an act of rebellion. It was my declaration of independence wrapped up in velvet ropes and champagne-soaked celebrations. Every night spent within its walls felt like stolen time—hours snatched away from sleep and gifted to pleasure instead.

And I loved every moment of it—from managing its operations to mingling with patrons who knew nothing about the club owner's double life. The thrill that surged through me as I observed deals being sealed behind closed doors matched no other high.

Sleep deprivation? That didn't bother me one bit. Compared to living a life shackled to a suffocating heritage, it was no contest. As long as I had Xyst, I had a taste of autonomy, and that was worth every minute of lost sleep.

I wrapped a towel around my damp hair and slipped into a silky robe, reveling in its softness as it slid over my skin. The intercom buzzed, announcing the arrival of my dinner. Eager to see my favorite delivery boy, I buzzed him in and hurried to the vestibule. With a wide grin, I swung the inner door open.

"Hey, Elliot," I greeted him, a bit breathless. "You're right on time, as always."

"Uh, hi, Ms. Genovese... Anastasia," he stammered, his cheeks flushing a brilliant shade of red. He held out the bag of food, his hands shaking ever so slightly. His father owned the Italian restaurant I often ordered from. It had immediately become one of my favorite places as soon as I'd moved here after graduation. I could remember when Elliot was just a thirteen-year-old boy in braces with a goofy haircut. He was currently home from college for the summer. Even after all this time, he was still a sweet guy. And although he had grown up a bit, he still got bashful around me.

"Please, call me Ana," I purred, tilting my head and giving him a cheeky little side-glance. "Everyone else does. So how's school going?"

"Okay...Ana," he managed to choke out, still blushing furiously. "School's good. I got all A's second semester." He shrugged, but the note of pride in his voice was obvious. "Here's your order: spaghetti carbonara and garlic bread. I added some tiramisu for dessert—on the house." His eyes roamed from my bare toes up to my eyes as he handed me the bag.

"Perfect, and thank you for the sweet treat," I said, taking it from him and letting my fingers linger on his for a moment longer than necessary. "How much do I owe you?"

"Um, it's twenty-seven fifty," he replied, his eyes darting around nervously.

"Here you go," I said, handing him two twenties. "Keep the change. And good job on those grades. I'm sure your parents were happy with that."

"Th-thank you, Ana," he stuttered, clearly flustered by our interaction. It was amusing how nervous he always was when he brought a delivery. I loved knowing I had that effect on him. It gave my ego the boost it needed.

"Anytime, Elliot. You always know how to make a girl happy on a Friday night." I winked at him before closing the door, leaving him standing in the hallway as my robe swished behind me.

Chuckling, I carried my dinner to the kitchen and poured myself a generous glass of red wine. The rich aroma wafted up, promising a bold flavor to accompany my meal. I took a sip, savoring the taste as it washed over my tongue.

I sat down to eat and wasted no time digging in. Twirling the pasta around my fork, I took a large bite, enjoying the salty tang of the pork within.

The bridal magazine caught my eye, and the irritation from earlier returned. I hated that I only had a little over a month of freedom left. For tonight, however, I would push those thoughts aside and lose myself in the intoxicating atmosphere of the club. And if Lucian was in the mood for a little private rendezvous, well...that would be the cherry on top.

"Let's get this show on the road," I whispered to myself, finishing my meal, feeling all full and warm inside. I glanced at the clock and realized I was running late. So I threw away the takeout container, shoved the tiramisu in the refrigerator, and dashed upstairs.

In my bedroom, I stood in front of my full-length mirror, pulled the towel off my hair, and let my robe fall to the floor. My dark hair cascaded down my back, still damp from the shower.

During the daytime, I had to be the obedient daughter, hiding who I really was beneath layers of restraint. But now that the sun had set and the moon had taken its place, it was my time to shine.

Turning to the mirror over my dresser, I blow-dried my hair and used a curling iron to tame the waves. Then, I began applying my makeup: a smoky eyeshadow and some dramatic eyeliner. I brushed on a deep-red lipstick, which matched my burgeoning confidence. With each stroke that transformed my face, I became more powerful—more like the fierce woman I was known as at Xyst.

Next, I turned my attention to what I would wear. I pulled a slinky black dress from a hanger, the fabric shimmering enticingly in the dim light. The plunging neckline showcased my very average cleavage, making it appear fuller than it was, while the hem stopped just below my butt, leaving little to the imagination. As I slipped into the dress, the silky material caressed my skin and hugged my curves. I wriggled my feet into a pair of sky-high stiletto heels that made my legs look endless and gave me an air of self-assurance.

With one last glance at the mirror, I grabbed my purse and headed downstairs.

Leaning against the kitchen counter, I pulled out my phone and ordered an Uber. While I waited for my ride, my mind drifted to Lucian again. Shivers went down my spine as I thought of how his strong hands always gripped my hips while his deep, breathy moans filled my ears. I found myself growing impatient for this night to begin. I had to relish my independence and live life to the fullest while I still had the chance.

A few minutes later, the Uber pulled up to the curb in front of my steps. I flew out of the apartment and slid into the backseat, mentally preparing myself for the frenzied pace of the club.

Xyst was my one indulgence, a slap in the face to the future laid out for me. It was where I traded whispers with the city's elite, where I was more than just a tactic in my family's strategy. My role at the club, the thrill of the gamble, the dance of seduction—it was me at my most alive. And tonight, like most nights, I was embracing that defiance. It was the only piece of my life that was truly mine, and I'd fight tooth and nail to keep it that way.

I was a boss lady at Xyst, ruling over a domain of nocturnal secrets. And for a few precious hours, I'd forget about the chains waiting to drag me back into my daytime reality.

Chapter Two

5/24

I sat nestled in the backseat of the Uber, tapping my fingers on my knee. The city lights flashed by, painting my skin in a kaleidoscope of colors.

"Take a right here, and make a loop around the block so you can let me off in front of Club Xyst," I directed the driver, not wanting to cross the street when he let me out. The anticipation of stepping into the club was like a heady cocktail that never lost its kick. My little black dress clung to me like a second skin, and in these high heels, I felt invincible.

The car took a sharp right before continuing on the same path I'd taken too many times to count. It took me back to the first time I'd walked into the place. God, how nervous I'd been. It was back when I had just started working at the Roosevelt Library. I had already been feeling suffocated by the monotony of my daily routine and was looking for something to challenge me. Scrolling through job ads on one of the city's local news sites one night, I'd happened upon an unusual listing. By the time I'd finally applied, I'd read the ad so many times that I knew it by heart. *Unlock the Night: Join the Xyst Team Now*—that was the headline that had caught my attention by sheer chance. The unusual ad had continued: *Are you craving excitement beyond the ordinary? Xyst, the city's most exclusive underground venue, is searching for charismatic and daring individuals to join our elite team. Our club members are the crème de la crème of society, indulging in nights filled with unparalleled luxury, hidden gambles, intoxicating rhythms, and mesmerizing encounters. We Seek: Individuals with a flair for drama, a passion for the nocturnal lifestyle, and those who can keep a secret. Become part of something more than just a job. Become part of the Xyst legacy. Are you ready to unlock the door?*

It had piqued my curiosity. And, sick and tired of being the good, obedient daughter everyone expected me to be, I'd applied. Little did I know then that it would change my life forever. Working at Club Xyst had opened up an entirely new world for me, full of excitement and independence. Eventually, I'd covertly used my trust-fund money to buy into the operation, and I hadn't looked back since.

"Thanks for the ride," I said as the car pulled up outside the club's entrance. I stepped out onto the sidewalk, only a few yards from the roped line where people waited to get in. Private members, as well as those who had registered online, could bypass the guy at the door. Anyone else had to wait in line until there was space available.

Music spilled out onto the street as I approached the door. Slade, our bouncer, greeted me with a grin. "Ah, our queen has arrived," he said with a wink. His towering presence made him perfect for keeping unwanted guests at bay, but he had a soft side that only those who knew him ever saw.

"Watch it, Slade," I replied playfully. "You'll give me a big head."

"You're looking heavenly as always," he said, moving to open the door for me while guiding a gentleman to the side with an outstretched arm.

"Watch out, or I might just start believing you," I teased him, returning his smile.

"Whoa, who's this angel?" a man standing nearby asked, eyeing me up and down.

"Sorry, mate," Slade replied, placing a protective hand on my lower back. "She's way out of your league. The lady may look like an angel, but she's wicked like the devil."

"Aw, but I love a challenge," the man protested, smirking at me.

"Good luck with that guy," I said to Slade, laughing and shaking my head as I walked past him and into the club.

The front room was a blur of activity tonight. I strode toward the bar area that ran the length of the left side of the dance floor. Gabriel, one of the other club owners, was pouring a drink with a flourish, his dark hair falling into his eyes. "Anastasia! There you are!" he exclaimed. "Thought you'd never show up."

Stepping behind the bar, I reached under the counter and pulled out the box where we stashed invoices, receipts, and such before taking them upstairs to the office. "Please, you know I wouldn't miss one of my scheduled nights here," I said, rolling my eyes.

"True, true. But hey, better late than never, right?" he said, returning his attention to the cocktail he was preparing for a customer.

"Right," I agreed. With that, I quickly reviewed some of the paperwork in the box. Seeing there wasn't anything urgent, I shoved it back inside and decided to deal with it later.

After tucking the box away, I headed downstairs to the underground gaming room. It was our most restricted area, a place for discreet clientele, secret deals, and high-stakes wagers.

As I entered, I spotted several familiar faces at one of the poker tables. Among them was the governor's brother, who raised his hand to me in acknowledgment. As I stopped next to the poker table, I watched him toy with a stack of poker chips. He let them drop in quick succession, and a rapid, sharp clacking noise resonated from the table. The distinct sound, familiar in the poker scene, signaled tension and contemplation. He repeated the motion, and the chips produced another crisp, satisfying clatter.

"Good evening, Mr. Harrington. A pleasure to see you again," I greeted him warmly. "How's Lady Luck treating you tonight?"

"Ah, Anastasia! Always a pleasure to see you too," he said, his voice dripping with the practiced charisma of someone used to being in the public eye. "And not so good these first couple of hands, but that's all about to change now that my lucky charm showed up. You know, I was just telling these fine folks about the time you took down that arrogant billionaire, Callahan, with three queens."

"Oh gosh, I remember that guy," I reminisced with a grin. "Nothing quite like putting someone in their place." I turned to address the other players—each person/man more powerful than the last—and nodded at one of our congressmen. "Gentlemen, is there anything I can get for you?"

"Another round of drinks would be lovely," replied Marcus Gates, a prominent financier.

"Only your presence at the table, pretty lady," another player chimed in, wagging his brows.

"Flattery will get you everywhere," I said, sliding my fingers along the top of his shoulders. With a wink and a raise of my chin, I signaled one of the servers to come over. "Best of luck to you all."

As I left them to their game, I heard my name over the hubbub of the room.

"Anastasia!" Lachlan, another co-owner, called out again from a shadowy corner behind the bar. I moved through the crowded room toward him, checking on each group of guests and stopping to chat along the way. The beat of the music vibrated through my entire body as I walked.

Eventually, I made it over to him and settled against the downstairs bar, breathing in the rich scent of aged whiskey before turning to survey the room. Club Xyst was alive with energy tonight. Clouds of expensive perfume wafted through the air. Voices deep in conversation boomed throughout the room, accompanied by the vigorous rustling of cards being shuffled and dealt.

"Hey, Lach, how's everything going?" I asked, my voice barely audible over the noise. "Are we making a killing at the tables?"

"Absolutely." He grinned. "The high rollers are in full force, and the house is doing well. We're making a killing at the bar here and upstairs as well," he added in his thick Irish accent.

"Excellent. And how's our liquor inventory holding up?"

"Fully stocked, as always," he assured me. "We're prepared for any party that comes our way."

"Good to hear." I nodded in approval. Then, glancing around, I asked, "By the way, have you seen Lucian?"

Lachlan's smile faded. "Ah, my brother is probably in the office fuming right now."

"Really? What happened?" I asked, concerned.

"Apparently, the New York State Liquor Authority and police are threatening to take away our liquor license," he explained, swallowing as if he were choking down a bitter pill. "Some spoiled twenty-year-old idiot got in here with a fake ID, got absolutely shit-faced, and ended up punching a cop just after leaving the club. The kid was with one of our regulars who swears he thought his younger cousin had turned twenty-one."

"Damn," I muttered, running my fingers through my hair. "That's not good."

"Yeah, Lucian's pretty pissed about it," Lachlan admitted, his expression growing grim. "It's a pretty big mess."

"Yeah, that's a serious situation. Losing our ability to sell alcohol would fucking ruin us," I said, gripping the edge of the bar and chewing on the inside of my cheek. "Well, I'd better go check on him. Thanks for the update, Lach."

"Any time, Ana," he replied, his smile returning.

The lively noise of laughter and conversation followed me as I ascended to the main floor. Here, the dim lights and music created a lively vibe, with the clinking of glasses and murmur of conversations adding to the ambiance. My heels, precarious on the slick hardwood floor, forced me to weave a careful path through the dense crowd to avoid a clumsy fall. The club was filled with an eclectic mix of individuals hanging out and having a good time. A signature aroma—a unique mixture of sweat and alcohol—permeated the place.

"Hey, how's it going?" I asked a group of regulars as I climbed a flight of stairs on the opposite side. Midway up, I turned and surveyed the club. The dance floor pulsed with energy, while the balconies above provided a more intimate setting for conversation and drinks. The club's design never failed to impress me. Each of the four levels catered to different types of pleasures. From intimate lounges to private party spaces, Xyst offered a unique experience to meet our patrons' every taste and desire. The top floor was reserved for our most exclusive members, who also had access to the underground gaming area.

Just as I topped the stairs, someone shouted my name. Damian Jasper, from the band Toxic Romance, called out, raising his glass in salute. I responded with a wave and a warm smile, continuing on my way. I laughed as I thought of a few years back, when he and his band had played gigs here for free on live band nights. Since then, he'd become super famous.

At the elevator on the second floor, a quick scan of my phone prompted the doors to open. I stepped in, pressed the button for the top floor, and was whisked away. The elevator's quiet hum was a familiar comfort after the club's loud buzz.

The doors opened to reveal our private office space. The calm, elegant ambiance here contrasted distinctly with the club's frenzied atmosphere. It was an oasis compared to the chaos below. Aria, our stunning, blonde personal assistant, glanced up from her reception desk and offered me a welcoming smile.

"Hey, Anastasia! What brings you up here?"

"Lucian," I replied. "I heard about the SLA issue."

Aria's smile wilted into a look of concern. "He's in the office, but be forewarned... He's not in the best mood."

"Thanks, Aria." I nodded before moving toward the office door.

I braced myself for what lay behind it. Lucian's Irish temper was not to be taken lightly. But as his friend and business partner, it was my job to help him work through this crisis. And that was exactly what I intended to do.

I knocked lightly, steeling myself for the confrontation ahead. "Lucian?" No response. I hesitated for a moment before turning the handle and stepping inside.

When I entered, I found him brooding by the window, his large frame silhouetted against the one-way glass. The dance floor and bar were visible below, but no one could see us. Lucian had discarded his jacket and rolled his sleeves up like he was preparing for a fight. He clutched his whiskey glass tightly, the amber liquid sloshing around with every strained movement he made. Anger radiated from him like heat from a flame.

"Hey," I said softly, closing the door behind me. "Lach told me what happened."

"Of course he did." Lucian's voice was low and gruff. "Can't keep anything to ourselves in this place."

"Lucian, we're all worried about the club. This isn't just your problem to deal with." I crossed the room and placed my hand on his shoulder, letting out a sigh as my fingers brushed over his tense muscles. "We'll figure it out together."

I leaned in, biting his earlobe playfully, but he stood resolute, with his arms crossed over his chest. I needed to rid him of this menacing attitude and knew just how to do it.

"Let's forget about all that SLA garbage for the moment," I whispered into his ear and slipped my arms around him from behind. Finally, his body relaxed slightly under my touch.

"Anastasia," he exhaled, turning to face me and wrapping his arms around my waist as my hands glided up his chest and around his neck. He let his hands rest on the curves of my hips. The coolness of his glass pressed against my lower back. His dark eyes were filled with a fire that sent shivers down my spine. "You always know how to distract me."

"Is that a bad thing?" I grinned, tracing a finger along the curve of his jaw. The scent of his cologne, mingling with the faint aroma of whiskey, made my head spin.

"Depends on the situation," he replied, smirking. "But right now, I'm in no mood for a distraction."

"Then I'll just have to change your mood," I whispered, pressing my lips to his. After giving me a throaty snarl, he opened for me. My body melted, the heat of his mouth and the taste of the whiskey chasing away thoughts of anything else. I let myself be consumed by it for a moment, but then the muscles of his shoulders stiffened again.

Ignoring his dark mood and taut shoulders, I pulled away a little and bit his lip hard. He jerked back, glancing at me with a mix of surprise and annoyance.

"Not now," he barked. "I have no patience for your antics at the moment."

"Relax, Lucian," I purred, brushing my fingertips along his unyielding shoulders. "My family has connections in the NYPD's sixth precinct—you know, the ones responsible for things here in the Meatpacking District."

I let my words sink in, watching his eyes narrow. His brow furrowed deeper as he considered what I was saying.

"Why else do you think we haven't been given a hard time for our underground gambling operation?" I asked. "They're well paid off, so don't worry. I'll handle it. Someone must not have gotten the memo about leaving us alone. Who knows?"

Lucian stared at me, suspicion clouding his eyes. "What kind of family has that kind of influence? How does a librarian by day know how to pay off cops?"

"Ah, well, my dear Lucian," I said with a playful smile, hoping I looked more confident than I felt, "everyone has their secrets." My mind raced as I tried to come up with a plausible story.

I hadn't told any of the guys about my true background. I certainly hadn't mentioned the arranged marriage contract looming over my head, and I wasn't about to get into that right now.

"Let's just say I have a rich uncle who's a politician," I lied smoothly. "He taught me a thing or two about making deals and keeping secrets." I leaned in closer until our breaths mingled in the air between us, whispering, "It's amazing what you can learn when you're quietly sitting at dinner and people forget you're there."

Lucian studied me for a moment, his gaze intense enough to set my skin on fire. Then he sighed, loosened his grip from around my hips, and took a sip of his drink.

"All right," he finally conceded, his voice low and rough. "I'll trust you to handle it. Just don't let this come back to bite us."

"Trust me, Lucian," I assured him, giving him a quick kiss. "I have no intention of letting anything jeopardize what we've built here." But as I stepped away, I worried that I might have overpromised on what I could do. Surely Uncle Luca would help me. It was his area of expertise, after all. At least I hadn't slipped up and told Lucian I came from a mob family. For now, my secrets were safe, and that was all that mattered.

He shifted his attention back to the bar on the other side of the window, knocking back the rest of his whiskey and running his thumb across his bottom lip, glaring at some unseen enemy. "You know if we lose our ability to sell alcohol, we'll lose this place. Everything will go up in smoke. This is no joke, Ana."

"Lucian," I said, stepping forward and tugging on his arm. "You need to snap out of this. Seriously, I will work it out. Why are you being such a jerk tonight? Love the confidence you have in me...*not*." I tried to slip my arms around his waist, but he shifted to the side.

"Leave me be, Anastasia," he grumbled, refusing to look at me, his worry holding him hostage.

But I wasn't about to let him wallow any longer.

"Enough!" I shouted, jerking him around and shoving him back so forcefully it caused his glass to fly from his hand and hit the floor with a thud. Stumbling back, he landed hard on his ass atop the large desk. The impact sent papers and office supplies tumbling to the floor, but I didn't care.

"Anastasia! What the hell are you—"

His protest died as I climbed on top of him, placing a knee on either side of his hips and pressing my lips firmly against his. His breath hitched, and his cock hardened beneath me as I ground against him.

"Ana..." he whispered, pulling away. But a hint of lust was beginning to replace his anger.

"Shut up and kiss me," I ordered.

Our mouths collided, tongues tangling and exploring with raw, unrestrained urgency. He slid his hands up my thighs and under my dress until he was gripping my waist tightly. While his fingers dug into my flesh, I devoured his mouth. With a low growl, he pushed me back and yanked off my dress in one swift motion, leaving me exposed in just a lacy black thong and sexy stilettos.

"Like what you see?" I teased, smirking at the way he raked his gaze over my body. Desire burned hot in his eyes, and I knew I had his full attention now.

"God, yes," he admitted, pulling me close and capturing my mouth again, biting and sucking on my lower lip. He trailed kisses down my throat, nipping at my pulse point before moving on to my breasts. I gasped when he sucked one nipple into his mouth while pinching and rolling the other between his fingers.

The sensation sent shivers down my spine, and warm wetness pooled between my legs.

"Damn, Ana, you're making such a mess on my pants," he huffed. I simply grinned and pressed myself against him even harder, grinding my hips against his erection.

"Can't help it," I replied breathlessly. "It's all your fault."

With a sudden surge of strength, Lucian lifted me off his lap, turned, and dropped me on the desk. The sudden impact sent tingles up my spine. Yanking me forward until my butt was at the edge and my legs dangled over the side, he wasted no time dropping to his knees. He gripped my inner thighs and used his elbows to spread my legs wide. Pulling my thong aside, he dove right into my swollen folds.

"Lucian," I gasped, clutching the edge of the desk as his tongue darted out to tease my clit. He knew exactly the best ways to touch me, swirling and flicking his tongue with all the right moves. My hips bucked against his face while he slid two fingers inside me, pumping them in and out in rhythm with his tongue's movements. The sensations were overwhelming, and I was close to coming apart.

"Please, don't stop!" I begged as the pressure built deep within me. His fingers curled, hitting that sweet spot that made me see stars. He intensified his efforts, driving me higher and higher until finally, I shattered, screaming his name as waves of ecstasy crashed over me. He continued to lap at my juices, prolonging my orgasm until I could hardly breathe.

When I had come down from my high, he stood, licking each of his fingers clean, a satisfied expression on his face. "Ana, you taste like the sweetest sin," he said, his voice rough with desire.

He unbuttoned his pants and shoved them and his boxer briefs to the floor. Stepping out of them, he made quick work of removing his tie and shirt. I stared, mesmerized by his tanned, muscular body and broad shoulders. His abs rippled with every movement. He was a masterpiece, sculpted by the gods. His drop-dead gorgeous build, coupled with his thick Irish accent, made me putty in his hands.

"God, you're so hot," I whispered, running my hands over his chiseled chest before reaching down to stroke his hard cock. "I want you to fuck me, Lucian. Let out all your anger on me."

His eyes flashed with lust before he leaned down to press his forehead against mine, inhaling deeply. His hands gripped my hips, and the tip of his cock pressed against my entrance, teasing me.

He moved to place kisses against the sensitive spot behind my ear, then tangled his fingers in my hair before he pressed his lips to mine with a bruising intensity. The taste of my own arousal lingered on his lips, mingling with the intoxicating scent of our combined desire. His strong arms hoisted me up, and I instinctively wrapped my legs around his waist as his throbbing erection nestled against my core.

"Tell me how you want it," he growled, his cock straining against me.

"Hard and fast," I commanded, my eyes locked onto his. "I want you to release all your pent-up angst. Show me how much you want me."

His eyes darkened as a predatory grin spread across his face. This man was ready to claim me completely.

Lucian flipped me over on the desk with a sudden force that made my pulse quicken. My face and breasts were pressed against the cool surface as he held me in place with one hand splayed over the center of my back. He positioned himself behind me, giving my ass a couple of firm smacks. I gasped, my fingers desperately seeking traction on the surface of the desk. He wasted no time seizing my hips and plunging his cock inside me. Oh, how I relished the delicious way he stretched my walls as his length filled me completely.

"Fuck!" I groaned, feeling every inch of every stroke. His fingers dug into my flesh almost painfully, the edge of the desk biting into my hip bones each time he slammed into me. His raw power only served to heighten my pleasure. Lucian didn't hold back, thrusting into me with an aggression that left me breathless and wanting more.

"That's it, Anastasia. Take it like a good girl. Let me hear how much you want my dick," he commanded as our skin slapped against each other. I moaned in response, loving the way he dominated me like this. As his thrusts grew faster and harder, my breasts slid back and forth against the smooth surface of the desk, my nipples growing sensitive from the friction.

"More!" I cried out, desperately craving the sweet torture he was delivering. Lucian obliged, raking his nails along my spine before gripping my hair and pulling my head back, exposing my throat to his hungry mouth. He nipped and sucked at my sensitive skin, leaving a trail of possessive marks that sent tendrils of electricity coursing through my veins.

As his relentless pace continued, the familiar coil of tension built within me once more. His arm snaked around my waist, and my breath hitched when his fingers dipped between my legs to find my throbbing clit. He rubbed tight circles around the sensitive bundle of nerves while continuing to fuck me from behind, driving me toward the edge of sanity.

"Lucian... I'm gonna come!" I gasped, clutching at the surface of the desk for support as my legs trembled with need. In response, he increased his pace, working his fingers in tandem with his cock to send me spiraling to the edge.

"That's it, come for me, Ana!" he commanded, and I obeyed, my orgasm ripping across me like a wildfire, leaving me breathless and shaking. My walls clenched around Lucian's cock, and with one final, deep thrust, he groaned my name and released his hot cum inside me.

As our entwined bodies shuddered with the aftershocks, he collapsed onto my back, pressing his forehead against the slick skin between my shoulder blades. We panted, a tangled mess of limbs.

"Anastasia," he whispered, lifting his head and pressing a gentle kiss to the nape of my neck. "You're incredible."

"I like it when you're angry," I replied, a smug grin on my face. He chuckled, his belly rumbling against my back.

The moment he pulled out and the cool air hit my sensitive skin, I spun around and pressed my lips onto his, twining my fingers behind his neck. Our kiss was soft and slow this time, a contrast to our rough encounter. When we separated, I was relieved to notice that the darkness in his eyes had receded, replaced by a playful glint. "Yeah, I needed that," he said, giving me a swat on the ass.

There was no time to linger though. The club's needs always took precedence, and we both knew the rules—just pleasure and release for both of us and then back to the business at hand. It was an arrangement that worked perfectly for our needs. I'd made it clear that whatever we did together would end the minute either of us started to catch feelings. When we first met, we had tried to ignore the sexual tension between us, but that hadn't lasted long. Since my freedom had an expiration date, I'd made sure to tell him up front that I had no interest in any sort of relationship or complicated feelings, that whatever happened between us would just serve to meet our needs at the moment. I'd never forget his reaction—first a stunned expression, followed by a huge smile. He'd told me he had recently gotten out of a relationship with a girl who was beyond manipulative and a total liar. Some time later, his brother Lach had told me how devastated Lucian had been by her betrayal. So Lucian had eagerly accepted my terms. It was an out-in-the-open sort of agreement we'd made to not only each other, but with the full knowledge of the other guys here at the club. No secrets, no apologies.

"Looks like someone's in a better mood," I teased, stepping away to gather my discarded clothes from the floor. "Already so much happier than when I first walked into your office, huh?"

"Can you blame me?" He smirked, pulling on his pants. "You always know how to put a smile on my face."

"Who wouldn't enjoy having someone like me to let off steam with?" I giggled, sliding my dress over my head and adjusting it back into place.

"True," he agreed, buttoning up his shirt. "We're quite the dynamic duo when it comes to this."

We quickly finished dressing. As I was running my fingers through my tousled hair, Lucian leaned in for one last kiss, his lips lingering against mine for a moment before he stepped away. "I'll catch up with you later," he said, adjusting his tie. "I need to get back downstairs."

"All right, I'll let you know about the SLA issue," I called after him, watching his retreating figure disappear through the office door.

Around 3:00 a.m., the club began to wind down. The patrons filtered out while staff cleaned up. I said my goodbyes to the guys, promising to see them tomorrow night. Exhaustion hung heavy on my limbs, but a satisfied smile played on my lips as I stepped outside onto the sidewalk. My body still hummed from my passionate encounter with Lucian.

I let out a sigh of relief when I noticed that Slade had already hailed me a cab for the ride home.

"Thank you, kind sir," I said cheerfully. He grinned and nodded. He was aware that the only reason I'd be this upbeat at this time of the night was because of my special relationship with Lucian. I didn't care if everyone knew. It was one of the best perks of owning a piece of Club Xyst.

As the car whisked me through the city streets, the adrenaline and excitement of the night dissipated, replaced by the comforting blanket of fatigue. By the time I reached my apartment, all I wanted was to slide between the cool sheets and surrender to a peaceful oblivion.

Once home, I stumbled through the door, kicking off my shoes and shedding my clothes, leaving a trail behind me on my way to my bedroom. The softness of the bed beckoned, and I eagerly collapsed into it, my body sinking into the welcoming covers.

Thoughts of my hectic night swirled through my head in a blur until returning to the fast and furious encounter I'd had with Lucian. Our connection—his heat, our passion, and the unspoken understanding that what we had was strictly for our mutual physical gratification—made me feel powerful. I didn't have any interest in dating. He was up front about any other women he'd been with, and both of us made sure we kept ourselves healthy and clear of any STDs. I chuckled softly into the pillow, wondering if my future husband would question why his so-called virginal wife already had an IUD.

Before sleep finally claimed me, I had one last surge of gratitude for the connection Lucian and I shared, even if it was only temporary. We had our own little world of pleasure, and for now, that was more than enough.

Chapter Three

5/27

The sound of my alarm pierced through the early Monday morning silence, but it barely registered. My head ached from sleep deprivation and the stress of a hectic weekend at Club Xyst. I groaned, cursing the necessity of getting up. My body protested as I dragged myself out of bed and into the shower. I was desperately craving coffee and breakfast that I simply didn't have time for. I had to get moving.

While the hot water beat against my skin, my mind wandered to the events of the weekend. Uncle Luca had come through for me, helping resolve the issue with the NYSLA that had threatened to yank Xyst's liquor license. It had been a doozy of a situation. The drunk kid with a fake ID had punched one of the most senior cops on the force. The cop had wanted to throw the book at us, and it had attracted quite a lot of attention to the club, threatening to unravel everything we'd built. Uncle Luca had stepped in and made sure the issue was swept under the rug. The cops involved would have a fatter bank account and conveniently have no memory of the incident.

My uncle was the only one in my family who knew about my involvement with the club, finding it amusing that I was able to keep it a secret from everyone else. As a powerful second in the Genovese family, he had connections and influence that never failed to amaze me.

It was rumored that he would soon be stepping up as the next Don—the top boss—of the Genovese family. He admired my tenacity and, for reasons I didn't know, had kept my endeavors with Xyst from my parents and Aunt Elena. With his help, the police in the 6th precinct were paid off, ensuring they wouldn't shut down the club's underground gambling operation.

"*Anastasia, I like how you come to me. Trust me. Most of those your age in the family are too afraid to even look me in the eye. Not you. You're a force to be reckoned with,*" he'd told me on Saturday when we met to discuss the liquor license issue. I smiled at the memory.

By Sunday, everything had been resolved. When I'd informed Lucian of the situation, he had raised an eyebrow, clearly amazed and curious—maybe even a little suspicious— about how I'd taken care of the matter so quickly. But, as usual, I'd just played it off as having good political connections. Thankfully, he hadn't questioned me further.

Once I finished showering, I dried my hair, applied a bit of makeup, and dressed for my library job. It was so annoying to have to wear my conservative attire after spending the weekend at Club Xyst, but it was necessary to maintain appearances.

As I stood in front of the mirror, adjusting my cotton blouse and skirt, I couldn't shake the dread that accompanied putting on my "good girl" persona.

"Back to the grind," I muttered, grabbing my bag and heading out the door.

The subway car rumbled beneath my feet as I clung to the pole, my fingers tapping an impatient rhythm. The guys at the club didn't know today was my birthday, and my parents and Aunt Elena, cold and selfish as they were, never celebrated it. The only person on this planet who truly cared about me and made me feel special was the man who shared my birthday—Nik. He was the only one who had ever loved me unconditionally, and we had been inseparable growing up. But that had all changed when I was sent to America to live with Aunt Elena under a new identity. That day marked the end of our childhood together—when we were ripped apart and sent down separate paths. I'd been shipped off to America while Nik remained in Russia. The Austen Elmhurst Preparatory Academy for Girls had become my prison, a place where I was forced to learn how to be a prim and proper socialite—a role I despised.

As the subway lurched forward, I stifled a yawn and considered finding a quiet corner in the library for a catnap once I got there. I'd barely slept over the weekend, and now exhaustion threatened to consume me.

The one good thing I had to look forward to today was seeing Nik. Although we were normally separated by a great distance, he never failed to show up on our birthday.

My mind wandered back to our first year apart. I'd struggled to adjust to life in the US. It had been such a lonely time for me. I hadn't spoken English at first and was totally unfamiliar with

American culture. On our thirteenth birthday, Nik had appeared out of nowhere at my school. He had somehow managed to find his way to Aunt Elena's house, borrow a motorcycle, and ride all the way to the academy.

That year, he'd given me a necklace with a white-gold pendant of a howling wolf. It was part of an interlocking pair. It served as a reminder of who I was and where I came from—that our last name, Volkov, was the Russian word for "wolf." Nik had placed the other half around his neck, declaring it a symbol of our unbreakable connection, not just as twins but as protectors of each other. We were akin to wolves who fiercely guarded their pack. This pendant, still resting close to my heart, was a constant reminder of our loyalty and the formidable bond we shared. It served as a powerful tribute to the fact that we were forever intertwined.

"This is one-sixteen; next stop one-two-five; stand clear of the closing doors!" the conductor announced, snapping me back to the present.

"Dammit," I muttered, realizing I needed to get off at this stop. I dashed for the doors, barely making it out before they slammed shut behind me. As I stumbled across the platform, the throng of people was unforgiving, pushing and shoving like a sea of impatience. I tucked my necklace into my shirt before heading up the stairs and out of the station, wondering when Nik would appear and how our birthday would unfold.

"Excuse me," I muttered, elbowing my way through the crowd, eager to get some fresh air.

"Watch it!" someone snapped when I bumped into them. I quickly apologized and continued on my way up the stairs.

Once outside, I navigated the busy streets toward the campus gates. Soon I was making my way across Kennedy University's campus. The scent of freshly cut grass was refreshing as the sprinklers coated each blade in fine mist. A pang of loneliness hit me as I watched the students rush to their morning classes, talking and laughing amongst themselves about their normal, everyday lives.

Genuine connection was something my life lacked. Although I was technically surrounded by people all the time—students here at the university, coworkers at the library, and my friends at the club—I spent most of my time alone. Sure, I'd had some girlfriends at school and in college, but after graduating, we'd all gone our separate ways. I was the only one who'd gotten a job at the university. I hadn't dated much either. It was impossible to explain why I had to remain a virgin for "the family's" sake. How did you tell a guy about mobsters loving their virgins and marriage contracts?

After signing on to work at Xyst and meeting Lucian, I'd gained the self-confidence to say *fuck that*. I at least deserved to experience good sex before getting locked into a lifelong situation with someone I couldn't stand. Lucian was hot as hell and had zero expectations. He was perfect, and although we didn't talk about why neither of us continued to want a no-strings-attached type of relationship, we respected each other, and I trusted things wouldn't get complicated.

"Hey, Anastasia!" a familiar voice called out, interrupting my thoughts. Twisting around, I spotted Sarah, one of my coworkers, waving enthusiastically from a nearby bench, coffee in hand. She stood and hurried to catch up, falling into step beside me. "You look tired! Rough weekend?"

"Something like that. It was nonstop," I replied vaguely, giving her a forced smile. I wasn't about to reveal the true reason behind my exhaustion. "How about you? How was your weekend?"

"Pretty uneventful. You know, the same old, same old."
She shrugged.

We reached our building, and I lugged open the large wooden
door, holding it for her. As she entered, she threw a question
over her shoulder. "Hey, what do you think about joining me,
Josh, and his buddy for dinner on Friday? Kind of a low-key
double date. William's great—works over in the Provost's office
as an auditor. Could be fun, right?"

Internally, I groaned. Not the matchmaking spiel again. Oh,
God, how I hated it when people tried to fix me up. It happened
all the time. Was there something about me that screamed
"desperate for male attention—please, set me up" or what?

"Um, thanks for the invite," I said, "but I've just met
someone, and he seems super nice, so I'll have to pass this time."
I hoped that would politely nip the blind date idea in the bud.

"Really? That's news! What's he like? Do I know him?
What's he look like? Where does he work?"

Great, now I'd opened up a whole other can of worms. "It's
super early on in the relationship, so I'm keeping it on the down
low for now. If it starts to go anywhere, I'll make sure to tell
you all the juicy details." I wiggled my eyebrows and veered off
toward my office. "See you later," I said, making a quick escape.

When I entered my office, I found a box sitting on my
desk, labeled: "New accessions from the Smithsonian" and a
note from Mr. Henley that read: *Organize, review, and enter all
pertinent information regarding these newly acquired documents
into the library's system.*

Curious, I opened the box and rifled through its contents.
I was surprised to discover historical documents from the early
1900s related to the Genovese crime family. I skimmed through
them, intrigued. One was a police file that had evidence showing
they were involved in bootlegging during Prohibition, while

another detailed their alliance with Al Capone. Carefully and methodically, I spent the next few hours examining everything in the box, finding other snippets of information about the family to which I now belonged. One particular document caught my eye. It mentioned how the Genovese family, along with several other mafia families, had been involved in an alliance called the Commission, in 1931. Another stated that Charles "Lucky" Luciano, the founder of the modern American Mafia, had been a prominent member of the Genovese family.

As I scrutinized the documents, I thought of my own family—the Volkovs. I didn't see them often, but when I did, it was either at our estate in Tacoma or at my grandmother's home in St. Petersburg. Although I spoke fluent Russian, my Northeastern American accent always gave me away as an outsider when I visited my homeland. My family had purposefully kept me in the dark about most things regarding the Volkovi Notchi. It was as if they thought ignorance would protect me. Or maybe it was to protect them.

All throughout the day, I kept checking my phone and watching the door, but Nik hadn't found me yet. It was unusual—he was always with me on our birthday. I couldn't shake the feeling that something was off. Maybe he planned to meet me at home? With that in mind, I tidied up my office and left campus.

When I passed by the bodega next to the subway entrance, I treated myself to a small, fragrant bouquet from their outdoor stand. It was my birthday after all. Once I arrived home, I tried calling Nik. No answer. A hint of worry crept into my chest.

I called my mother, only to receive no response. I debated calling my father, but decided against it. He wouldn't care where Nik was if he wasn't doing something for him, nor would he care about anything else I had to say. His apathy toward me was ridiculous.

While I waited there with nothing else to do, I thought about Nik, about how different he was from our father. He despised working for him. It pained me to see him trapped in a life he'd never wanted, but I still had hope that one day, we could both break free from our family's dark legacy.

"Where are you, Nikolai?" I whispered, gazing at the bouquet, which was now in a vase sitting on the table.

Shaking off the worry, I headed to my bedroom and slipped into my comfiest sweatpants and an old T-shirt before coming back downstairs and collapsing onto the sofa. The sketches of my wedding dress from the renowned designer, Isabella Leclair, lay scattered on the coffee table. I picked one up and examined the intricate lace detailing. This dress was the closest I'd ever get to feeling like a princess. At each fitting, the design came more alive. During the final fitting, I'd stood gazing in the mirror, marveling at how glamorous the dress was, with its fitted waist and chapel-length train. The dress would soon be finished and delivered. Despite its luxurious beauty, all I could think about was how getting married would be like slamming the door closed on my own jail cell.

"Broodmare," I muttered under my breath, thinking of how my only purpose in life seemed to be producing heirs and forever connecting three powerful mafia families by blood. I hated everything about this life—the patriarchy, the criminality, and the complete disregard for human decency. My time as a Xyst club owner had given me a taste of freedom, but that would vanish once I was forced to marry.

It was ridiculous that, in today's world, arranged marriages were still a thing. And it was even more pathetic that I was supposed to maintain my virginity. I laughed as I thought of how I'd finally shaken free of that rule and enjoyed every steamy moment with Lucian. Mobsters loved their virgins and trophy wives, but I didn't care. Both the Volkov and Genovese families should be grateful I was going along with their plans and hadn't run off. All I wanted was a life free from the constraints of my mafia legacy. But deep down, I knew running away wasn't an option. They would hunt me down and make me pay.

"Francis Aloysius Moretti," I said out loud, chuckling at the ridiculous name of my soon-to-be husband. Frankie was hardly a catch. He was forty-six, shorter than me, and demanded I wear nothing but flat shoes. The man had a potbelly and never worked out. He was always sequestered in his midtown office, counting the Moretti's millions. Our mandatory Thursday night dates over the past six months had been nothing short of torture for me. All he ever talked about was what other people had and what they were doing, always eager to flash his Amex Black Card at Casa Cipriani. If I ate more than half of the food on my plate, he'd make snide comments about me gaining weight.

"Creep," I murmured, picturing his smug face. I despised him, but I'd been raised for this type of marriage. My mother and my aunt had drilled it into me that my purpose in life was to marry a high-ranking mafia man, and then I could have all the lovers I desired. What a twisted way to live.

After a few more minutes, I headed up to bed and tried to distract myself with a book. But I couldn't focus, and as the evening wore on, I kept glancing at the clock, hoping against hope that Nik would show up. As midnight approached, I reluctantly began to accept that this would be the first time we wouldn't spend our birthday together. At the thought of not seeing him on our special day, a sadness overcame me, and eventually, sleep claimed me.

5/28 early morning

I woke up with a heavy heart, the sting of Nik's absence lingering. I grabbed my phone and started texting everyone in the family.

No response.

Panic began to claw at my insides, and fear twisted my stomach as I got up and tried to start my day.

Something wasn't right.

Gut-churning worry gnawed at me, a relentless beast that refused to be ignored. In desperation, I decided to call Aunt Elena, hoping for some answers. With a sigh of resignation, I pressed the numbers on my phone screen, my fingers trembling slightly.

I told her about Nik not showing up for our birthday yesterday and that he hadn't even texted me. I explained that I'd tried him several times and had even called my mother, who hadn't answered either. Elena didn't seem too concerned, telling me she hadn't heard from Nik in many months. That in itself wasn't unusual, but she hadn't spoken with either my mother or father in weeks, which was indeed strange, considering the wedding was only a month away. Before hanging up, she promised to try to locate them and that she would let me know as soon as she did.

But that wasn't good enough. My gut told me I had to go and try to find him. Surely, there'd be someone at the Volkov estate in Tacoma who could give me some answers, and if not, I'd fly my ass right on over to St. Petersburg. One way or the other, I was determined to connect with Nik.

I called Lucian. "Hey, I need to go out of town for a...family emergency. I'm not sure how long it will be and wanted to give you and the guys a heads-up that I probably won't be able to work this weekend." As I spoke, I tried not to sound too rattled.

His response was immediate, his voice laced with concern. "Ana, what's going on? Is there anything I can do? Tell me and I'll make it happen." His Irish accent softened his tone, adding a layer of warmth that did little to quell my anxiety.

I hesitated, unsure of how much to reveal. The situation was full of potential complications and danger—two things I'd always tried to keep Lucian away from. But he deserved to know why I wouldn't be at Xyst this weekend.

"I can't get a hold of my brother, and he was supposed to come see me yesterday," I began slowly, trying to find the right words to avoid alarming him too much. "There's trouble back home."

"Trouble?" he asked with a note of apprehension in his voice. "What kind of trouble are we talking about here?"

I sighed heavily, wishing for once that life could be simple. "Just family stuff." I meant for my response to come off casually, so as not to worry him too much.

There was a pause on the other end before he responded. "Are you sure you should go alone? I'm not feeling so good about your safety, especially knowing that your family has the kind of connections to make shit like the SLA stuff just go away."

"I'll manage. I just need to find my brother and see what's going on. Don't worry. I should be back in a week," I assured him, attempting to keep the tremor out of my voice despite the nagging fear in my gut. "Just...keep things running smoothly at Xyst this weekend for me, okay?"

After promising him I'd check in later, I ended the call and rushed to book a flight and request an Uber to JFK.

I worried the corner of my mouth with my teeth as I hastily threw my essentials—clothes, shoes, toiletries—into a duffle bag, all in record time. I bolted out of my apartment just as the Uber arrived.

The city lights were still twinkling in the early dawn as we sped toward the airport.

Getting checked in at the ticket counter was a close call. I'd cut it far too close to the departure time. The agent gave me a sympathetic smile as she handed back my driver's license and boarding pass—first-class seat, thankfully—but her kindness couldn't put a dent in my mounting anxiety.

Navigating through security was another hurdle I overcame by sheer force of will. The race against the clock gave me something to think about besides worrying over Nik. I ran through the airport and made it to the gate just as they were making the final boarding call.

As I settled into my seat on the plane, relief washed over me. Soon, however, a gnawing unease started twisting my stomach into knots again. The plane's engines roared to life, and while we ascended, I found myself gripping the edges of my phone, staring at the darkened screen, willing Nik to respond.

Something was terribly wrong—I could feel it in my bones. As the miles between New York and Tacoma shrank, my worry grew. I had no idea what awaited me there. A sense of foreboding clung to me like a second skin throughout the long flight.

Chapter Four

5/28 morning

After arriving in Tacoma, I took an Uber to the Volkov estate on Fox Island. It was still early in the day, since I'd gained three hours traveling west. Windblown police tape greeted me, wrapping around the property like a sinister ribbon. The sight sent chills down my spine. From the looks of it, the tape had been here for months. The lawn and flower beds had been ignored. The grass was knee-high, and weeds were growing out of control. Very strange.

The gated entrance stood open, but police tape blocked any vehicles from entering the driveway. I told the driver to let me out by the mailbox. He looked at me like I was crazy for getting out here in the rain, but I didn't say anything, acting like I'd expected this situation. I gave him a reassuring smile and grabbed my bag before shutting the door.

Confidently, I stepped onto the driveway and ducked under the tape. My heart was racing and adrenaline was pumping, but I made sure to maintain a calm demeanor so as not to arouse suspicion. After idling there for a minute, the Uber driver finally took off.

In the past, there had always been someone here to greet me. I didn't have any sort of key or code to get in, but I knew the place fairly well, so I decided to go around back and break in through a service entrance. I found a landscaping brick in a flower bed and used it to break the door's window and let myself in. Quickly, I shoved my bag into the coat closet and made my way farther into the house. The place was a mess. Broken items were strewn about, and there was not a single computer or electronic device in sight. Meandering through the first floor, memories from my occasional visits here reminded me of how formal and stuffy my relationship was with my parents. Dinners were like dining at a three star Michelin restaurant where casual chit chat was unacceptable. The only good thing about coming here had been hanging out with Nik. When he could get away from my father, we'd always have the best of times. My heart pounded as I dialed Nik's number again and searched the place over, but he never answered.

What the hell was going on?

Suddenly, distant police sirens disturbed my search. They were getting closer by the second. Realizing I must have set off some sort of silent alarm, I bolted for the garage. In my haste to enter one of the cars, my phone slipped from my grasp, clattering onto the floor and into a drainage grate. "Shit," I cursed under my breath, but I couldn't afford to waste time retrieving it. The sirens sounded as if they were nearing the driveway. Breathlessly, I got into the driver's seat of the nearest vehicle. Lucky for me, the keys were in the ignition and the garage door opened when I pressed the button for it.

Torrents of rain lashed at the windshield, distorting my view as I frantically maneuvered out of the driveway and onto the road. How would I ever explain who I was or why I'd broken into the house? A house surrounded by police tape. I had no way of proving I was the daughter of the man who owned the place—a man who operated a crime syndicate. Even if I could prove my true identity, I was bound by secrecy to protect the family and the plans for me to marry Frankie. No, I just needed to get away and hope they didn't follow me.

Of course, I had terrible timing. Just as I turned out of the driveway, police cars descended like a swarm of angry hornets. Panicking, I gunned the engine, making the tires skid against the slick asphalt. The wailing sirens sliced through my nerves, making it impossible to think straight. All I wanted was to get away from them somehow. I'd never been chased, and I was terrified that if they caught me, they'd trace me back to the Volkovs, ruining the many years of hard work everyone had spent developing my new identity.

The rearview mirror reflected a menacing parade of flashing red and blue lights. They closed in fast as I careered down the winding country road. The rain-soaked landscape sped by in a blur of green and gray, but I only pushed harder on the accelerator.

The shrieking sirens and the terror threatening to burst through my chest spurred me to race recklessly through each twist and turn. My knuckles turned white on the steering wheel, my lips trembling from the adrenaline. The world outside morphed into a kaleidoscope of blurred colors and bright lights. Everything was moving too fast.

The car groaned under my command, its tires skidding precariously on the rain-soaked pavement as I pushed it beyond its limits. A sharp turn loomed ahead—too sharp, too unanticipated. I spun the wheel desperately, but it was futile.

Time seemed to slow down. The car careened off course with a screech of protesting rubber, hurling toward an ominous silhouette of a tree looming in my path. At that moment, every detail was amplified—the dreadful crumple of metal folding in upon itself as it met unyielding wood, the shattered glass raining down around me like diamonds.

The airbag deployed with a violent burst, slamming into me like a punch from a heavyweight boxer. It stole my breath away and filled my nose with the bitter tang of burned rubber and powdered chemicals. My body was whipped back and forth inside the car like a rag doll. Then my head smacked into the side window with a sickening crunch. Pain erupted throughout my body like wildfire—raw and all-consuming.

A jagged shard of metal came flying through the window and sliced open my forehead, and warm blood began trickling down into my eyes, blurring what little sight remained. My ribs screamed in protest. Each gasp for air was a struggle between breathing and utter suffering.

As consciousness began to ebb away, the shrill wail of approaching sirens grew louder. The world around me became dim, my body succumbing to the overwhelming pain and shock.

I gave a final shudder before darkness claimed me, swallowing the last vestiges of reality as I slipped away from the chaos and into—

Chapter Five

5/28 morning

"**F**uck!" I banged my fist against the cold concrete wall. I couldn't believe I'd been stuck in this eight-by-eight hellhole overnight and missed Anastasia's birthday for this FBI bullshit. Every year, without fail, I'd been there for her. Now, she was probably thinking I'd blown her off with no explanation. She would think I didn't care, which was worse than any beating I could have taken.

Two days ago, I had landed at SeaTac to handle the last formalities of the transfer of my father's estate trust. As my Pakhan, Viktor Volkov was always entangling me in Volkovi Notchi business. For this particular assignment, my job had been to ensure that all the documents were in order, according to my father's instructions, so they could be signed and made official by the next day when the FBI's seizure would no longer be enforced.

The plan had been simple: verify everything, jump on an early flight to JFK, scoop up the little sis from the library, and celebrate her birthday as she deserved. But no, they'd snatched me right at the airport, just as I was about to board my flight.

Sitting here on this stiff, uncomfortable cot, I chuckled and thought about how Anastasia always rolled her eyes whenever she heard me call her my *little sister*. It was technically true, since I was twenty-two minutes older, but she would argue she was the more mature one.

Thinking about her sitting by herself in her modest brownstone, waiting for me, pissed me off all the more. Long ago, I had promised to always look out for her, protect her, and make sure she was safe and happy. Since the day they'd shipped her off to the States and tried to erase her identity—changing her name as if that could scrub away who she truly was—she had been my responsibility and would remain so until my last breath. Ana was the only one who had ever had my back unconditionally, the only damn person who loved me just as fiercely as I loved her.

Now here I was, wasting time in this dump, trapped by the FBI on some trumped-up charges just because I was Viktor Volkov's son, while she was all alone, wondering why I'd never showed. This was not how I'd planned things to go. Not at all.

Since the age of twelve, I'd been my father's lackey. I'd never gotten a formal education, but trust me, the school of hard knocks had taught me plenty. My father—if you could even call him that—had ensured I'd gotten my hands dirty early on and learned all the devious tricks of his trade. But unlike him, I found no pleasure in the power plays and violent games. Sure, my hands were stained with blood, but that wasn't something I was proud of. I had no choice; if I wanted to stay alive, I had to not only follow orders but also prove my loyalty, which he tested regularly.

But this life, his way, wouldn't be my endgame. I'd been building something on the side, a network of companies. I'd slowly and carefully made my way in this world, establishing my own empire so that Ana and I could rid ourselves of all things mafia. I now had a conglomerate of enterprises. Perhaps they were not all legal in some countries, or squeaky clean, but hell, they were a damn sight better than the shit my father was involved in—drugs, human trafficking, or stealing from any sucker too slow to pay attention.

I leaned back against the wall, trying not to inhale the stench of mildew and sweat that lingered in the cell's air, and thought of my sister again. Ana was the only pure thing in our twisted family. I despised the underhanded scheming of my parents and my aunt, who had traded her happiness for unsavory alliances with American crime families like the Genovese and Morettis. If they only knew that they themselves were pawns in Viktor's grand plan to take over, they'd never have gone along with accepting my sister as blood payment to seal the alliances.

I sighed. God, how I was ready to get out of this cell. It was ludicrous of me to have thought I could avoid ending up in American legal custody. I was Viktor's son and second, after all. Really, I should have expected this. Despite my careful planning and the distance I maintained from Viktor's dealings, his shadow loomed large over my life.

But this was particularly bad timing. And now I'd ruined Ana's birthday.

I was confident the Volkov family attorney would spring me soon. Harrison Tate was the best in the business when it came to mafia transactions. Tate was a sharply intelligent man who had served the Volkov family for years. With a remarkable blend of loyalty and legal acumen, he'd kept much of their empire intact through various crises.

Leaning my head back against the wall, I closed my eyes. All I could do was bide my time.

Soon, the metallic clinking of keys approached. The cell door swung open, and a stern-faced police officer stood there, another officer not far behind him. "Volkov, interrogation room. Now. You know the drill. Hands out in front of you."

I stood up slowly, stretching my limbs as if I had all the time in the world. My movements were deliberate, calculated to show no hint of concern. I held my hands up and pressed them together. He slapped the cuffs around my wrists.

The two officers marched me down the narrow corridor. The echo of our steps bounced off the concrete walls, a reminder that I was their prisoner. As soon as we entered the interrogation room, which felt like a freezer, one of the officers shoved me into a chair next to a lone table under the glaring fluorescent lights. I rested my cuffed hands on the table in front of me and sighed, doing my best to project an image of calm and control. This little game they were playing was irritating—and a waste of my time.

The place was what you'd expect in a city police station: drab beige walls and a dull gray, scuffed-up floor that looked like it hadn't ever seen a mop. On the wall directly facing me was a one-way mirror, underscoring that every move I made was being watched.

"All right, Mr. Volkov," Agent Reynolds said as he strode into the small room, his lips in a thin line and his eyes hard as steel. We'd become acquainted yesterday, right before I'd informed him I wouldn't speak to him without my attorney present. It was then that he'd let me know I'd be staying for a while. "Let's have another chat before your attorney gets you out of here."

He sat opposite me, his eyes boring into mine. His female counterpart, Agent Johnson, joined us in the room, shutting the door behind her.

"You're going to tell us everything you know about your father's plans to reestablish the drug trade here in the Northwest," he said. "We know he sent you to take care of the matter. So, before you get yourself into any real trouble, how about you cut your losses and talk to us? We know you were supposed to meet someone at JFK. Who?"

I leaned back in my chair, crossing my arms. "Go ahead and ask away. Say what you want, but I've got nothing for you. You'll find I'm not my father. I suggest you check your facts before making assumptions about my involvement." I kept my voice cool and met his gaze without fear. I wasn't going to let these FBI agents intimidate me. I'd been on my way to visit Anastasia, so they had nothing on me. "Visiting family. What's wrong with that?" I kept my voice even, hiding the protective surge that raced up my spine whenever I thought of my sister.

"You expect us to believe that?" he pressed, narrowing his eyes.

"Yeah, I do," I replied unflinchingly.

"Your father is a fugitive, Nikolai," Agent Johnson said, chiming in. "And here you are, trying to step into his shoes. Look, we know you're involved in your father's businesses." Her voice dripped with disdain. "So why don't you make things easier on yourself and tell us about Viktor and the Volkovi Notchi's plans?"

"Like I told you before, I was in the UK for the past year, working hard, trying to earn a living." I picked at my nails, smirking at their futile attempts to manipulate me. "I have done nothing wrong, and you know that as well as I do."

"Maybe nothing we can prove yet, but we will be keeping a close eye on you," Agent Reynolds threatened, clenching his jaw.

Just then, there was a knock at the door, and a uniformed officer poked his head in. "Agents, Mr. Volkov's lawyer has finalized his release. He's free to go," he said almost apologetically.

"Looks like my ride's here," I said, getting up from my chair and holding my cuffed hands out. With a huff, Agent Johnson pulled the key out of her pocket and unlocked them. "You two enjoy watching me live my life." I resisted the urge to rub my wrists where the metal had been biting into them.

Leaving that interrogation room was like thawing out after coming inside from a snowstorm—a sudden relief, but it still made you kind of numb. Once the cuffs were off, the officers didn't waste any time guiding me through the busy station at a quick pace. The other staff were all caught up in their own world of paperwork and phone calls, so they didn't pay much attention to me. It was just another day for them, but for me, this was my first taste of freedom in over twenty-four hours.

With minimal fuss, I followed the officer through the maze-like hallways to the processing area. Briefly, we stopped to sign off on my release forms—no charges, no fuss. I barely registered the clerk's monotone instructions as I initialed here and signed there.

Next up was the property room. The officer there read off a list of my items as they were handed back to me: phone, wallet, watch, suitcase, computer case. When this process was completed, I checked each one, starting with my watch. It was thankfully unharmed, so I strapped it on. I then flipped through my wallet, found all my money still there just as I remembered, and shoved it in my back pocket. Next, I checked my phone—it was at fifteen percent battery—and quickly pocketed it. Finally, I examined my suitcase and computer case. No signs of tampering. Still, the relief of having my things back didn't quite erase the sting of having them taken in the first place. With a huff and a shake of my head, I walked toward the door. I'd wasted enough of my day in this place and wanted to get going.

5/28 midday

I met Harrison Tate in the police station lobby. He was waiting with that "I just won" smile plastered across his face. Harrison was a slick lawyer who knew how to play the system.

"Let's get you out of here," he said. "We've got a lot to cover, and you've got places to be." Together, we walked out to where his sleek black X5-M was parked in the pouring rain.

As we drove away, he began updating me on everything related to our family estate on Fox Island.

"With the completion of the trust for your family's estate, including all of Viktor's *legal businesses*, Anastasia is now officially the sole beneficiary, and I am the trustee overseeing it all. Everything has been meticulously cleaned up, reorganized, and made legitimate." He greedily chuckled to himself. "And the best part is, Miss Anastasia has no clue. Your father was a smart man, shipping her off to boarding school, giving her a new identity, and ensuring she was a US citizen. Her reputation as a pretty young socialite will mask any links to the Volkovs. No one knows Anastasia is related to the family. She's a perfect cover."

I wanted to punch the smug asshole right in the mouth. "Nothing of this better come back on her," I said harshly, glaring at him.

"No worries. She's under the protection of the Genovese family—and soon the Moretti family as well. No one will mess with her," he replied casually, as if being in the middle of a mafia crime family takeover was no big deal.

My time was ticking. I had to get us out from under all this mafia bullshit—that is, if I could.

Tate continued to fill me in on what had happened to the estate back in December, after Viktor had taken off. "It was thoroughly searched—ransacked, you could even say. They went through every inch of the property, so assume everything there is now public knowledge. They removed all the electronics too. The place is a mess, really," he said, pursing his lips.

"Good thing I never trust any 'smart' device," I mused. "They're all open to surveillance." There were many ways to listen in on just about any person on the planet. I knew because

I had done it often. My mind raced as I considered all the ways they could have bugged our home. "We need to get rid of everything with connective technologies—TVs, fridges, pretty much everything that runs on some sort of power and has a chip. Plus, I want the entire house swept for bugs."

I'd seen enough in my line of work to be jaded. My company specialized in keeping the world's elite safe from prying eyes, and if I couldn't trust a device, it was as good as trash.

"Ah, I have just the people for that," Tate said, a glint in his eye. "There's a security organization that specializes in such matters, well-known for their prevention of hacking. Their parent company is an outfit called DarkMatter Defense, based out of Kyiv, but they have a large operation here in Seattle."

"Really?" I raised an eyebrow, amused that he was suggesting the very company I owned. That fact—and my status as a world-class hacker—was something I guarded fiercely, even from my father and Tate. "Make the arrangements then. They sound like our best bet."

Tate continued to babble on about security concerns, his knowledge ancient, from a decade ago. I nodded, barely listening. My mind was on Anastasia. I needed to make it up to her for missing our birthday somehow. Scrolling through the ridiculously long list of calls I'd missed while in jail, I came across her name. She had called earlier today and last night. Dammit, she must have been desperate to find me. Of course, she had no idea I'd been sitting in the slammer. I dialed her number, each ring twisting the knot of guilt tighter in my chest.

Voicemail.

"Hey, it's Nik. I'm so sorry I missed seeing you yesterday. I'll explain everything soon. Just...stay safe, okay? Call me as soon as you get this. Love you, little sis."

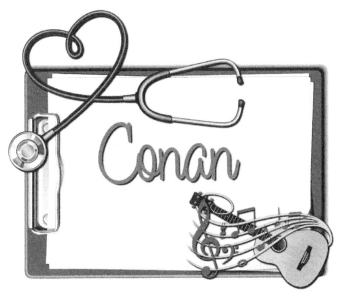

Chapter Six

5/28 morning

At St. John's Hospital, things could change in a heartbeat. One minute we would be doing routine checks, and the next we were in the midst of an adrenaline-fueled emergency. It was all a part of being at a frontline level II trauma center. We always had to be ready for the worst-case scenario, even though we often had long periods of quiet, like right now.

Leaning against the nurses' station, I gulped down my third energy drink of the day, eyes on my brother, Atticus, as he finished up scribbling the last notes on a patient's chart.

"You sure you don't want to switch jobs for a day? I could use a break from all the surgical procedures," he joked, glancing over at me and stretching his back with a theatrical groan. His role as an attending emergency department physician sometimes left him envious of my more predictable nursing duties.

"And miss out on handling all the paperwork and patient hand-holding? Never," I shot back with a smirk, snatching the clipboard from him.

"I'd trade the scalpel for your blood pressure cuff any day. At least you get to sit once in a while," he bemoaned, rolling his eyes as he tucked his pen into his scrubs pocket. Turning away, he pulled the next clipboard out of the rack and headed down the hallway.

"Like all nurses do is take patients' vitals," I snapped, letting out a groan. He just waved the chart in the air and kept on walking. I loved him, but sometimes he could be such a douchebag.

I left the nurses' station and made my way to room seventeen to see my next patient, Mrs. Jenkins. She was an elderly woman who had been admitted several hours ago because of a sudden spike in blood pressure—her reading was 201/104. Not good. Pushing open the door, I paused, taking in her startled expression. It wasn't unusual for patients to be taken aback when they first laid eyes on me. I didn't exactly fit the stereotype of a nurse. My large, muscular frame and the array of tattoos running down my arms and hands often made me look more like a hit man than a healthcare professional.

Mrs. Jenkins glanced up at me, her eyes wide with something akin to fear, then quickly looked down.

"Good afternoon," I began, softening my voice as much as I could. "I'm Conan, and I'll be taking care of you today." She flinched slightly at my introduction, a reaction I'd seen more times than I could count.

"Oh, I-I see," she stammered, her eyes flicking to my tattoos before darting away. Her hands fidgeted nervously.

I smiled gently, going to stand beside her. "It's all right. I know the tattoos can be a bit surprising. I promise I'm here to take good care of you."

She gave me a tentative smile, carefully avoiding looking directly at my inked arms. "It's just...you're not what I was expecting," she admitted.

"Understandable." I laughed softly.

Unfolding the blood pressure cuff, I carefully wrapped it around her slender arm. I made sure it was snug but not too tight, just above her elbow, where the brachial artery pulsed beneath.

I attached the other end to the digital monitoring machine. After double-checking the connections and ensuring the cable was securely plugged in, I pressed the start button on the monitor's interface. The machine emitted a series of soft beeps as it began tracking her vital signs.

Next, I tried to find a way to connect with her in a more personal way, to show her the person I was behind the ink. "You know, when I'm not at work, I like to play the guitar. Would you like to see a video? I think it might be a song you know."

Raising her brows, she nodded. I had piqued her interest. So I pulled out my phone and found a video of me playing an acoustic version of "Here Comes the Sun" by The Beatles—a song I figured would be familiar to most people. I let her hold the phone as I moved to check her other vitals. With the stethoscope pressed against her chest, I instructed her to take deep breaths while I listened for any abnormalities. Next, I attached the pulse ox to her fingertip. This provided a real-time reading of her oxygen saturation levels. Then came the placement of an IV line in her arm. Everyone hated this part, but it ensured we had immediate access for medications if needed. As the music played and I gently tended to her, her expression softened, and she even began to hum along quietly.

"That's lovely," she said with a faint smile when the song ended. "You're very talented."

"Thank you." I was pleased to see her relaxing. "Music helps me unwind. I'm glad you enjoyed it."

While the machine beeped softly in the background, I told her about the other tests we'd be performing. "We're going to check your electrolytes and enzymes, maybe get a chest X-ray and a brain scan, just to rule out any possibility of a stroke or heart attack. It's all routine, just making sure we cover all our bases."

She nodded, her earlier fear now replaced by grandmotherly warmth. We continued chatting for a few minutes about music and her favorite songs. When I left her room to chart her vitals, I chuckled, remembering her horrified expression when I'd first walked in. It was always interesting to observe how people reacted to meeting me for the first time. If she'd seen all the tattoos on my torso or the giant skull across my back, I doubt she would have ever relaxed. It often took time to show people that beneath the tattoos was a caregiver committed to their comfort and health.

The day was rolling along when I managed to snatch a rare quiet moment with Atticus in the break room. He'd just brewed a pot of coffee when I walked in and flashed me a quick grin over his shoulder.

"Black as midnight, strong as an ox. Just how you like it," he said. "Want a cup?"

"Sure, it will complement the three energy drinks I've already had," I said, flopping down into the nearest chair and breathing in the scent of freshly brewed coffee that was wafting through the room.

"I've noticed you've been hyped up all day by the way you've been hustling," Atticus said, setting my cup down in front of me and taking the seat beside mine.

His eyes were weary, but he was still sharp as a tack, as always. Hospital life did that to you—drained you physically yet fueled you emotionally.

"So, how's Nurse Ratched doing?" he asked, a smirk spreading across his face. He'd taken to calling me that ever since I'd controlled a particularly violent patient with nothing but a steely glare and a stern reprimand.

"Keeping things running smoothly," I replied, blowing over the surface of the piping hot coffee before taking a sip. I savored the bitter taste and then continued, "Even managed to win over Mrs. Jenkins today."

"Mrs. Jenkins? The elderly lady in hypertensive crisis?"

"Yep. Showed her a video of me playing 'Here Comes the Sun' on my acoustic, and she was putty in my hands."

Atticus chuckled lightly, a smirk playing on his lips. "You've always had that magic touch with the ladies."

"Yeah, yeah—especially the grannies," I said, rolling my eyes. "Hey, heard through the grapevine that Samantha's switching to days. Must be a relief, huh?" I nudged him with an elbow, watching his face for the smile that always came when Samantha was mentioned.

With a crooked smile he nodded, brushing a hand through his hair, a sign he was mulling something over. "Yeah, she's really excited about it. Working nights has been tough after the kidnapping ordeal. Her therapist thinks switching to a more normal daytime routine will be beneficial for her mind and body. I'm just relieved that the press and legal chaos from the Volkovi Notchi mess is finally settling down. I wish we'd caught Viktor Volkov that night. It's frustrating that he and his top men just disappeared. Even though he's probably holed up in Russia somewhere, you never know when that snake might come back to strike again."

"Yeah, that whole thing was such a nightmare," I said. "I still can't believe something like that could happen right here in Tacoma. At least Samantha has a lot to keep her busy. She must be excited—not just about the shift change, but also about the big wedding coming up. How are the preparations going?" I grinned, imagining the bash that would celebrate those two finally tying the knot.

Atticus took a long sip of his coffee before responding, his expression softening. "She's up to her ears with the planning. You know Samantha; she's all wound up about the details. She wants to keep working right up until the big day. I suggested she take some time off, you know, to relax and hang out at home more. Murphy would love the company."

I laughed, picturing the tiny shih tzu that had more toys than any dog I knew. "That pup's living the dream. But you know Sam, always on the move. I bet she's just not wired for downtime."

"Yeah, she wasn't having any part of cutting back her schedule. Said she'd get bored staying at home." Atticus shook his head lightly. "I get it though. After everything with her kidnapping and the mafia, work helps her feel grounded and gives her something to focus on. She says staying busy keeps her mind off...everything that happened. Can't blame her really."

"Tough as nails, that one. Most people wouldn't be able to jump back into life so quickly after such an ordeal, but Samantha—she's faced down her demons and is still standing strong."

"Exactly why I fell for her," Atticus muttered, almost to himself, his lips curling into a small smile. "She's got this resilience that just blows me away. Doesn't let anything keep her down for long."

Just then, the intercom buzzed to life, calling for a trauma team to assemble. We tossed our cups in the trash, ready to dive back into the fray.

When I entered the trauma area, a voice came in over the dedicated radio speaker. It was unmistakably my brother Braxton, his tone urgent and strained.

"St. John's, this is Medic Four. We're en route with a critical patient and need a trauma team on standby. ETA ten minutes. Over."

I grabbed the radio and pressed the button to respond. "Received, Medic Four. This is Nurse Thorin at St. John's. Can you provide more details on the patient's condition and confirm vitals and interventions? Go ahead, Medic Four."

"Hey, Conan, it's Brax. We've got a bad one. Female, late twenties, involved in a high-speed MVA. Car wrapped around a tree. Required extrication with the jaws of life. She's unconscious and unresponsive, Glasgow Coma Scale at 3. Significant facial and cranial trauma with a deep laceration across the forehead. Multiple superficial cuts and bruises across her body, but no obvious fractures to arms or legs. We've intubated and have an IV running. BP is ninety over sixty, pulse one twenty and thready. Administered twenty milligrams of etomidate and a hundred micrograms of fentanyl for sedation and pain. We're maintaining c-spine precautions and have started cooling measures. How do you copy?"

"Copy that, Brax. We'll get all set up on our end. Trauma team is assembling now. Drive safe, and keep us posted if there are any changes in her status."

I set down the radio mic and turned to Atticus, who had been standing behind me. "Sounds like a rough one," he said. "Let's get everyone ready and the on-call specialists here."

As the team mobilized, the siren's distant wail grew steadily louder. I prepped a gurney with the help of a fellow nurse, making sure we had everything necessary for immediate intervention: trauma shears, gauze, additional IV supplies, and a portable X-ray machine on standby.

While we gathered all the necessary materials and instruments, I also took the time to prepare my mind. The tension in Braxton's voice had hinted at the severity of this crash, and the fact that the jaws of life had been used meant this patient could be in bad shape. It was a grim picture. We had to be on top of our game.

The scene erupted into organized chaos as the ambulance backed into the emergency bay intake area. Several police cars pulled up alongside it, their lights silently strobing. There was even a truck from one of the local news stations pulling into a parking spot outside.

The ambulance doors flew open. Braxton was the one first out, guiding the gurney. The other paramedic joined him to wheel the woman into the triage area. She lay motionless. What I could see of her face was ashen and smeared with blood. Her long, dark brown hair was matted against her skull.

"Let's move, people!" Braxton called out as the other EMT and a couple of our techs transferred her to the hospital gurney we had readied. Her neck had been carefully stabilized with a cervical collar, and they remained vigilant in protecting it as they moved her. When she was settled, they placed the portable ventilator next to her.

Suddenly, I was startled by the popping of camera flashes. A man near the door held his camera at arm's length and pointed it at the woman, clicking away.

Stepping forward, I blocked the guy with my body. Being a thick six-three came in handy sometimes. Thankfully, one of our security staff moved to usher the photographer away.

I got to work and swapped out the blood-soaked gauze on the patient's forehead for fresh pads while keeping an eye on the monitors, tracking her vitals. When I caught sight of the deep gash beneath the gauze, I winced. It was worse than I'd imagined.

Braxton leaned in and briefed us about the incident. "She broke into the Volkov estate, triggered alarms, and took a car. Drove like a bat out of hell in the rain before wrapping it around a tree. Even with side-impact airbags, it looks like her head hit the window hard enough to shatter the glass."

The presence of police suddenly made sense.

"No ID on her. Nothing in the car either. Nothing that tells us who she is, not even a phone," Braxton continued. "Police are still at the estate, trying to ID her."

Atticus's brow furrowed deeply, and he shot me a questioning glance. It seemed we had both noted the mention of the Volkov name.

My chest tightened as I looked at her. Despite the blood and bruises marring her face, there was something strikingly beautiful about her, almost ethereal.

At that moment, the local reporter returned. He started trying to muscle through the nurses, techs, and police, throwing out questions about her possible ties to the Russian mafia's Volkovi Notchi. Atticus stepped up and addressed the man. "You need to leave. This isn't a press conference. Hospital policy and patient rights," he stated, his tone brooking no argument. He gestured to one of the police officers nearby. Reluctantly, the reporter backed off, and Braxton turned to block him from coming any closer.

"Blood for type and cross, full panel, and coags," Atticus called out to the charge nurse, who nodded and hurried to draw the necessary samples.

Atticus moved to the patient's side, assessing her pupils and checking her response to stimuli. "Dilated and sluggish on the left," he noted grimly. "Hang a unit of her blood type as soon as we know it," he directed one of the nurses. "We need to stay ahead of the blood loss."

As we worked, cutting away the patient's clothing and removing her jewelry, we assessed every inch of her for additional injuries. I wondered what her story was, who might be waiting for her to come home. This part of the job—the intersection of clinical detachment and intense personal connection to strangers we fought to save—was a constant challenge for me.

"Let's get her into Trauma One, stat!" Atticus said, his commanding tone snapping me back to reality. We moved swiftly, following the stretcher into the trauma room.

"Blood pressure's dropping, eighty-five over fifty. Heart rate's a hundred and thirty and climbing," I reported, attaching the blood pressure cuff and ECG leads. My hands worked automatically, but my mind was unusually focused on the patient's pale, haunting face.

"We need to stabilize her before we can even think about imaging," Atticus instructed, frowning as he administered an IV push of epinephrine.

As we worked, I had a strange feeling I couldn't shake off. I was drawn to this woman, protective of someone I didn't even know. It wasn't just her looks. There was a vulnerability that called to something deep inside me.

"Conan, keep an eye on her stats. Let me know the minute she's stable enough for a CT," Atticus said, moving to examine the cut on her forehead more closely.

"Got it," I murmured, adjusting the IV line. "We'll take good care of you," I whispered to her, even though she couldn't hear me.

The room quieted down as her condition stabilized. The rush of activity gave way to the steady beep of the heart monitor and the soft whir of the ventilator.

As the team prepared her for further testing, my thoughts raced. Who was she? What had caused her to run from the police so recklessly? And why did I feel such a strong pull to protect her?

"Imaging's ready," someone announced.

Stepping up next to her, I carefully stabilized her neck while we prepped to move her to imaging. "Let's get her to CT now," Atticus said, and together we all worked like a well-oiled machine, hustling the gurney down the corridor.

While we wheeled her toward the imaging suite, her face remained eerily calm under the harsh fluorescent lights.

"We're almost there," I muttered, more to myself than to anyone else, checking her vitals again. The rhythmic beeping of the heart monitor provided a small comfort—that is, until it suddenly spiked.

"Atticus, her heart rate's climbing—one hundred seventy... one hundred eighty!" I called out.

No sooner had I spoken than her body began to convulse violently. The stretcher shook as her arms and legs flailed uncontrollably.

"Seizure! She's having a seizure!" I shouted. Immediately, I lowered the side rails of the stretcher and attempted to hold her head in place to prevent further injury. "She needs diazepam, now!"

Atticus raced back to the trauma room and returned within seconds, syringe already in hand. He administered the medication intravenously, his movements precise as always, while I maintained my hold, ensuring the patient didn't harm herself.

The convulsions slowly ebbed. The incident had drawn a small crowd of medical staff, but I was solely focused on her, my hands held firm, keeping her steady despite the rush of adrenaline going through me.

When the seizure passed and her body finally relaxed, I continued to keep a close watch on her breathing, ensuring the endotracheal tube stayed properly placed and her respiration remained steady. The crisis was over, but our window to diagnose her injuries was narrowing.

With the seizure under control, Atticus smacked his hands together, eager for us to get moving. "Let's get her to CT now. We need to rule out intracranial bleeding or swelling," he said with a decisive edge. "Time's critical."

We arrived in the imaging suite, and as she was wheeled under the scanner I placed a reassuring hand on hers, a silent promise of protection. The CT machine whirred to life. My thoughts churned. I thought of all the potential complications. Seizures could indicate a traumatic brain injury, and time was not on our side.

By the time the scan was completed, the tension in the air had eased slightly, but the concern for our Jane Doe hadn't. We wheeled her to the ICU, where they would be better able to monitor her fragile condition.

"We're set up in ICU Room Twelve," I relayed to the team as we entered the intensive care unit. The ICU team was ready, and a group of doctors and nurses gathered to take over. The handoff was swift but thorough. I briefed them quickly, summarizing everything from her arrival to her current condition. "Severe head trauma, recent seizure managed with diazepam, awaiting further imaging results."

They nodded along, taking notes and asking pointed questions about her vitals and the timeline of her care. When they wheeled her to her new room, I felt a pang of concern, but I knew she was in capable hands. This was their realm, where they turned tides, battling inch by inch for every patient's recovery.

Stepping back, I watched them hook up her monitors and adjust her medications. It was hard to leave her side, but my part, for now, was done. I trusted these colleagues implicitly. They were skilled professionals. As I walked away, my mind replayed the intense events of the last hour. I hoped we'd done enough to give her a fighting chance.

When I returned to the ED, I found Atticus reviewing the preliminary CT results on the portable screen. "No immediate signs of hemorrhage," he said, "but she's definitely got a concussion. I'm sure the folks over in the ICU will keep a close eye on her for any changes."

Throughout the rest of my shift, I found reasons to pass by the ICU. And each time, I paused to check on Jane Doe. Every visit left me more intrigued and invested in her well-being. Despite the flurry of activity that defined emergency department life, thoughts of her lingered at the back of my mind as I continued with my other responsibilities.

Midway through my shift, I pushed through the door of the break room and found Atticus there, staring at the TV mounted in the corner. The local news was on. He barely glanced over at me as I entered, scrutinizing the images with a troubled expression. He had a cup of coffee in hand but didn't seem interested in drinking it.

"Come watch this," he said, pointing at the screen.

I moved closer and leaned back, resting my elbows on the counter. The journalist who had annoyed us earlier stood outside the entrance to the hospital's emergency department.

He was recapping the accident's brutal details. The image of the mangled car wrapped around a tree flashed up, grave against the rainy backdrop.

"What are they saying?" I asked.

"They're just giving the details about the wreck now." Atticus's brow furrowed as he listened. The reporter described how the unidentified woman had broken into the Volkov estate, stolen a car, and then led the police on a high-speed chase that had ended in disaster.

"The car was demolished," I pointed out as I moved to grab a bottle of water from the fridge. Then I leaned back on the counter again.

The reporter continued, detailing the absence of any identification on the woman and informing viewers how the police had returned to the mansion, finding nothing there with which they could identify her.

"And as for her fingerprints, found at the Volkov estate, the police report that they've found nothing in their system. For now, she is a complete unknown," the reporter concluded, promising to dig deeper into her identity and motives.

Atticus shook his head, muttering, "Do you think she could be tied to the Volkovi Notchi? With all the heat on that organization after kidnapping Sam, it's weird she'd just break in."

I shrugged and took a sip of my water as I thought about his question. "Nah, it doesn't add up. If she was connected to them, why break in? And why run from the cops in such a panic? If she knew the Volkovs, she'd have known better than to trigger alarms and steal a car. She'd understand the lay of the land better than to end up wrapped around a tree. Sounds more like she panicked and realized too late she was in over her head."

"True." Atticus nodded, keeping his gaze fixed on the screen while the newscast moved on to another story. "But then, why was she there? Nothing besides the car stolen, no signs of anything else disturbed. If she's not connected, what's her angle?"

"Maybe it was a dare or something random? Maybe it's a case of being in the wrong place at the wrong time?" I suggested, trying to come up with any scenario that would fit the bizarre facts.

"Could be," he agreed, though his voice was tinged with skepticism. "But a dare that leads to a high-speed chase and a crash? Seems extreme."

The TV continued to hum in the background as I considered the possibilities. The report had given us more questions than answers.

"Whatever the reason, she's in terrible shape now," I said after a moment, pushing off from the counter. "And with no ID and the police not having any information on her, she's a mystery on all fronts."

Atticus drained the last of his coffee, crushing his cup in his hand before throwing it away. "Well, for now, she seems to be doing as good as can be expected under the circumstances. Let's just hope she wakes up with some answers."

I nodded, though worry nagged at me. "I'll head back to the ICU and see how she's doing in a little while."

Something about Jane Doe's story—and the rumors of her mafia ties—bothered me. It was a puzzle with too many missing pieces, but it was one I wanted to figure out.

Several hours passed. Before punching out of my shift, I headed to check on Jane Doe one last time. The corridors of St. John's were quieter now, but as I approached the secured doors of the ICU, a now familiar voice disrupted the calm.

"Excuse me, Doctor, a moment of your time?" Niles Johnson, the persistent reporter from KING Channel 5 News, positioned himself squarely in my path, notepad at the ready.

"I'm not a doctor. I'm ED Nurse Thorin," I corrected him, not breaking my stride or even giving him the decency of looking in his direction.

Niles followed me, undeterred. "Right, Nurse Thorin. Can you update us on the condition of the woman from the crash? The one involved in the Volkov estate break-in?"

At that, I stopped and faced him, my patience wearing thin. "Look, I can't discuss any patient details with you. It's against hospital policy and a violation of patient privacy."

"But the public has a right to know, especially given the connection to the Volkovi Notchi crime organization," he pressed, his voice gaining an edge. "And how is Samantha doing? Considering her past with them, people are curious."

God, of course. I should have known that, as soon as I mentioned my last name, he would make the connection to Samantha and her kidnapping. All the press around that ordeal had finally quietened down, and this incident was going to cause lots of new speculation. What were the odds of someone breaking into the Volkov estate and ending up in our ED under the Thorin brothers' care? What was the likelihood of all three of us being on shift at the same time and caring for someone tied to the Volkovs? Maybe I should stop and pick up a lottery ticket on my way home.

"That's none of your business, Jensen. Samantha's fine, and she has nothing to do with this incident." I gritted my teeth, feeling a rush of protectiveness.

Niles shot back, "I'm just here on public grounds, gathering information for a story under the protection of the First Amendment, Nurse Thorin."

I scoffed. "Freedom of the press doesn't give you the right to harass patients or hospital staff. Now, if you'll excuse me." With that, I brushed past him, swiping my badge to enter the ICU.

I made my way to Jane Doe's room and paused next to her bed. There she was, lying unconscious, her features tranquil despite the jungle of tubes and wires attached to her. She looked like some kind of refined princess from a storybook, all grace and mystery, resting in a glass case—a sleeping beauty, untouched by the real world.

Standing there, watching her, I felt like a damn monster—a guy covered in tattoos, each one a marker of past fights and darker days. My exterior might have been tough, but it was nothing compared to the ugliness trying to claw its way out of my heart. My childhood had left me jaded and untrusting. I had always put on a good front, acting like the easygoing golden retriever who didn't take life too seriously. But ever since I was a kid, I'd known life mostly sucked. So why not live in the moment? If life had taught me one thing, it was that none of us were guaranteed a tomorrow.

I leaned in, keeping my voice low as the monitors beeped in the background. "I've got your back, pretty angel. I won't let any more harm come to you." It was more than a promise; it felt like a vow. Being this close to her, I couldn't shake the feeling that fate had thrown us together for some higher purpose. Here I was, a beast, and there she was, a beauty—our lives slammed together by some twist of destiny.

Feeling a lingering sense of duty, I straightened up and headed back out, only to find Niles waiting like a vulture. But my mind was still back in that room with her. She and I, we were worlds apart and yet inexplicably linked. This wasn't just about protecting her from the prying eyes of the world—it was about protecting something more, something I couldn't explain.

"Did you see her?" Niles asked, sounding like an incessantly annoying mosquito. "What can you tell us about her condition?"

My frustration boiled over. "I told you to back off," I growled, stepping close enough to see him reconsider his stance. Without another word, I pushed past him.

I reported the incident to the on-duty nurse manager before walking out to my Jeep, my curiosity about our Jane Doe hanging over me like a cloud.

Chapter Seven

5/28 afternoon

Tate and I rolled up to the sprawling estate to find a couple of Tacoma police cruisers parked out front, their lights throwing splashes of blue and red across the front of the building. We'd barely stepped out of the car when a cop marched over to us, his face all business.

"Gentlemen, can I be of some help to you?" he asked. "This is a private home, and it's currently being searched by the police." He crossed his arms, as if that would somehow intimidate us.

Tate didn't miss a beat. "I'm Harrison Tate, trustee of the estate. This property was recently transferred to a trust under my management." He opened the back door of his car and rummaged around, snagging his briefcase. After flipping it open, he showed the cop the deed and trust documents.

The officer perused the paperwork. "I need to confirm a few details about the information you've provided," he told us before pulling out his radio and speaking into it. After several minutes of back and forth with various individuals, he nodded and turned back to us. "Everything checks out. The chief says Mr. Tate was just at the station, and he knows all about the ownership change. We're just wrapping up our search here." He eyed me suspiciously and sighed but proceeded to run us through the morning's chaos.

"A few hours ago, someone broke in through the service entrance and tripped the surveillance alarms we had set up in conjunction with the FBI," he said. "Seems like she hadn't made it far inside when our sirens spooked her. She bolted, took one of the estate's cars, and...well, ended up wrapping it around a tree down the road—critically injuring herself."

The cop paused as his radio crackled with chatter from another officer. "She had no ID on her and is currently listed as a Jane Doe over at St. John's. If she pulls through, she'll be facing charges for breaking and entering, theft, and property damage, among others."

Tate rubbed his chin and glanced over at me, his brows pinched tight. I was taken aback by this whole situation. What were the chances that something like this would happen the day after the ownership of the estate changed hands and I was locked up? This had *mafia* written all over it.

"Mr. Tate," the officer began, "this woman who broke into the estate earlier today...do you have any idea who she might be?"

"No clue," he replied. I racked my brain for any woman that could be involved, but no one came to mind. Tate nodded, scribbling notes. "Thank you, officer. Please keep us updated on her condition and any legal steps we need to take regarding the charges." Reaching once again into his briefcase, he pulled out

75

a couple of business cards and handed them to the officer, who stuck them in his shirt pocket and walked away.

I couldn't shake the feeling that there was more to this situation. Tate and I went to the service entrance and surveyed the damage there. It wasn't much, just some broken glass.

"Replace this with a metal security door and deadbolts," I said to Tate. "Let's get a crew out here. There are lots of changes I want to make right away. I wonder if this was a professional job or random? Looks to me like she knew the most vulnerable way in."

"Suspicious for sure," he said. "With Viktor, there could be any number of folks interested in seeing what they might find inside." He pressed his lips together tightly and shook his head. "I hope your father was careful about his privacy, even at home."

"He was, but as you know, he left unexpectedly and in a hurry." My sixth sense told me something bad was up. I always got this feeling in my gut before I was hit with bad news.

We watched the police finish up, and the red and blue lights disappeared one by one as they cleared out, leaving us to ponder the mess that was now ours to sort out.

Once inside the house, I immediately set to work reestablishing the security measures we'd previously had in place. I needed to make sure we were protected from additional break-ins and prying eyes.

The rest of the day blurred into a frenzy of activity. We coordinated with the DarkMatter crew to sweep the house for bugs, remove and dismantle any potentially compromised devices, and install new surveillance tech. The crew had no idea who I was. They only knew the boss man had ordered the best guys from the firm to haul their asses over here, pronto, and install the highest level of security. I oversaw everything, ensuring no stone was left unturned.

It was late when things finally started to calm down. Exhausted, I flopped down onto the living room sofa and flicked on the TV, hoping to catch something mindless so I could unwind. Instead, the local news was on, and the anchor was discussing a critical accident involving an unidentified woman, who was now at St. John's Hospital. I knew instantly from the image of the car that they were reporting on our break-in.

My heart nearly stopped when a picture of the beautiful Jane Doe flashed up on the screen. Despite all the bruises and the large cut on her head, her features resembled someone I knew far too well—Anastasia.

Just then, one of the DarkMatter crew, who had been finishing up for the night, came in, holding a cell phone.

"Excuse me, sir," he said. "Found this in the garage, near where the stolen car was parked." I took the phone, and my gut twisted.

He followed me into the kitchen, where I pulled out my laptop from its bag. I connected the phone to the computer and began hacking into it. Even though my laptop had been taken into police custody when they'd hauled me in from the airport, I hadn't been worried about them accessing any of the data. I had everything locked down tight. My paranoia and skill were unmatched. Moments later, I was in, and what I saw floored me. The contacts, the photos—it was Anastasia's phone. My mind hadn't had time to process the images from the news, but this confirmed what I'd seen. Fuck!

It hit me like a punch to the gut. Anastasia really was the woman in the crash. How had she ended up here? I needed answers, and I needed them now. Whatever it took, I was going to find out what happened and make sure she was safe.

I slammed my laptop shut, frustrated. I told the guy from the firm to head on out and see to it that everyone else had left, giving him fifteen minutes before I set the alarm system.

I needed to be at the hospital with Anastasia, making sure she was all right, but that was exactly what I couldn't do. Being linked to her now, with the shitstorm surrounding the Volkovi Notchi, would only drag her deeper into the sleaze I was trying to keep her out of.

Fury and worry bubbled inside me. I couldn't risk tying her to our father's criminal empire. With no other choice, I dialed my father in Russia.

The familiar yet always foreboding ringback tone echoed in the quiet room as I waited for him to pick up. When he finally answered, his voice was gruff and detached. "Nikolai, what is it?"

"It's Anastasia," I said, keeping my voice steady despite my simmering rage. "She's been in an accident here in Tacoma and has been hospitalized. She's in critical condition."

There was a pause, then, "Sit tight. I'll send some men. Do not go to her. It's too risky. My men will handle the situation discreetly. They can ensure her safety and manage the fallout without tying her—or you—directly to the Volkovi Notchi."

I hated how he always treated me like some idiot. "And what am I supposed to do? Just wait?" I snapped. The idea of being passive while others took action grated on my every nerve.

"Yes, Nikolai, you will wait and keep things under control on your end. We can't afford any more surprises. And don't forget you have a job to do. Reestablish the trades and routes we discussed before." His voice was now a dangerous growl, putting me on edge. There was no hint of concern for my sister. God, how I fucking hated this bastard!

"What about Aunt Elena, Luca, and her friends back in New York? Should I contact them and let them know?" I asked.

"No. I'll call Elena. She'll ensure no one comes around looking for your sister. We can't risk the wedding getting postponed, or worse, called off. Your job is to get that girl to the church on time, keeping the situation under wraps. You got it?"

"Yes, sir."

The phone went dead.

As much as I loathed my father, I couldn't let him down. If I didn't follow his orders, not only would he question my loyalty, he might also go sniffing around my personal affairs—discover my ownership of DarkMatter. Viktor would kill me without hesitation if he thought I was a threat to him or the business ventures of the Volkovi Notchi.

With a mind full of worry, I prepared a late-night snack and retreated to my bedroom. Thoughts of Anastasia intertwined with concerns over the mafia families she was tangled up with— the Volkov, Genovese, and Moretti. How could I save her from this life? And how could I take out the Thorin brothers without jeopardizing everything I'd built?

My thoughts raced as I tried to find the answers to questions that seemed impossible to solve. I needed solutions, and fast. The stakes were too high, the game too dangerous. But for Anastasia, I'd risk it all.

5/29

I tossed and turned all night. In the early morning, I blinked away the remnants of a poor night's sleep, cursing the restless night that had refused to grant me any peace. With a groan, I rolled out of bed. I couldn't stand it anymore. I had to see Anastasia, even if just a glimpse, to confirm she was alive and still fighting. The thought of her lying there unconscious gnawed at me.

Throwing on my clothes, I rushed out the door, heading for the hospital.

When I arrived, it was still early, so the hallways were quiet, a hushed sanctuary of pale walls and antiseptic smells. Following the signage, I made my way to the ICU, but a nurse stopped me cold. "Only immediate family beyond this point," she said firmly before badging through the door.

I lingered there, my frustration mounting. If I claimed to be her brother, I'd risk exposing her—and me—to all sorts of unwanted attention. Dammit, she was just beyond those doors, and there was nothing I could do.

A dark thought crossed my mind. Were the Thorin brothers around? The desire for retribution seared through me. I was in Tacoma because of them, and indirectly, so was she. It was their fault we'd been forced into this situation, their fault my sister suffered. I considered finding Dr. Atticus Thorin and ending him. That would check a box off my father's list. But the risks were too high. It would only draw more attention to Anastasia.

With a heavy sigh, I turned away from the ICU and left the hospital, my mind made up. I would work with my father, reestablish our presence here in Tacoma, and keep my cover.

I swore to myself that I would never let Anastasia down again. Whatever it took, I would be there for her, protect her, and ensure her safety. And if the Thorin brothers dared to cross my path, they'd learn firsthand the wrath of a Volkov.

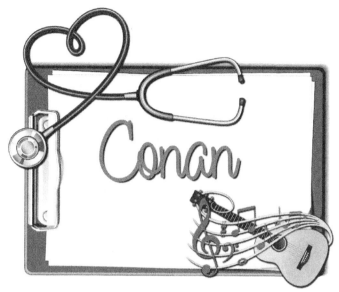

Chapter Eight

5/29

My shift at St. John's hadn't even started, but I was already strolling through the quiet hallways of the hospital on my way to the ICU. I'd gotten here early today. I needed to see for myself how she—my Jane Doe—was doing.

When I reached the ICU, Emily Everett, one of the night shift nurses, was updating a chart at the nurses' station just outside of Jane Doe's room. She glanced up and smiled.

"Morning, Conan. You're here early," she said, keeping her voice at a whisper to not disturb the quiet of the ICU.

I moved to stand in the open doorway of Jane Doe's room.

"Just wanted to check on our mystery guest from last night. How's she doing?" I asked, my gaze drifting over to the bed where she lay. She was all cleaned up and tucked in. Her dark chestnut hair fanned out over the crisp white pillow that cradled her head, framing her face in a silky halo. God, how I wanted to run my fingers through her hair and prove to myself she was real, but I knew better than to cross that line.

Emily chuckled softly as she moved past me and into the room. I realized I'd been staring at our Jane Doe with a goofy expression on my face. "The pretty lady is doing much better than when she came in. That's for sure," Emily said, stepping aside so I could see the monitors better. "Her heart rate's steady, blood pressure's looking good, and oxygen levels are strong. We're all surprised she didn't break any bones in such a violent collision."

I stepped further into the room and leaned over to see Jane Doe better. The deep bruises on her arms and throat were an alarming shade of purplish black, a terrible reminder of the crash's severity. "Bruises look rough, but it's good there's no broken bones," I said, adjusting the blanket slightly, careful not to disturb her.

"Definitely lucky on that front," Emily agreed. "Seat belt and airbags did their job. They just left their marks is all. She's mainly suffering from the overall trauma that comes along with a high-impact crash."

I nodded, scanning the monitors. The numbers there told a story of positive progress. "Good thing she thought to buckle up in her race to get away from...well, whatever she was running from in a stolen car," I said.

"Oh, and about that." Emily's eyes darted to Jane Doe's face. "We were told that Tacoma PD is going to post a guard at her door, and as soon as she's medically able, they will take her into custody to be arraigned for the various crimes she committed."

"Hmm, good to know." I turned my attention to the sutures on her forehead, placed as if a plastic surgeon had done them. Just what I'd expect from Atticus. "How's the head wound?" I asked.

"Healing well. She'll have a scar, but the sutures are looking good. They should heal nicely if we keep infection at bay." Emily's fingers lightly touched the edge of my girl's brow as if to emphasize her point. "She didn't stir much last night, but when the doctor checked her pupils a few minutes ago, they were responsive and reacted normally. She's in a good spot."

"Responsive pupils—that's great to hear. Any timeline on reducing ventilator support?" I asked, already thinking ahead about her recovery phase.

"The docs are planning to wean her off the ventilator in the next couple of days—if she keeps improving at this rate," Emily added in a cautious but optimistic tone as she made a note in the chart.

I stepped closer to Jane Doe's side, observing her quiet breathing. The rhythmic rise and fall of her chest was reassuring. The ventilator hummed, a constant companion in the sterile room. Her face remained peaceful, despite the severity of her injuries.

For reasons I couldn't explain, I felt a compulsion to listen to the sounds in her chest. "Do you mind if I listen to her lungs?" I asked, pulling the stethoscope from around my neck.

"Sure, go ahead."

I listened intently to the clear sounds of her breathing and strong heartbeat. "Lungs are clear. Surprising after right middle lobe atelectasis," I said after a moment, hanging the stethoscope back around my neck.

"Yeah, she's a fighter. I think her athleticism is helping her recovery."

"Thanks for the update, Emily. I'll swing by later to check on her progress." My gaze lingered on Jane Doe for a moment. She was no longer just another patient; she was mine to protect until someone who loved her found her.

"No problem, Conan. I'll keep you posted if anything changes." Emily turned and left the room, moving to check on another patient.

Before I walked away to start my shift, I leaned down and whispered, "You're doing a great job, pretty angel. Just keep taking one breath at a time."

I stepped out of the ICU area. The hospital was slowly waking up. I took a deep breath, the taste of hospital coffee now appealing as I prepared to start another day at St. John's.

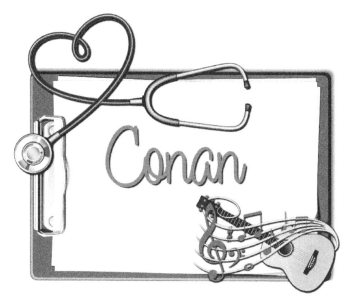

Chapter Nine

5/30

The next morning, I'd barely clocked in for my shift when my phone started vibrating in my pocket. It was a text from Atticus: *Break room. Now.* That tone, even in a text, meant trouble, so I hustled down the hallway.

Bursting into the break room, I found Atticus planted in the corner of the room, gritting his teeth, crossing his arms, and staring up at the TV. The room was empty except for us. The screen showed the reporter—Niles Johnson, from Channel 5— once again camped outside our emergency department. He had that familiar smug look plastered across his face as he spoke into the microphone. His overly slick appearance and pompous demeanor grated on my nerves.

I joined Atticus in front of the TV, fixing my eyes on the screen. "What's he saying now?"

"They're running a 'Do you know this woman?' segment," Atticus muttered disgustedly. "Look at this. They're using the photos of her from the scene of the wreck as they extricated her from the car and from when she was brought in."

On the screen, images flashed of Jane Doe, bloodied and unconscious, her face barely recognizable.

"—and if anyone recognizes this woman or has any information about her actions leading up to the accident, please contact local authorities or us here at KING Channel 5 News."

"They're using her accident photos? That's low," I huffed out.

"Listen to this," Atticus said, his voice tight.

Niles started recapping how she'd broken into the Volkov estate, stolen a car, and led police on a wild chase that had ended at the base of a tree.

"The individual did not appear to know whose home she was breaking into," Niles was saying. "Authorities have found no links to the man who led the notorious Volkovi Notchi crime syndicate. At this point, all our findings indicate she stumbled upon the property by accident."

"And they just blast her face all over the news, no regard for her privacy," I spat out, rubbing my fingers across the stubble on my chin. Niles continued his narrative by detailing her pending charges.

"They know nothing about her situation. She could've been desperate, scared..." I sighed, thinking of her lying there in the ICU, unaware of the circus her life had become.

"Yeah, but since when did the media care about the why? It's all about the spectacle," Atticus said, shaking his head.

"And now, that asshole has turned her into a target by asking viewers to play detective," I said.

Niles continued, "As far as we know, she has not regained consciousness, and no one has come forward recognizing her. Remember, if you have any information about this woman, please contact local authorities at the hotline number below."

More images of the crash site and Jane Doe being wheeled into the hospital appeared on the screen, a blatant invasion of her privacy.

"This is bullshit," I growled. "He's got no right. Those were taken once she was in our care, during her treatment. That's confidential."

"Yeah, and there's no respect for her condition or the circumstances. It's like they've already tried and convicted her," Atticus scoffed, then jabbed the remote to turn off the TV. "She's being treated like a criminal before she even wakes up."

"Has anyone called legal about this?" I asked, already pulling out my phone, ready to make the call myself.

Atticus nodded. "I called them the moment I saw what was going on. They're on it, but you know how these things go. Freedom of the press gives these vultures a lot to hide behind, and public interest validates what they're doing."

I pocketed my phone, clenching my fists at my sides. "It's not right. She's not even awake to defend herself, and they're painting her as some criminal mastermind."

"We've done all we can for the moment," Atticus said, motioning toward the door. "Let's get back to work. Patients need us more than we need to watch this garbage."

Nodding, I followed him out of the break room. The images we'd seen of Jane Doe were burned into my mind. With every step I took toward the ED, I became more and more pissed off. This media storm was going to be a battle, and I was ready to fuck up one Niles Johnson.

Chapter Ten

5/30

Since attempting to visit Anastasia in the hospital, I had thrown myself into Volkovi Notchi business, forcing myself to carry out my father's orders. I had a lot to accomplish—including setting up new drug routes and establishing a private communication system between our contacts in Tacoma and my father in Russia. My effort to distract myself from Anastasia's condition was relentless, but it felt like I was moving through a fog.

The day became a blur of phone calls, meetings, and secret deals. I knew the importance of my work, the necessity of maintaining our operations, but my heart wasn't in it. Every task was tainted by the gnawing worry for my sister.

Anastasia's car crash had left her unconscious and in serious condition, and her identity was unknown to the hospital staff. I wanted nothing more than to rush to her side, to be there when she woke up, but I couldn't risk it. Visiting her would mean identifying myself, leading authorities to ask questions about our ties to the Russian mafia. It was a risk I couldn't afford to take.

Frustration simmered beneath my calm exterior. I checked the news obsessively, searching for any mention of the mysterious Jane Doe. Each report was a reminder of my helplessness. The image of her lying in that hospital bed ate at me. I was torn between my obligations to our father and the desperate need to protect my sister.

I clenched my fists, forcing myself to focus. There would come a time when I could be with Anastasia, when I could explain everything and make sure she was safe. Until then, I had to play my part, maintain the facade, and keep our enemies at bay.

Desperate for more direct information, I put my hacking skills to use, infiltrating the hospital's network to access employee data. After some thorough research, I identified a nursing tech, Maria Hobbs, who worked in the ICU, and decided she was my in. I was well-versed in the art of bribery. Maria had a lot of debt and could use the money. I sent her a few anonymous messages, stealthily introducing myself and making sure she knew I could reach her anytime, anywhere. I then wired a hefty sum of money to her checking account.

More where that came from if you provide me with information on one of your patients. The Jane Doe from the wreck out on Fox Island. Nothing you can't easily do, nothing that would jeopardize your job, I texted her. I knew that would get her attention.

It took her a while to respond. *How much money are we talking about?*

Double what I sent you every time you do what I ask, I replied.

It didn't take two seconds before she was all in.

I instructed her to send me a copy of Jane Doe's complete case history and pictures of her too. I wanted to see every wound on her body.

The first photo Maria sent shattered me. Anastasia was hooked up to a ventilator, bruises marring her skin. It hit like a physical blow. This was all my fault. If not for my detainment by the FBI, Anastasia wouldn't have rushed to our Tacoma estate. She must have flown in because I hadn't met up with her. She knew I'd never miss seeing her on our birthday, and it was out of character for me not to keep her informed. When she reached the estate, she must have panicked, seeing all the police tape and the house ransacked, thinking something awful had happened to me. And then she had fled because she didn't want to answer questions about our family.

The guilt was crushing, but I couldn't change the past. I had to focus on helping Ana as much as I could right now. With Maria on board as my eyes and ears, I could keep close tabs on Ana and devise the best strategy to extricate her from this situation. For now, I had to bide my time and wait for the right moment to act.

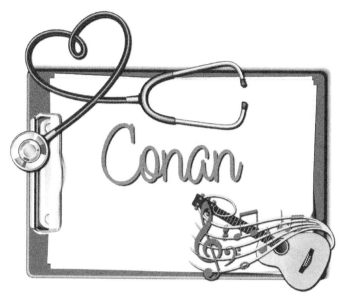

Chapter Eleven

5/31

Daylight was already spilling through the windows when I started my shift the next day. The ED hummed and hustled, but despite the constant rush, a part of my mind was elsewhere, stuck in the ICU where my Jane Doe had been the last few days.

By midday, I'd handled everything from broken bones to a kid who'd swallowed a coin. Once I was able to snatch a moment amidst the madness, I made a beeline for the ICU. A Tacoma PD officer now sat by her door, just as Emily had forewarned. The officer, a broad-shouldered guy, eyed me as I approached.

"Good afternoon," I nodded, flashing my hospital badge without breaking stride. "Just checking in on the patient."

He gave me a curt nod, not questioning my presence. Inside, the room was still and peaceful, with the machines beeping softly in the background. Jane Doe was still unconscious, but she was looking less like a car crash victim and more like someone deeply asleep. Her breathing was even, and the bruising had faded into a softer purple hue. It didn't look as harsh now.

For a moment, I stood there watching the soft rise and fall of her chest under the thin hospital blanket. Then I checked her vitals on the monitor, confirming my girl was stable, and slipped out as silently as I had entered.

Once I'd left the ICU, the normal racket of the hospital didn't bother me as much. It was like a weird pause button got hit in my head every time I saw her.

Throughout the day, I made the quick checks on my sleeping beauty a regular thing, stealing moments between patients or whenever I managed to get a break. I couldn't resist the pull to see her, even with the ED buzzing like a kicked hornet's nest. Each time I entered her room, I noticed little changes—a decrease in swelling here, a reduction in bruising there. Her body was mending, and her brain scans didn't show any new concerns. The progress she was making kept my worst fears at bay.

6/1

Fast-forward through another whirlwind of patients and paperwork, and it was the end of my shift—my last before the weekend kicked in. I made one final stop at the ICU, needing to see her, knowing in my gut something important had happened.

This time, the door was slightly ajar, and the officer gave me a knowing look and a half smile as I approached. Inside, the change hit me like a slap. Her ventilator was gone. There she was, breathing on her own with a simple nasal cannula in her nose supplementing her oxygen. The machinery that had been her constant companion since her arrival was now gone.

I was drawn to the edge of her bed, and placed my hand on her arm. "You're looking beautiful today, my angel," I murmured, keeping my voice soft. "Breathing all on your own, huh? That's what I like to see."

For the first time, I had an unobstructed view of her face. Without the endotracheal tube, mouthpiece, tape, and mask, her features were undistorted, peaceful. The cut on her forehead was the only sign of the hell she'd been through. She was beautiful—stunning, actually. It knocked the wind out of me, a feeling that hit somewhere deep, where I didn't do feelings. I took her hand in mine. Its cool limpness ate at me. How had such a divine creature ended up like this—and all alone? She deserved better.

After brushing a strand of hair from her cheek, I leaned over her. The desire to place a soft kiss on her forehead was almost overwhelming. Instead, I made her a promise. "In the middle of chaos, there you were—mine to care for, mine to protect."

A whispered vow I would keep.

Moving back before I did something stupid, like actually kissing her, I checked her IV lines and made sure everything was properly in place, even though I already knew it was. Anything to stall, to spend a few more moments with her. I checked the monitors. All her vitals were good. There was nothing to do except have patience and hope she'd come around soon.

I stood there a bit longer, just watching her. "Tomorrow's my day off, but I'll come by and bring my guitar and play you some tunes. I bet you'd like that."

When I finally left the room, the worry I'd been feeling over her injuries began to lift, replaced by a strange anticipation. Tomorrow, I'd be back for a little music therapy. I'd seen for myself over the years how music or even reading to ill or seriously injured patients could help them. Maybe I could help her find her way back.

I shut my apartment door behind me with a thud, kicking my boots off. A waterfront condo on Point Ruston was a great place for a single guy like me to live. I didn't have many requirements, but what I did need was a place I could enjoy. This community had a movie theater, restaurants, bars, fitness facilities, and a mile-long waterfront trail system. Living here meant convenience, entertainment, and beautiful views! My one-bedroom apartment that overlooked the choppy blue-gray waters that Tacoma was known for, was an ideal place for me. I was a hometown kind of boy.

As I made my way to the kitchen, a couple of boats bobbing in the distance caught my eye through the expansive windows. I tossed my keys onto the granite counter. Although the apartment was small—and cost more than I liked—the simplicity of the layout, the clean lines, and the comfortable decor suited me just fine.

I went to the fridge and pulled out the fixings for a sandwich—some leftover chicken, mayo, pickles, and a couple of slices of bread—and slapped it all together on a plate.

Grabbing a beer from the fridge, I popped the cap off and took a long drag, the cold liquid hitting the spot. With my plate and beer in one hand, I grabbed my laptop with the other and settled onto the bar stool. As soon as I pressed it open, the screen lit up and the processor hummed.

I started typing, searching for any updates on Jane Doe. Nothing new popped up—just the same recycled crap from earlier. Frustration simmered in my chest as I took another bite of the sandwich.

My mind wasn't on my dinner; it was tangled up with thoughts about the woman who'd crashed into my life. I took another swig of beer, letting the bitterness wash over my tongue, the cold of the bottle comforting against my palm. I stared out the window, watching the lights flicker along the boardwalk below.

"Shit," I muttered, rubbing my temples. I couldn't get her out of my head. The mystery woman lying unconscious in the hospital bed was doing a number on my mind. I felt like I needed to help her somehow but wasn't sure where to start.

When I'd polished off the last bite of my sandwich, I pushed back from the bar and stretched. My muscles ached for rest, the result of the long shift at St. John's and the heavy leg day I'd done at the gym after work.

I ambled over to the couch, turned on a late-night talk show on the TV, and sank into the soft cushions, letting their comfort ease my weary bones. The host's banter was just funny enough to distract me from all that had been going on with my Jane Doe.

After a while, sleep tugged at me, but it remained elusive. Her image danced behind my eyelids every time I closed them.

"Dammit," I muttered under my breath, raking a hand through my hair in frustration. With an exasperated sigh, I heaved myself off the couch and clicked off the TV. The apartment was plunged into darkness save for the dim illumination coming from the streetlights and marina outside.

The cool silk sheets welcomed me as I slipped into bed. Even so, sleep refused to come. Jane Doe's face and her possible connection to the Russian mafia still lingered in every corner of my thoughts.

My gaze wandered over to the digital clock on the bedside table. 12:07 a.m. glowed back at me. I had to get up early if I was going to make the ICU's early visiting hours. I groaned before rolling onto my side, trying desperately to fall asleep—to no avail.

"Fuck this," I growled, throwing off the covers and heading for the bathroom. Maybe a hot shower would help.

As the water battered against my weary body, I tried to focus on the sensation of the steam and the smell of the soap. Anything but her.

Just then, my phone rang. I turned off the shower and stepped out, steam billowing around me like a blanket. Wrapping a towel around my waist, I padded across the cold tiles, leaving damp footprints in my wake.

I picked up my phone from the counter, and Cassidy's name flashed on the screen. Cass was a girl I occasionally hung out with or hooked up with. I'd met her a couple of years back when she started working out at the gym down the street. She was a sassy little blonde flight attendant who was living life to the fullest, and I respected her for that. Our encounters had been casual and uncomplicated, and we always had fun together.

"Hey, Conan," she said, her voice slightly slurred, a clear sign she was a bit tipsy. "Can I come over? I'm just down the street with some friends."

Perfect timing. I needed a distraction, and sleep wasn't on the horizon anyway. "Sure thing, Cass. The code to open my door is four-two-seven-seven."

After hanging up, I brushed my teeth and stared into the mirror. I wasn't getting any younger, and I wondered if I'd ever find a woman who I could trust with my heart.

Doubtful.

I dried my face and headed toward the front door.

Before I even reached it, there she was, stepping inside, wearing a hot-pink crop top and short jean skirt. She teetered slightly on her heels, eyes sparkling with that familiar mischievous glint.

Cassidy's laughter filled the space as she made her way over to me, her perfume—sweet and citrusy—wafting in along with the humid night air.

"Missed you, big guy," she purred, pressing her body against mine. Her hands wasted no time exploring the contours of my chest, making their way up and behind my neck. I hadn't bothered dressing, so I was only wearing the towel I'd slung around my hips.

"Missed you too, Cass," I said, sliding my hands around her waist.

Cassidy stretched up on her tiptoes, and then her lips found mine, hungry and demanding. The taste of tequila lingered on her tongue. I pulled her closer, deepening the kiss, my hands roaming over the curve of her hips and the small of her back. She responded eagerly, tangling her fingers in my hair and pulling me down to her level.

We stumbled toward the bedroom, shedding clothes along the way. Her top hit the floor, followed by my towel. She giggled, unsteady on her feet, and I scooped her up, her laughter turning into a soft moan as I kissed her neck. Her skin was warm and smooth, with a faint trace of sweat from the summer heat.

As soon as I set her on the bed, she shimmied out of her skirt. Her bra came off next, revealing her perfectly perky breasts. I took a moment to admire her—the way her body moved, the way she bit her lip, how her eyes darkened with desire. Then she was on me again, tugging my hand and dragging me to her mouth in a searing kiss that left me breathless.

We fell back onto the bed, a tangle of limbs. Cassidy's nails raked down my sides, sending shivers through me. I hooked my fingers under the waistband of her thong, removing it in one swift motion. She gasped, arching her back, and I took the opportunity to kiss my way down her body, tasting the salt of her sweat mixed with her natural sweetness.

Her hands gripped my shoulders, pulling me back up to her. "Fuck. Me. Now," she demanded, voice husky with desire.

I didn't need any more encouragement—I needed release. I positioned myself between her legs. Her glistening core was making me hungry, and I was eager to taste her, but that would have to wait. The sensation of entering her was electric, a jolt of pleasure that made both of us moan. Cassidy wrapped her legs around me, urging me deeper, digging her nails into my arms.

We moved together in the natural rhythm we always found, the bed creaking beneath us. Her needy little noises filled the room, mingling with my own grunts of gratification. It wasn't long before we climaxed together and collapsed on the bed. She draped an arm over my chest, her breathing steadying as she drifted into sleep.

I stared at the ceiling, the afterglow fading as unbidden thoughts crept in. Cassidy's soft snores filled the room, but my mind wandered back to the ICU, to the mysterious Jane Doe. She was still unconscious, alone, and vulnerable. There was something inexplicable drawing me to her, something deeper than just professional concern. With Cassidy, sex was instinctive, almost mechanical. Don't get me wrong, she always delivered in bed, and now had been no exception, but I wasn't emotionally connected to her. I didn't have that unexplainable craving for her I saw in other men's eyes for the women they loved. Maybe that wasn't in the cards for me.

For whatever reason, every time I shut my eyes, Jane Doe's face was there. No matter how wrong it felt, or how much I knew I shouldn't, I couldn't help but want her. I didn't feel good enough for her, but the desire was undeniable.

I wasn't a virtuous man. Broken, living for today, never any guilt for living my life on my own terms, a playboy with no remorse—that was who I'd always been. The things I'd done throughout my life, the choices I'd made—she deserved better. She deserved someone like one of my brothers, someone good and noble.

Atticus was the perfect one—an attending ED doc, loads of money, always did the right thing—and now he had the perfect woman by his side. Braxton wasn't so different from Atticus. Not only did he and Atticus look like they could be twins, but their penchant for perfectionism and being the hero everyone wanted made them wildly successful. But me, the baby brother, almost seven years younger than Atticus, I'd always been the hellion. I was the guy who wasn't afraid to taste all that life had to offer. The one who'd done crazy shit like fly down the steepest hill on his bike as a kid—even though it had ended with a broken arm and a deep scar on my knee—just to be noticed occasionally.

Living in my brothers' shadow wouldn't have been so bad if I'd had competent parents. Sure, my mother and father had looked great from the outside looking in. But the truth of them was shitty at best. By the time I was eight, my mother had put herself in the ground drinking herself to death. A little more than a year after she'd passed, my father died from a widow-maker heart attack. It had been a lot to deal with—even though none of us had been close to the self-absorbed, workaholic who never made time for any of us.

Although the three of us brothers had shared the same miserable childhood, we'd dealt with it differently. I'd always been determined to live and let live, and I'd had loads of fun, but where had that gotten me? Lots of lovers, but no love. I was on friendly terms with just about everyone I'd ever met, but I had no close friends. I'd eventually managed to make it through college and had chosen nursing as a profession because the money was decent and I enjoyed helping people. It was the one thing that had given my life purpose. But now, it was just a job, a daily grind. I'd become jaded working in the emergency department for so many years. When I'd first started working as an ED nurse, I'd felt like a superhero, like I mattered in the world. Not too many years in, though, my cape had become tarnished with the realities of the human condition. Now, I wanted more out of life—something that was real, something that wasn't here today and gone tomorrow.

Watching Atticus and Sam find each other had stirred something deep within my soul. I wanted what they had but didn't know where to find it. Maybe that was why this Jane Doe had shaken me. Deep down, I knew she was different, and it gnawed at me in so many different ways. Why had no one recognized her or come for her? Why would a beautiful goddess like her steal a car and run from the police so recklessly? How could she be so utterly alone?

At the same time, I couldn't help but be pissed off at her too. Her carelessness and lack of self-preservation had nearly gotten her killed. Did she honestly think her actions would have no consequences? What if she'd crashed into a minivan, killing a bunch of little kids? What the fuck had she been thinking?

A part of me wanted to protect her, but there was also a part that wanted to knock some common sense into her. I'd never been a saint. Forgiveness wasn't my thing. But something was nagging at the edges of my conscience, compelling me to find all of her missing pieces and put her back together again, to find out if she was worth my effort or was just another self-absorbed, shallow woman who believed she was above the laws of human decency. I'd give her the benefit of the doubt for now. My gut told me she was the kind of woman worth figuring out.

Cassidy stirred beside me, her hand slipping off my chest. I rolled away from her, trying to escape the thoughts gnawing at me. Closing my eyes, I forced myself to sleep, but it was fitful, my mind unable to let go of the image of Jane Doe lying helpless in that hospital bed.

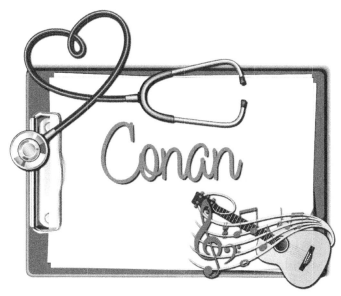

Chapter Twelve

6/2

My alarm blared, shattering sleep's hold over me before dawn had even begun to crack. I groaned and rolled over, reaching out to hit snooze on my phone, which was sitting on my bedside table. It was supposed to be one of my days off, a day to do something fun or relaxing, but there wasn't time for that today. Shaking my head, I forced myself to get out of bed.

Cassidy lay sprawled across the sheets, her breathing steady and deep. I moved slowly, careful not to jostle the bed as I slid out from under the covers. Her scent lingered on my skin, a mix of her perfume and the heat of our night together. I went into the bathroom and took a super quick shower, the hot water washing away the remnants of sex and sleep. Running a brush through my long hair, I tied it back with a hair tie, then dressed in a pair of jeans and a black T-shirt.

In the kitchen, I grabbed an energy bar from the pantry, chewing on it while I scribbled a note for Cassidy. I explained that I didn't mean to be rude by leaving early, but I had to help with a patient at the hospital. Then, I listed out the breakfast options: eggs, bacon, toast, cereal, bagels, and fruit. I made sure to mention the coffee setup—filters in the drawer, coffee in the canister, and the machine ready to go. I ended by telling her she was a beautiful, amazing woman who brought a lot of light into my life, and I valued our friendship more than she probably realized. Lastly, I told her to stay safe and that I'd see her next time.

I folded Cassidy's top neatly and placed it on the kitchen island, setting the note on top. Her laughter from last night echoed in my mind as I moved around the kitchen, tidying up and setting a few things out for her breakfast. The memory of our wild romp played in my head, a reminder of just how much I'd needed the distraction. The intensity, the raw passion—it was just what I'd been seeking to push aside my bizarre, obsessive worry for the unknown woman in the ICU, even if only for a little while.

I packed my guitar in its case, pulled on my black combat boots, and headed out the door, locking it behind me. I was eager to spend some time with my Jane Doe and see if she had any reaction to me or my music.

As soon as I arrived at the hospital, I stopped at the ICU nurses' station, where Emily sat shuffling through some charts. Her eyes lit up when she saw me.

"Hey, Conan. Back again?" she asked, her brows arching playfully.

"Yeah, just wanted to see how our girl's doing today and maybe play for her," I said, hoisting my guitar case up so she could see it over the counter.

"Actually, she's showing some promising signs. After you left last night, we did a whole battery of tests—motor responses, reflexes, and an EEG. She even had another CT scan."

I raised an eyebrow. "And?"

"She's hanging in there. Reflexes are better than expected, and the EEG didn't show anything worrying. The CT scan was clean too, with no new issues. She's tough. I'll give her that." Emily flipped through some pages on her clipboard.

"That's damn good to hear. How's she doing with consciousness? With those results, it seems like she should be coming around."

"Still out, but with responses like these, it's just a matter of time. You know how TBIs affect everyone differently," she said with a shrug.

Nodding, I glanced toward Jane Doe's room. One of the four different police officers I'd become acquainted with over the last few days sat by the door. I approached him, my boots thudding softly on the tiled floor. He'd seen me enough to know who I was even when I wasn't wearing my scrubs.

"I'll be sticking around for a bit," I said. "Gonna play some tunes for her. A little music therapy." The officer just nodded, barely glancing up from his phone.

Inside her room, I set the guitar case down gently, then popped it open to pull out my favorite acoustic guitar.

Pulling up a chair beside her bed, I propped my boot on the edge, leaned back, and began the soft, familiar intro to a timeless rock ballad, "Nothing Else Matters" by Metallica. My fingers found their rhythm, moving over the strings with practiced ease.

My girl's face was peaceful, framed by her long, wavy chestnut hair. Even in stillness, she looked stunning. As I played, I watched her closed eyes, noting every movement under their lids and every flutter of her lashes. It did seem like she could hear me. Maybe the music was reaching somewhere deep inside her.

Over the next few hours, I kept playing for her. The soft melodies filled the room as I sang along. Every so often, her face twitched, and I took that as a sign to keep going, pouring more feeling into every chord and word.

Time slipped by unnoticed until a different nurse, from the day shift, popped her head in to give me a gentle reminder: "Visiting hours are wrapping up. It's time to go."

I nodded, finishing the last verse in a whisper. Then I placed the guitar back in its case, clipped it shut, and stood up, giving my back a good stretch before approaching the bed.

My gaze lingered on her for a moment. "See you tomorrow, my pretty warrior," I whispered, my voice barely audible over the soft beeps of the remaining monitors. I could've sworn I saw her brow furrow before I stepped out of the room. Maybe she was near to regaining consciousness.

Chapter Thirteen

6/2

Music, like a lasso, tugged at my awareness. Soft strands of a familiar melody drifted along like wisps of mist in my mind, awakening something from the murky depths of nothingness in my mind. Each flicker of recognition drew me closer to consciousness.

There was a voice too. I focused on it as it tapped at the fringes of my mind and enticed me tenderly back to the present.

I tried to move, but found I was encased in something thick and unyielding. It was like being buried beneath the icy-cold remnants of an avalanche.

And then the pain seized my attention. I could no longer hear the melody or feel the voice's warmth wrapping around me.

Stabbing pain erupted against my skull, and the cold turned to fiery tendrils. They began racing through every vein, nerve, and fiber of my being. Each breath was like inhaling shards of glass. Panic started to take over, but I couldn't move—I couldn't get away from the fire.

Calm down. Just calm down and focus.

My mind was hazy and thick, as if I was half asleep or in some drug- or liquor-induced stupor. Confusion and fear swirled around, muddling my ability to comprehend.

Where was I?

What was happening to me?

Wait...what was my name?

The answers were there, but as soon as I tried to snatch a hold of them and force them to connect, they evaporated. Dammit, I knew they were there. It was like when a word was on the tip of your tongue, but it just wouldn't come. The circuits in my brain were misfiring. Why couldn't I recall my own name?!

The faint notes of a song danced across my mind once again. I compelled myself to focus only on the deep, soothing timbre of the voice that was singing. I told myself to breathe in and breathe out to each strum of the guitar's strings.

I was alive and breathing on my own. All I needed was a little time.

Little by little, I calmed myself enough to gather clues about my circumstances. I was resting in a bed. I could hear soft, mechanical beeps and swooshes. And there was a stale antiseptic smell coming directly into my nose. It took what felt like forever for me to connect the dots. I was in a hospital.

That explained the pain. I didn't like feeling helpless or out of control. I had to stop and assess my current situation and break down the events that had landed me here.

Fingers—I tried to curl them into a fist, but with all my effort, they barely brushed against the smooth surface they rested on.

Toes—they wouldn't wiggle, but I knew they were there.

Eyes—I just had to open them. Let someone know I was here. But no, they wouldn't obey my command.

I was frozen inside my icy crypt. My only saving grace was the voice—*his* voice, each note sung with a gentleness that was like a lifeline cast across the turbulent seas of my mind. I clung to it, the intonation blending with the gentle plucking of guitar strings and somehow softening the sharpest edges of my pain. I swallowed. This motion that should've come naturally was now a forced maneuver.

But soon I found that each breath was getting easier, a little less like inhaling glass. Each note of the song brought me one step away from the precipice of panic.

As I lay there, tethered to life by the melody, something encouraging began to happen. The darkness that swirled around the edges of my consciousness receded a bit, pushed away by the warmth of his song. The fear that had clutched my heart started to dissolve, replaced by a deep, overwhelming gratitude. Here in this sterile hospital room, amidst the beeping machines, his music was my sanctuary.

I wanted to tell him. I wanted to open my eyes, to speak, to let him know that his presence was my only comfort. But my body refused to cooperate, and I remained a silent, invisible listener, my voice locked deep within.

Then, another voice pierced the serenity—a woman's voice, crisp and professional, saying, "Visiting hours are wrapping up. It's time to go." A simple sentence, yet it fell upon my ears like a sentence of doom.

Desperation surged within me, an urgent plea for him not to leave. I needed him. His voice was the only thing keeping the darkness at bay. But I was powerless, my thoughts unspoken, my pleas unheard. I wanted to cry out, to beg, to hold on to the man.

"See you tomorrow, my pretty warrior," he whispered. Then, the sound of his footsteps—a soft shuffle—faded away. With the absence of his voice, the cold void descended immediately, enveloping me once more.

More questions hit me. Why did he sound so worried? Did I know this man? He claimed me as his, but I had no memory of him. But then again, my mind was a jumbled mess. Did I have a memory of anyone?

A single tear escaped, tracing a warm path down my cheek. The comforting blanket of his music had been ripped away, leaving the bleak reality of my solitude to press down upon me.

As the door clicked shut, a heavy darkness rolled over me again, thick and suffocating. Everything went dark once more—the pain, the fear, and the loneliness merging into an oppressive force that dragged me into the realm of sleep.

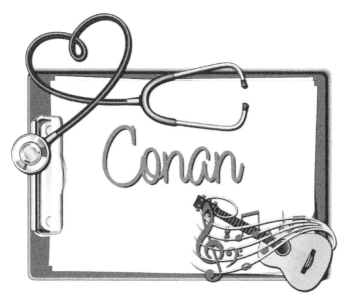

Chapter Fourteen

6/5 evening

Studying my Jane Doe's face as I played, I could have sworn her eyes opened. I jumped to my feet and leaned over her bed to see if she was awake. But no, her eyes were shut tight. Frustrated, I'd plopped back down into the chair, which gave a loud scuff, and heaved a sigh. The song, "Say Something" by A Great Big World, came to mind, so I began playing the notes. I loved its discordant melody, but in my version, I sang that I was *not* giving up on her, hoping she'd get the message. Just as I was finishing the song, one of the nurses reminded me that visiting hours were over and that I needed to leave.

After strumming the last chord of my evening set, I packed up my guitar and made my way out of the ICU. This was my last day off. The previous two days—during both the morning and evening visiting hours—I'd sat here in my sleeping beauty's room, watching her as I played and hoping she would awaken. I had developed quite the following among not only the ICU patients and staff but also the police officers assigned to watch over Jane Doe. Damn, did I hate calling her that. I was eager for her to regain consciousness so I could learn more about her—find out her name. She'd been here and unconscious for nine days, and I was beginning to wonder if she'd ever wake up.

I hadn't talked to Atticus in a few days, so I headed over to the ED on my way out to see if he had any news regarding her ties to the Volkovs. The familiar chaos hit me as soon as I badged open the automatic doors that separated the rest of the hospital from the ED.

Bethany spotted me as soon as I entered, her eyes brightening despite her obvious fatigue from a long shift. Her dark hair was staging a playful escape from her ponytail, sticking out around her face. "Hey Conan, how's your mysterious lady doing?" she called out, leaning against the nurses' station.

I shrugged, sliding my guitar case onto a nearby chair. "She's the same. I've been playing some guitar for her, hoping it might spark something to get her to wake up."

Bethany's eyes sparkled with mischief, a smile playing on her lips. "A guitar serenade, huh? You're really into this Jane Doe, I see. I've never known you to get so infatuated with a patient before. What gives?" She laughed. "Sounds like someone's got a bit of a crush."

A flush crept up my neck, a rarity for me. "Nah, it's nothing like that. It's just that...she's been alone for too long. No one's come looking for her. It's messed up. She's the first Jane Doe who hasn't been found after a day or so, y'know? Feels shitty to leave her all alone like that."

In truth, I was captivated by her. It wasn't only that she was gorgeous; it was also the unexplained circumstances surrounding her.

"Sure, sure." Bethany chuckled, pushing off from the counter. "Whatever you say, big guy. I've just never seen you this hooked on a patient—or any woman for that matter. Well, except for that momentary crush you had on Sam," she said, smirking. Bethany was an expert at harassing me.

I cracked a smile, uncomfortable with how close to home her words hit. "Well, there's a first time for everything, right? By the way, have you seen Atticus?" I asked, changing the subject before Bethany could dig any deeper.

She glanced at her watch and then back up at me. "Should be done soon. I think he's wrapping up with a patient in room six."

Before I could take a step in that direction, Bethany stopped me. "Hey Conan, did you hear the good news yet?"

I raised an eyebrow, curious. "What's up?"

"Samantha's moving to the day shift next week. We'll actually get to see her in the daylight for a change!"

A smile broke across my face. "Wow, that's awesome. We should all go out and celebrate. Grab dinner or something."

Bethany's eyes sparkled. "That's a great idea! I'll text Sam now." With that, she whipped out her phone and started tapping away.

I left her to it and headed toward the clinical workstation, where I spotted Atticus leaning back in his chair with his hands clasped behind his head. He seemed lost in thought, his eyes narrowed in concentration.

"Hey, Atticus," I said, interrupting his contemplation. He looked up, tilting his head slightly in curiosity.

"Conan, what's up?"

I leaned against the workstation and asked in a low voice, "Heard anything new from the FBI or Tacoma PD? Or maybe something from Colton about Viktor Volkov or the Volkovi Notchi?"

Colton, Atticus's close friend from his time in the Navy, had helped rescue Sam from Viktor's kidnapping plot back in December. If anyone could squeeze information out of law enforcement, it was him.

Atticus straightened up, resting his arms on the desk. "Actually, yeah. Colton called me yesterday. The Volkov estate was sold a few days ago—on the day of Jane Doe's break-in. The private deal listed the property as now being owned by a trust, with some New York City socialite as the beneficiary and an attorney up in Seattle as the trustee. Seems a little too coincidental, don't you think?"

"The day after her wreck, huh?" I mused, grazing my thumb over my lower lip. "That timing doesn't sit right with me either. Could our Jane Doe be the woman from New York?"

"I wouldn't think so. If she owned the place, why would she break in and run from the police? That doesn't make sense," Atticus said, his eyes narrowing. "But I don't believe in coincidences. Something's definitely off about the whole thing."

I nodded, an icy knot of apprehension forming deep within my gut. "Do you think Jane Doe might be tied to the Volkovi Notchi?"

"It's a possibility we can't ignore," he said, drumming his fingers on the desk. "I know you've taken a close interest in her and have been spending a lot of time with her, Conan. Just be careful, all right? She's a patient, first and foremost, and brain injuries can make things...complicated. Especially if she's got a troubled past or dangerous ties."

I shifted uncomfortably. "I get it, man. I'm keeping it professional. But damn, she's been there alone for days. No one's come looking for her even with all the press pushing out her pictures. It's tearing me up."

Atticus sighed, running a hand through his hair. "I know, and I'm not saying don't care. Just…watch your step. She'll be in a delicate place emotionally when she wakes up, and if she's connected to the Volkovi, it could spell trouble. We don't need more of that, especially not with Samantha's history. She's still having nightmares about what happened. Her therapist has been great at helping her rein in her panic attacks, but she doesn't need a setback."

I clenched my jaw, thinking about the risks. "Understood. But I can't just walk away from her, Atticus. No one should be that alone."

"Yeah, I agree. For all we know, she could have gotten herself into some trouble with the Volkovi. They could be looking to do her harm. Who knows?"

"On a lighter note," I said, "while I was playing for her the last couple of days, she had some rapid eye movements, and her face was twitching a bit. I could have sworn she even opened her eyes for a second. I think she might be close to waking up. Hopefully, she'll be able to tell us something about herself or the Volkovi soon."

Atticus raised his eyebrows, his lips curving into a cautious smile. "That's promising. Keep me posted, okay? Oh, and make sure to keep your eyes open, little brother."

I pushed off from the counter and headed toward the chair where I'd left my guitar. "Always do," I said over my shoulder.

Grabbing my guitar case, I slung it over my shoulder and pulled the strap tight against my back. As I walked past Atticus,

I added, "I'm heading out. Tell Sam I said hello and we need to get together soon for dinner."

"Will do. Have a good night," Atticus said, giving me a nod and turning his attention back to the computer screen.

"Night," I called out as I headed toward the exit.

Chapter Fifteen

6/5 evening

The chords of a guitar and the voice of the man I'd come to rely on as my mental savior gently woke me from sleep. Each time he visited, the damaged parts of my mind healed, growing stronger, helping me remember and accept that I was still alive.

I was determined to see him, to let him know I was awake. Summoning all my force of will, I squinted, peeling my sticky eyelashes apart. Piercing bright light slammed against my retinas, splitting my skull wide open. Instantly, I squeezed them shut. Pain and confusion swirled around like dark wraiths, poking and nudging at my mind, threatening to pull me back into the void I'd been so desperate to escape.

He stopped playing, and I heard the rustle of clothing. Was he standing? He must have noticed me open my eyes! If only there was something he could do to end this nightmare I was stuck in.

But no. After a moment of silence, the chair scraped against the floor. With a sigh, he started into a new song. He sang that he was *not* giving up on me, and his voice had such a commanding intensity that I knew he believed his words alone could break through the thickness in my brain and release me from my silent bonds. God, how I wanted them to.

As he had done during his other visits, he continued to play and sing until someone told him it was time to go. The chair softly creaked under his shifting weight when he stood. A muffled thud followed as he settled his guitar into its case, followed by the metallic clicks of the latches. And then he walked away, his footsteps shuffling across the floor. I couldn't bear for him to leave.

I had no concept of time, and I had no idea what had landed me in such a predicament, but my instinct was to fight—to resurface and find answers.

Every inch of my body ached. Gravity seemed to press down three times harder than it should have. Oh my God, I had to break free.

Anger and frustration simmered deep in my core. The monitor keeping time to my heartbeat ratcheted up. The pounding in my skull sent a shock wave of pain cascading through every nerve. There was nothing left for me to do but scream.

I unleashed a shrieking sound unlike any that had ever come from me before. I squeezed my eyes tight, and my face contorted from all the emotions that had been bound and twisted inside me for however long I'd endured this ordeal. Unable to remain still a moment longer, I bolted upright, and the noise morphed into a wail that went on and on for what seemed like eons.

A gentle hand stroked the side of my arm. "Shh, you're okay. Just take some slow, deep breaths for me." I recognized the kind voice; it belonged to one of my nurses.

Gulping in a huge breath, I stopped screaming. Each inhale and exhale sounded loud in my ears. The nurse tried to guide me to lie back, but I fought her, keeping my eyes shut as I flailed around.

"How about I raise the head of your bed so you can rest upright for now?" she calmly suggested. The bed rattled, and soon the mattress rose to meet my back, allowing me to relax against it.

I swallowed hard and ever so cautiously peeked through my eyelashes, taking in my surroundings for the first time. As my eyes adjusted to the light, I slowly opened them to see a nurse with a kind, round face standing next to the bed. Another nurse stood in the doorway, syringe in hand, at the ready.

"See, you're okay," the kind nurse said. "You were in a car accident a while ago, but you've come a long way. Soon, we'll have you up and about. For now, you have to try to stay still and allow yourself to adjust, to finish healing." She checked some of the tubes attached to my arms. "Can you stay calm, or should I have Katie over there give you some medicine to help?"

"No!" I said, the word coming out in a rasp. "Please, no more meds." The scratchiness of my voice surprised and irritated me.

She laid her hand on top of mine.

"Don't touch me!" I shouted.

"Okay, no worries," she said, turning and waving off the other nurse and taking a step back. "I'm sure you're feeling very confused. My name is Emily. If you need me, just push this button." She handed me a remote control that was attached to the side of the bed. "Sit here for a minute while I get you some water to sip on. We're in no rush. I'll be right here to help you and answer all your questions."

Emily quickly brought a cup of water with a straw. She advised that I go slow and only drink a little at a time. The cool liquid helped temper the flames in my throat. She told me to relax for a few minutes and maybe watch a little TV before the doctors came by to check on me. I thanked her but chose to sit in silence. I needed to gather my thoughts.

Shifting my hands to my lap, I stretched out my fingers. All present and functional, thank God. My eyes slid up my arms. Stuck in my wrist was…what was that thing called? Oh yeah, the word was *IV*. There were bruises too, an entire road map of them. Carefully, I raised my knees, sliding the bottoms of my feet along the smooth fabric beneath. I checked to see if I could wiggle my toes. Yes, they all seemed fine as well.

I was overwhelmed and groggy. My thoughts were disjointed, like I was physically having to push them uphill just to connect one with the next. I had so many questions. What happened? Where was I? What day was it? I glanced around for clues. Outside, the sun was low in the sky. It must be evening. Oh, wait, maybe the day was just dawning?

I didn't know who I was or how I'd gotten here. I had so many questions. And each question demanded an answer, but I had none. Zero.

The walls seemed to close in around me. My breaths became quick and frantic. I knew I had better get it together. If I didn't, they would come back with more drugs. My brain was bleary enough as it was. I didn't want that to happen.

My chest tightened, each breath shallow and rapid, my pulse pounding in my ears. I gripped the edge of the bed, my knuckles turning white, trying to ground myself. Panic clawed at my mind, threatening to drag me under, and I fought desperately to stay in control, to not let the fear consume me.

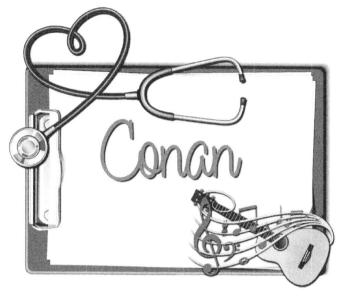

Chapter Sixteen

6/5

Just as I pushed through the doors and stepped out into the cool evening air, my phone buzzed in my pocket. I pulled it out, expecting a message from someone I knew, or some spam, but it was a text from Emily in the ICU. The message made my heart jump: *Jane Doe's awake, disoriented, and freaking out. Can you come by? Might help to have a familiar presence.*

"Shit," I muttered, spinning on my heel and charging back through the ED corridors. I caught Atticus just as he was about to disappear into another room. "Hey, Jane Doe's awake!"

His head snapped up, eyes wide. "Seriously? All right, go. I'll be there soon if I can."

I nodded and sprinted toward the ICU, my boots thudding loudly against the floor.

As I passed the hospital's gift shop, something caught my eye—a small, fluffy teddy bear perched among some gift baskets and flower arrangements. A thought struck me. Maybe something soft and nonthreatening would ease her nerves when she saw a big-ass tattooed guy entering her room. I dashed in, grabbed the teddy bear, threw some cash at the clerk without waiting for change, and kept moving.

The ICU was as quiet as ever, so I slowed down as I approached her room, not wanting to burst in like some kind of storm.

"Hey, Emily," I panted when I reached the nurses' station, brandishing the teddy bear like a carnival prize.

"She's been pretty upset since waking up," she replied.

Quietly, I peeked into Jane Doe's room. There she was, the woman who had consumed my thoughts for days. She didn't notice me standing there as she leaned against the pillows, her eyes wide and darting around the room in panic. Her breathing was rapid, and she looked ready to bolt, but even in her current state, she was still unbelievably beautiful.

Chapter Seventeen

6/5

Out of nowhere, a man's massive, tattooed hand appeared in the doorway. It held a little teddy bear in an almost comically gentle way, making the plush little guy dance and swing from side to side as he wiggled it and kept the rest of himself hidden from my view. He made the bear bob up and down to the rhythm of the song I could barely place by Bob Marley, maybe. "Be happy, you're awake and a beautiful sight. It's gonna be a good day, no troubles to fight. Smile now, everything's gonna be all right," he sang, making up his own lyrics just for me and perfectly matching the bear's antics. The playful and silly melody brought a smile to my face despite the terrible situation.

As I sat there in bed, tangled in too many wires and tubes, with my heart hammering in my ears, a storm swirled in my head.

Everything was too much—too bright, too loud, too unknown. But as I watched the bear swing from a hand that was as big as a shovel and tattooed with small patterns that moved with every little gesture, it was hard not to chuckle. The absurdity of it helped keep my panic at bay. The corners of my mouth twitched with soft laughter, and I leaned back into my pillows, watching this odd little scene unfold.

When the man finally walked into the room, the air seemed to shift with his presence. The scent of his cologne—subtle but distinctly masculine—was familiar, like the sound of his voice and made me relax a little. I couldn't believe the size of him. He was a mountain of a man, with muscles bulging under his tight shirt, each movement showing off the ink that swirled over his arms like a personal gallery of stories. This was the type of guy you'd think twice about crossing on a dark street. He moved with the kind of confidence that came from knowing he could take on the world and win. Yet, there was a warmth about him that hinted at a softer side.

Silently he walked toward the corner of the room, then shrugged off his guitar case and leaned it against the wall.

I caught myself staring, taking in every detail—from his shoulder-length dirty-blond hair half tied back in a bun to the blue scrubs barely containing all his inked muscles, down to the black boots on his feet. His appearance, so bold and imposing, made me self-conscious. Here I was, a mess, with tangled hair and a goofy-looking hospital gown draped over my body, and there he was, looking like some badass street fighter.

When he turned to face me, I dropped my gaze, embarrassed over how awful I must look. I dragged my eyes slowly back up to his face, tracing the lines of his tattoos along his arms and neck, over his chiseled jawline, and up to his eyes. When our eyes met, his breath seemed to catch for a split second, and his playful grin softened into something more intense. For a long while, he didn't speak, just stared.

Then, shaking his head as if to clear his mind, he stepped closer. In a voice low and smooth like melted chocolate, he finally said, "When your gaze met mine just now, I found myself lost in those icy blue sapphires. They're like the place where the tumultuousness of the sea meets the tranquility of the sky, stealing my breath and every word I had planned to say."

His poetic words lingered in the air between us, and my cheeks warmed, the heat spreading across my face. I couldn't help but be drawn to him, despite knowing nothing about him—or myself, for that matter.

Then it hit me—the voice. That voice had filled the silence of my dimly lit mind, had kept the haze of unconsciousness at bay over the last who knew how many days. I looked at him, really looked at him, trying to reconcile the voice with the man standing before me. He was nothing like I had pictured. How could someone so...threatening-looking carry such calm warmth in his voice? His presence had helped to pull me out of wherever I'd been trapped in my mind.

Tears sprang to my eyes. My hand flew to my mouth, emotions overtaking me.

His face melted into an expression of concern, and he closed the distance between us in two long strides, setting the teddy bear down next to me.

"I brought this little guy to make you smile," he said, giving me a crooked grin. "Figured he's less intimidating than I might be at first glance."

I smiled, drawn in by his straightforward charm and unexpected tenderness.

"Yeah, maybe just a tad less," I said with a note of sarcasm.

At this, the big guy laughed, tilting his head back slightly. "I'm Conan, by the way." He stepped back to give me some space, though every inch of him radiated a protective stance. "I'm the nurse who took care of you when you came into the emergency department, and I've been here with you, playing music, hoping it might help somehow."

"Nurse?! You...you're a nurse?" I choked out. Looking down, I realized I was wearing nothing but a hospital gown. Oh, God, how humiliating. "Sorry, I just—"

"Don't worry. No apologies are necessary. I'm used to it," he said, rubbing the back of his neck and chuckling. "I'm a damn good nurse. Once patients get over the initial shock, they're good with it. The ink actually can be a good conversation starter."

"Oh, it's not the tattoos, or your size, or—" I flailed my hands about like an idiot. "It's just that I'm rather underdressed. Have no idea where my clothes are or when I lost them."

"You have nothing to worry about. We're all respectful of patients' privacy. Besides, we've seen it all in the emergency department. I just wanted to stop by and make sure you were doing okay." He dropped his head to the side and gave me a half smile. "Hope the music therapy has helped you these last few days? My brothers ride me hard over playing for anyone who will hold still long enough."

"It did. You have no idea," I said in a rush. Overwhelmed by embarrassment and the memory of lying here paralyzed and unable to communicate, I grimaced. The throbbing in my head started up again, and I dropped my gaze, reached over, and picked up the teddy bear. I ran my fingers over its little paw, avoiding eye contact with Conan. "Thank you. It's hard... My mind is a blurry mess. I'm not sure what's real and what's not, but I do remember your songs. They're the only thing that's kept me from going completely mad."

"That's good to hear. I love playing. Don't stress over what's happening. Brain injuries are tricky. It will take time for you to heal and for your mind to sort everything out. So tell me, are you hurting anywhere? How are you feeling otherwise?" Concern was etched onto his handsome face.

"I...I don't know," I admitted, my voice shaky. "I don't even know what my name is. Sounds stupid, I know, but I only have broken pieces."

I forced myself to look up at him and smile as best I could. I didn't want him to think I didn't appreciate everything he'd done for me. There was something about Conan that made me feel safe, even amid all this chaos and confusion.

"Hey, it's all right," he reassured me, his vivid emerald-green eyes locking onto mine. "I'll help you figure this out, okay? I promise."

"Thanks. Really," I whispered. My heart sped up with gratitude and a feeling of a connection I couldn't quite explain. The mechanical beeping of the machine behind me echoed the increased tempo.

"Any time," he replied. His smile reached his eyes, lighting them up as he glanced over at the monitor. "And now that you're awake, I'm sure it's just a matter of time before your mind is able to reconnect all your memories."

His assurance, simple and firm, anchored me. I nodded, feeling safer. I was strangely at ease with this giant with tattoos and tender eyes.

"Do you know where you are?" he asked gently.

I tried to think, but my thoughts were sluggish, as if I were trying to wade through a thick fog.

I glanced around. "A hospital," I managed to say.

"Yes, you're in a hospital," Conan affirmed. "But do you know what city?"

"New York City?" I guessed, plucking the name from the top of the swirling confusion in my mind.

Conan shook his head. "No, actually you're in Tacoma, Washington. Quite a ways from New York. Does that ring a bell?"

I stared at him, my confusion deepening. "Tacoma? I've never been to Tacoma...I don't think," I whispered, the realization unsettling me.

Before Conan could respond, a tall man with dark hair and a white coat appeared in the doorway. It was a doctor. He leaned against the doorframe, frowning down at a chart.

Conan continued, "Do you know what day or month it is?"

I paused, a distant memory flickering to life in my mind. "Is it...May? My birthday month maybe?" That seemed right—and important somehow—but who knew? I was grasping at straws.

"It's June fifth," he said. "You arrived here on May twenty-eighth."

The room spun a little as the panic started to creep in. That was a lot of days to be unconscious. Just how bad were my injuries? My breathing quickened, and I shouted, "I don't even know my own name!"

Conan was quick to react, coming to sit on the edge of the bed next to me. He reached out, gently cradling my face in his hands, and pressed his forehead against mine. His touch was solid and comforting.

"You're going to be okay," he whispered, exuding a quiet confidence that reassured me. "I'm here with you. You're not alone in this. In time, you'll remember. You've been fighting a hard battle, sweet angel." As he spoke, his breath brushed softly over my lips.

He leaned back, his hands falling on top of the stuffed bear. "You know what? I'm gonna call you Angel if that's all right. I can't stand you being called Jane Doe like you're just some nobody. I think Angel fits because you kinda swooped into my life outta nowhere, and there's this...ethereal beauty about you."

The nickname, under the circumstances, touched something inside me. It was silly and sweet, and despite my inner turmoil, I found myself liking it. "Angel," I repeated, smiling slightly. Deep down, regardless of my current helplessness, I knew I was strong—that I was no angel. But with everything so jumbled, I had to let that go for now and accept his help.

Conan's tenacity, the solidness of his hands, the nickname—it all felt strangely right. "Thank you, Conan," I whispered, trying to steady my breathing. "Thank you for being here for me."

"I'll be here as long as you need me, Angel. We'll get through this together."

The doctor, whom I'd forgotten was standing at the door, cleared his throat and stepped into the room. His cool, professional air contrasted with Conan's more rugged demeanor.

Conan jumped to his feet, turned, and let out a breath, relaxing his shoulders. He stepped back, allowing the doctor to approach my bed.

"Good evening. I'm Dr. Atticus Thorin," he said with a nod, his eyes scanning the chart briefly before meeting mine. "I treated you when you first arrived in the emergency department, and I'm also Conan's older brother." He glanced over his shoulder and flashed Conan a quick half smile.

I glanced from one to the other, searching for the resemblance but not seeing much. Dr. Thorin continued speaking, but I struggled to pay attention to what he was saying. "You're experiencing what we call traumatic amnesia, likely due to the concussion you suffered. Which means you've lost memories formed before the accident. It's caused by damage to the hippocampus, a region of the brain that plays a crucial role in the consolidation of information from short-term to long-term memory. It's common in patients with significant head injuries. Essentially, your brain is protecting itself while it heals."

His brow furrowed slightly in concern. "How are you feeling physically? Any discomfort from the seat belt, or perhaps pain in your arms and legs?"

I hadn't thought about it until he asked. Hesitantly, I lifted the edge of my hospital gown, peeked under it, and caught sight of the dark greenish bruises marring my skin. I inhaled sharply—more from surprise than pain—while recoiling from the sight.

"The bruising may look severe but is expected, given the nature of your accident," Dr. Thorin commented, making a note on the chart. "And your breathing? Any difficulty there?"

I hesitated as I considered this, aware of a slight tightness in my chest that I hadn't noticed before. "My chest feels a bit heavy." Swallowing hard, I grumbled, "And my throat feels like I drank razor blades."

"That's consistent with a condition you had upon arrival—right middle lobe atelectasis," he explained. "It required intubation at the scene of the wreck, and you were placed on a ventilator to assist your breathing. It's not uncommon for patients to feel some residual effects from the mechanical ventilation, such as soreness or a hoarse throat."

All the details made my head spin.

Conan said gently, "Maybe we can go over this in bits and pieces, huh? Give her some time to adjust."

Atticus nodded, his expression softening. "Of course. You're in excellent hands here in the ICU, and the team has noted your good progress. If this continues, you'll soon be moved to a private room and eventually outpatient therapy. You've made remarkable progress so far." He turned to Conan. "Let me know if you need anything."

With a final smile and a nod to me, he left the room.

Conan moved closer. "Don't worry about all that right now," he said. "Just focus on today, on this moment. We'll tackle everything else as it comes."

His words, simple and direct, helped ease my mind after the torrent of information Dr. Thorin had unleashed.

"So he's your brother, huh?" I asked.

Conan chuckled, shoving a hand in his pocket. "Yeah, there's three of us Thorin brothers. And you're not going to believe this, but all of us worked with you just after your wreck. Braxton was the EMT who scooped you up and brought you to our ED."

"Whoa. That's a lot to take in." I shifted slightly on the hospital bed, wincing from the dull ache that seemed to run through my entire body. "Tell me everything you know about me and what happened," I pleaded, desperate for any information that could help me regain my lost past.

Conan dragged the armchair closer to me and perched casually on the edge. Hesitating, he rubbed the scruff of his beard before beginning his explanation. "You didn't have any ID on you when you arrived. Police didn't find a phone either. What we do know...well, it's kind of a wild story."

I chewed on my lower lip, bracing myself.

"You broke into a large home on an exclusive estate property," he said, watching my reaction closely. "When the police showed up, you took off in one of the homeowner's cars. It was a stormy morning and raining hard."

I gasped. "Stolen?" I tried to imagine myself doing any of that, but my mind was blank.

He kept going. "You were driving really fast and ended up going off the road, wrapping the car around a tree. They had to use the jaws of life to get you out."

I absorbed his words, an image of twisted metal and shattered glass forming in my mind. "Sounds like I'm lucky to be alive."

"Damn right you are," he agreed, smiling. "And you were smart enough to buckle up. You might be the safest car thief I've ever heard of."

Despite the situation, I chuckled. "Happy to be alive, but not feeling so lucky right now." I knocked my index finger against my head. "Every part of me hurts, and I can't remember who I am or much else."

His expression softened. "I might know someone who can help you with what you're going through. Atticus's fiancée had a traumatic brain injury not long ago, after she dealt with some... pretty serious stuff. I'll ask her to come by and talk to you. You'll like her a lot. She's a fiery little thing."

Our conversation was cut short when Emily knocked on the door. "Conan, this isn't normal visiting hours," she said with a friendly yet professional demeanor. "We need to check on our patient."

Conan stood, his large frame towering over me once more. "Right, right. Just so you know, Jane Doe is going by the name Angel now," he told Emily, grinning widely.

Emily looked at me, a giggle escaping from her. "Is that the name you're choosing, or is Conan choosing for you?"

Glancing over at him, I nodded. "Absolutely my choice."

"Good night, Angel," Conan said as he walked away, his voice making me all tingly inside. As soon as I lost sight of him, my face fell, and I slumped over, heaving a defeated sigh. Noticing my disappointment, Emily gave me a knowing smile.

"Don't worry, he left his guitar. He'll be back."

After Emily left, I lay back, thinking about Conan's return. The thought made my stomach flutter. Despite the dreadfulness of my situation, I found myself looking forward to seeing him again. The butterflies in my stomach seemed to agree.

Chapter Eighteen

6/6 - 6/9

The last few days had passed in a fog of amnesia, each awakening a disorienting plunge into an unfamiliar world. They'd stepped me down from the ICU to a progressive care unit three days ago, and now I was finally in a regular hospital room. It felt like I'd lived a month in this hospital, but it had only been a couple of weeks since my accident. The progressive care unit was quieter and less intense, which was nice, but something about hospital care made me crave the outside world like never before. Hopefully, this new room would give me a little privacy.

Conan, the nurse who had kind of adopted me since I'd landed in the emergency room, was a great distraction through it all. On his breaks, he would often pop in with a milkshake or some fast food, making the hospital seem less like a prison and more like some kind of weird dorm. He talked—a lot—and through his stories; I was getting to know not just about him but about his brothers and Samantha too.

Although he was careful not to say anything that might bring back bad memories, I could tell he was curious to figure out who I really was. He had been great, but even he couldn't stop the waves of frustration that hit me hard when the neuropsychologist visited. Dr. Schneider had come by a few times, trying to jog my memory using various techniques and even hypnosis, but he'd had no luck—my past remained a blank slate.

When I wasn't doing sessions with the neuropsychologist, seeing various therapists, or being visited by Conan, I vegged out a lot by watching TV and trying to read. Reading was tough at first; my brain functioned like it had short-circuited, but gradually it was getting better. I could now get through a few chapters without feeling exhausted. It was progress, I guess.

Now that I'd been moved to a regular room, I was looking forward to starting physical therapy in the gym. I had a gut feeling that I used to be super active. Maybe I was a runner? Or did yoga? Who knew? I was curious to find out. It was weird, but moving my body felt like the one thing that might help me connect with who I was before all this.

The transition from room to room hadn't been easy. Each move had brought a mix of relief and anxiety. It was bizarre, being so disconnected from myself while my body ticked off all the boxes on the recovery list. Perhaps it was the lingering uncertainty about who I was or what my life had been like before the accident that unnerved me. Sadly, while my body healed, my memories lagged far behind. Some were muddled, but most were still missing entirely because of the amnesia.

Just as I'd finished settling into my new hospital room, there was a knock on the door before it clicked softly and swung open. A woman wearing leggings and a cute sports top breezed in.

When she took a step closer, I noticed a nursing badge attached to a lanyard around her neck. She seemed to be about my age and had an easy smile to go along with her fiery red hair. Everything about her lit up the room. This woman was instantly likable. She had to be the one Conan had told me about.

"Hey there! You must be Angel. I'm Samantha, but you can call me Sam. I work down in the ED alongside Conan and Dr. Thorin. Well, I'm actually engaged to him, so I guess it's okay to call him Atticus since I'm not on duty. I'm still getting used to the idea of marrying a doctor I work with." She giggled. "Do you mind if I come in and hang out for a while? I heard you've been through quite a lot, kinda like what I've experienced myself."

"Sure, I could use some company. So far, no one claims to know me." I rolled my eyes and gave a half-shrug.

"God, that has to suck. At least when I fell and cracked my head on the concrete, I woke up with most of my memories and was surrounded by people who cared about me. I didn't recall what happened just before, but it was a crazy scene, so that was probably for the best." She pulled a chair closer and plopped down onto it.

I shifted slightly on the bed, trying to get more comfortable as I turned toward where she sat—intrigued by her openness and willingness to not sugarcoat my situation. "It's nice to meet you, Sam. Conan has mentioned you a few times."

Sam smiled. "Oh, God, can that man talk. Am I right? He's been worrying over you since the moment you came through our doors."

The thought of him worrying about me sent a thrill skittering down my spine. "Yeah, he can for sure talk a lot. But I have to admit, though, that I loved him singing to me. I swear it was his music therapy—as he called it—that triggered me to wake up.

His voice was like warm honey on a hot buttered biscuit. I could listen to it all day. And, oh, was he particularly pleasant to wake up to!" I sighed.

Sam laughed again. I guessed she could tell by the look on my face where my thoughts had drifted off to.

She leaned in a little, and the playfulness in her face faded into a more serious expression. "I wanted to come and see you because, not too long ago, I was pretty much where you're at now. I had a traumatic brain injury and figured I might be able to offer some...I don't know, insider advice, or just an ear. Conan told me a bit about what you've been dealing with...the amnesia and all. I can't imagine how discombobulating it must be. After my injuries, there were so many things I had to work through just to feel safe again."

I appreciated her straightforwardness. There was no pity in her tone, just an understanding that came from a lived experience.

"Conan said you were involved with some serious stuff," I probed, curious despite myself.

She let out a bitter chuckle. "Yeah, 'serious stuff' is one way to put it. A Russian mafia organization called the Volkovi Notchi kidnapped me. Ever heard of them?" At my shake of the head, she continued. "Well, it was terrifying. They're really bad news. There was a shoot-out in a warehouse at the Port of Tacoma. Atticus, Conan, and their brother, Braxton, came to the rescue along with a security team."

It sounded like the plot of a crime thriller, not something that could happen to a person in real life. "That's insane. I can't believe that happened to you."

"It's definitely one of my least-fond memories," Sam said dryly. "The head of the mafia syndicate in this area, Viktor Volkov, managed to escape with a couple of his thugs. They're probably in Russia now. We don't know who all is involved or if they're still trying to hurt us. But we know he's out there somewhere."

I sat up a bit straighter, my heart thumping. The idea of such violence was horrifying. "That sounds awful, Sam," I said. An icy shiver made the hair on my arms stand up.

"It's like living with a constant shadow over your head, knowing that someone could be lurking around waiting to kill you." She paused, glancing down at her hands. "And the not knowing is the hardest part. I still get nightmares, and it sucks because it's not just me it affects—it's Atticus too." A wave of melancholy crossed over her face.

"Having to look over your shoulder all the time... You're brave, Sam. No one should have to live in that kind of fear."

She shrugged, brushing off the compliment. "We do what we have to, right?"

As she revealed more details about her abduction and the sinister dealings of the mafia, the name "Volkov" snagged in my subconscious. With each mention, the unease grew in my mind.

Samantha leaned back in the chair and sighed. "And honestly, Viktor Volkov is just the worst sort of scum. It's like his heart is made of that cold Russian ice or something. The stuff they were into—drug dealing, human trafficking, kidnapping, you name it—was so, so bad." As she spoke, her hands moved to emphasize each word.

At the third or fourth mention of that name, something snapped inside me, triggering a rush of fragmented images. A vivid, jarring memory burst through the fog that had clouded my past. I saw a ruthless man with a snarl on his face. Power and danger rolled off him in waves. Next to him stood a striking woman. She had sharp features, and her lips were painted a bold red.

The room faded, and Samantha's voice became a distant buzz as the memory consumed me. My face twisted in pain, my body went rigid, and my gaze locked onto something only I could see while I began to relive a heart-wrenching separation.

The scene played out on the steps of a massive estate. A giant, ornately decorated wooden door loomed behind the man and woman. The woman's hand reached out and clutched my forearm painfully tight, pulling me away from a boy who stood frozen next to the vile man. The boy's eyes met mine, helplessness and anger filling them as the woman forcefully dragged me toward a waiting car. In desperation, I kicked my legs against the stone pavers, my screams piercing the air, but it was no use. The man shoved the boy through the door before disappearing inside the house and slamming the door shut.

"Angel? Hey, are you okay?" Samantha's voice penetrated the haze. She gently touched my arm.

I blinked, the room snapping back into focus. She was now standing next to the bed. "I...I just remembered something," I said in a shaky whisper.

"What was it?" she asked, stroking my arm reassuringly.

"It was...confusing. Children being pulled apart. It was just so sad." The words were inadequate to describe the intensity of the memory, but they were all I could muster. The pain of being dragged away from someone I loved twisted my insides, but I couldn't tell if it was my own memory or something I'd seen on TV.

"Children?" Sam repeated, her brow furrowing in confusion.

"Yeah, it's all a bit jumbled. But it felt very real." I rubbed my temples, as if I could smooth out the creases of my disheveled thoughts.

"Was it someone you know?" she prodded gently.

"I'm not sure. It was too disjointed for me to make sense of it fully." The connection to the name Volkov lingered in my mind, but I chose to keep it to myself, unsure of what it meant or how it tied everything together.

Sam gave my hand a reassuring squeeze. "It's okay. These things might take time to piece together. And hey, if you need someone to talk to, or if anything else comes back to you—any memories or feelings—just know I'm here, okay?"

"Thanks, Sam," I said, managing a smile. I was grateful for her support, even as the shadows of my memory loomed large in the back of my mind.

Without warning, the door to my hospital room swung open, and Conan's massive frame filled the doorway. Despite his intimidating appearance, he radiated warmth and happiness like a human golden retriever.

"Damn, Angel, look at you! You're looking great today!" he exclaimed, grinning from ear to ear. "It's good to see you out of the PCU and in a private room. This is a serious upgrade!" Walking up next to my bed, he swept his arms wide, assessing the small room.

"Oh yeah, I'm sure I look great with this scar running across my forehead and over my brow," I said sarcastically.

Conan leaned in closer, dropping his hand to the mattress next to me, and gave my head a closer look. "Well, if you ask me, it looks totally badass, like a villain in a movie. You raise that brow at somebody and give them the evil eye, and they're gonna think twice about crossing you." He gave me a wink. "If I were you, I'd keep it. It's sexy as hell—like a well-placed tattoo—and in that, I'm an expert," he said, standing up and raising the hem of his shirt to his collar.

At the sight of his ripped abs, covered in a montage of inked images, I gasped. I swallowed hard as my eyes traced his V-cut to the edge of his pants, where a hint of a red-lipstick tattoo made me want to take a taste.

Before I could respond, he released his shirt and swooped over to Samantha, effortlessly hoisting her off the ground in a bear hug. "How's my favorite sister-in-law?"

Samantha laughed, kicking her dangling legs slightly. "I'm not your sister-in-law yet, Conan! Put me down, you big oaf. This is not the place for rowdiness."

Conan chuckled and set her down, his eyes crinkling at the corners. "Since when did you start caring about being proper? Atticus's influence, I bet. You used to be fun."

Samantha put her hands on her hips, feigning indignation. "Excuse me? I'm still fun. It's just that someone has to be the adult around here."

"Oh, yeah?" Conan teased, a mischievous grin spreading across his face. "Bet you haven't even touched those video games I left you guys. Atticus too stiff to learn how to handle a controller?"

Samantha shot back with a playful smirk, "Oh, we've been playing, just not the kind of games you're thinking about. Let's just say Atticus has his hands full."

Conan groaned. "Jesus, Sam, there are things a brother just doesn't need to get a visual of! Already been there and done that. I'll never be able to get the cabin-hot-tub incident out of my mind."

"Shut up! Don't even go there," Sam retorted playfully, pretending to be offended.

While I listened to their banter, the heaviness that had settled over our earlier conversation dissipated, and I found myself smiling, genuinely amused by their dynamic. It was a welcome distraction from the dark memory my mind had dredged up after Sam shared her terrifying mafia ordeal with me.

"All right, you two, that's too much information," I cut in, chuckling. "Keep it out of the gutter, will you? My imagination is already running wild."

Conan pulled up a chair next to Sam's, his gigantic frame making it squeak in protest as he sat down. "So, what were you guys getting into? Anything I can help with?"

"Just hearing about the mafia goons that kidnapped Sam when a disturbing memory flashed into my mind," I said, glancing at Samantha, who nodded. My face fell, and I worried my lower lip with my teeth.

Conan's face softened. "Anything new pop up that's bothering you?"

I hesitated. Images of the stern man and woman were still vivid in my mind. But I shook my head slowly. "Just bits and pieces. Nothing clear enough to make sense of yet."

"Well, if there's anything you remember, any detail that may lead us to figure out your identity, you know we're here for you, right?" Conan frowned in concern, his usual bravado tempered in light of the seriousness of the situation.

"Yeah, I know," I assured him. "Thanks, Conan."

He nodded, then stood up, stretching his back with a grunt. "All right, I'll let you ladies get back to it. I just wanted to stop by and say hi. Sam, try not to corrupt my older brother too much, yeah?"

Samantha waved him off, shaking her head. "Ha! Me? Corrupt him? That's a good one." She walked with Conan toward the door, and he stopped and gave her a quick side-hug.

"Well, you did manage to break through all that ice surrounding his 'bachelor for life' heart. I'll give you that," Conan said with a smirk before walking out.

Samantha rolled her eyes and chuckled, but I caught the blush that crept up her neck. As she brushed off Conan's departing shot, he spun on his heel and returned to the doorway, a second thought bringing him back into the room. "Wait, I almost forgot," he said, his gaze softening as he looked at me. "Pretty soon, they'll kick you out of here. I bet you can't wait."

I managed a weak smile, but the thought of leaving wasn't as comforting as he probably imagined it was. "Yeah, and straight into a jail cell with that cop watching me like a hawk," I muttered, nodding toward the officer stationed outside my door.

Conan glanced at the officer and grimaced. Turning back to me, he leaned in, lowering his voice. "Don't worry, I'm gonna help you with that. Atticus and I have been talking. He's got a lawyer friend who's already on board to help with your case at the arraignment."

His words should have eased my mind, but a chill ran through me instead. "But what if I did something terrible?" I whispered. "What if I actually broke into that place or...or worse?"

"Hey," Conan said, his voice firm, "we're gonna figure it out. And if you remember anything about why you might have been at the Volkov estate or why you ran, just tell us. It may help clear things up."

A wave of nausea passed through me at the mere idea of having any association with such people. I shook my head. "I can't imagine I'm tied to people like that, to a mafia crime family. It just doesn't fit. Mafia, crime...it's not me. I don't remember much, but I know I'm not like that."

The distress must have shown clearly on my face because Samantha quickly interjected, "If you were friendly with the likes of them, you wouldn't have been running away like your life depended on it. We don't think you're one of them, but maybe you were caught up in some sort of entanglement with their dealings, like what happened to me because of my dad."

Conan nodded. "Let's put that aside for now. Soon you'll be out of here and hanging out with me. You've got to know that'll be a—"

His words were cut short as two Tacoma police officers stepped around him and entered the room.

"Good afternoon, Miss. I'm Detective Brady from Tacoma PD, and this is Officer Miller," he said, indicating a female officer behind him. "We need to ask you a few questions. This is regarding what happened on the morning of May twenty-eighth—when you broke into the old Volkov estate, stole a car, and fled from police before crashing into a tree." He walked further into the room, with Miller trailing behind him.

Conan stepped in between me and the officers, his size instantly filling the space like a protective barrier. "Is this necessary, guys? She's still recovering and just getting her bearings," he asked, his tone respectful yet firm.

My stomach churned, and I braced myself for the interrogation to come.

Without responding, Detective Brady glanced at Conan, then back at me. "Miss, before we proceed with any questions, I need to inform you that I have a warrant for your arrest and inform you of your rights." He paused, ensuring I was paying attention. "You have the right to remain silent. Anything you say can and will be used against you in a court of law. You have the right to an attorney. If you cannot afford an attorney, one will be provided for you. Do you understand these rights as I have read them to you?"

I nodded, feeling a lump forming in my throat. "Yes, I understand."

Detective Brady sat down in one of the chairs beside my bed, his partner moving to stand just behind him, effectively forcing

Samantha and Conan to stand at the foot of the bed.

"Ma'am, we need to go over what happened," he said, making no effort to ease into the questioning. His tone was more accusing than inquiring. "You're facing serious charges: evading police, reckless driving, trespassing, car theft, and breaking and entering."

I stared at him, my mouth dry. The words barely made sense, and his harsh tone made it worse. "I...I don't remember any of that. I remember nothing before waking up here. I can't explain something I don't remember," I stammered.

"That's convenient," the officer said sarcastically. "But amnesia or not, you were found at the scene in a stolen car after having broken into a home. Once you're medically cleared, you will be taken into custody, transported to the station, booked, and brought to the courthouse for arraignment."

His partner, who had remained quiet thus far but was equally imposing, leaned forward slightly and said, "With all of these charges. You'd better hope you can find a way to post bail, or you won't be going anywhere."

The room spun a little. My heartbeat roared in my ears, fast and loud, drowning out their voices. The walls seemed to close in on me, and I struggled to catch my breath.

Samantha, who had been quietly observing, stepped in swiftly. "That's enough," she said sharply, moving to stand on the other side of the bed. "She's clearly not in any state to discuss this right now. And as a nurse in this hospital, I'm telling you, you're causing her unnecessary distress."

The stern officer looked like he wanted to argue but glanced at his partner and then back at me. I was still shaking and struggling to breathe. Samantha was in her element, standing there confidently and not backing down.

"You need to leave. Now," she insisted, pointing to the door. "This woman is under our medical care, and I will not allow you to jeopardize her recovery."

Reluctantly, the officer stood up and gave me a long look. "We'll be back once the doctors clear you to be discharged," he said gruffly. And with that, they both left the room.

Once they were gone, Samantha reached for the controller attached to the bed, raising it so I could sit up straighter. "Breathe with me, Angel. In and out, slowly," she instructed, counting for each breath.

I followed her lead, though each inhale was sharp, and each exhale was a bit shaky. Gradually, my breathing evened out. The room stopped spinning, and the trembling subsided.

"Thank you. I've never experienced anything like that before," I whispered once I could speak again.

"Don't mention it," she said, giving my shoulder a reassuring squeeze. "I've suffered from panic attacks since I was a little girl. You're going to be okay." Samantha gave me a comforting smile. "Why don't you plan on coming to stay with Atticus and me once you're out on bail? Our new house is ridiculously large for just two people, and you can even babysit Murphy."

I paused, a little taken aback. "You guys have a kid?" I asked, imagining a toddler running around a sprawling living room.

Samantha burst into laughter. "Oh, no, not a kid. Murphy is our almost eight-month-old shih tzu puppy. He's a handful and loves attention."

I smiled at the thought of babysitting a playful puppy. But then I was snapped back to reality. "I don't have any money. Even if the bail is small, I won't be able to pay for it. I don't even know who I am, so there's no way I could find anyone willing to pay to get me out."

Conan waved off my concerns with a dismissive hand. "Don't worry, Braxton knows the chief of police. They're old friends. And Atticus is getting you the best attorney. I'll cover the bail. It's no issue."

I chewed on the inside of my cheek, my anxiety flaring up again.

"Money's not a problem, Angel," Conan said. "I've got it covered. You can pay me back whenever, or not at all. I just want you out and safe."

I tried to protest, the idea of owing such an enormous debt weighing heavily on me. "I can't just take your money, Conan—"

"Seriously, stop worrying about it," he insisted, his voice firm yet kind. "I wouldn't offer if it was a problem. Focus on getting better and sorting out your memories."

Reluctantly, I nodded, accepting his generosity with a heavy heart. "I don't know how I'll ever make it up to you guys, but I promise, somehow, I will."

Samantha smiled. "You don't owe us anything. Just get yourself back on your feet. That's payment enough."

Conan glanced at his watch, his brows rising. "Shit, break ended ages ago. Gotta get back to the ED." He turned to leave, then paused at the door. "Just hang in there, all right?"

Samantha stepped back. "I've got to head home as well. I'll set up a room for you. You focus on getting your strength back. We'll handle the rest."

When they left, I lay back against my pillows. The room abruptly felt too big and too empty. I was alone with my swirling thoughts again. It was almost too much to believe that Conan, Sam, and even Dr. Thorin were willing to help me so generously. To them, I was a complete stranger, yet here they were, coming to my aid. Their support was surprising and hard to accept, but I guessed there truly were good people out there, and I just happened to have been lucky enough to meet them in my darkest hour. They hadn't asked for it, but they had my utter loyalty, and somehow, one day, I would figure out a way to repay them.

Samantha's stories about the Volkov family consumed my mind, stirring a dark fear. Was I connected to the mafia? The thought terrified me. Despite the support from Samantha and Conan, anxiety about my past—and my potential ties to an organization as sinister as the Volkovi Notchi—nagged at my conscience. I shivered, hoping against all odds that my past was not as dark as I was beginning to think it might be.

Chapter Nineteen

Evening 6/9 - 6/10

The TV hummed as I flicked through channels, looking for something, anything, to distract myself from my constantly churning thoughts. My hand froze on the remote when the local news logo flashed onto the screen underneath the scene of a horrific car wreck that evoked a feeling of déjà vu. A second later, a newscaster, poised and polished, appeared on screen.

"Tonight, we update you on the mysterious Jane Doe case," the anchor began. The screen split, with the image of his face on one side and a series of disturbing images on the other. My heart pounded as I realized with a sickening jolt that the bloodied woman in those pictures was me.

While the anchor droned on, details of my accident materialized in my mind like a nightmarish, slow-motion film— metal twisting, glass shattering, the caustic, metallic taste of blood. The sharp, visceral memory of pain shot through me as I remembered fleeing the dark Volkov garage. I'd been in a panic, the urgent need to escape overriding everything else. I still couldn't piece together why I'd run or what I'd been running from, but the anchor's mention of the Volkov name kindled a flicker of recognition.

"And as police prepare for her discharge from the hospital, they hope she will be able to shed some light on the incident that left her hospitalized and with amnesia," the reporter continued.

My battered face appeared on the screen again, and anger surged through me. It was invasive, seeing myself like that, displayed for all the world as some evening-news spectacle. I'd received no calls from worried family or friends—just endless speculation from strangers. No one had come forward to claim me. I'd had no tearful reunions with relieved friends. Just silence. Was I really so alone? Did no one miss me at all?

The news shifted to another story, but the damage was done. I turned off the TV. The screen went dark and plunged the room back into silence.

Lying back, I tried to process the flood of emotions—the fear, the frustration, the loneliness.

The realization that no one cared about me, that I was utterly alone in this world, hit me hard. Tears welled in my eyes. God, was I such a terrible person?

I stared up at the sterile white ceiling. At least there were a few kind people who'd reached out to help me. My thoughts drifted back to one of Conan's visits—how he'd swaggered in with that cocky grin of his and a bag of those disgustingly sweet treats he claimed were *"just what the doctor ordered."*

"Yeah, 'cause sugar comas are totally therapeutic," I had teased, but he'd just winked and ruffled my hair, his large hands

surprisingly gentle. He loved those doughnut holes and could pop two in his mouth at once.

His presence always seemed to make the room warmer. I found myself drawn to his tattoos, curious about each one and the story they told. His rough exterior contradicted the kindness in his eyes when he looked at me. This paradox drew me in—it was a mystery I wanted to unravel. The protectiveness in his voice when he spoke to me sent fiery little tingles straight between my legs.

Then there was Samantha, with her fiery attitude and that unfiltered sass that made even Conan blush. Chuckling, I thought about how she and Dr. Thorin were such an odd match—him with his formal and meticulous ways, and her with her feisty, unapologetic gusto. Outside the hospital setting, I wondered how they managed to get along. I was curious about their unlikely pairing and eager to get to know them better. Was Dr. Thorin more relaxed at home?

I sighed, rolling onto my side as I tried to find sleep, my mind stubbornly replaying Conan's last visit. I hoped I wasn't tied to some other man, because there was no denying my attraction to him. As sleep finally began to claim me, my last thoughts drifted to what it might be like to be held by him, for him to touch me not just in passing but with intention—with desire.

The sun was barely up when Samantha burst into my room, one arm laden with what looked like an entire rack from her favorite boutique while she dragged a suitcase behind her with the other hand. She flopped the armful of clothes onto the small round table in the corner and turned toward me; her face lighting up with excitement and mischief.

"Rise and shine, Angel! It's makeover time. I brought you some essentials." She lugged the suitcase up onto my bed, flipping it open to reveal more clothes, some shoes, and an array of toiletries and makeup. "I figured you'd want something other than hospital chic for the rest of your stay and grand exit."

I eyed the contents, my cheeks heating up. It was all so overwhelming. "Sam, this is too much. I can't accept all this. You planning on dressing me up for a runway or a mug shot?" I joked, trying to infuse some humor into the situation to mask my embarrassment.

She shot me a knowing look, placing her hands on her hips. "Girl, with how good you're going to look, you'll be ready for either." She tossed me a pair of leggings, a sports bra, and a tee. "Here, start with these. Comfy enough for physical therapy and loads better than the hospital gown you've been sporting."

"Sam, you've practically brought an entire store here."

With a smile, she waved off my protest and started pulling out more items. "Here, you've got some comfy stuff to relax in, some workout gear for your PT, and something a bit nicer for your...um, photoshoot down at the station."

I couldn't help but chuckle at her phrasing. "Photoshoot, huh? If only the booking and arraignment were more like a day on vacation."

As I stepped into the bathroom to change, I heard her rummaging through the suitcase. "You know," she said contemplatively, "when those mafia goons trashed my place, I was left with pretty much nothing. It sucked having to accept help, especially from Atticus. I was so used to handling things on my own."

"Yeah, boy can I relate," I said as I slid into the clothes she'd tossed me. Wearing real clothes for the first time in weeks felt so nice. I'd never appreciated how great everyday things were until

I had to go without them. These comfy leggings and this T-shirt made me feel like a million bucks. Oh God, how badly I wanted out of this hospital and out from under whatever legal matters I'd gotten myself into.

When I walked out of the bathroom, Sam was holding up a bottle of shampoo like it was a trophy. "But I learned it's okay to let others lend a hand. We all need a boost sometimes. Consider this me paying it forward. One day, when all this is a distant memory, you'll help someone in need, and it'll feel just as good."

"Thanks, Sam. Really. I don't know what I'd do without you, but I promise I'll pay you back."

She waved off my concern with a flick of her wrist. "Don't sweat it. Just focus on getting out of here. Besides... Good news, Atticus's attorney has sorted out your booking and arraignment so they coincide with your release. Everything will happen on the same day. One less thing to worry about, right?"

"So, I'll be crashing at your place for a while, huh?"

"Yes, I've got your room all set up. I can't wait to have another girl staying in the house, because it's always filled with Atticus and his two rowdy brothers. I could use a little more estrogen in the place to balance it all out. Even the dog is a boy."

I laughed, thinking about her surrounded by the Thorin brothers. Based on what I'd learned from being around Conan and Atticus, they all had intense personalities.

"After you're done with the arraignment, I've got a big dinner planned to celebrate your release from the hospital and all. Atticus loves to cook in his fancy kitchen. It's one of his favorite pastimes. Bethany, my best friend, is coming over along with the boys. It'll be a great way to take your mind off everything that's happened and have some normalcy," she said, smiling from ear to ear.

I raised an eyebrow. "Oh good, from jailbird to party animal, all in one day. Let's hope the only bars I ever see are made of chocolate. Hospital food is bad enough. I can only imagine how awful food is in jail."

"Exactly!" she said, laughing.

She finished unpacking and showed me everything she'd brought. It felt like Christmas. She was making this whole daunting process seem like it was no big thing. With a friend like Sam, maybe I could get through this whole ordeal.

"I've got to get to work, but I'll be back soon," she said, heading for the door. "If you need anything, tell one of the nurses to call me."

"Will do. And thanks again for everything. I'm still stunned by it all. If you ever want to give up nursing, you could have a second career as a personal shopper for the rich and famous."

That made her laugh as she walked out and closed the door behind her.

The things she'd brought not only got rid of the sterile hospital vibe but also sparked a flicker of hope inside me. As I sifted through the clothes again, I was finally able to imagine an end to being confined in the hospital. Freedom had never sounded so good. I was motivated all the more to work hard in the gym to get my strength back.

A little while later, a tech came to my room with a wheelchair. "Are you ready for some PT?" he asked.

"Sure, but what's the wheelchair for?" I asked, squinching up my nose.

"Procedures. You've got to prove you're safe to get down there on your own before you can go without a ride." He shrugged.

"Do I need to bring anything with me?"

"Nope, just a good attitude and comfortable clothes. Looks like you've got that covered," he said. Then he swept his arm out dramatically as if offering me a spot on an amusement park ride.

I smiled and plopped down in the chair, and then we were off, the dutiful officer in tow. As fast as the tech was walking and taking the turns, you would have thought I was in a race car, not a wheelchair.

The PT gym was bustling when we got there, filled with the sounds of machines whirring and weights clanking. Liz, my physical therapist, greeted me, clipboard in hand. "Ready to work hard today?" she asked, her eyes twinkling with challenge. Liz had worked with me every day since I regained consciousness, ensuring I was physically able to perform basic tasks and would be safe once we moved to the gym.

"Let's do it," I replied, pulling my hair back into a ponytail with a hairband Sam had brought me.

We began with a warm-up—some simple stretches that should have been easy. I reached for my toes, felt the pull in my hamstrings, and was surprised by their resistance to my efforts. Next, Liz guided me through a series of arm circles and shoulder shrugs, which loosened me up but also highlighted how stiff my body had become.

"Now, let's see where you're at with some resistance bands," Liz suggested, handing me one of the lighter ones. As I pulled my hands outward, stretching the band, I found the resistance unexpectedly fierce. My arms trembled from the effort. "It's okay, Angel. Take it slow," Liz encouraged as she noted my struggle.

"I don't want to take it slow," I shot back out of frustration, but I continued on with the rest of the sets.

I switched to some small dumbbells. The weights, seemingly light, felt like boulders in my hands. I gritted my teeth as I lifted them. I could barely complete the three sets without my arms shaking. After doing several more types of exercises, exasperation bubbled up. I was dismayed at how weak I was. But I set my jaw and pushed through.

"Let's work on your core strength," Liz directed after I set the weights down. I did some basic sit-ups and planks. Each movement was a battle, my core muscles quivering with each lift. "You've got this, Angel," Liz kept saying, standing by my side.

Next, we moved to legs, using various machines. The weights, which were set lower than I would have liked, were still an intense challenge, and I found myself getting even more disgusted with my lack of fitness. This wasn't me. I used to be fit, athletic even. I might not be able to remember my past workouts, but in my heart, I was certain I had always been strong and healthy.

"Time for some cardio to wrap this up," Liz announced, and we moved to the long line of treadmills facing the floor-to-ceiling windows. I started with a slow walk, gradually increasing the speed. Soon my breaths were heavy, my heart pounding as if I was running a marathon. I met Liz's gaze, expecting pity. But there was none. Just a fierce sort of expectation. "Every rep is a step back to who you were, Angel. You're doing great."

Finally, we ended with some cooldown stretches, which gave me a moment to catch my breath and reflect. I was dripping with sweat, breathing hard, and my muscles ached, but making it through the workout session felt like a small victory.

I caught my reflection in the mirror—a flushed face with an ugly scar—but at least I was up and moving. Weak or not, today I had started my journey to get the hell out of this place.

"I'll see you tomorrow, right?" Liz said as she wiped down the equipment.

"Absolutely," I responded.

Liz had made a note in my chart that I could walk between my room and the gym rather than ride. I would have been excited if it weren't for my constant Tacoma PD chaperone. It was so embarrassing. I swore I'd never get myself into this kind of situation again. Ugh!

I headed back to my room, taking each step slowly, my body reminding me of the workout I'd just completed. Despite my physical weakness, today a fire had been lit inside of me. Even though I was shocked by my body's limitations, I wouldn't let this setback define me. Each day was a chance to regain a part of myself, and I was determined to keep fighting, no matter how tough it got. Tomorrow, I'd be back, ready to push even harder.

When I swung open the door to my room, Conan was there, sprawled out on the chair next to the bed like he owned the place, flipping through a magazine. His eyes lit up when he saw me, and a cheeky smile spread across his face.

"Damn, if it isn't the hottest patient in the hospital," he teased, his eyes slowly tracing the lines of my body, starting at my face and working their way down to my toes before bouncing back up. "Those leggings should come with a warning label."

That made me laugh, and as I leaned against the doorframe—still catching my breath—I felt a rush of my old self return. That workout might have wiped me out, but I was ready for his flirtatious wordplay.

"Watch it, big guy, or you might need an *eye-raping* warning label yourself," I said, giving him a coy little side-eye.

Leaning forward, he set the magazine down and propped his elbows on his knees. His build made the hospital chair look like it was made for children. "So, when you busting out of this joint? I go to a pretty hardcore CrossFit box. You think you're ready to train with me once you're out? Or would that be too much for a pretty little princess like you?"

His teasing struck a nerve.

Walking past him and trying not to let him see how spent my muscles were after that pitiful workout, I grabbed a bottle of water from the bedside table. Conan got to his feet, his sheer size dwarfing me. Standing this close to him for the first time, I realized how small I was.

I smirked, popping the cap off the water. "Oh, please. You wouldn't be able to keep up. I might not remember my workouts, but I have a feeling I was pretty in shape."

Conan crossed his arms, pretending to size me up. "Is that a challenge, Angel? Because you have to know I never back down from one of those."

I rolled my eyes and popped my hip out, jamming my fist onto it. "Oh, so you're one of those guys who can't back down from a challenge, huh? How original. Your ego must be a full-time job to maintain."

"Are you seriously rolling your eyes at me and getting mouthy? I thought your amnesia would come with a better sense of survival, my sassy angel." His voice had dropped to a low, gravelly timbre, sending a shiver down my spine.

I let out a defiant laugh. "Who knows, maybe that's my innate personality coming to the surface and erupting out of my mouth? I can't be held responsible for anything I say these days."

"That may be true, but the eye roll—that was all you, sweetheart. And if there's one thing you need to know, it's that doing that will get you more than you bargain for with me."

Oooh, I wanted to ask him so badly if that was a promise, but the way he was towering over me, nostrils flaring and pupils blown wide, I didn't dare. I swallowed hard and chose to change the subject.

"Hmm, I believe I've always liked finding a good bargain, but your price seems a little much." I gave him a half-shrug, taking a step back to put a little distance between us. Heat was rising from the center of my chest to the top of my head.

He squinted and smirked, knowing good and well he'd rattled my cage and drawn out the trouble-seeking side of me that lurked beneath the surface. "Angel, I do have to wonder just who you are."

"Well, if you figure that out, let me know. Because I don't know who the hell I am." I meant for my words to sound teasing, but they came out with a sharp edge. All this banter and innuendo was more than my poor broken mind could handle.

He laughed, and the corners of his eyes crinkled, giving him a roguish appeal. Damn, was this guy hot, and here I was, a sweaty, scarred mess, taking him on as if I was wearing my best pair of stilettos. Time for a U-turn.

I slapped on my charm-school smile and straightened my back. "It was so nice of you to drop by today, but I seriously need a shower. I'm a grimy mess," I said, hoping he would get the hint that it was time for him to leave.

Conan raised an eyebrow, stepping closer with a grin that spelled trouble. "Need help with your back? I'm pretty handy with a washcloth."

I laughed, shaking my head at his audacity. "Dream on, Conan. It'll take more than your charm to get that kind of privilege."

He mock-gasped, placing a hand over his heart, feigning offense. "Ouch, you wound me. And here I thought I was irresistible. Women are usually dragging me into their shower, not the other way around."

"Well, I'm not just any woman," I shot back, turning to gather my shower things.

"You got that right," he agreed with a nod. "All right, guess I'd better stop joking around and leave you to it then. How about

I bring you dinner later? Something better than the dreaded hospital meat loaf?"

"That sounds amazing," I said. "And if you're coming back, don't forget your guitar. The food's great, but your music? That's what I could really go for. Oh, and maybe one of your old T-shirts for me to hang out in."

Conan laughed, heading for the door. "Oh, God, what have I gotten myself into with you? I think I've created a pint-sized diva!"

His laughter echoed down the hallway as he walked away, leaving a smile on my face. It felt good to have moments like these—light, teasing, almost normal. It was a reminder that not everything in my world was heavy and complicated. With each banter-filled visit, Conan not only brought a piece of the outside world but also a piece of *me* back to life. I was already looking forward to what he would bring back for dinner—food, music, and maybe just a little more.

Chapter Twenty

6/10 evening

The anticipation of Conan's visit kept me glancing at the clock every few minutes. As I waited for him to arrive, I rummaged through the clothes Samantha had brought me earlier. Among them was a casual but flirty light heather-gray off-the-shoulder top, which paired perfectly with some comfy black leggings. It was just the right mix of cozy and cute—ideal for a night in but nice enough to show I was making an effort for the company I was expecting.

I spent a good while in front of the small bathroom mirror, working on my hair until it fell in soft waves around my shoulders. A touch of makeup enhanced my light blue eyes, making them pop. I was doing this for me, I told myself, but the flutter in my stomach at the thought of Conan's reaction indicated otherwise.

There was a firm knock on the door that snapped me back to the present. "Come on in!" I called out on the way out of the bathroom. Conan stepped into the room, his arms loaded with bags that smelled like heaven. He grinned when he saw me, his eyes doing an appreciative once-over.

"Hope you're hungry, because I might have overdone it." He grinned, setting the bags down and starting to unpack. "Wasn't sure what you'd like, so I got a little bit of everything."

"Looks like you bought out the whole restaurant," I joked, helping him lay out an array of dishes on the table by the window: spaghetti and meatballs, lasagna, carbonara, chicken parmigiana, shrimp Alfredo, and garlic bread. He even brought raspberry tea and a bottle of wine, plus some torta tenerina and a bunch of those cute little red-and-white butter mints.

"Planning to feed the entire floor, or just us?" I asked.

"Eating is serious business." Conan shrugged, giving me an easy smile. "But remember, just one glass of wine for you tonight. Gotta take care of that head of yours."

His concern warmed me more than any wine could. I nodded. "Doctor's orders, huh?"

"Something like that." He chuckled, pouring me a small glass before filling his own.

"Not sure what I like," I admitted, looking over the feast.

"Let's make it fun then. We'll share and try a bit of everything. Can't go wrong with Italian, right?" He handed me a plate.

We started with the spaghetti, both of us making appreciative noises as we ate. Next, I twirled a forkful of carbonara and took a bite. As soon as the creamy richness burst on my tongue, something clicked. I paused, holding the fork just outside of my mouth, and got lost for a moment in a sudden rush of images. The room faded away as a memory surfaced—me, laughing as a young delivery boy blushed at my teasing, the familiar comfort of my home around me. Then another flash of memory hit me—a cozy, warmly lit kitchen, laughter, and the same dish in front of me.

"Angel?" Conan's voice was tinged with concern. He reached over, gently brushing a strand of hair from my face.

I blinked, and the room snapped back into focus. "I...I just remembered something. Carbonara is my favorite. I always order it from this little Italian place just a few blocks from where I live. There's this young delivery boy—oh, how he gets so flustered every time he comes by—I flirt just to watch him turn red," I said, giggling. "And, from the memory, I think I live alone..."

Conan's expression shifted from worry to amusement. "Got a thing for younger guys, huh? Sounds like you are quite the heartbreaker." Then his smile softened. "But hey, that's great you had a happy memory. I bet it means more are on the way. Looks like you're getting your life back piece by piece."

We continued eating, the tension from my flashback dissipating into easy conversation. Every so often, Conan would make a joke or I'd laugh, and it felt like we were just two people having dinner, not a patient and her nurse navigating the complicated aftermath of amnesia.

After we'd polished off what must have been half the menu of an Italian restaurant, Conan patted his stomach, declaring a need for a music break. "Gonna grab my guitar from the car. Hang tight, okay?"

With him gone, I took the opportunity to clear away the remnants of our feast. I stacked and bagged the empty containers, replaying the day's conversation in my mind. Conan really was something—with his straightforward charm and that rough-around-the-edges vibe that somehow made him even more enticing. I was particularly looking forward to hearing him play again. His singing voice seemed to smooth out the sharp edges of my shattered memories.

By the time I'd arranged the pillows against the raised head of the bed and settled cross-legged on the soft blanket, Conan was back, guitar in hand. He flashed me a playful grin and plopped down at the foot of my bed, tuning his guitar.

"Where's the case?" I asked.

"Oh, I left it in the car. I grabbed it and ran back inside. It was just easier than having to stop and let your guard check it out. He took forever with the food. I'm surprised it wasn't cold by the time I got in here."

I shook my head and huffed out a sigh. God, how annoying to be constantly babysat. Was a guard really necessary? Did someone think I would run out of here with nothing but my broken mind?

Without missing a beat, Conan started strumming a tune that stirred something in the recesses of my mind. When he started singing "Fast Car" by Tracy Chapman, my mouth dropped open, and I couldn't suppress my shock or the smile that followed. He caught my reaction, and his grin widened.

"Too soon?" he flippantly asked.

With a laugh, I shoved his shoulder, then let my hand fall to the bed beside his guitar, which rested on his thigh. Leaning into him, I curled my legs up and to the side, tucking myself comfortably around him as he continued to play.

He sang with a teasing edge, and I was mesmerized by his playing. I watched, almost hypnotized, by his ability to use such big hands to deftly finger the notes and pick the guitar strings with ease, making complex movements look simple. It was hard to believe that hands big enough to palm a basketball could manipulate the frets with such precision. The music vibrated through the mattress, resonating not only with my emotions but sending tingles through my body. I was getting turned on, growing wetter with each strum, and I had to clench my thighs to keep from reacting to my raw impulses.

His voice, deep and mellow, layered another dimension of sensation over the physical vibrations. The sound he produced didn't just travel through the air; it moved through me, making everything inside me hum. I couldn't tear my eyes away from his fingers.

By the time he'd finished the song, I was so wrapped up in his playing and the sound of his voice that I hadn't realized how much my imagination had run wild. I was having a vivid daydream about those very fingers, imagining how well he could play—me—and betting mentally that he could make me sing too.

Conan cleared his throat, yanking me back to reality, and I realized he'd finished his song. He had a knowing smile on his face. I'd been caught in the act, staring a bit too intently, my thoughts wandering to places they probably shouldn't. My cheeks heated up instantly. Trying to recover, I dipped my head, biting my lip in a mix of embarrassment and lingering thrill.

Conan just chuckled. He seemed to know exactly the effect he had on me. He shifted to retrieve a bottle of water from the nearby tray. Seizing the moment, I stretched across him, my hand grazing his side as I snagged a few butter mints from the pile. Unwrapping one, I popped it into my mouth and started crunching it loudly.

He raised an eyebrow. "You're supposed to let those melt, not demolish them. You should savor the peppermint flavor as it lingers on your tongue," he teased.

Mischievously I glanced over at him and unwrapped another mint, this time holding it between my fingers and licking it slowly and deliberately. Conan watched wordlessly, running his fingers across his lips as I tucked the candy into my cheek with an impish smile.

"I see you're one who likes living dangerously," he said, giving me a full-on smirk.

I rolled my eyes and let out a sigh.

"What did I say about rolling your eyes?" he growled, picking up his guitar.

My easy laughter blended with the soft strumming. He began Kenny Chesney's "Take Her Home," his voice a soft hum that filled the room with a sweet melancholy. The soothing melody and his soulful voice made everything else fade away, and I found myself lost in the moment.

When the last notes of the song had trailed off into the stillness of the room, Conan set his guitar aside and turned to face me, his eyes locking with mine in a gaze that seemed to drill right into my core. He inched closer, and I got lost in the flecks of gold in his green eyes.

For a moment, we just sat there, the space between us charged. It was as if an unseen magnet was drawing us together. My breath hitched, my heart thumping against my ribs like it wanted to break free.

He leaned forward, cupping my cheek as he traced my lips with his thumb. I dared not blink or breathe out of fear of giving in to the temptation of desire swirling around us. His lips hovered over mine, close enough that I caught the minty freshness of his breath.

Then the tension snapped, and our lips met softly, tentatively at first, coaxing a response I hadn't planned but couldn't resist.

His kiss grew hungrier, more urgent, as one arm encircled me, pulling me into him while his hand moved to tangle his fist in my hair. His strength was unmistakable, not just in the hold he had on me, but in the gentleness he managed despite it. I melted into his embrace, my hands finding the back of his neck, drawing him deeper into the kiss. The lingering taste of mint on our tongues only amped up the craving within me.

The kiss intensified, and in that moment, nothing else existed—no hospital rules, no murky past, just the undeniable connection that sizzled wherever our skin touched.

But as quickly as the moment had come, it shattered. Conan pulled back, his face full of regret and something darker, more intense. He swallowed hard, sliding his hands down my arms before pushing me away, leaving me cold and confused.

"I'm sorry," he murmured, the words rough around the edges. "I shouldn't have done that. Nurses don't kiss their patients."

I sat there, stunned, my lips still tingling from his touch. Part of me wanted to pull him back, to taste his lips again, to lose myself in that rush. But in reality, I realized the kiss had been a stolen moment. My memory was still patchy, and Conan was a nurse at this hospital. We couldn't do this.

"It's okay," I managed to say, forcing a small smile onto my lips. "We just got caught up in the music, that's all."

His eyes were full of torment, as though he was torn between what he wanted to do and what he thought he should do. "You're right. Forget that it ever happened," he said quickly, standing up. He took his guitar in hand and stepped back. "It's getting late. I should go."

And he was gone before I could even reply.

After the door clicked shut, I lay back against my pillows, my mind racing. His departure left an empty space in my soul. It was just a kiss...but the thrill of it had sparked fantasies that I couldn't allow myself to wish for. If he only knew what I really wanted to do to him, even *he* would blush.

As I lay there, the hospital room seemed more confining than ever—like a cage keeping me from freedom. Even though my brain was a dysfunctional mess, it didn't mean I wasn't a woman with a healthy sexual appetite. I might not remember my partners, but I knew without a doubt I was no virgin. During one of the many discussions with my doctors about the tests they'd conducted, both while I was unconscious and those I'd consented to after waking, they'd assured me that my IUD was still properly placed and that my labs showed no STIs. There had also been no alcohol or drugs in my system on the day of the wreck—news I'd been happy to hear. It was strange knowing I'd had sex but not being able to recall any details. Somewhere deep down, though, my instincts told me I relished it. I supposed that was why I craved what I couldn't have—at least for now—with Conan. But one thing was clear: I *would* have my wicked way with him. It was just a matter of time. No hospital rules or professional boundaries would keep that attraction from igniting once we were both free to explore it.

Chapter Twenty-One

6/11 through 6/22

The last ten days had gone by painfully slow.

Each one had rolled into the next, a blur of relentless routines that were both comforting and suffocating. A range of rehabilitation treatments—from the exhausting to the mind-numbing—filled my schedule. Physical therapy was the only one I looked forward to. It wasn't just the physical exertion that helped; it was also the one thing that made me feel like I was truly doing something to fight back against the fog in my brain and the annoying weakness in my muscles. For that one hour a day, I could channel all my frustrations into pushing against the limits of my recovering body. Outside those sessions, my reality was increasingly constrained by the barrage of therapies aimed at unlocking my mind, which remained stubbornly closed off.

Particularly grating had been the neuropsychologist, a man whose smile seemed permanently absent. He poked and prodded at my psyche like I was some strange phenomenon to be studied. "This might jog your memory," he would say, introducing yet another set of bizarre tests. I didn't have any problem meeting with a therapist who wanted to talk. I craved conversation. Any human contact beat sitting in my room feeling like a pound puppy nobody wanted. But Dr. Schneider was an odd man with no personality who treated me like a science experiment. He was uninterested in small talk or understanding my feelings in any genuine way. Yuck. No thanks.

Worse than the therapies, though, was the silence from Conan. Since the kiss, he hadn't shown up. He hadn't even sent a message through Samantha.

She had been wonderful, dropping by with a laptop, some books, and more clothes, trying to keep my spirits up. Earlier today, when I'd finally dared to ask about Conan, she had swiftly steered the conversation elsewhere. But I needed to know, so I'd pushed her for an answer. Her eyes had shifted between me and the doorway as she picked up the TV remote and turned up the volume. Then, she'd leaned in and whispered, *"I can't say too much, and when you get out of the hospital and all, Conan will explain. He'd be all sorts of pissed off at me if I told you anything. Let's just say he has good reasons not to come see you, and you shouldn't be mad at him. It's something that's beyond his control. Just so you know, HR really doesn't want me hanging out with you either. Hospital policies are complicated, but it's nothing you should worry about. Trust me on this, okay?"*

I'd slowly nodded in agreement. Her words hadn't made any sense, but I let it go, not wanting to get her in trouble or push her away. My best guess was that the hospital didn't want its staff hanging out with criminals like me. I bet the guards told the higher-ups about how Sam and especially Conan had been visiting me a lot. Couple that with Conan's obvious regret for kissing me, and I couldn't blame him for steering clear of me. But it still hurt that he made no effort to explain after spending so much time with me. He could have at least sent a note with Sam or something. Maybe I was being petty, but he of all people should know how disappearing would affect me. I didn't understand, and it was really pissing me off. But what could I do about it? Absolutely nothing.

After Sam's visit, I dove back into searching for any clues as to who I was, using the laptop she'd brought me to comb through the internet.

I'd already spent hours scrolling and typing queries into search bars in hopes of uncovering anything that might give me a hint. Over the last week I'd perused social media sites and news archives, looking for anything a normal person would have out there. But it was like I didn't exist. I even took a picture with the laptop's camera and uploaded it for a reverse-image search. Nothing. No matches. It was unnerving. How could someone my age not exist online?

As my frustration mounted, I redirected my energy into learning more about the Volkov family and the notorious dealings of the Volkovi Notchi. If I couldn't find anything about myself, maybe I could at least determine why my first memory that had come back was full of fear, why that name kept raising red flags.

Finding information about the Volkovs wasn't difficult, considering the violent showdown at the Port of Tacoma that Sam and the others had gone through just six months ago. The articles painted a vivid picture of a ruthless crime syndicate involved in human and drug trafficking, smuggling, violence, and corruption. I read about Samantha's ordeal, the shootout, and Viktor Volkov's role in it all. The stories were harrowing, reminding me of the potential danger I could be in once I was outside of these walls, especially if I was connected to them in some way as I suspected. I had hoped to find pictures of the family in hopes that they would stir a memory, but I couldn't find any. Mafia types must really know how to stay under the radar.

Despite finding no direct link to myself and the Volkovs, the fear that I was somehow entangled with them ate at me. It all seemed too coincidental—my presence at the estate, fleeing in one of their cars, and the fact that no one had come for me. But then again, maybe no news was good news. Maybe my lack of a digital footprint was a shield, protecting me from a past intertwined with criminals.

With all the uncertainty, I threw myself harder into my workouts, each session fueled by anxiety and loneliness. Every rep, every set, helped me build strength—not just physically but mentally. If my past was going to come back to haunt me, I would be ready. I'd make sure of it. But deep down, I couldn't shake the feeling that somehow my life was tangled up with the dark legacy of the Volkovi Notchi. And not knowing how worried me more than anything else.

I was more than the sum of discovered—or undiscovered—facts. And if my past wouldn't come to me, I'd build a future that didn't need it. But the question of who I'd been before all this remained. This was a puzzle I was determined to solve, with or without Conan's help. No matter what truths lay buried, I would face them head-on. After all, wasn't that what survivors did?

6/23

As I zipped up one of the suitcases Samantha had brought me, the reality of leaving the hospital tomorrow hit me hard. It was the closing of one chapter and the uncertain start of another.

Tomorrow morning, the hospital room I'd grown to know so well over the last two weeks would be only a memory, and I'd be walking into the harsh confines of a police station.

Earlier in the day, Samantha had come by with news that both lifted and sank my spirits. She'd been bubbling over with reassurance, telling me that Dr. Thorin had everything arranged for my discharge and subsequent arraignment. "*You'll be out on bail before you know it,*" she'd said with a confident smile. The attorney they'd hired was optimistic and apparently armed with a slew of information that could help my case. This news was supposed to be comforting.

Yet, as I folded another shirt, the reality of handcuffs, mug shots, and fingerprints clawed at me. It felt degrading—the prospect of being paraded around like a criminal. Samantha had tried to lighten the mood, instructing me to pack up and prepare for a new start at her place. "*Just think of it as moving from one room to a much nicer one. It'll be like a long sleepover,*" she had joked.

I appreciated her—more than she probably knew. But as I placed the last item in the second suitcase, my thoughts drifted to Conan. He had completely vanished. I still hadn't heard a word from him, and it stung more than I cared to admit. I worried about how this could affect things with Samantha and even Dr. Thorin. The last thing I wanted was to bring drama into their lives. But the more I thought about it, the more determined I became to clear the air with him once I was out of here. It was ridiculous for Conan to avoid me like this.

Finally, almost everything was packed, my life neatly contained in two suitcases except for what I needed for tonight and in the morning. I sat on the edge of the bed, looking around the dimly lit room. It was strange to think I wouldn't see it again.

I climbed into bed and tried to find a comfortable position, my mind racing with what the next day would bring. Despite the softness of the pillows and the quiet of the room, sleep didn't come easily. But eventually, exhaustion overtook the anxiety, and I drifted off into a restless sleep peppered with dreams of courtrooms and unfamiliar faces.

Chapter Twenty-Two

6/24

By the time the alarm on the laptop sounded, I'd already showered and dressed and was preparing for what would undoubtedly be one of the most critical days of my life. Sam had brought me a very conservative pink button-down blouse, some charcoal-gray dress pants, and a pair of black flats. I looked more like an accountant than a reckless woman who had broken into a home and stolen a car. My hair, which I usually wore down, needed to look tidy. So I brushed it back into a sleek, low bun, securing the stray strands with a light hairspray. This style not only kept my hair off my face but also lent an air of professionalism and modesty to my appearance.

With that done, I sat and looked out the window, nervously waiting for the day to begin and wishing I could disappear. Within a few minutes, Samantha breezed into my room. Atticus followed, his expression serious but kind as he carried an empty duffle bag.

"Morning, Angel!" Samantha said, taking the bag from Atticus and setting it on the foot of my bed. "Today's the big day, huh? We'll take your stuff to our place and then meet you for your arraignment. Let's put anything you haven't already packed in this bag."

"Thanks, Sam. I don't know what I'd do without you guys," I said, swallowing hard.

There wasn't much left to pack—just some toiletries, the clothes I'd slept in, and the laptop. It was all I owned in the world, and it wasn't much. But it was better than the nothing I'd come to the hospital with.

Atticus stepped forward. "Okay, let's go through what's going to happen today. In a few minutes, a nursing tech will roll you in a wheelchair to the patient pickup area downstairs. That's where the police will take you into custody. Don't worry; it's all standard procedure."

My heart thudded uncomfortably at the mention of police custody, but Atticus's calm demeanor helped dampen the spike of panic. "They know about your condition and have been briefed to handle everything smoothly," he said. "So you don't need to worry about that part. Just follow their lead, okay?"

I nodded, trying to muster a smile. "I'm just nervous, you know?"

Sam reached out and squeezed my arm. "We'll be right behind you. I'll make sure to be at the courthouse before you even arrive."

Atticus continued, "You'll ride with them to the station. They'll process you—fingerprints, mug shot, the usual—but remember, it's just a formality at this point."

The thought of the handcuffs and the police car made my heart race. Nervously, I scanned their faces, trying to find some courage. "What if things go south?"

"Hey," Samantha said in a sharp tone, a flash of her sass showing. "You've got the best friends in Tacoma. We won't let you down."

"Yeah, we get you're nervous," Atticus said, giving me a crooked grin as he picked up the duffle and one of the suitcases. "Keep in mind, this is a process you have to go through, and it'll soon be over. Plus, I've wrangled tougher situations over breakfast. This is just a walk in the park. The moment it's over, we're heading straight home. Sam's got a big dinner lined up."

"Home," I said, trying out the word. Would anywhere ever truly feel like home if my memories never returned?

The police officer standing guard leaned in the door. "All right, folks, it's time to go," he said.

A tech rounded the corner just then, pushing my ride. "Time for your grand exit," he said with a smile, helping me into the wheelchair.

I sat motionless while we made our way through the hallways and down the elevator. My stomach churned with anxiety. The moment of truth was approaching fast, and there was no turning back now.

When we approached the hospital's main doors, cameras started flashing, and the murmur of the crowd grew louder. The officer led us to the doors, somewhat blocking me from the sight of those waiting just beyond.

"Ready?" the tech asked, giving me a sympathetic glance.

I nodded, my throat tight. There wasn't really a choice.

As soon as the doors swung open, I was inundated with the roar coming from the mass of people waiting outside—shouts from reporters, calls for my attention, camera shutters clicking wildly. I squinted against the bright sunlight. The humid air immediately blanketed me, a striking contrast to the recycled coolness of the hospital. I was momentarily disoriented.

"Miss, can you tell us who you are? Can you tell us what happened?" a reporter yelled, edging closer.

"Why were you at the Volkov estate? Are you involved in some sort of criminal activity?"

"Where is your family?"

"What's your name?"

So many questions to which I had no answers.

Several additional police officers promptly appeared at my side, forming a barrier between me and the cameras. One officer, a tall woman, stepped in front of me before addressing the crowd, saying firmly, "Please, give her some space."

Despite the chaos, her presence was reassuring. She and another officer helped me stand. The discreet click of handcuffs being secured around my wrists was almost drowned out by the clamor. My hands were gently but firmly secured in front of me, and a jacket was draped over my shoulders, hiding me from the eager cameramen.

"We're going to walk straight to the car," the female officer instructed, her tone low and calm amid the cacophony.

People swarmed like vultures, hurling questions at me, but I remained silent, focusing on putting one foot in front of the other. I was guided toward a waiting patrol car, expertly shielded from the prying eyes of the crowd. I kept my gaze down, watching the concrete move beneath my feet.

Once we reached the car, the door was opened for me, and I was helped inside. "Watch your head," the officer said. I ducked into the vehicle, the scent of old vinyl and coffee greeting me.

The door shut with a solid thud, cutting off most of the noise from the reporters. The occasional flash of a camera was visible through the tinted windows. I cast a fleeting glance at the curious faces. Their features blurred into a sea of hungry eyes and eager mouths, all vying for a piece of my story.

"Are you okay?" the officer in the passenger seat asked, turning slightly to check on me. "That was quite the zoo. I think everyone's heard of the mysterious Jane Doe."

"Yeah, I'm just...overwhelmed," I admitted.

"We'll be at the station soon, and we'll take care of everything there," she assured me in a kind voice.

As the car pulled away from the hospital, the noise of the crowd faded into the background, replaced by the soft hum of the engine and the occasional crackle of the radio. I leaned back against the seat, the fabric cool against my skin, letting the motion lull me into a semblance of calm. What awaited me was unknown, a path as unclear and unnerving as the fragmented memories that occasionally haunted me. But in this moment, all I could do was sit back and watch the world move by, a silent observer of my own life's unfolding drama.

Soon after arriving at the police station, the door of the patrol car swung open, and the officers ushered me into the bustling environment of the booking area.

"Right this way, ma'am," one of them said, guiding me to a desk cluttered with papers and a computer that looked like it had seen better days. He sat down and pulled out a form, clicking a pen. He was a middle-aged man with a scruffy beard and an impassive expression.

"We need to get some information down," he stated, turning the monitor slightly to face him. "What's your full name?"

I shrugged, my chest tightening at the question.

"They told me you had amnesia, but I still have to ask. Procedures and all. You'll be listed as Jane Doe," he said before continuing.

"Date of birth?" he asked, fingers poised over the keyboard.

"I...I don't remember," I admitted, and not for the first time, the blank spots in my memory plagued my mind.

"That's okay. We'll keep moving through the form, giving you the opportunity to tell me anything you do remember."

He went through a list of questions, none of which I had answers for, and then hit the enter key hard, catching my attention. "Okay, now that's done, we're going to do a quick search, just routine."

He looked up, meeting my gaze briefly before turning to a female officer who stood ready nearby. "Can you take her to get searched and then to fingerprinting?"

She stepped forward, her face all business. "Come with me."

I rose from my seat, and she led me down a narrow hallway to a small room, where she had me remove my shoes. After I'd complied, she patted me down with swift, practiced moves. She checked under my arms, around my waist, and down my legs. Her hands were brisk and impersonal as they checked each potential hiding spot for contraband.

"All clear," she announced, gesturing to my shoes and then for me to follow her once more.

Next came the fingerprinting. Even though my prints had been taken at the hospital, they did it again here. I rolled each fingertip, one by one, over the cool glass as instructed by a young officer, who tried to make small talk to ease the tension. I'd never seen anything quite like the scanner they used.

The mug shot was next. I stood against a height chart, a camera pointed at my face. "Just look straight ahead," the person behind the camera instructed. It flashed twice, and I blinked against the bright light. A brief memory surfaced in my mind. This camera was the same type as the one that had been used for my driver's license. I recalled holding the card in the palm of my hand. It had the words *New York State* printed at the top—a clue to where I was from that I would keep to myself for the time being.

"Let's get you checked out by the nurse," the officer said. We moved to a small clinic set up within the station. A nurse greeted me with a tired smile.

"We just need to do a quick health screening and a drug test," she said. "I'm going to check your vitals and take a small blood sample." As she explained this, she wrapped a blood pressure cuff around my arm. The pump hissed, and I watched the numbers flicker on the digital display.

"Blood pressure looks good," she noted, jotting down the results. "Now for the blood sample." She took a minute to open what she needed and label the tubes.

"I know they found no drugs in your system on the day of the accident, but we need to do this as part of the booking process," she added. Gently, she took my arm. The needle prick was sharp but quick, and soon she was applying a small bandage to my arm. "All set here. You're okay to be processed further."

They led me to a holding area to wait for my arraignment, and as I took a seat on the bench, the reality of my situation seemed to settle fully. The holding cell was unwelcoming and bleak, the walls a grimy shade of gray. The air was stale, filled with the lingering scent of disinfectant and something less identifiable but equally unpleasant. A couple of other women were already there. Both kept to themselves. One was curled up on a thin mattress in the corner, her eyes closed but not quite at rest, while the other sat upright on a bench, leaning her head back against the wall.

I hugged myself to keep warm, trying not to think about my shitty circumstances. It was a relief when they finally called my name and led me out of that depressing place.

An officer escorted me to a car, which transported me to the courthouse. The ride was short, with the police vehicle cutting efficiently through the city traffic. The courthouse buzzed with activity while they ushered me into a pre-trial holding area—a small room with a table and four chairs. I sat and rested my cuffed hands on top, picking at my nails since I had nothing else to do.

After what felt like forever, but was likely only a few minutes, the door opened, startling me. A well-dressed older man in a suit stepped in. His expression was all business as he approached me, a folder tucked under one arm.

"Ma'am, I'm Marcus Donovan," he said, introducing himself quickly. He sat down in front of me with a briskness that suggested time was a luxury. "I'll be representing you today. We don't have much time, but I need you to understand what's going to happen."

He opened his folder and pulled out some documents. "You're being charged with several serious offenses," he began, his eyes flicking to mine before he quickly ran through the list of charges. His words were straightforward, his tone professional but not cold. "However, I've just received some potentially pivotal information that might help mitigate your situation. Given your circumstances, we have a strong case for leniency."

I nodded, absorbing his words with a growing sense of bewilderment. "What kind of information?"

Mr. Donovan didn't bother looking up from the papers he was reviewing. "Let's just say it could significantly alter the outcome today. For now, just follow my lead in court. Answer the judge's questions succinctly, and let me do the talking."

Before I could ask anything more, he checked his watch and stood up abruptly. "I need to go file these documents and prepare. Trust me, I'll do everything I can."

He exited the room as quickly as he had arrived, leaving me to process his assurances and vague promises.

When the time came, an officer removed my handcuffs. "You don't gotta wear these for your arraignment," he said. After that, he escorted me into the courtroom through a side door. The spectator's gallery was full of people. The judge's bench loomed large to my left. Every eye was on me as I was led to my seat.

Mr. Donovan appeared at my side. "Just stay calm," he said in a voice so low I could barely hear it over my hammering heart. Despite my anxiety, his presence was reassuring.

The room became quiet when the bailiff, a stern-faced man with a voice that commanded attention, called out, "All rise!" We stood in unison, shoes squeaking and clothes rustling, as the judge entered.

He was an imposing figure, an older, distinguished gentleman with white hair and a black robe. His expression was impossible to read as he took his seat at the bench and signaled for everyone to be seated.

An air of formality instantly settled over the room. The judge glanced around with a measured gaze before speaking. "This is the case of the State of Washington versus Jane Doe, and we are here today for her arraignment on the following charges," he announced. The judge looked off to the side expectantly at a woman standing to his right.

The clerk proceeded to read out the formal charges against me. "The defendant is charged with grand theft, breaking and entering, trespass, reckless driving, evading arrest, and several counts related to the property damage resulting from a motor vehicle accident and break-in," she stated clearly, her voice echoing slightly in the cavernous room.

A cold dread settled over me. Each charge was like a weight added to my shoulders. I tried to keep my composure, glancing briefly at Mr. Donovan, who gave a subtle nod, reminding me of the discussion we'd had earlier.

Once the charges had been formally declared, the judge looked directly at me. "How does the defendant plead?" he asked solemnly.

"Not guilty, Your Honor," Mr. Donovan responded on my behalf, his voice steady and confident.

"Very well. Everyone may be seated," the judge stated, making a note on the file in front of him. "We will now proceed with the review of the documents and evidence related to this case."

Mr. Donovan sat next to me. His earlier disclosure hovered in my mind as I tried to steady my nerves for whatever came next. He leaned in and whispered, "I'm going to request a meeting in the judge's chambers. There's a compelling reason to discuss the unique circumstances of your case privately."

He stood, addressing the court with an assertive tone. "Your Honor, if I may request a brief recess for a bench conference in your chambers? There are significant developments from the property owners involved that directly impact the proceedings today."

The judge considered this for a moment, his gaze shifting between Mr. Donovan and the prosecutor. "Very well, Counsel. We'll have a brief recess. Let's sort this out in chambers."

Mr. Donovan gave me an encouraging nod before gathering his documents and departing. The prosecutor, a middle-aged woman, followed suit, glancing over at us with a contemplative expression. Her heels clicked against the wooden floor as she and Mr. Donovan made their way to a large oak door behind the judge's bench.

The room buzzed quietly with conversation once they were out of sight. As I sat there, lost in thought, the hum of whispered speculations from the gallery barely registered in my ears.

After what seemed like an eternity, the door reopened. Mr. Donovan stepped out first, a subtle but visible relief in his posture. The prosecutor followed, her expression neutral yet somehow resigned.

Mr. Donovan's smile was the first actual sign that the news was good. "We have a positive update," he announced as he reached my side. The prosecutor nodded slightly to me, an acknowledgment of the decision reached behind closed doors.

"We've all agreed that the charges related to the property damage, trespass, and theft should be dismissed," Mr. Donovan said. "The statements from the estate trustee and the owner of the property where the accident occurred were very clear. They have no interest in pressing charges, considering your medical condition and the other circumstances. Evidently, the new owner of the estate is extremely wealthy and doesn't want to waste her time on what she considers trivial matters."

My brows shot up. I wondered how wealthy the woman must be to not care about me totaling her expensive car.

"And," he added, "given that the police were unable to find any criminal record, and since you were the only person injured, there's a consensus that pursuing other charges would not be in the public interest."

The prosecutor, stepping close to the table where I sat, added in a firm voice, "We believe this is a fair resolution given the unique factors at play here. The state sees no benefit in further penalizing Ms. Doe under these conditions."

Mr. Donovan turned back to me, his eyes serious yet kind. "This means we're essentially looking at a resolution that involves some financial restitution on your part but no criminal charges. We'll need to go back before the judge to make it official."

The judge re-entered the courtroom soon after, and the formalities resumed, but now there was an air of conclusion rather than contention.

Everyone remained silent as we awaited the judge's decision. He looked over the documents laid out before him and then addressed us.

"The new owner of the estate, represented by attorney Harrison Tate, has expressed that pursuing charges against Ms. Doe for the trespass, breaking and entering, theft, and property damage is neither worth his time nor effort," the judge said, his tone measured and clear. "Similarly, the owner of the property where the car hit the tree has stated that, considering Ms. Doe's injuries and amnesia, further prosecution is unnecessary. He also refuses to press charges."

He paused, looking down at me from the bench. "Now, regarding the charges of reckless driving and evading the police, this presents a complex issue. Ms. Doe's fingerprints and DNA have returned no matches in any criminal databases. This suggests that this is her first offense."

I sat there with my hands clasped in front of me, listening as the judge continued, his voice echoing slightly off the room's high ceiling. "In light of these circumstances, and with the support of Dr. Atticus Thorin—a well-respected member of this community, who has offered to assist and house Ms. Doe during her outpatient rehabilitation—it seems fair to take a compassionate approach."

Everyone in the room seemed to be holding their breath as the judge leaned forward, his gaze stern yet not unkind. "Therefore, I am allowing the charges against Ms. Doe to be dismissed. However, Ms. Doe will be required to pay court fees and a sum of five thousand dollars to cover a portion of the costs incurred by the city. This amount will be divided between the Tacoma Police Department and the Tacoma Fire Department EMS to cover some of their expenses."

He looked directly at me once more. "Ms. Doe, do you understand the terms laid out? Do you agree to these conditions?"

I nodded, exhaling, allowing my relief to sink in. "Yes, Your Honor. I understand, and I agree to the terms."

"Very well." He made a note on the paperwork in front of him. "That concludes this matter. Ms. Doe, I trust you understand the leniency being afforded to you today. This is your one and only get-out-of-jail-free card. Make sure you use this chance wisely."

"Thank you, Your Honor," I managed to say, my voice steady despite the turmoil of emotions inside me.

With the rap of his gavel, it was done. I was free of the charges, thanks to the unexpected advocacy of those who had nothing to gain from helping me. Turning, I spotted Samantha, who smiled supportively, and Atticus, who gave me a nod of approval. Conan sat next to them, looking relieved.

Mr. Donovan leaned in close and said softly, "Atticus has taken care of all the costs. The money the judge mentioned, it's all sorted. I will complete all the paperwork on your behalf over the next few days."

I blinked, the words taking a moment to register. "Thank you," I whispered, turning back to Atticus as tears welled in my eyes.

"Let's get you out of here so you can have a fresh start," Mr. Donovan said with a small, victorious smile.

I stood, and the courtroom seemed to spin slightly. My legs felt like they might give out, but Mr. Donovan was right there, quickly taking my elbow and steadying me. Overwhelmed, I reached out and hugged him, surprising him and myself with the sudden show of emotion. "Thank you so much," I said. He patted my back awkwardly.

"Go on now. They're waiting for you," he said, gesturing toward the gallery.

When I turned, the sight of Samantha and Atticus standing there—smiles wide and eyes bright—pulled a laugh from me. I rushed to them, and we fell into a group hug.

"You did it, Angel," Samantha squealed, squeezing me tight.

Atticus gave me a firm, reassuring pat on the back. "I knew it would all work out."

Pulling away, I noticed Conan off to the side. He was clutching a big bunch of colorful flowers in one hand and standing uncomfortably, his other hand buried deep in his pocket. He looked up with a sheepish expression, eyes wide and apologetic—exactly like a kid caught stealing cookies but hoping to be forgiven.

He took a hesitant step forward, his usual bravado absent. "Angel, I'm...I'm really sorry for not being around these last few weeks," he said, his voice rough around the edges.

This man, who was usually so sure of himself, was standing here in front of me looking all unsure and regretful. It did funny things to my heart.

"I had to stay away," he said. "There were reasons, good ones, I swear. I'll explain everything once we're back at Sam and Atticus's place." His hand shot out, giving me the flowers.

I nodded, relishing the earnestness in his eyes. "Okay. We'll talk later," I agreed. I was unsure what this was all about, but willing to hear him out. For now, the relief that this was all over was enough to keep the smile on my face.

"Let's get out of here," I said, following behind Samantha as she and the others turned to leave. We walked out of the courtroom and into the hallway.

Before we'd reached the courthouse exit, I nearly collided with a man who stepped directly in front of me. He was about my age, with dark hair and intense light blue eyes that locked onto mine in a way that sent a shiver down my spine.

"Do I... Do you know me?" I blurted out, the words slipping from my lips before I could think. There was something familiar about him. A nagging sensation at the back of my mind screamed I should know who he was, yet the details were just out of reach.

He said nothing, just stared at me, not moving an inch to let us pass. His intense behavior threw me off-kilter. I felt a strange mix of recognition and confusion, but no words came from him. He merely continued with that deep, penetrating stare.

"Hey, buddy, you need to step aside," Conan barked, ratcheting up the tension, his tone sharp with a protective warning. He stepped up beside me, his presence reassuringly solid.

But the guy didn't flinch or so much as blink in response. He never took his eyes off me. His expression remained unreadable. It was unsettling, the way he held his ground, unaffected by Conan's size or the obvious threat.

Conan wrapped an arm around my shoulders and shot a look at Atticus, who nodded subtly, ready to intervene if needed.

With a protective squeeze to my arm, Conan shouldered the man aside—not gently—done with the strange, silent confrontation. The man stumbled a bit but regained his balance. He kept his gaze locked on me while we moved past him.

"Who was that?" I whispered to Conan as we hurried out of the courthouse.

Conan shook his head as his brow furrowed. "No idea, but I didn't like how he was looking at you. We'll make sure he doesn't follow us."

As we walked away, I glanced back over my shoulder. The man still stood there, watching us leave, a strange, almost pained expression on his face. It was a look that tugged at my heart. But for now, I had to let it go.

Chapter Twenty-Three

6/24 evening

Stepping into the bright sun of a warm summer day, I paused and shut my eyes. Before this morning's ride to the police station, I hadn't been out of the hospital since waking up—and that had been almost a month. God knew I'd never take the sun's radiant warmth on my face for granted ever again.

Sam and Atticus were making small talk as they made their way across the parking lot. I stopped, taking a minute to enjoy the sun, and took a couple of cleansing breaths. When I opened my eyes, I found Conan standing next to a hunter-green Jeep that had its doors and top off. Atticus was opening the passenger door to a black Mercedes across the lane. I wanted nothing more than to ride with Conan and feel the breeze rush across my skin, but I wasn't ready to talk about his disappearing act, so I walked over and got in the car behind Sam.

The ride to Atticus and Samantha's house was filled with a strange mixture of optimism and tension. The odd encounter with the intense guy at the courthouse still lingered in my thoughts, but having all the charges dismissed was a huge load off my mind.

Sam turned up the radio and sang along with a song. Trying to relax and make myself mentally move on from all that had happened, I focused on the flowers in my lap, tracing my fingers over the stems and soft petals. It was sweet of Conan to get them for me. I wondered if, in my old life, other men had bought me flowers. Something in the back of my mind—the place where my memories were locked away—told me no one ever had.

Sam turned, peering over her shoulder. "It will take us only a few more minutes to get to our house. It sits on a lot overlooking the water in the Horsehead Bay area. We moved in a few months ago, and I still have a hard time believing I get to live there."

"Thank you guys again for allowing me to stay in your home," I said. "Hopefully, I'll get my memories back soon and can get out of your hair."

"It's not a problem," she said. "Seriously, we have plenty of room. I can't wait for you to meet Bethany and Braxton. Well, actually you have met Braxton, since he was the EMT who brought you in the morning of your wreck." Sam reached over and ran her fingers through the back of Atticus's hair. He glanced over, and she smiled as he rested his hand on her leg. The love between them was obvious.

"That's right. You'd told me my misadventure was a family affair," I said with a soft laugh.

After another song came and went, we turned onto a long driveway dappled with sunlight streaming through the trees. It led to a stunning home nestled in a lush, wooded area. The tall trees and expansive lawn were a far cry from the sterile hospital environment I'd left behind.

"Wow," I breathed out, genuinely impressed by the sprawling estate. "This place is incredible."

"Thank you! And because of Atticus's obsession with security, it's probably safer than Fort Knox. Since the kidnapping incident, his protective paranoia has been in overdrive." Samantha laughed as we approached the security gate. "Atticus installed this sci-fi system that includes cameras and sensors for everything. I wouldn't be surprised if he knows every bird that flies over and every squirrel that visits a tree."

When we pulled into the garage, my eyes caught the gleam of something spectacular—a red 1967 Firebird convertible. It sat there like a piece of muscle-car history, perfectly preserved and radiating a vibe of untamed freedom. How I knew the details of the car, I didn't know, but I did. Now if I could only figure out what my name was, I'd be getting somewhere.

As soon as Atticus parked, I opened my door and stepped out, drawn to the vehicle like a magnet. "That's a gorgeous car," I remarked, running my fingers lightly over the hood, appreciating the smooth finish.

Atticus followed me over and ran his hand over the back fender with a fondness that made Samantha snort. "This beauty is fully original," he said. "Haven't changed a thing since I got her except for maintenance items."

Samantha rolled her eyes. "Oh, she's definitely the other woman in our relationship. Once, Bethany and I took her for a spin to the grocery store. Thought Atticus was going to stroke out when I told him."

From the garage, I watched as Conan pulled into the driveway and parked. I was still holding the bouquet he'd given me. I wanted to ask why he'd stopped visiting, but I shelved that thought when he got out and walked toward me. Now wasn't the time for that discussion. He crossed over to the other side of the garage, joining us by the Firebird.

"Thank God nothing happened to his precious car," Samantha continued. "That might have crossed a line I could never uncross." Her tone was light, but there was a thread of sincerity that told me how much the car meant to Atticus.

After admiring the Firebird for another moment, we walked across the garage and into the door leading to the main floor of the home.

The instant the door swung open, a blur of fur and energy—Murphy, the shih tzu puppy, I guessed—tore around the corner. As we made our way further in, I watched him zip from one end of the living room to the other with such excitement that his little paws barely seemed to touch the ground.

"Look at him go!" I laughed, scooping him into my arms as he was making another pass. His curly tail wagged furiously, and he licked at my face as if I were made of his favorite treats. While I held him, I wondered if I had a pet waiting somewhere for me, missing me. The thought was unsettling. Thankfully, it didn't resonate with that place in my mind where my memories were stored. It would kill me to find out I'd abandoned a furry friend.

Conan grinned, watching us. "He's got endless energy, doesn't he?"

"He's just the cutest thing ever," I said, scratching the dog behind his ears. He settled contentedly into my arms.

Conan and I followed Samantha and Atticus into the open living room kitchen area, which was as vast and beautifully appointed as the outside suggested. The spacious living area with large windows framed magnificent views of the dense trees surrounding the property and the bay behind the house. The decor was elegant yet inviting. It was the type of home I'd love to have one day.

"I can see why you chose this place. It's absolutely stunning," I said to Atticus, who seemed pleased with my reaction.

"It's safe, quiet, and yeah, it has enough tech to keep the bad guys at bay," he replied, his voice carrying a hint of something darker.

Samantha nudged me gently, giving me a reassuring smile. "And it's got plenty of room for guests, so make yourself at home. Follow me, and I'll show you to your room." With that, she led me upstairs. The hallway was lined with black-and-white images that seemed carefully chosen, pieces I recognized but couldn't put names to.

After a brief tour of the upstairs, she showed me to the guest room, which was on the opposite side of the house from where she and Atticus slept. "You'll have plenty of privacy here," she said. It was a beautifully decorated room with a plush king bed and a view of the bay.

Crossing the room, she opened the closet. My suitcases from the hospital were already there. She then pointed to the en suite. "You should have everything you need in here, but let me know if you're missing anything."

She returned to where I was standing and picked up a gorgeous little bright blue bikini that was lying neatly folded on the bed. "I hope you like it," she said, holding it up. "Thought we could celebrate the solstice, the full moon, and your liberation tonight with dinner and a swim."

She handed me the bikini, and I held it out in front of me, shimmying my shoulders. "Ooo, it's a sexy little thing. Thank you. I love it. Maybe I'll get my memories back tonight if I do some kind of pagan ritual dance under the moon," I joked, and we both burst into laughter.

"You never know," she said. "Magic is more common than you'd think on nights like this. There's always more babies born on full moons than at any other time."

"Whatever it takes to get my memories back, I'll do it. One of the docs told me that since I've been getting some of them back as I experience familiar things, it's a good sign that they may all come back."

"Well, then getting out of the hospital environment and back to a normal life should really help you. I'm guessing having the charges dismissed today will take a huge load off your mind too."

"Oh God, you have no idea. Just going through the booking and arraignment process was a humiliating ordeal. I can't imagine how awful it would have been to go to jail." I shuddered just thinking about it.

"I'm so glad it all worked out for you. I know all too well how life can throw us some wild curveballs. I never imagined in a hundred years that I would get tangled up with the mafia. Six months ago, my life was turned upside down, and thankfully, I had some good people come to my rescue. These Thorin brothers are special men," she said in an appreciative tone.

"I still can't believe all that happened to you. It sounds like something straight out of a movie. I'm so lucky to have had you guys—especially you, Sam—come to my rescue."

"All right, all right, enough of this serious talk. How about you go ahead and change out of those dress clothes?" Samantha suggested. "Those have got to be miserable. I'm just gonna throw some shorts over a swimsuit. I'll meet you back downstairs when you're ready. We're keeping it super casual tonight, just dinner by the pool."

Once I was left alone in the room, I took in my surroundings. An overwhelming sense of gratitude washed over me. Samantha and Atticus had given me a safe haven. Their kindness was more than I could have asked for when I needed it most.

As I changed into the swimsuit and pulled on a pair of shorts, I made a silent promise to pay them back somehow for all their generosity and help. They had been so welcoming, and they'd never asked for anything in return. For the past month, I had felt like I was caught underneath an ocean's rolling wave, but now, I could finally breathe.

I made my way downstairs, still adjusting to the idea that I'd be staying in this beautiful, sprawling house with people who, just weeks ago, were strangers to me.

The laughter and chatter ahead pulled me in. I paused before entering the kitchen, soaking in the energy of the pre-dinner chaos radiating from the room.

"Hey, Angel! Come join us. We're just getting the food organized!" Samantha called out, her hands full of colorful veggies destined for the grill.

I stepped into the kitchen, watching Atticus as he expertly seasoned some steaks that were lying on a cutting board. Inhaling deeply, I took in the scent of herbs and spices that mingled with the smoky aroma wafting in from the outdoor kitchen by the pool.

"Smells amazing, Atticus," I said, admiring his culinary skills as he moved to start assembling chicken kabobs. He grinned and pointed a skewer at a charcuterie board laden with cheese and sliced meats. "Thanks. Just wait until you taste it. How about you help us get all this outside? You can take that to the table on the patio."

Sam and I carried the various trays and other stuff outside, setting up for what promised to be a fantastic cookout. The late afternoon was warm, and the music playing from various speakers around the house created a fun atmosphere.

Beside a spacious teakwood dining table that perfectly complemented the luxurious patio and poolside ambiance,

Conan wrestled with putting together an old-fashioned hand-crank ice-cream maker. "This'll be worth the workout," he promised as he set it to the side.

"Angel, wait till you try Conan's homemade strawberry ice cream," Samantha said. "He's got a secret recipe." She laughed, nudging me with her elbow as we laid out the chips and dips.

"Yeah, wait to be amazed," he added with a wink, popping a grape into his mouth. Then he straightened up and looked around at us. "All right, who's thirsty? There's beer and wine." He gestured to a large galvanized tub filled with beer, various bottles of wine, canned cocktails, and water.

"Do you have anything strawberry flavored?" I asked, my eyes lighting up at the thought.

"I bet we do," he replied with a grin. He fished around and found a can in the bucket, grabbed a glass, filled it with ice, and poured the Straw-Ber-Rita before handing it to me. He served Samantha her favorite blush wine and snagged a bottle of water for Atticus. "Here you go," Conan said. Atticus accepted the water with a nod. Then Conan grabbed a beer for himself.

"Thanks, Conan," Samantha said, taking a sip of her wine. I took a grateful drink of my icy Straw-Ber-Rita. It was dessert in a can.

As we worked, the banter flowed as easily as the wine and beer. Conan kept pouring for everyone except Atticus, who I found out didn't drink.

Samantha, with a mischievous glint in her eye, started teasing Atticus about the house's history. "He bought this fortress so I wouldn't have any ghosts of girlfriends past to worry about."

Atticus, standing by the grill, shot her a smirk, tossing a towel over his shoulder. "And what promise did I make you, huh?"

Samantha blushed slightly, but before she could reply, Conan cut in, his voice booming across the patio. "He swore he'd fuck you on every surface of this new house, didn't he?" He laughed heartily as Sam playfully slapped his arm.

"I can't believe you told him that!" Samantha fired back an exaggerated glare at Atticus, her cheeks reddening further.

Conan leaned in close to Samantha. "Oh, no, I overheard him say it loud and clear the night he asked you to marry him. Trust me, neither of you excels at keeping your voice down."

Leaning in my direction as if he were going to whisper something privately, but still speaking plenty loud, he said, "It's not easy to spend the night in this house. I warn you, Angel, you'll practically experience everything they do alongside them."

Samantha rolled her eyes, her comeback swift. "Oh, like you're one to talk. Don't let him fool you. It's not like Conan's shy. He's kissed nearly every girl he's ever met! He doesn't have a prudish bone in his body." She giggled. "He's even kissed me before."

"And you loved it," Conan retorted.

"Yeah, about as much as making out with a basset hound after it's slurped up half its water bowl," she quipped.

Before she could dodge him, Conan scooped her up in an exuberant hug, peppering her face with sloppy kisses. Samantha squealed and swatted at him while Atticus pretended to be outraged.

"Get the fuck off my wife," he demanded, his chiseled jaw tightening as he moved toward Conan. Conan let Sam go and turned toward Atticus with his fists up. A smirk formed at the corner of Atticus's lips as he threw a mock punch at Conan, who ducked.

"She's not your wife yet."

The two men started a high-spirited scuffle, throwing air punches and sparring around the patio. Laughing, Conan grabbed Atticus in a light choke hold.

"You know, I should have let the hospital fire your ass for not being able to control what the fuck you do with your mouth," Atticus grumbled, though the crinkles at the corners of his eyes betrayed his jest.

The atmosphere shifted subtly, the laughter dying down as Conan released Atticus, his face turning serious. "You swore you wouldn't mention that in front of her," he muttered, glancing my way.

I awkwardly stood there, tilting my head in confusion. Samantha glanced over at me and stepped in. "Okay, time out. Conan, maybe now's the time you should explain to Angel what happened after you kissed her."

Everyone turned and stared at me, and Conan's embarrassed expression made my stomach twist with dread. He cleared his throat, motioning for me to follow him toward the pool, where we could talk with a bit more privacy. As we walked to the far end, Sam and Atticus turned back to their tasks.

Chapter Twenty-Four

6/24 evening

The evening sun glinted off the gently lapping water as Conan and I sat down at the edge of the pool, dipping our feet into the surprisingly warm water.

"So, you just vanished after that kiss," I said, my words sharper than I'd intended. "What gives?"

Conan shifted, placing his fist next to my hip as he leaned in closer. "Look, Angel, I didn't mean to be a dick to you. Staying away was the last thing I wanted, but I had no choice." His jaw was clenched tight, and his face—only inches away from mine—had a look on it I'd not seen before. His frustration was palpable. Clearly, he was pissed off. The heat in his eyes and the way his nostrils flared made my breath hitch.

I tried to keep my composure, despite the chaos swirling inside me. "I...I'm sorry. Let's just drop it. It's not worth worrying

197

about," I said, my words stumbling out in a rush. What the hell could his problem be? With heat rushing up my neck, I turned, preparing to slip into the pool to escape further confrontation, but he reached out with his big ole giant hand and captured my chin between his thumb and forefinger, forcing me to face him.

"You're wrong. It is worth worrying about," he said. Then he took a long breath, his stare unflinching as I blinked in stunned silence. "You deserved better—as a patient and someone suffering from a TBI. You have amnesia for Christ's sake. It was unprofessional, bordering on perverse, of me to kiss you or take advantage of you. I'm a fucking nurse—your nurse—who was responsible for your initial care. I was in a position of power over you when you were at your most vulnerable. What I did was wrong, a big mistake. That's on me, not you, and for that I'm sorry."

My mouth dropped open, but words wouldn't form. I shook my head, trying to clear the whirlwind of embarrassment and anger. Did he honestly think I was so pathetic that a fucking kiss could possibly damage me somehow? I smacked his hand away from my chin.

"It was only a simple kiss," I said. "It's not like you threw me against a wall and fucked me until I didn't know my name—not that I know my name, but you get my drift. Besides, I all but fell into your lap and begged you to kiss me. No need to be dramatic. It was no big deal." I huffed, rolling my eyes so hard it hurt.

He dropped his chin to the side and arched his brow as his tight lips curved into a half-smirk. "Sorry, didn't mean to imply that a kiss from me was any big deal. As gorgeous as you are, I'm sure back in your real life you have men falling at your feet. So, let me rephrase. In a hospital environment, none of the staff should ever allow themselves to participate in an inappropriate interaction with a patient. I not only did that, but was caught in the act."

"What?!"

"Yeah, just as I was about to pull away from our kiss, I looked up, and your ever-diligent guard was staring straight at me from the doorway."

My lips formed a silent *O* as understanding dawned.

"That's why I bolted. I went to Atticus, and he not-so-gently advised me to self-report before the guy told on me. I swear, if we hadn't been standing in the middle of the ED, he would've punched me right in the face," Conan confessed, a rueful grin flickering across his face.

I couldn't help but chuckle, despite the seriousness of the situation. "So, what happened then?"

"I self-reported. But I didn't expect the chain of events to unfold like they did. Let's just say Administration wanted to fire my ass. If it hadn't been for Atticus threatening to leave and take Sam with him, I wouldn't have a job. It could have cost me my career. Instead, they agreed to put me on probation and restrict me from leaving the ED except when given specific permission by the charge nurse." He shook his head and shrugged his shoulders in disbelief.

"So, of course, the gossip mill has had a field day with all the speculation about what I did," he said. "Worse, it impacted Sam. Administration found out she'd taken a special interest in you and demanded she stop. I'll give it to her though. She stood her ground, telling them it was her duty as a nurse to provide help to those in need. She told them her relationship with you was professional and dared them to prove otherwise. They let it drop, but not without warning her to watch her step because of how the press was treating the whole mysterious Jane Doe situation and her possible ties to organized crime." His head dropped,

Evie James

and he ran his hand over the back of his neck. "For me, it's been a *big deal*."

My hand shot out to his knee, his bare skin warm to the touch. "I'm so sorry, Conan. I never in my wildest dreams could have imagined all that would happen. Oh my God, I feel terrible that every single person who has reached out to help me has had to suffer. I...I don't have words to tell you how awful I feel."

He covered my hand with his, and then his head snapped up, a broad grin spreading across his lips. "I should have just waited for you to get to Atticus's house."

I felt his smile all the way to my toes. How could I resist wanting a taste of those lips? But after all he'd been through, I bet he would never take another chance on the girl with the broken head. Fuck, what a shame.

Trying to detour away from the seriousness of our conversation, I teased, "Oh, so you think you've earned the right to kiss me again?"

In one swift motion, he pushed off from the ground and sprang to his feet. For a big guy, he had some moves. He extended his open hand, which I more than happily accepted, and helped me up to my feet. Then, pulling me to his chest, he leaned down and whispered in my ear, "Like Samantha just said, I do like kissing the ladies."

Before his words could completely register, Sam let out a high-pitched squeal and ran to bear-hug a woman with long, dark brown hair.

Atticus raised his eyebrows in surprise. "Looks like I need to scrutinize the security system, because I could have sworn the front door was locked."

Sam, still hugging the woman, tossed over her shoulder, "Nah, I updated the protocols, giving Beth her own biometric access."

Sam let the woman go and strolled over to Atticus, planting a kiss on his cheek. "I knew you wouldn't mind." She chuckled.

Turning toward Conan and me, she shouted, "Hey, you two, come over here and let me introduce Angel to my best friend!"

When we joined them, Sam made a quick introduction. "Angel, this is Bethany, another nurse from the ED at St. John's. Beth, this is—"

"Oh, I know exactly who this is. She may not have a name, but she's totally famous," Bethany said, throwing her arms around me in a big hug. I stood there with my arms pinned to my sides, swaying back and forth.

"Beth, let the woman go," Conan said. "You're freaking her the fuck out. Give her a minute to adjust to your hyperactive nature." He rubbed his fingers over the creases in his forehead.

Bethany let go, pushed me up against Conan's side, took his hand, and draped his arm over my shoulder. "Don't worry. She's all yours. Wouldn't dream of stealing her away from you." Catching my gaze, she winked and headed to the grill, where Atticus stood, checking the temperature of the steaks.

The laughter that bubbled up from my throat felt good, cleansing even. I started swaying to the rhythm of the song that was playing on the speakers—"House Party" by Sam Hunt. "So, what now?" I asked him, the tension finally lifting between us.

"Now?" Conan paused. A playful glint appeared in his eyes. His fingers glided down my arm, and he took my hand, spinning me around in time to the music. "Now, I guess we try to be friends without complications."

"Friends with no strings attached?" I asked as we continued to dance. The phrase rang a bell, tugging at the hidden part of my mind.

"Exactly." He grinned. "But you gotta know that I value honesty. I may not have many friends, but I'm completely loyal to those I do have. Anyone who knows me knows that my friends mean the world to me, and I'd go to war for them. I'd give my life for my brothers and those I call friends. Honesty is at the heart of trust, and trust doesn't come easy to me. I want to trust you, my Angel, and I want you to trust me. So no secrets between us, okay?"

The intensity of this man's fierce declaration—his request for honesty—made me feel like some sort of sacred bond was being formed. I didn't know if I had the emotional fortitude to live up to his expectations.

Just then, a man who looked an awful lot like Atticus strolled out the back door and onto the patio, interrupting the moment and leaving Conan's question unanswered. "Hey, guys," he said, snagging a handful of chips.

"Brixxie! Hey, brother! Long time no see," Atticus said, pulling a longneck from the ice-filled tub. Pressing it into his palm, he gave him a one-armed hug.

Conan, still holding my hand, pulled me over to the man. "Angel, this is my other brother, Braxton."

Braxton took the side of my arm in a firm grip. "You look a hell of a lot better than when I picked you up. How are you doing?" My breath caught at the sight of his big, beautiful smile. Damn, the Thorin brothers had good looks in spades.

"I'm doing great," I said. "All fixed up...well, except for the giant black hole inside of my head," I chuckled, shrugging my shoulders.

"At least you haven't lost your sense of humor," Braxton smiled, turning back to Atticus. "When's the food gonna be ready? I'm starving."

"Soon. You guys have a seat and enjoy your drinks while Sam and I finish up," he replied.

Conan, Braxton, and I sat down at a large wooden table and took in the view of the bay that ran along the edge of the property. We laughed and talked while the evening slid into a warm, balmy night. Braxton raised his beer, nodding toward the setting sun. "Longest day of the year. Perfect night to share good food with friends and family. Happy summer solstice, or as the Vikings call it, Midsummer! *Skål!*" he shouted, and we all clinked our glasses and bottles together.

Bethany, already a bit tipsy, flashed a wicked grin and chimed in, "Ooo, after dinner, we all need to go skinny-dipping." She leaned toward me, giggling, and took a quick sip of her wine. "Last fall, Sam and I went skinny-dipping in the hot tub at their old place. It was an act of rebellion after Atticus made up a bunch of ridiculous house rules when she first started staying with him. We systematically broke every single one within hours. What choice did he give us with such outlandish demands?" She and Sam both laughed out loud.

Atticus's head whipped around, and he shot us an exasperated look as a smirk curved over his lips. "Oh, that night will be forever burned into my memory," he said. "Someone had to lay down the law, didn't they, Samantha?" He leaned over and kissed her on the cheek before giving her butt a hard smack, nearly causing her to drop the platter of grilled corn she was attempting to set on the table.

She yelped, and her face flashed beet red, but the way she bit her lip told me that the hot-tub incident was a fond memory.

Atticus smiled, a glint of nostalgia in his eyes. "Yeah, with a friend like Bethany, I thought Sam needed a whole list of rules. Nothing too crazy, just something to keep these girls in check. Not that it did a bit of good."

Bethany quipped, "Please, you were just too uptight! You needed someone like me to shake things up. Sam needed a partner in crime."

"*Partner in crime* is an accurate description, all right. You're always trying to corrupt her and make her a wild woman like you," Atticus said, laughing as he scraped his fingers through his hair.

Bethany laughed too, shoving Conan's shoulder. "Nothing's wrong with having a little fun. Right, Conan? You can't tell me you're not the free spirit of the family, the one who keeps things interesting. You know how to have a good time while also keeping an important day job."

"Barely," Atticus shot back with a sarcastic laugh.

"Don't drag me into this," Conan said, pointing his beer bottle at Bethany.

At that, everyone laughed. While we waited for the food to come off the grill, we sat back and sipped our drinks, the conversation flowing easily. I mostly watched, taking note of the group's dynamics, intrigued by their deep connections and contrasting personalities. It was during this lighthearted banter that Conan segued to a more serious discussion.

He leaned back, beer in hand, and gave me a half smile. "Everyone here knows I'm an open book...well except Angel, that is. You guys might call me a free spirit, but it hasn't been all fun and games, as you know. I wouldn't want Angel to get the wrong idea about me."

He gave me a long look before continuing. His eyes were a silent reflection of some inner turmoil. I could tell he wanted me to know there was more to him than just a playboy.

I leaned in, fascinated by the change in his tone.

"Yeah, Atticus has always been the serious one, keeping everything bottled up," he began carefully. "It almost cost him his happiness too. But thanks to Sam, he's learning to let go a bit."

He hesitated, gathering his thoughts, then said, "You don't know this as the others do, but things were pretty rough for us brothers growing up." Conan's eyes traced the patterns on his beer bottle. "When I was six, our mom...she tried to end it all. Survived that only to die from drinking herself to death two years later. Dad followed a year after when his heart gave out."

The silence that followed was heavy. Even Murphy, the pup, seemed to sense the shift, settling down by Conan's feet.

There was more than met the eye with Conan, and I wanted to find out more.

"It was a messed up time," he continued softly. "Atticus, being the oldest, had to step up fast, taking care of Braxton and me. He was barely sixteen. Imagine that—having to suddenly be the man of the house." Conan's voice was tinged with a rawness that made my heart ache for him.

Bethany nudged him gently. "But you turned it around, right? You're not that wild kid anymore."

Conan nodded, his brow furrowing slightly. "I didn't understand it all back then. I just knew our parents weren't around like they should've been. After they both died, I just...lost it. Yeah, I was definitely out of control for a while. As I got older, you could say I was a guy with a chip on his shoulder, looking for a good time and without a worry as to who got hurt in the process. Getting into a brawl was the only thing that made me feel much of anything. Pain was always a good reminder that I was still alive. So, anyway, I moved to Huntington Beach the day I turned eighteen, started surfing, doing drugs, partying like there was no tomorrow. I used people—especially women—and lived only for the next thrill. It was a shitty way to treat those around me. But at the time I didn't care. I lived from moment to moment. Man, Atticus had to bail me out more times than I can count."

"Still do," Atticus shot over his shoulder.

Conan paused, glancing over at Atticus and then at me for the briefest of moments before taking a sip of his beer. "Eventually, I realized I wanted something more. Seeing Atticus, how his work mattered, how he saved lives...it got to me. Made me want to feel like I was worth something to someone. So I got my ass enrolled in college. But I knew there was no way I could go through all the hoops for medical school, not to mention there was no way in hell I'd ever get into one. Nursing wasn't just a random choice; it was a way for me to make a difference too. And yeah, the mostly female colleagues didn't hurt," he added with a wry smile.

As I glanced around at everyone, I could see they already knew Conan's truths by the way they nodded and gave him empathetic smiles. It occurred to me that this was his way of sharing his story with me, a part of his keeping the no-secrets pledge he'd made before. What I didn't know was whether I deserved his trust. What if, in my real life, I was a horrible person...the kind no one looked for when they suddenly went missing?

"But here's the kicker," Conan said, leaning closer, his voice dropping to a contemplative whisper. "For a long time, I never wanted the whole white-picket-fence life. Marriage, kids, the whole straight-laced path—it never appealed to me. After what I saw at home, how could it? I saw too much go wrong to ever want that. And the whole societal expectation thing—it wasn't ever for me either. I like the ED because, like me, it's intense— immediate. You make a real difference, and then you move on to the next crisis. It fits with how I've always lived."

Samantha nodded. "It's tough, breaking away from what you're supposed to want." She patted his shoulders from behind, gazing down at him with a kind expression before returning to help Atticus with the steaks and chicken coming off the grill.

"Yeah, but here's the thing," Conan said, looking over at me with a half grin. "Being in the ED, you see the worst day of someone's life, every day. It makes you appreciate the good moments and the real connections you make. And that's what

I'm after."

The group fell quiet, mulling over his words. Then Bethany broke the silence. "Well, I say cheers to finding our own paths, no matter how messy."

Glasses clinked once more, the conversation giving way to an acceptance of the histories we all carried.

The flickering lights around the pool cast a soft glow on everyone's faces as we settled back and grazed the finger foods on the table before us. I smiled, feeling fortunate to have stumbled into this quirky, caring group of people.

Soon, Atticus and Samantha began serving dinner. Steaks, chicken kabobs, and grilled vegetables were placed on the table alongside the charcuterie board and a platter of fruit. The table was overflowing with food, and everything smelled as great as it looked. Everyone served themselves, piling their plates high and settling in for the meal.

As we dug in, the conversation drifted toward darker topics— to the infamous Volkov estate.

"You know, I read online about the Volkovi Notchi and your kidnapping, Sam," I said, a shudder running through me despite the warmth of the evening. "It's horrifying, all that they were into—human trafficking and drugs. Damn, that shit's for real."

"Yeah, those Russians were bad news," Samantha replied, her nose wrinkling in disgust. "And after everything they put me through...I can't believe Viktor Volkov and his goons got away."

Conan nodded, adding another piece of steak to his plate. "The Russian mafia is the worst of the worst—society's gutter rats. They did a lot of damage to a lot of lives in this part of the country. I'm just glad you got out of that mess mostly unscathed, Sam."

"We were all stunned by the extent of it," Atticus added in a somber tone. "Makes you wonder who'd buy such a place, knowing its history."

Samantha glanced over at Atticus. "I'm curious who the woman is and what she'll do with the place."

"That's the million-dollar question," Conan said, reaching across me and grabbing the platter with the grilled veggies. "Whoever it is, she's gotta have some serious guts or no clue about the estate's past."

"Yeah, someone with deep pockets and hopefully better intentions," Atticus added, tearing off a bite of chicken from a skewer with his teeth. "From what my buddy Colton found out, the owner is a wealthy socialite from New York City who bought the property for investment purposes."

I mulled over why someone from the New York social scene would be interested in a property in Tacoma. The strangeness of that nagged at my missing memories. Somehow, I had a feeling that most NYC girls would hardly know Tacoma existed, much less buy investment property here. Recalling the image of my driver's license, I once again got a sense that I was somehow tied to New York.

The subject was dropped, and we continued eating, turning to lighter small talk. When we were finally winding down, Conan excused himself. He soon returned, lugging the old-fashioned ice-cream contraption in his arms. "Time for dessert, and you're all gonna work for it!" he announced with a grin, setting up the machine on the counter near the grill. He poured the ingredients into the basin before putting ice around the edges and a generous helping of rock salt on top of the ice.

Everyone took turns cranking, and it turned into a mini competition of who could crank fastest. When it was my turn, Conan stood close, offering unnecessary tips. "Careful now, it's all in the wrist action."

I rolled my eyes and shook my head. "You've got to be kidding."

He leaned next to my ear and whispered, "Didn't I warn you about rolling those big beautiful blue eyes at me?"

"Yeah, yeah, yeah," I said, patting his stomach as I moved around him to return to my seat. "You just finish cranking that off." I smiled at the low growl he made behind me.

When he began to serve the soft strawberry ice cream, he playfully dabbed a dollop on my nose. Chuckling, I grabbed a spoonful to flick back at him, but my aim faltered, and it plopped onto the ground. Murphy, ever the opportunist, darted over and lapped it up.

After we finished our dessert, we cleared the table, cleaned up the dishes, and put everything away.

Bethany, leaning against the kitchen counter with her chin resting on her palm, gave me a sideways glance.

"Angel, have you noticed Conan here following you around like a lost puppy?" she asked with a teasing lilt to her voice. "I swear, I've never seen him like this around anyone."

Conan, who was in the midst of drying a plate, paused. In one quick motion, he twisted the towel into a makeshift whip and cracked it over Bethany's backside, causing her to yelp and back away with her hands up in the air in surrender. He threatened to pop her again, but she ran out to the patio. He rolled his eyes at me as his ears reddened, giving away his embarrassment.

"Oh, so you can roll your eyes at me? Mm-hmm, I see the double standard." The corners of his eyes crinkled, and a bright smile lit up his face, sending fiery tingles straight to the apex of my thighs.

Outside, Bethany screamed, and then there was a splash. I turned to look. Braxton stood laughing at the edge. He had helped her enter the pool the hard way.

Once the dishes were done, the rest of us headed out to join them for a night swim. The temperature was just right. Murphy, not one to be left out, splashed alongside us, his tiny legs paddling energetically.

After a while, Conan floated over to me, nudged my arm, and nodded toward the house, where Atticus and Samantha were already retreating. "Goodnight, guys," Atticus called. "It's time for the old guy to turn in. Thanks for coming tonight. It's always good having you over." He slid his hand around Samantha's waist and squeezed, causing her to squeal.

"Those two are in no way tired. Trust me on that one," Conan whispered, his brows bouncing. "Atticus just wants some alone time with his lady."

Bethany, catching on, laughed. "Well, we'd better clear out then. Don't want to interrupt the romance. Come on, Braxton, let's let these lovebirds have their nest."

"Yeah, it's getting late, and some of us have early mornings," Braxton added as he and Bethany wrapped themselves in towels. "Beth, I'll give you a ride home, and you can pick up your car in the morning," he offered, sliding into his loafers.

"That'd be great. I was just about to order an Uber."

She and Braxton disappeared into the house.

With just Conan and me in the pool, the night became quiet and calm. The soft underwater lights made the surface of the water shimmer, casting a magical glow around us. Conan, stretching out on a pool lounger, drifted lazily, while I perched on the edge with my feet in the warm, inviting water.

I gazed up at the full moon and then back down to the water, noticing its silver light reflecting off the pool's surface. The atmosphere was peaceful, almost dreamlike, and I couldn't remember the last time I'd been so at ease.

Conan floated closer, his eyes half-closed as a contented smile played on his lips. "You look like you're enjoying yourself."

A warmth that had nothing to do with the pool meandered through my chest, spread to my core, and settled between my thighs. "This is the most relaxed I've felt in ages," I admitted, letting my hand trail through the water. "The whole setup here is incredible. It's like going on a posh vacation."

He chuckled, the sound coming from deep in his belly. "Yeah, it's pretty great. Nights like this make all the crazy shifts in the ED worth it."

I slipped into the pool, the water enveloping me like a gentle hug. Then I swam toward him, the distance between us closing with each kick. The moonlight highlighted the contours of his face, making his features even more striking.

As I floated closer, Conan reached out and pulled me to him, his hand rough against my skin. The desire between us thickened the air. I placed a hand on his chest and, without breaking eye contact, traced the ridges of his abs with my fingers. His skin, wet and warm, seemed to pulse under my touch.

Holding onto the edge of the float with one hand, I shifted my gaze to where the fingers of my other hand glided along his contours. His tattoos, now on full display, were an eclectic mix. Some appeared to be badges of honor, while others were clearly souvenirs of a life well-lived. "You've got some really interesting tattoos. Looks like a lot of history inked on your skin."

He lay still, with one hand tucked up under his head and the other resting on his belly, watching my fingers trace one of the images—a red flag starting low between the V-cut of his hips and disappearing under the waistband of his shorts. He froze as my fingers moved lower.

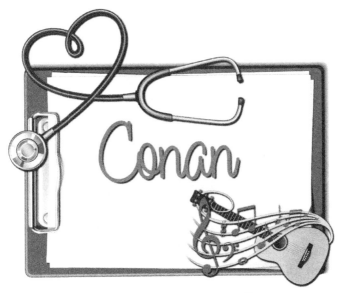

Chapter Twenty-Five

6/24 night

This woman's touch was like fire straight to my groin. I was instantly hard and wanted nothing more than to throw her against the side of the pool, feast on all she had to offer, and fuck her thoroughly. But the fact remained—she had no idea who she was or the life she'd had before the wreck that brought her to me. No matter how badly I wanted her, it wasn't an option.

I seized her hand before she went any further and slowly shook my head. "No." Every man had his breaking point, and I could only resist so much.

Angel pursed her lips into a pout, squinching her eyes in frustration. Irritation was etched across her face, her brow furrowed and her nose crinkled. She crossed her arms and let out a huff, clearly not happy about being stopped, and allowed space to come between us. The expression on her face was almost comical, but I knew better than to laugh. She was really worked up, and there was something oddly endearing about her fiery reaction.

I floated lazily on the pool lounger, letting the cool water lap against my skin, enjoying a rare moment of peace. My eyes closed as I let myself relax—that was, until Angel gave my float a hard shove, flipping me into the water with a huge splash.

The shock of the water hitting my skin woke me up real quick. I surfaced, sputtering and shaking the water from my hair, only to see Angel swimming away, her laughter echoing across the patio. "You're gonna pay for that!" I called out, diving after her.

She was fast, but not fast enough. When she reached the edge of the pool and grabbed onto the side, trying to pull herself out, I closed the gap between us, wrapping my arms around her waist.

"You're not getting away that easy," I growled. In one swift motion, I spun her around and pinned her against the wall, planting my hands firmly on either side of her head, trapping her in place. The water sloshed around us, up to her shoulders, and her wide eyes met mine, filled with surprise and something else—something that ignited a fire within me.

My eyes traced the silvery scar cutting through the perfect skin of her forehead. I raised a hand, softly trailing my wet fingers over the mark. "You're beautiful," I murmured, locking my eyes onto hers. She let out a soft gasp.

Her eyes darted to the water, and she tried to pull away, her cheeks flushing a deep pink. "Don't," she murmured, turning her head. "That thing makes me look like a monster."

I tilted her chin back toward me, brushing my thumb against her jaw. "Bullshit," I said firmly. "You look fierce. This scar is a badge of courage, showing you're a survivor."

Her pupils dilated, and she bit her lower lip. My touch had affected her. The blush spreading down her neck—and the way her chest rose and fell as she all but panted—told me she was not only embarrassed but aroused, and it was driving me wild.

I leaned in closer until our noses were almost touching. "You think this scar makes you ugly? No. When I see it, I see strength." I kissed the scar, then moved to her temple, trailing kisses down to her jaw.

She shivered, resting her palms on my chest.

Lust pulsed through me, raw and undeniable, but the nagging concern of not taking advantage of her held me back. I was teetering on the edge of control. Every nerve in my body screamed to take her right then and there, but I couldn't let myself cross that line—one she might later regret. Not with her amnesia, not with her unknown past hanging over us.

It was my duty to protect her.

I didn't want to be the guy *who couldn't control what the fuck he did with his mouth,* as Atticus had put it. She needed more time to heal, more time for her memories to return.

With a sigh, I let my hands slide down her sides, feeling the curve of her waist and the swell of her hips beneath the water. My desire for her was overwhelming, the tension between us electric. I needed to make sure this was what she truly wanted— to make sure she was in a good place mentally.

I allowed my body to sink under the water until my feet were planted on the bottom. Then, in a single fluid movement, I pulled back and pushed off with a powerful kick. I swam to the other edge of the pool, needing a moment to collect myself.

When I surfaced, I folded my arms on the pool deck and rested my chin on my clasped hands, staring out at the night.

The silence between us stretched, thick with tension. We were locked in a silent standoff. She wanted me—that much was clear—and dammit, I wanted her too. It was a battle of wills, of restraint and desire, and for now, I had to be the one to stand my ground.

"Fuck," I muttered under my breath, trying to shake off the urge that kept gnawing at me. I had to focus and take deep cleansing breaths just not to get a hard-on. Palming a handful of water, I splashed it over my face. The coolness of it did little to quell the heat coursing through me though.

I thought about how wrong it would be to fuck this woman, how taking advantage of her when she was in this state would be making a move I couldn't take back. She was vulnerable, even if she didn't show it. Even if she tried to act tough, there was a fragility to her situation that I had to respect. I had to remember who she was right now—a woman without her past, without her memories.

I was leaning against the edge of the pool, lost in thought, when I heard the faint sound of water being disturbed. Angel was gliding through the pool, her strokes smooth and nearly silent. Then the rhythmic sound halted, causing me to glance around.

Out of nowhere, she yanked my swim shorts down to my ankles.

I jerked, completely shocked. Angel, of all people, had the guts to pull a stunt like that. When she came up for air, she was treading water in the middle of the pool. She locked her eyes onto mine and gave me a smug grin.

Reaching down, I retrieved my shorts and threw them out of the pool, watching them land on the patio with a wet slap. When I turned back, her eyes widened, and her brows shot up. But then that smug grin of hers reappeared, and she rolled her eyes—taunting me, provoking me.

"I have no shame, Angel," I said, crossing my arms over my chest and staring back at her. "And you shouldn't tempt the devil."

She laughed. "Maybe I like living dangerously."

"You're playing with fire," I warned, swimming toward her, the water parting smoothly around me. "What's your endgame?"

She shrugged, her lips curving into a sly smile. "No endgame. Just living in the moment."

I reached her in a few powerful strokes, stopping just inches from her. Sparks of tension flew between us. "You're pushing me to my limits," I said, reaching out to brush a wet strand of hair from her face. "But don't think I won't push back."

Her breath hitched, her eyelashes heavy with desire. "Then push back, Conan."

Clenching my teeth, I fought the urge to lose myself in her. I couldn't let things go too far, not with her in this state. But damn, she made it hard.

I slid my hands around her waist, pulling her close until our bodies were pressed together in the water. "You're driving me insane," I murmured against her ear. Reflexively, my hands traced the curves of her ass. "But I can't do this."

She looked up at me, her eyes wide. "Why? What's holding you back?"

"You deserve better than a quick fuck in a pool," I said, reluctantly releasing her. "You deserve everything I can't give you."

Her expression softened. "Conan, I want you. Here—now. Let's stop complicating things."

The words struck a chord, but I shook my head and started to turn. Without warning, she leaped onto me, wrapping her arms and legs around me. Unable to think straight, I pulled her toward me once more, our bodies colliding in the water, our lips meeting in a heated kiss. Fuck, did she taste good. Her hard nipples, only covered by the thin fabric of her swimsuit, pressed against my chest, and all I wanted to do was take one between my teeth.

But I had to push her away while I still had a shred of control. With all the strength I could muster, I lifted her and flung her backward. There was a loud splash behind me as I turned toward the stairs.

The water's surface rippled from her fall, lapping against the edge of the pool. Her hands smacked against the surface as she broke through, coughing and sputtering. I winced at the sound of her struggle.

"What the hell is your problem, Conan?!" she shouted angrily, her voice garbled by the water. I paused, my steps faltering.

I spun around to face her. The pool lights highlighted her wet, furious face as she dipped under and then resurfaced with her hair slicked back. Her eyes blazed with frustration, demanding that I explain myself.

"Angel, I—"

But she didn't let me finish. "One minute you're all over me; the next you're shoving me away," she said, treading water. "You're giving me fucking whiplash." She massaged her neck to emphasize her point.

As I often did out of habit when searching for things to say, I pulled the hair tie off my ponytail, then scraped my fingers through my hair before tying it back up again. "You don't understand. This isn't about you. It's about me trying to do the right thing."

"The right thing?" she scoffed, her voice steadier now. "What's so wrong about this?"

Taking a deep breath, I turned to face her fully. "You're not just some girl I can fool around with. You deserve more than that. And with everything you've been through, the last thing you need is me complicating things further."

She glared at me. "I think *I* get to decide what I need, Conan. And right now, I need you to stop treating me like I'm fragile—broken."

With my arms crossed and my chin held high, I clenched my jaw. "Angel, listen. Of course I want to fuck you," I said, being blunt, as was my nature. "But I'm not about to take advantage of an innocent girl." I stared at her, trying to keep my resolve.

Angel's eyes sparked with defiance. "I'm not a child, and I'm far from innocent."

I heaved a sigh and turned my back to her, making my way to the pool's steps. The water lapped around my waist as I moved, but the coolness did little to calm me.

"You put on a good show, playing the fun-loving laid-back type of guy one minute and the indifferent badass the next. But I can see through your act!" she called out. "You're more of the tortured-soul type."

"Nah," I said over my shoulder, keeping my tone light. "I'm always easy, go with the flow, you know?"

"No, you're not," she said. "You might be lying to yourself, but I see the truth. You're a man who puts on a good front so often you believe your own bullshit."

Her words stopped me in my tracks. Once more, I turned to face her. The distance between us seemed like a million miles. "You think you've got me all figured out, huh?"

She swam forward, making it to a spot where she could stand her ground only a few feet in front of me, and glared at me, her eyes fierce. "I didn't say that. I may not remember much from before the accident, but I remember everything after. The songs you sang to me and the way you sang them...they were all about heartache and sadness. All I could do was listen and absorb your pain alongside my own."

She fired off a couple of the song titles and recited a few lyrics. "And what about when you sang the song 'Hurt' by Johnny Cash, which is about becoming a shell of a man and losing everyone you love? Or that song 'Creep' by Radiohead about feeling like an outsider who is unworthy of affection, a man who is inadequate and full of self-loathing. You can't fake that kind of emotion. I could go on and on. Remember, you've spent hours with me—and I heard every word."

I swallowed hard. Her insight hit closer to home than I wanted to admit. "You're reading too much into it."

"No, I'm not," she insisted. "Your tattoos tell a story too. The skull on your back, the black widow on your neck, the bloody axes, the broken heart—all intermixed with the sexy women. You try to paint yourself as some badass, but I see the truth. You're not just the easygoing live-and-let-live guy. In reality, you're more like a jaded, brokenhearted little boy who lost his momma way too early and who has a giant, sensitive, *although scarred*, heart that has been hurt too many times."

I clenched my fists at my sides, the truth in her words stinging. How did she perceive so much? I had always buried my past beneath a facade of indifference and charm. But she had seen right through that.

"Why are you giving me such a hard time?" I asked, attempting to maintain my calm.

"Because I see you, Conan. The real you," she replied, her tone softening. "And I want you to see me too."

I took a step back, needing space to process. Her insight was like a punch to the gut, and I had to remind myself to stand strong against the temptation she represented, even though my body craved hers.

Still not convinced that hooking up with her was something I could do—or maybe it was the beer making me more argumentative than normal—I chose to push back with logic. "How do you know you're not a virgin, or perhaps married?" I asked, throwing caution to the wind.

Angel didn't miss a beat. "Trust me, I'm no virgin. I might not remember having sex, but virgins don't have IUDs or wild fantasies about what they'd do to you playing around in their minds." Her lips curled into a wicked grin.

"What about a husband?"

"If I had a husband, don't you think he'd come looking for me? If anyone gave a shit about me, they would have shown up by now. Obviously, in my past life, I must have been a loner or a loser. The kind of person no one cares about or notices when they disappear. What does that say about me? No wonder you don't want any part of me. I get it."

I blinked, her words hitting me like a freight train. I wasn't going to listen to this level of self-deprecation from her. "Shut the fuck up!" I snapped, unable to keep the anger out of my voice. "There's no way you're alone or unwanted. Can't be. I've spent plenty of time with you. You're smart, funny, sensitive, not to mention drop-dead gorgeous. I meet people all day every day in the ED, and trust me, you are head and shoulders above most of them."

Angel's eyes narrowed, skepticism flickering in them. "You're just saying that to make me feel better." Her tone was softer now, almost fragile. She would hate to know I actually did think that because of her injuries, so I kept it to myself.

"I'm not lying," I barked, my frustration boiling over. "You're amazing, and if people from your past haven't shown up, it's their fucking loss. Not yours."

She scowled fiercely. "Then why won't you be with me? Why are you holding back?"

I rubbed my hands over my face, trying to gather my thoughts. "Because, my Angel, you deserve someone who can give you everything without any reservations. And right now, I'm not sure I can be that guy. You've been through so much. The last thing I want to do is take advantage of you or one day be a regret."

Angel backstroked to the side of the pool. Spreading her arms out along the edge, she leaned her head back and stared up at the full moon. She remained silent for a long time.

"There's one thing that does make me unsure. I know I'm not a shy wallflower, Conan," she began. "But I've had dreams—confusing ones. Sometimes I'm this quiet, studious girl, and other times I'm a wild party girl who takes exactly what she wants. I don't know who I am or which of those personas actually fits, but I do know life is too short not to live in the present."

As she spoke, I watched, unable to look away. Her face was so incredibly beautiful, illuminated by the moon. For a beat, neither of us spoke. I exhaled a slow breath.

She gazed up at the stars with a melancholy expression. Even from where I was standing, I could see the unshed tears glistening in her eyes. "What if I never get my memories back? Am I supposed to live life in limbo or move on?"

I stayed silent, watching her breath. I wanted to freeze time, to hold on to this moment forever. No woman had ever affected me this deeply. Maybe it was her innocence—the fact that she was a blank slate due to her amnesia, free to write her story anew without the weight of past memories. God, how I longed to help her fill those empty spaces.

"You know, in the vast timeline of the universe, our lives are but fleeting moments," she said. "Everything is temporary—the worst of times, the best times—especially the best ones. We only have so many years to experience love and life as humans. We should embrace every moment, even the painful ones, and love them, all of them, no matter the pain or the pleasure, because they are all part of our journey."

She took a deep breath, speaking thoughts that I could never put into words.

"Heartache, grief, agony—they all teach us, shaping who we are. There's no wasted experience if we learn from it. Our willingness to fail determines our capacity to grow. The clock never stops ticking. The only regret you'll have is not striving harder for what you truly wanted when it was right in front of you."

Her insightfulness hit me hard. She was right. The sand in the hourglass never slowed down, and we only had so much time to reach for what we wanted.

Bringing her focus back to me, she threw up her hands, her eyes flashing with annoyance. "I have to move on at some point," she said, biting her lip. "I can't just live here with Sam and Atticus. I have to figure out how to take care of myself. I deserve to live a normal life like everyone else."

She paused, inhaling sharply. "And...how dare you get up on some sort of moral high horse and judge me for being a goddamn woman with needs and wants?"

Her words hit me like a punch. I stepped back, my mind racing. "Angel, it's not about judgment. It's about acting with integrity. You're in a delicate place right now. I don't want to be the guy who takes advantage of that."

She pursed her lips, irritation etched across her features. "Maybe I don't need you to protect me. Maybe I just need you to see me as a person who deserves to live, to feel, to want."

Hesitating for a moment, I breathed in the scent of chlorine and summer air. "I see you, Angel. Trust me, I do."

Her eyes softened, the fire dimming but not extinguished. "Then show me, Conan. Show me that you see me."

I scrubbed my hand over my chin as her words resonated in my mind. Dammit, she had a point, and I had no retort for her logic. I wanted to argue, to push back, but she had me pinned. She was so fucking smart and confident, and that turned me on more than I cared to admit. But the last thing I wanted was to take advantage of her. I stood at the end of the pool, unsure what to say or how to react. She had me cornered, and no matter which way I moved, it felt like the wrong decision.

If I pushed her away, she'd think I wasn't interested. But if I gave in, I'd be taking advantage of her.

"Angel—you're making this so hard."

"It's not about making things easy or hard. It's about being real," she replied, her gaze unflinching. "I want you to see me for who I am, just like I see you."

Stabbing my fingers into my wet hair, I gripped my head in frustration, torn between my desires and being the kind of man she deserved. "You don't make anything simple, do you?"

She shook her head, a small smile playing on her lips. "Never."

Dropping my hand to my side, I took a couple of steps toward her, my resolve crumbling as she dipped back into the water and resurfaced. "Fine, you want the truth? You're right. I've been hurt. But that doesn't change the fact that you deserve better than this. Better than me."

"Maybe," she said softly. "I'm not asking for perfection, Conan. I'm asking for you."

I stared at her—conflicted. This woman had a way of cutting through my defenses, seeing the parts of me I tried to hide. And damn, did I want her.

"I'm warning you. I'm not a hero. I'm not even close."

"Ever thought I might just want you, flaws and all?"

Her arguments were like a drug, intoxicating and impossible to resist. This was just the beginning, and I knew it was going to be one hell of a ride.

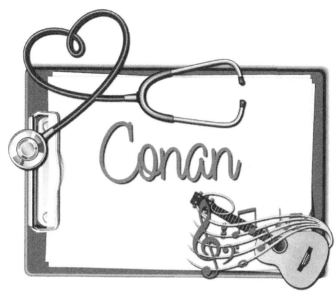

Chapter Twenty-Six
6/24 night 6/25 early morning

With a coy look and a half grin, Angel let her hands drift to her shoulders, the water lapping along her collarbone. She slid her fingers under the straps of her bikini top, letting them fall into the water—a slow striptease. She reached one hand behind her back and, with a flick, unclasped her top. Her eyes stayed locked on mine, her smile broadening as she flung the top onto the pool deck, making my mouth water.

Frozen in place, I watched as she dipped down into the water, wiggling her hips. The sight of her bare breasts made my dick stand at attention. Then she tossed the bottoms of her swimsuit out as well. Her boldness made my blood race.

My gaze drifted down. The moonlight glimmering on the water's surface highlighted her every move. Her expression morphed into an impish smile, and she turned and carefully pulled herself up, water streaming down her back—ass—thighs as she faced the bay in the distance. The moon's illumination caught the droplets on her skin, making her look like a damn goddess.

She placed her knee on the edge of the pool, giving me a tantalizing glimpse of her dark pink lips, then flipped herself around to sit on the edge, dangling her feet in the water. Like a siren luring me in, she stared down at me seductively. "I'm not trying to prove anything, Conan. I'm just being honest. I know what I want, and I want you."

Heat flared in her eyes as she scrutinized me—daring me to make a move.

My control was slipping, her boldness pushing me to the edge. I had to make a choice, and every second made it harder to resist.

Angel slowly placed one foot, then the other, on the edge of the pool. She pressed her knees together, and water streamed down her shins, over the tops of her feet, and dripped from her cute little toenails that were painted hot pink. Then her knees separated and fell open, and she leisurely spread her legs wide, exposing her juicy pussy. I nearly lost my shit right then and there. My Angel wanted what she wanted, and that was me. Never in my fucking life had I seen something so damn inviting. The water glistened on her belly, falling in thin rivulets over her mound and down the creases of her thighs. The folds of her pussy were now on full display for me. My dick got rock-hard, even in the waist-deep cool water.

When she brought the fingers of one hand to her mouth, my gaze followed. Her tongue swirled around the two middle digits before they disappeared between her lips. The sight of her cheeks hollowing as she sucked sent my mind spiraling with thoughts of those lips wrapped around my cock. She trailed saliva-coated fingers down to tease one of her nipples, making it perk right up. Her other hand moved south, fingers dancing over her wet folds before settling on her clit. She circled her sensitive nub with her middle finger, and her back arched in response to the delicious friction. My eyes locked onto hers as she let out an intoxicating moan. This made my dick throb beneath the cool water, completely betraying any sense of control I thought I had.

Those crystal-blue eyes of hers...they cut through all the bullshit and pierced my soul. I was forever lost to her. That twenty percent angel, eighty percent devil mix made me want to dive headfirst into whatever underworld she'd take me.

As if reading my mind, Angel curled her lips into a sly smirk and she began giving me one hell of a show. She spread her legs wider, utterly captivating me.

"God, I want to feel your dick inside me." She moaned as she slipped one, then two fingers into her wetness. I swallowed hard, trying to stay still and just watch her sexy performance. My cock twitched, aching to replace her fingers—to be the one making her moan and writhe.

Her fingers fucked her pussy mercilessly, pulling out only to sweep her sweet juices over her clit.

Her moans grew louder, more desperate. Then her orgasm ripped through her, making her groan loud enough that it echoed around the pool.

My control was slipping. Her boldness and pleasure-filled face pushing me up to the breaking point.

There she sat on the edge of the pool, writhing from the orgasm she'd just given herself. I couldn't take it any longer, so I shot through the water like a fucking torpedo, reaching where she sat, legs still stretched wide. "Your pussy looks good enough to eat," I growled.

She spread her legs for me like she knew it was going to be my last meal. And hell, maybe it was.

Reverently, I kneeled between her legs, hooking her thighs in my elbows, breathing in the intoxicating scent of her arousal. I lifted her ass and pulled it forward until it was hanging over the edge of the pool, giving me full access. Then I peppered her thighs with soft kisses before darting my tongue out and flicking her clit. Enveloping her in the warmth of my mouth, I feasted. Her gasp was music to my ears, spurring me on as I sucked and licked her sensitive nub. The tangy sweetness of her juices made my mouth water, and I couldn't help but moan at the exquisite flavor.

"Oh God, yes!" she shouted, her hands gripping the pool's edge as if her life depended on it.

My fingers slid into her wetness, curling in search of her most sensitive spot while I continued to feast on her clit. Her hips bucked, her breathing becoming ragged as my fingers brushed against that magic button. The combination had her squirming beneath me. Instead of tipping her over, I withdrew my fingers, replacing them with my hungry tongue. It pumped relentlessly in and out of her, my teeth grazing her clit while my thumb circled her puckered hole, applying just enough pressure to make her gasp. To my pleasant surprise, she pressed against my finger. I savored the thought of taking her there too.

Angel's legs began to shake uncontrollably, her cries growing desperate as she reached the brink of another orgasm.

"Conan!"

Her walls clenched around my tongue, her body convulsing with ecstasy while she screamed my name. The sight of her writhing in pleasure, completely lost in the sensation, was enough to make me ready to burst.

I scooped her up effortlessly and carried her toward the steps of the pool. Her legs wrapped around my torso. Her pussy settled against my throbbing cock, the sensation making me all the more desperate for release.

Before I climbed the first step, she wriggled out of my hold, falling back into the water and laughing. She grabbed my hand and spun me around. Confused, I cocked my head to the side, arching a brow.

"Sit," she commanded, pushing me onto the top step of the pool. The water lapped against my ass as my shaft stood tall, like a flagpole, out of the water.

She lowered herself onto her knees on the step below me until her face was level with my aching erection. Glancing up at me with that wicked grin of hers, she took it in her hand and licked the head slowly, her tongue teasing the sensitive frenulum. My Angel was eager to indulge in her own feast. Her other hand cupped my balls while teasing the strip of skin behind them, eliciting a deep groan from me that vibrated against her lips. She giggled, and I almost lost my mind.

"Shit, Angel, don't do that to me. I want to savor this for as long as I can," I growled as her tongue swirled around the head of my cock and down along the back of my shaft.

Her lips and hands worked in tandem, bringing me closer to my release. Soon she started pushing my cock deeper into her mouth and taking me into her throat, stroke after stroke until tears were streaming down her cheeks. She didn't gag or show any sign of pain, but I couldn't stand to push her beyond her limits. I gently withdrew from her mouth, not wanting to hurt her.

Angel rested her head on my thigh, gasping for air. Feeling the need for release, I pulled away from her and lifted her in my arms once more. I carried her over to a poolside chaise, positioning myself on top of her. As her legs wrapped around me, I put one foot on the ground.

"Conan," she whispered, her breath hot against my ear. "I want you inside me."

"My Angel, you have no idea how much I've been craving this," I breathed out, thrusting into her tight heat in one smooth motion. Our bodies moved together, our desire for each other insatiable. The sounds of our passion filled the air, punctuated by the slap of skin against skin.

"Ah, what the fuck!" I yelped as an unexpected, wet sensation on my balls caught me off guard. I jerked back and caught sight of Murphy, Samantha's little white shih tzu, going to town on my nether regions.

"Murphy!" Samantha's voice rang out from the doorway. "What are you doing?!"

"Shit," I muttered, annoyed as hell but struggling not to laugh. Angel's eyes widened in shock as her hands flew up to cover her face.

"Conan, you're corrupting my dog!" Samantha screeched, her face turning a deep shade of red. She threw her hand over her eyes but couldn't resist peeking through her fingers.

"Hey now, your damn dog is the pervert here," I shot back, grinning despite the absurdity of the situation. "He just licked my balls!"

Angel let out a muffled giggle, her body shaking with laughter as she rested her forehead on my chest.

Samantha, still mortified, pleaded, "Come here, Murphy." She tried to coax him away with a promise of a treat from the fridge. "You want some turkey? Come on, sweet boy, let's get you something better to eat."

I gave no fucks. I pulled out and scooped Angel up into my arms, carrying her past Samantha and straight up to the guest bedroom she was staying in. While we ascended the stairs, she buried her face in my neck, laughing and blushing at the ridiculousness of it all.

Once we were in the bedroom, I moved to toss Angel onto the bed, but she clung to me like a koala, pulling me down with her. We rolled over to the center of the bed in a tangled mess of limbs, laughing uncontrollably. I scooted back and propped myself up against the pillows, resting my head against the wall.

"Okay, enough playing around," I said, my tone firm but lighthearted. "I don't like to play games, Angel—I like to fuck."

"Me too," she replied with a devilish grin, straddling my hips. My cock twitched in anticipation, desperate for release.

In a single graceful move, Angel impaled herself on my dick, her tits bouncing in my face. It was the hottest thing I'd ever seen, and I fought to hold back a groan. She began to ride me like a goddamn stallion, and soon our bodies were moving in heated sync.

"Mmm, fuck!" I roared as we picked up speed, the sound of our skin smacking against each other spurring me on.

"Conan, you feel so good inside me," she moaned, throwing her head back as our bodies moved together, slick with sweat.

"Angel, you're driving me insane," I hissed, my fingers digging into her ass. She rode me with wild abandon as I heaved her up and down on my cock even harder, making her whine. I grinned. This was what I needed—this raw, unbridled passion. Her nails dug into my shoulders as she cried out in pleasure. The sensation of her tight, wet pussy gripping my dick made me feral.

"Don't stop! I'm so...so close," she stammered, her breath hot against my face. Her blue eyes were glazed with lust as she looked down at me. I reached up to cup her perfect breasts, my thumbs flicking over her sensitive nipples as she continued to bounce on my cock.

"Damn, your tits are incredible," I told her, leaning up to capture one of her nipples in my mouth. I swirled my tongue around the hardened tip before gently nipping it between my teeth. She cried out, tangling her fingers in my hair. I switched to the other nipple, sucking it hard between my lips.

"Shit, Conan, I'm gonna come..." She panted, her body trembling as she neared her climax. My hands slid down to cup her ass, and I skimmed my fingers between her cheeks to tease her puckered hole, which was dripping with her own juices. Slowly, I eased one finger in just past the first knuckle, making her gasp. She seized my dick in an iron grip.

"Oh, fuck!" she screamed, her orgasm crashing through her like a tidal wave. She flung her head back. There was nothing better than watching my Angel fall to pieces. Her pussy pulsed around me, and it was the most incredible sensation I'd ever felt. I couldn't hold back any longer. With a guttural groan, I slammed into her one last time, my climax exploding through me as I filled her with my cum.

Our bodies shuddered together, limbs entwined, while we rode out our intense orgasms.

"That was... Fuck, that was amazing," I whispered, my voice hoarse.

"Mmm," she purred, collapsing onto my chest. She pressed a soft kiss to my neck before draping an arm over my shoulder, her body warm against mine. "It really was."

She took deep, ragged breaths, attempting to steady herself. We stayed like that for a while, as we came down from our rapture.

"Aren't you glad you gave in to me?" she asked. "Maybe you won't be so hard to convince next time." She let out a soft chuckle.

I smirked. "You say that as if I'm done with you, my Angel. But I'm just getting started. You opened the gates and released the beast. Now you're going to learn just what I meant when I warned you about me taking advantage of your innocence."

With a swift, decisive action, I flipped her over onto her belly and shoved her knees up under her, positioning her just right, ass in the air.

"Seriously?" She gasped, glancing back at me with wide eyes. "You're ready for round two already?"

"Can't help myself," I admitted, rubbing my already-hard dick along her butt crack and onto her back. A shiver ran down her spine. "You turn me on like no one else."

"All right then," she said in a sultry and eager voice. "Let's test your stamina."

"My girl's a greedy little devil, aren't you?"

In reply, she wriggled her ass against my cock.

I positioned myself behind her, relishing the sight of her perfect ass. Gripping her hips, I brushed her wet pussy lips with the tip of my cock and slowly pushed into her, moaning softly as her warmth enveloped my thickening shaft.

"You dare to question my stamina from this position, my Angel?" I growled.

"Mm-hmm," she taunted.

With that, I hammered my cock into her, my gentleness long forgotten in the wake of how she provoked me. My girl was no angel in bed; she was my vixen, my personal addiction.

"Stroke that clit of yours while I fuck you," I demanded. "I want to feel you squeeze around me again."

"Like this?" she asked, putting her fingers in a *V* shape and sliding them down between her legs. She began stimulating her clit while adding friction to the sides of my dick at the same time.

"Perfect," I grunted, pounding into her wet heat. The way her walls tightened around my dick drove me wild. The arm that held her weight began to shake, so she twisted her fingers into the sheets, providing her the leverage to return my thrusts stroke for stroke. With each one, the tip of my cock pulled all the way back to the edge of her entrance before slamming against her back wall.

"Fuck…Conan," she moaned, and I could sense her approaching climax. Her breaths started coming in short gasps as her body tensed.

"Come for me, Angel," I commanded, feeling my orgasm building as my balls tightened.

With a cry of pleasure, she shuddered. Her walls clenched around me, waves of ecstasy crashing over her.

I couldn't hold back any longer. I pulled out and let my hot cum shower her back, painting her skin with the evidence of our passion.

"Wow," she breathed heavily, turning to look at me with wide eyes. "I didn't think you had that in you."

"Never underestimate me, my Angel." I grinned, admiring the sight of her flushed face and heaving chest.

Sliding one leg off the bed, I reached over and lifted her in my arms, then carried her to the shower in her en suite bathroom, our lips locked in a passionate, never-ending kiss. Without releasing her, I reached an arm in and turned on the hot water.

While we waited for it to heat up, I plopped her ass on the vanity. I couldn't stop kissing her, couldn't get enough of this woman. Every time those icy blues gave me her attention, fiery tendrils shot from my core to my groin. There was no rational explanation for why I was blazing toward this woman like wildfire. Nor was there any denying it either.

"My Angel, you're all mine now," I whispered, stamping a kiss on her forehead. "Let's get cleaned up."

With that, I lifted her off the counter and guided her into the shower. When we stepped under the spray, she jumped away— the water was a bit too hot. I moved to block it from hitting her and quickly adjusted the temperature as her laughter filled the steamy air.

"Let me help you," I murmured, reaching for the soap. Standing naked before me, she nervously crossed her arms in front of her chest. I took my time tracing her form with my eyes, then cocked my head to the side. "So now you're shy?"

Biting the corner of her lip, she placed her hands on my chest. "No, just feeling exposed. The lights of the shower, the closeness...the nakedness. It's all just very real, standing here as you scrutinize me from head to toe."

"I'm not judging you, beautiful. More like stunned that you're standing before me."

I gently pulled her against my chest. She wrapped her arms around my waist, sighing as she relaxed into me. Reaching over to the bottle of bath gel, I squirted a handful into my palm and lathered my hands up behind her. Then I caressed her skin, running my foamy hands from the nape of her neck down her back and over the curves of her ass. After I was finished, I shifted her into the warm spray. She let out a mellow sigh against my chest. I took the time to drink in this moment, running my fingers over her back and tracing the curves of her sides. She was the perfect fit for me.

Forcing myself to break out of the trance I'd succumbed to, I groaned and moved her so I could grab the shampoo. I squirted it into my palm and applied it to her long locks, tenderly stroking her scalp and running my fingers through her hair while she rested her forehead on my pec. Turning her within my arms, I guided her head under the spray, carefully rinsing her hair. Then I added conditioner to her lengths and repeated the rinsing process, leaving her hair smooth and tangle free. Remembering the hair tie holding my hair back, I pulled it out and shook my hair like a wet dog. She giggled, reaching up and running her hands through it.

Stepping back, I took her chin with my thumb and gave her a soft kiss. With my fingers, I combed her hair up into a high, crazy bun, securing it with the hair tie. Now that I had full access to her long, slender throat, I couldn't help but trail tender kisses along it. It would have been easy to lose myself in her, but I stepped away to add more soap to my hands. I scrubbed them together, creating lots of foamy goodness before placing my hands on the sides of her neck. Moving from her neck, over her shoulders, and downward, I explored every curve and crevice of the rest of her body. The intimate touch, combined with the hot water and steam, reignited the fire between us.

She rose on her toes, wrapping her hands around my neck, and pulled me in for a demanding kiss.

"Your turn," she said, taking the soap from me and repeating the process on my body. She even climbed onto the bench and tenderly cleaned and conditioned my hair. God, did her touch make my head spin. Her skin glistened under the water, and my cock hardened once more as she ran her fingers over it with soap and rinsed it clean. Angel noticed, biting her lip and giving me a playful grin. "Already?" she teased. "You really are insatiable."

"I'm fucking bewitched by you, my little devil in angel's wings," I replied, wrapping my fingers around her tiny waist and pulling her close. Sitting down on the bench, I hoisted her up to stand over me and positioned her feet on either side of my hips. Her wet pussy hovered just above my face—the perfect height for me to taste her again. She gasped when my tongue found her clit. I began licking it and sucking it between my lips while my hands wrapped around her ass. I could smell her arousal and taste her desire.

"Delicious," I growled, sinking my tongue into her sensitive folds. My hands forced her harder against my mouth while my fingers teasingly brushed against her puckered hole. She gasped again, louder this time, gripping my hair as I sucked on her clit.

It wasn't long before her body tensed up. Just before she came, I lowered her onto my rock-hard cock, growling in pleasure when her tight walls engulfed me once more.

"Ride me, Angel."

She ground her hips in rhythm with mine and held my face as we kissed passionately. I gripped her tightly, driving her up and down my shaft as we moved together in perfect sync.

"Come with me, my Angel," I growled, my climax building. She nodded, her eyes locked onto mine with an intensity that sent heat down my spine.

"Conan!" she screamed, her walls squeezing me tight as her orgasm washed over her. The sensation pushed me over the edge, and we came together in a powerful release that left us both breathless.

"God, I can't believe it," she panted, resting her forehead against mine. "You're amazing."

"For you, anything." I pressed one last lingering kiss to her lips before helping her stand and turning off the water. As the steam cleared, I stepped out and grabbed a fluffy towel from the cabinet. Carefully and slowly, I rubbed it up and down her body, making sure every inch of her skin was dry before doing the same to myself.

"Conan...I think I might've gotten more than I bargained for with you," Angel admitted, her legs shaking slightly from exhaustion. "You've got quite the insatiable appetite and the ginormous ever-ready dick to go with it." She laughed as a bright smile lit up her face.

Scooping her up, I carried her to the bed and laid her down gently.

I spooned up against her. She fit perfectly against me, like a key sliding effortlessly into its lock. As she drifted off to sleep, I traced the lines of her face and the curves of her body, marveling at the connection we shared.

Soulmates, true love, and forever were just fairy tales—but then I met her.

It didn't make sense. Hell, I'd spent my whole life dodging anything that even hinted at real feelings. I'd always been the guy who kept it light, never letting anyone get close enough to see the cracks beneath the surface. But Angel had fallen into my life—quite literally—and changed everything. When she was brought into the ED, bloody and unconscious, something had shifted inside me. I couldn't leave her side, not then and not now.

For a month, I'd watched over her as she lay there, vulnerable and angelic. The amnesia had stripped her of her past but not her spirit. Even though she didn't remember who she was, she faced each day with a kind of grace and resilience that left me in awe. No vanity, no pretense—just pure, natural beauty. And that kindness, man, it blew me away. She had every reason to be angry at the world, to feel lost, but instead, she was grateful, gentle, and strong.

There was something about her that drew me in deeper than I'd ever thought possible. Maybe it was how she saw me—not as some carefree playboy but as someone worth getting to know. She didn't judge me for my past or the walls I'd built around my heart. She accepted me for who I was in this moment, and that scared the hell out of me. Yet it also made me want to protect her with everything I had.

I'd never been one to get attached, but with my Angel, it was different. I could envision myself in her future—not as a fleeting presence but as something real and lasting. Falling for her was like jumping out of a plane without a parachute—dangerous and thrilling. I didn't understand it, but I was falling hard and fast, and there was no stopping it.

This woman, with her strength and kindness, had broken through the barriers I'd carefully constructed, and I was okay with that. My Angel was more than just a woman in my life; she was becoming my reason to fight, to protect, and to love. And damn if that didn't make me feel more alive than I ever had before.

My life would never be the same after tonight.

Chapter Twenty-Seven

6/25

The aroma of espresso stirred me awake, dragging me from the depths of sleep. As I stretched, my muscles and most intimate places ached and tingled from a night well spent. Conan had lit a fire in me—a blazing wildfire that engulfed my senses and left me craving more. I'd needed his touch and the lust in his eyes more than I'd ever thought possible. He had a way of tethering me to the now when my past was nothing more than a hazy mirage. The intensity with which he had taken me was as terrifying as it was thrilling. Every move he made was just right, as though he was attuned to all my wants and needs.

His hands had explored every inch of my body with reverence, tracing patterns on my skin that left me shivering in anticipation, only to be followed by his lips tracing the same journey, leaving me desperate for more. God, how I loved that he took his sweet time, stretching out each moment and prolonging every possible pleasure.

With Conan, I mattered. I was even treasured. The way he looked at me—like I was the only woman worth knowing—filled me with a sense of belonging that had been absent since waking up in that sterile hospital room.

Every stroke spoke volumes about his longing for me; every smoldering gaze screamed of his need. Yet he never took without giving first. Each kiss he imprinted on my skin held promises of bliss; each caress sent waves of pleasure crashing over me until all thought evaporated and only raw sensations were left.

Afterward, he'd cradled me so close, and our bodies had tangled together as if attempting to meld into one. His steady heartbeat and protective hold reassured me that I mattered. He saw me as stunning when I was shattered, significant when I felt inconsequential. And even though I couldn't recall who I used to be, Conan reminded me of who I was—a woman desired and cherished for just being herself.

Rolling over, I reached out, searching for him, but his side of the bed was empty and cold. I peeked around the room and into the en suite, but there was no sign of his massive form.

I rose and quickly took care of my business, not bothering to run a brush through the tangled bird's nest that was now my hair. I threw on a pair of soft pink shorts and a heather-gray T-shirt that hung off my shoulder, then made my way downstairs barefoot. The wooden steps were cool beneath my feet as I followed the enticing aroma of coffee all the way to the kitchen.

Atticus, Samantha, and Conan were already up and dressed, ready for their shift at St. John's. The sight of them in their scrubs whiplashed me right back to the hospital. God, how much I'd hated being in that place. Although...seeing Conan's ink-wrapped muscles bulging against the constraints of the fabric did make tingles erupt in my belly. The thought of playing naughty nurse games later kicked my imagination into high gear.

Atticus cleared his throat, breaking me away from my dirty thoughts. Conan noticed the way I was ogling him and smirked. I turned my attention to Atticus, who handed me a freshly poured cup of espresso from his fancy coffee machine.

"Looks like you could use this more than I could at the moment," he said, cocking his head and giving my hair a judgmental once-over.

"Morning, sleepyhead," Samantha said, spreading cream cheese on a bagel. "Don't pay him any mind. Want some breakfast? We've got bagels, cold cuts, fruit...the works."

"Thanks," I said, taking a sip of the rich espresso. "What's with the big spread?"

"Gotta fuel up for the chaos of the ED," Conan said, shoving a bagel into the toaster. He winked at me. "Didn't mean to wake you. You must be exhausted after yesterday."

"Yeah, yesterday was...a lot," I said, sitting on a barstool at the island. "But honestly, I'm more tired from a certain someone wearing me out last night." I bounced my eyebrows a couple of times, hoping to get a rise out of Conan.

Samantha burst out laughing. "Well, after what Murphy and I saw, I'm not surprised. Poor dog. I think you and Conan might have permanently scarred him with what he witnessed by the pool!"

"Oh God," I groaned, cheeks burning. "Sorry about that."

"Well, it's his own fault. Murphman is the one who interrupted us," Conan shot back, raising his hands in mock surrender. "And, hey, if he learned anything, it's how to have a good time."

Atticus shook his head. "I'm sure Murphy will survive. He's seen worse."

"Besides, no shame here," Conan said, grinning at me. "You all know that. Right, Atticus?"

Atticus nodded, keeping his expression deadpan. "Absolutely. Conan's shamelessness is well-documented."

"Too late to tame him now," Samantha quipped, handing Conan a clean plate.

I laughed, savoring the warmth of the espresso as I peeked over the rim of my cup. Samantha set a plate of toasted bagels and fruit in front of me, and we dug into breakfast. Soon we were chatting about the day ahead.

After polishing off his food and setting his plate in the sink, Conan walked up next to me and said softly, "Seriously though, I didn't mean to wake you. You must be tired after just getting out of the hospital and dealing with the arraignment."

"Oh, I'm tired all right, but it has nothing to do with the hospital or the arraignment." I smiled up at him through my lashes. "Don't worry. I'll take it easy and be good to go when you get back later."

He cupped my cheek and stamped a kiss on my forehead. "It won't be too late when I get home, so plan on some more music therapy." He grinned, nodding toward the living room. "My guitar is next to the hearth. I'll play all your favorite songs tonight."

"Home, huh?" Atticus said, cocking one of his sharp brows at Conan. "So, you've decided to move in with us? Are you going to start paying rent too?"

"Nah, you know what I mean, you little fucker," Conan said with a shake of his head and a roll of his eyes. "You know I love my place over in Ruston. It might not be an ostentatious fortress like this place, but it has everything I need conveniently within walking distance."

Samantha and I both chuckled, watching the brothers verbally spar.

Atticus stood up, straightening his shirt. "All right, time to head out. Hope traffic's light this morning. Conan, you riding with us, or are you taking your Jeep?"

"I'll drive myself. I've got errands to run after I get off," Conan said, grabbing his keys.

Samantha started clearing the plates from the island.

"You guys get going. I'll clean up," I offered.

"Are you sure? This kitchen is like a sci-fi spaceship," Samantha warned.

I waved a hand dismissively. "I'll figure it out. Go, save lives."

As they gathered their things and headed for the garage, Samantha glanced up, her eyes widening. "Oh, I almost forgot! Angel, I have your personal items from the ED. They were in my car from where I brought them home from the hospital yesterday."

I glanced up, curious. "My personal items?"

Already heading toward the garage, Samantha explained, "Yeah, when the EMTs brought you in, you didn't have much on you. No purse, wallet, or even a phone—"

"We had to cut off your clothing because of your injuries," Conan added, walking back to where I sat. "I don't remember there being anything except maybe a pair of shoes. I was too focused on keeping your neck aligned and dealing with that gash on your forehead."

I cringed, heat creeping up my face. "So everyone saw me naked? Including you guys?!"

Atticus nodded, sympathy in his eyes. "Yeah, it was quite the introduction. But don't worry; we've all seen worse."

Conan reached over and squeezed my hand. "You're a trooper, Angel. Don't sweat it."

Samantha returned with the paper bag a couple of minutes later and set it on the counter. "Here you go. Just to warn you, there may be blood on whatever's in there. We usually plop a person's stuff in the bag in a rush, and then it gets labeled and stored."

"Okay, thanks for letting me know." I stared at it, curious but not ready to deal with memories that might be provoked by blood-covered shoes.

Before they left, Conan gave me a sweet kiss. "Take it easy while I'm gone, okay?"

"I will," I said, rising from the island to get going with the dishes and dismissing him as I started rinsing off the plates.

Then they were out the door, leaving the house quiet. Murphy trotted up to me, his tail wagging. I couldn't resist slipping him a piece of leftover turkey. The silence felt strange after a month of constant activity and noise in the hospital.

As I finished cleaning up, my mind went over everything that had happened. The support I'd received from everyone had been incredible, but I was still uncertain about my memories and anxious about the future.

I took the bag from the emergency department upstairs and dropped it on the dresser, still not ready to face what was inside. The soft, luxurious bedding called my name, and I couldn't fight the urge to take a nap. I was hoping some rest would help clear my head. Murphy jumped onto the bed and curled up beside me. His soft snores and occasional snorts were comforting, and eventually, I drifted off.

I woke up some time later and rubbed my eyes before stretching out across the bed and letting out a groan. The aroma of espresso lingered faintly in the air. My sleep had left me groggy. A shower would be the perfect way to shake off the remnants of my nap.

I padded to the bathroom, appreciating the cool tile under my feet. The place was a dream. I'd not gotten well acquainted with it yesterday because I'd been in such a rush to change when I first arrived. Then, later, I'd been high on endorphins and lost in my arousal with Conan. When I glanced at the shower, memories of his ginormous hands on my skin sent heat skirting to my lower belly. The man knew how to play me better than his guitar. My head was still spinning from the many orgasms he'd given me. Somewhere in the back of my mind, I knew it had been an exceptional night of pleasure, regardless of who I'd been with in the past. I was surprised I hadn't had any flashbacks, but then again, Conan had demanded my full attention.

Exploring a bit, I found the immaculate space was stocked with everything imaginable—high-end soaps, shampoos, and other toiletries, plush linens, and even a fancy blow dryer and curler. I selected a peony-scented bodywash and some rich, moisturizing shampoo and conditioner. Then I turned on the water, adjusted it until it was just the right temperature, and stepped under the luxurious spray.

The warm water cascaded over me, washing away the morning's soreness. I sighed in relief. Silky bubbles from the bodywash glided over my skin as I lathered up. I wished I could stay in here all day, but I needed to get going, so I moved on to washing my hair. The steam enveloped me as I massaged shampoo into my scalp, creating a cocoon of comfort while the peony-scented air sent my imagination off to some tropical island.

I reached for the conditioner and worked it through the ends of my hair. For a few minutes, I allowed it to sit, standing under the spray before finally rinsing my hair thoroughly. Turning off the water, I stepped out and wrapped myself in a plush towel.

After that, I took my time drying my hair with the blow-dryer, enjoying the way it fluffed up under the warm air. I decided to style it in a high ponytail, using the hair tie Conan had given me last night. I couldn't help but smile at the memory of him pulling it out and shaking his long dirty-blond hair like some golden retriever. The man might have had others convinced he was the carefree *good boy*, but I knew better. He was more like the German-shepherd type.

Feeling refreshed, I dressed in my favorite leggings and a cute summer top, finishing the look with a pair of sneakers. The mirror reflected someone ready to face the day, even if I didn't feel entirely that way inside.

While I was tidying up the bathroom, I remembered the bag Samantha had brought home from the ED. Curiosity tugged at me, so I headed over to the dresser where I'd dropped it.

After retrieving it and setting it on the bed, I studied it, wondering if whatever was inside would trigger any memories. My heart pounded as I opened it and pulled out a pair of black ankle boots. They were covered in dried blood and had a funky smell.

While I held them in my hands and scrutinized them more closely, a sharp pain shot through my head, and I doubled over, clutching the boots against my thighs. A memory slammed into me with brutal force.

I was in a bedroom—*my* bedroom, in a brownstone—pulling on these very boots. The room was bathed in early morning light that cast long shadows on the wooden floors. The faint scent of fresh flowers wafted in the air. I was rushing around, packing my bag in a hurry, filled with an inexplicable sense of urgency.

The flashback was intense, each detail vivid and overwhelming. It came like a tidal wave, crashing over me and dragging me under. I gasped for breath because the pain that accompanied the memory was like a vise tightening around my head.

But at the same time, I had a glimmer of excitement. I knew where I was from...where I lived. My home was on a quiet side street in Chelsea. I had a life in New York City. The realization gave me something solid to grasp onto, and a piece of my identity slipped back into place.

Despite this small victory, the details were still fuzzy, and the memory left me trembling. I had to lean against the edge of the bed to steady myself. I was both exhilarated and terrified by the fragments of my past coming back to me.

As the pain subsided, I wiped away the tears that had welled in my eyes. This was progress, even if it hurt. A piece of my puzzle had emerged, and I clung to it tightly, determined to put together the rest of my story, no matter how painful it might be.

Standing, I looked inside the bag, still open next to me once more, and took a deep breath. My head ached from the intensity of the flashback, but something nudged me to search the bag. At the very bottom was a small envelope. My hands grew clammy as I pulled it out and tore it open. There, nestled inside, was a necklace with a howling wolf charm. As I studied it, I realized that it must be only one half of an interlocking pendant. Its white gold shimmered hypnotically under the soft light of the bedroom as I dangled it in front of me.

Out of nowhere, a violent rush of memories hit me. My vision blurred, and my head pounded as if someone had driven an ice pick into my skull. I clutched the necklace, its cool metal digging into my palm, and suddenly, the dam burst.

Nikolai's face appeared in my mind—his determined expression when he showed up on our thirteenth birthday, riding that borrowed motorcycle. I remembered the joy that had washed over me as he placed the necklace around my neck and declared our bond unbreakable. We were protectors of each other, just like wolves guarding their pack.

Then came the darker memories of an earlier time—being torn away from him, from all that I knew, and sent to live in an upstate New York boarding school. I saw the faces of my Russian family and their stern expressions as they reminded me of my duty to the family.

Images and feelings assaulted me in rapid succession. Fast-forward, and I was standing in Club Xyst, where I had secretly become part owner. The music, the lights, the clandestine deals in dark corners—it was all a part of my life, a life I loved. The club was a sanctuary for the rich and famous, a place even the governor of New York frequented. My heart pounded as I remembered the thrill and danger of it all. The club, with its underground gambling, bars, and escort services for the city's elite, was where my true self could come out at night. By day, I was a conservative librarian—but that was a cover story for prying eyes, a prison I'd been stuck in for years. I lived in a world where luxury and crime intertwined, hiding my true identity.

Another flash: I was in the lavish Genovese home, my aunt Elena reminding me of my duties as Anastasia Genovese. I recalled the constant pressure to live up to the family name, the parties, the whispers of arranged marriages. Then the bitter taste of bile rose in my throat as I remembered *my* arranged marriage to Frankie Moretti, a man I loathed, to solidify an alliance between crime families. I winced when an image of his smug smile appeared, recalling the weight of an engagement ring I refused to wear except on our weekly dates, a ring that was like a shackle on my finger. My stomach turned at the thought of our upcoming wedding, a trap I couldn't escape. The fact that I'd accepted my fate without a fight made me all the more nauseated. Why had I never considered resisting...escaping to lead my own life?

My knees buckled, and I collapsed onto the floor, clutching the necklace to my chest. Sobs racked my body as the memories continued to flood in—both the warmth of Nikolai's protectiveness and the cold reality of the life I was expected to live. My head throbbed with the intensity of it all, each memory like a shard of glass piercing my brain.

Through my tears, I remembered the happier times with my brother, our shared birthdays, and the unwavering loyalty we had for each other. But these were intertwined with the brutal realities of our mafia ties, the power plays, and the constant fear of retribution.

The pain was crushing, both physically and emotionally. My mind whirled with the onslaught, as if my entire life was being played on fast-forward. Good and bad, joy and sorrow all mingled together in a violent storm that left me gasping for air.

The torrent of my tears mixed with the flood of memories. It was as if I had been reborn into a world that was both familiar and alien. The weight of my past bore down on me, and I struggled to come to terms with who I was and what my life had become.

I was no longer Angel. I was Anastasia Volkov, daughter of a Russian mafia Pakhan—the very man I now knew had kidnapped Samantha and tried to kill her, the Thorin brothers, and others here in Tacoma. My life was a twisted web of betrayal and duty. The overwhelming surge of memories threatened to drown me, but amidst the chaos, one thing became clear—I had to reclaim control of my life, no matter what it took.

"Anastasia Volkov," I muttered to myself, tasting the name on my tongue. Daughter of Viktor and Valentina, the notorious leaders of the Volkovi Notchi crime syndicate, the very group that ran the city where I had found temporary refuge.

My name had been changed to Anastasia Genovese after my aunt Elena married into the American mafia. Growing up as a New York mafia princess, I'd been bound by traditions and alliances. I was a pawn in a game of power and control. My life had been manipulated, every move dictated by others.

After meeting Conan and experiencing a taste of freedom, I couldn't go back to that life.

But there was a big problem—Frankie Moretti. The marriage contract had been signed long ago to form an alliance between our families. The wedding was scheduled for June twenty-ninth—less than a week away. The thought of the contract made me want to vomit.

I thought about Club Xyst and my friends—Lucian, Lachlan, Julian, and Gabriel. They must be worried sick about me. What did they think had happened to me? Had they gone searching for me, delving into my secret life? Worry began to rise in my chest. Viktor would do anything to keep my true identity hidden, including murdering anyone who stood in his way.

Flashes of my special relationship with Lucian made me shudder. He was the reason—the only reason—I'd learned how to thoroughly enjoy sex. It was strange to think about how similar Lucian and Conan were, how they knew how to play my body. Yet, Conan was different... I'd given myself over to him both physically and emotionally even though what we had was still in the beginning stages. I was his blank journal, open to whatever story we wanted to write together.

I adored Lucian, but we'd always had a firm understanding that our relationship was no strings attached. There could never be anything permanent between us, so it was easy, controlled. But with Conan, we were just two normal people getting to know each other with the possibility of...falling. Now, though, that possibility was shattered. There was no way I'd involve him in the nightmare that was my life. No, he deserved so much better than what I could ever offer. Hell, who was I kidding? I had nothing to offer. How was I even going to explain to him who I was now that I knew what my father had done to him and those he cared so deeply about? It was best for me to slip out of his life and figure out how to protect him before either of us caught feelings.

"I need to get out of here," I whispered, panic setting in. "I can't let them get hurt because of me."

The knowledge of Viktor's ruthlessness sent shivers down my spine. He would order a hit on the Thorin brothers without a second thought. Atticus, Samantha, Conan—they were all at risk because of my mere presence in their home.

Tears streamed down my face. I had to protect them all. I had to leave and face my past, find Nikolai, and figure out a way to escape the mafia's grip. I couldn't let the people who had been good to me suffer because of my screwed up life.

With a shuddering breath, I wiped away my tears, determination replacing my fear. Finding Nikolai was my top priority now. He was the key to finding a way out. But first, I had to get out of here without drawing any attention to myself.

I stood up, my resolve strengthening. "This ends now," I muttered, slipping the necklace over my head. The pendant rested against my chest, a reminder of who I was and the strength that was in me. I would need every ounce of that strength if I was to save the people I cared about.

The clock was ticking. I had to act fast.

I moved to the bathroom sink and washed my face with cold water, hoping to lessen the swelling and blotchiness of my face. My mind spun with questions. Where did Nikolai fit into all this? The memory of him stepping in front of me and blocking my path at the arraignment flashed in my mind. At the time, I had brushed him off as some curious guy trying to get a glimpse of the

Jane Doe from the wreck. Why the hell didn't he say something to me? Why did he act like he didn't know me?

Anger bubbled up inside. Why hadn't he come to the hospital? If he knew where I was, why stay away? Was Viktor keeping him from me, or was Nikolai just as filthy as our father? The thought of my twin being involved in our father's dirty dealings twisted my gut.

"Why didn't you come to me on our birthday, Nikolai?!" I shouted, feeling the sting of his absence all over again. Every year, no matter what, he had found a way to be there—but not this year.

I paced the room, trying to think. I needed answers. Although I dreaded what I had to do next, I couldn't stay here and put these good people at risk. Viktor wouldn't hesitate to kill them if he thought they were harboring me.

The best thing I could do was leave and find Nikolai. Maybe he was at the Volkov estate on Fox Island. Normally, if he was in town, that was where he would be staying. But now, with the change of ownership, I had no clue. Just then, I remembered tucking my bag in a closet inside the house on the day of the wreck…and losing my phone in the garage. I needed those things in order to function. The laptop Sam had given me was helpful, but it wasn't the same as having a phone with all my contacts, apps, and passwords. Not for the first time, I wondered about the New York City socialite who now owned the estate. She had to be involved in the mafia, but was she Russian or American?

I bet the woman had never even laid eyes on the place, and if anyone was there right now, it would be Nik. There had to be a connection between him and the socialite; I just knew in my gut. I didn't want to take the time trying to use the laptop to hunt for a roundabout way to contact him, because that might attract attention.

Not having my phone was annoying, so I decided to just wing it and order an Uber out to the estate. I was grateful Sam had given me a gift card to buy a few essentials while I was in the hospital. I hated not having control over my life or the ability to act independently. Hopefully, I could sneak in and get my things and then get out quickly if Nik wasn't there.

I glanced at the clock. It was still early, so I had time before anyone came home to leave without getting caught. Somehow, I'd explain it to them later. I couldn't imagine their reaction to finding out who I was. What an honest-to-God clusterfuck my life had turned into.

Grabbing a small backpack, I packed some things, taking only the essentials.

Murphy padded over, jumped up on my knee, and nudged my hand with his wet nose, as if he knew exactly what was happening. I scratched behind his ears. "All right, buddy," I said softly. "Time for me to go."

I leaned against the doorframe of the guest bedroom, trying to steady my nerves. Leaving this place meant stepping back into a world I hated, but I didn't have a choice. I had to protect the people who had shown me kindness and find a way to reclaim my life from the grip of the mafia.

"I can do this," I said to Murphy as we headed down the stairs. "I have no other choice."

Just then, it hit me hard that the amnesia hadn't been a prison—it had been an opportunity for a fresh start. The wreck, the mental freedom I'd experienced over the last month, had changed me forever. I stood there in limbo between a past I no longer called my own and a present that wasn't real.

I glanced around the living room and, taking a final, resolute breath, headed out the door, ready to face whatever came next.

Chapter Twenty-Eight

6/25

During the drive to Fox Island, I was as tense as a tightly wound spring. I sat back, my mind firing off a thousand questions a minute. Why had Nikolai acted like he didn't know me at the arraignment? Was he under Viktor's orders? That thought made my blood boil. The idea of him being involved in kidnapping Samantha and plotting against the Thorin brothers gnawed at me. If he'd had a hand in that, I'd make sure he answered for it.

The estate slowly came into view, looming ominously against the tranquil forest of the island. The mansion was a monstrosity that screamed old money and power. It had an air of intimidation about it and was completely out of sync with its peaceful surroundings.

I leaned forward once we were close to the edge of the property. "Just here is fine, thanks," I said, keeping my voice even. The last thing I needed was to storm in through the front gates like a bull in a china shop. Caution was my ally here.

The driver shot me a questioning look through the rearview mirror, his eyebrows drawing together in confusion. Clearly, dropping a passenger off in the middle of nowhere wasn't his usual fare. But he didn't press me, just nodded and pulled over. As soon as the car came to a full stop, I slipped out, my nerves tingling with anticipation.

The car pulled away, leaving a cloud of dust behind. I took a moment to survey my surroundings. The estate was quiet—too quiet. It appeared well maintained, not like a place left to fend for itself as I remembered from the day of the wreck. The grass was freshly cut, the flower beds were neat and free of weeds, and there was no sign of police tape.

No cars were in the driveway, which helped me relax a bit. The place seemed deserted, but I knew better than to let my guard down, so I moved cautiously, my every sense heightened. Gusts of salty ocean air hit my face, and the scent of pine from the surrounding forest grounded me. I walked along the edge of the property, my sneakers crunching on fallen leaves and twigs.

Slipping through a gap in the hedge, I found myself closer to the back of the mansion than I'd guessed. A bit of a lucky break. The garden was immaculate, filled with blooming flowers and neatly trimmed bushes. It was the kind of place you'd expect to find in a glossy magazine.

I scampered forward and crouched behind a row of rose bushes. The mansion's back entrance was a few yards away. The house was dark, no lights on anywhere that I could see. Maybe no one was here, and I could get in and out quickly. How long could it possibly take to check the closet for my bag and run down to the garage for my phone? God, I hoped they were still there. Taking one last look around to ensure no one was watching, I made my move.

I reached the service entrance—the same one I'd slipped through a few weeks ago—in only a few hurried steps. To my disappointment, the door had been replaced with a metal one. There was no way I'd be able to get through it. Leaning down, I picked up a stone and grazed my thumb over it, wondering whether I could break the window and climb in. I had to assume a security alarm would sound, like the firing of a starter's pistol in a race, once I smashed it. Get in, get out—that was all I had to do. I paused, listening for any signs of life inside.

Nothing.

I took a deep breath, steadied my nerves, and with a quick move, struck the pane with the rock. The shattering of glass was loud, making me wince. Using another rock, I broke out the remaining glass. I tossed my backpack in and then slipped inside.

I had barely gotten a few steps in when I heard rapid footsteps coming toward me. My heart hammered against my ribs as adrenaline surged through me. I tensed, my muscles coiling for a confrontation.

Within seconds, a shadow descended on me. A hand grabbed my arm, twisted it behind my back, and forced me to the ground. I struggled instinctively, but I was overpowered and pinned to the ground with a knee in my back.

"Get your filthy hands off me!" I spat, kicking out.

"Anastasia?" The grip loosened, and I rolled over to find Nik staring down at me in shock.

Recognition flickered in his eyes, his expression morphing from fury to shock. "Ana? Holy hell! It's you? I could've killed you!" he bellowed, his voice echoing off the walls, the Russian accent thicker with emotion. "The only reason I didn't pull my gun was because I didn't want to make a bloody mess in the house and have to clean it up!"

"Nik, you idiot! Get off me!" I shoved him away, fury and relief mingling inside me as I scrambled to my feet.

He ran a hand through his hair, letting out a deep sigh. "I thought you were just another unfriendly trying to take me out. This place was empty since the FBI raided it last December, until I arrived a month ago. When I got here, I discovered it wasn't just the FBI that had taken a look around. I sure as hell never expected you to show up unannounced and break in. Surely you know better than to be so damn reckless!"

For a while, we stood there, catching our breath. Suddenly, Nik's face broke into a grin, and he pulled me into a giant bear hug, lifting me off my feet and spinning me around.

"God, Ana, I can't believe it's really you! Are your memories back? Are you okay? How did you ditch the Thorins?" He set me down but didn't release me, scanning my face for answers as he held me by the arms.

My relief at seeing him for the first time in over a year was short-lived. The anger I'd pushed aside when my memories of him returned came rushing back. I shoved him away, my hands trembling with rage. "Why didn't you come to the hospital, Nik? Why didn't you acknowledge me in some way? You left me helpless with nothing and no one! How could you be so cruel?"

His face fell, guilt replacing the joy. "Ana, I...I was trying to protect you."

"By ignoring me? By letting me think you didn't care?" Tears stung my eyes, but I blinked them back, refusing to let him see me cry.

Nik reached out, but I stepped back. "I'm sorry," he whispered. "I thought it was the only way to keep you safe from

Viktor. He's more dangerous than you realize."

"Safe?" I scoffed. "I was lost, alone, and terrified. You had no right to make that decision for me."

Nik sighed, rubbing his face. "I was trying to navigate this predicament without getting us both killed. But you're right, I should have been there for you. I'm sorry, Ana. Truly."

I crossed my arms, glaring at him. "Sorry isn't good enough. How about you start by explaining why you didn't come and visit me on our birthday like you always have in the past? Or why you didn't come to the hospital when you found out about the accident? Oh, and how about at the arraignment, when you stepped right in front of me, refusing to move?" I snapped, still high on adrenaline.

Nik grabbed my face in his palms, his touch rough but familiar. "Ana, you think I'd miss our birthday on purpose? You know I'd show up unless I absolutely couldn't."

"Then why didn't you?"

"I arrived in Tacoma to take care of some business before flying out to New York. Just as I was about to board, the FBI picked me up. They hauled me down to the police station and held me for questioning in relation to Volkovi Notchi activity."

My heart pounded at the mention of our father's crime syndicate. "How long did they keep you?"

"Overnight. I got out the next day and tried to call you, but you never answered."

He dropped his hands and stepped back, his expression tightening. "I tried, Ana. I tried a bunch of times. When I finally made it out to the estate, it was swarming with cops. Some crazy woman had broken in."

I folded my arms defensively and fixed him with an icy glare. "Funny. You know good and well that woman was me. I had no idea the house had been raided six months ago. And with your disappearing act, what was I supposed to do—sit on my hands? Of course not. So I came to find you as fast as I could get here. I was shocked to find the house in such disrepair and wrapped in police tape. Someone's always been here when I arrived, but not this time, so I had no choice but to let myself in. Then, out of nowhere, there were police sirens, and I knew I'd triggered an alarm. You had vanished, and I had no plausible explanation to give the police for why I would break into the house—that is, unless I linked myself to our father, and we both know how disastrous that would have been." My gaze dropped to my toes and then shot back up as my shoulders sank. "I'll admit, I got nervous, panicked, and ran because I didn't want to blow my cover."

Nik rolled his eyes. "And *we both know* how that ended," he said, his voice rising. "You took a car and wrapped it around a tree. You nearly killed yourself, Anastasia. Do you realize how lucky you are to be alive? How could you be so rash?"

"Rash?" I yelled. "The wreck wasn't my idea of fun, Nik! Nor were the weeks since then. I had amnesia, and not one single person came to look for me, to help me. I was a destitute Jane Doe. Thank God for good people like Samantha Sheridan and the Thorin brothers, who helped me not only because it was their obligation as medical professionals, but also because they are genuinely kind people. Without them, who knows where I'd be?! And you had better believe I'll do everything I can to protect them from Father."

He scoffed, his gaze hardening. "You realize that those same people nearly toppled our entire family. You're talking about loyalty to strangers who've been working with authorities to bring down the Volkovi Notchi. Don't forget where your loyalty lies, Ana. Keep in mind who puts food on your table and keeps you breathing. You can't make friends with enemies like the

Thorin brothers."

His words ignited a fire within me, and I couldn't hold back. "So, I should just be a good little mafia princess, huh? Keep quiet and know my place?" I shoved past him, stomping toward the kitchen, and opened the refrigerator. Its cool interior was a brief respite. I grabbed a bottle of water, the plastic crinkling loudly in my grip.

"Exactly, Ana. Keep your head down so someone doesn't take it off!" Nik called out from behind me.

I turned, water bottle in hand, my anger coiling in my gut. "And what? I should just forget that they cared for me when you didn't?" I unscrewed the cap, my movements jerky with pent-up frustration.

Nik leaned against the doorway, his eyes shadowed, jaw clenched. "It's not that simple, and you know it. We were born into this life, Anastasia. It's not about what we want; it's about survival."

"But at what cost, Nik? At what cost?" I asked quietly, my voice breaking. I took a long gulp of water, but the cool liquid did little to quench the dryness of my throat. Fury boiled up inside me, and I hurled the bottle of water into the sink, making it explode all over the place. I grabbed a pan resting on the counter, spun around, and threw it at Nik's head with all the rage I could muster. He deflected it effortlessly, a reminder of the lethal skills that made him so formidable.

As it clattered to the ground, he lunged forward, pinning my hands against the cool edge of the granite countertop. With his face inches from mine, he yelled, "You better start behaving, Ana!"

"Behave?" I screamed back, struggling against his iron grip. "If this wreck and losing my memory taught me anything, it's that life's too damn short to be miserable, to be traded among crime families like some kind of broodmare! I'm done with this mafia lifestyle, Nik. I want out. I'd rather be dead than live like this."

"Shut the fuck up, Anastasia!" he growled. "You think you've had it rough? You've been given everything in life for free. I was left behind in Russia at the mercy of our father's vicious hand and his every sick whim. How dare you complain?"

He leaned close again, his eyes blazing with anger. "How many men and women have you killed, Ana? How many bodies have you had to dispose of? How many times have you been beaten to within an inch of your life by not only our enemies but also by our own father?"

His questions stung. I took a deep breath, realizing how terrible Nik's life had been since we were separated as children. Guilt flooded through me, and my rage dissipated. I stopped struggling as the reality of Nik's life, the suffering he endured, sank in.

Nik's body relaxed, his muscles easing as he sensed my resignation. He stepped back, releasing my hands. "Let's go sit down in the living room and discuss everything like civilized people."

Still frustrated but willing to listen, I wrapped my arms around myself and followed him out of the kitchen. My steps were stiff, each one heavy with the burden of our shared legacy.

As Nik and I entered the living room, I noticed the drastic changes. The decor was sharper, more masculine than I remembered from past visits. It had been stripped of the old, lavish embellishments.

"Looks like you've been busy," I said.

Nik nodded, then moved further into the room. "Yeah, since Viktor was run out of Tacoma because of the incident last December, it was decided that I would take over his operations here. On our birthday, the FBI and police had just wrapped up their investigations, releasing it back to Viktor. What a coincidence, huh? He had his attorneys reorganize all his US assets, and I was here to oversee the deal. Since arriving a month ago, I've been doing lots of renovations so that it better fits my needs."

Raising an eyebrow, I shot back, "Did you get the approval of the New York socialite who bought this place? Are you her lackey too?"

Nik chuckled, sinking into one of the new leather sofas, gesturing for me to join him. "You've got a sharp tongue, Ana. The woman who bought the estate is beautiful and smart. I'd do anything for her. She has my complete loyalty."

Jealousy flared up inside me. "Who is she, Nik? And why would you or Viktor ever agree to sell the estate to her?"

Nik burst into laughter, which spiked my anger. Fidgeting, I reached under the collar of my shirt and pulled out my necklace, twisting it around my finger, waiting for him to stop.

He caught his breath and schooled his features. "The socialite is none other than you, Anastasia."

I paused, processing his words. "Me?"

"Yes, you," he said, his grin widening as he thoroughly enjoyed my confusion. "Viktor instructed his attorneys to transfer the estate and all his legal business assets into a trust with you as the sole beneficiary. Since you were raised by Aunt Elena and Luca Genovese—and you're an American citizen with no ties to the Volkov family—you provided the perfect cover to divert the FBI's attention. That's why I had to make a stop in Tacoma before coming to see you in New York."

I sank into the chair opposite him, my mind racing. "No wonder the owner refused to press charges against me for breaking in, stealing, and wrecking a car." I chuckled. But the realization didn't solve my bigger problem. "Nik, this is…well, I don't know exactly how I feel about this, but I meant what I said before. I want no part of the mafia lifestyle."

Nik's smile faded a bit, and he leaned forward, resting his elbows on his thighs. "But, Anastasia, we can't just choose to say no to all of this. You don't have the option of walking away from this family, let alone the Genoveses. And soon the Morettis, after you marry that goon."

"I have to leave, Nik. I'll never have a life if I'm forced to marry Frankie. We have to figure out how to get out from under it all."

He ran a thumb across his lower lip and grimaced. "Ana, you don't have a fucken clue what you're asking for."

"Then how about you enlighten me? Trust me, I'm sick and tired of being in the dark… You have no idea."

Nik sighed, running a hand through his hair. "I'd do anything for you, but what you're asking for is nearly impossible. I'm not in a position to fight our father yet."

The word *yet* hung between us, loaded with potential.

"Yet?" I prodded. "Have you been thinking of a way out?"

He had just opened his mouth to reply when his phone rang. Snatching it from the coffee table, he glanced at the screen, his expression turning solemn. "I have to take this, Ana."

I stared at him, raising a questioning brow, but he held up a finger to his lips as he answered the call. My stomach twisted when I recognized the booming Russian voice on the other end. But before I could react, Nik shot me a brutal look, signaling me to stay quiet. It was Viktor. He was demanding an update on—me.

"She's out of the hospital and made it through the arraignment," Nik said, "but she's not herself. She's in a rehab center now and still has amnesia. She didn't even recognize me at the arraignment." His tone was laced with feigned frustration.

I listened, heart pounding, as Nik continued weaving his story. "The girl doesn't know who the hell she is. There's no way she can marry Frankie Moretti a week from now."

Viktor's voice roared back, loud enough for me to hear every venomous word. "I don't care if the bitch can't put two sentences together! She's going to marry Frankie, and on time. I don't care if that girl is a babbling idiot. You make that wedding happen."

Nik's jaw clenched. "I get it, but she's a mess. How do you expect—"

"I said make it happen, Nikolai!" Viktor bellowed. "And those Thorin bastards, deal with them! I want them dead. No more delays!"

"Yes, sir."

Viktor said slowly and ominously, "Figure it out and make the wedding happen. And if she's of no value to the family, kill her." With that, he hung up, leaving a heavy silence in the room.

I shuddered, the chill of his words slicing through my chest. It was one thing to have secondhand knowledge about the ruthlessness of my father, but hearing him speak of me so dismissively, so coldly—it cut deeper than I could have imagined.

I swallowed hard, the reality of my situation setting in. "Nik, I...I have to warn Conan, Atticus, Samantha, and Braxton. They've been nothing but kind to me, and now they're in danger—because of me."

Nik's face tightened as his brow furrowed. "I'm sorry you heard all that, Ana. But that's who Viktor is. He's a merciless killer. But at least now you know he will stop at nothing to get what he wants."

I nodded, my thoughts racing. The idea of bringing danger to those who had helped me was unbearable. "Sam and the Thorins need to know who I am—everything. Even if it means they'll hate me afterward. I can't let them get hurt. I've got to warn them."

Nik leaned back into the sofa, his face shadowed with concern. "You've always been too kind for our world, Anastasia. It's why I've done everything to keep you out of it."

Tears welled in my eyes. "I can't believe how naïve I've been. All these years, I thought Mother and Father cared, at least in their own way."

Nik's eyes were full of sorrow. He seemed exhausted from the burden of a life spent living under the thumb of our father. Despite everything he had been through, Nik was still my brother, and we were in this together. "And you've been stuck dealing with him, all because he wants to keep me as a bargaining chip. It's not fair to you either, Nik."

Nik shook his head. "It's been my life's mission to keep you as far away from the family business as possible. Viktor has used the threat of involving you to keep me in line."

My heart broke. My brother had borne so much to protect me. "Nik, I had no idea..."

He sighed, a rare vulnerability softening his features. "Walking in Viktor's footsteps, constantly having to prove my loyalty...it's exhausting. But what choice do I have? He's not just our father; he's a vicious killer to those who cross him."

We were both trapped in this life, victims of a merciless family legacy.

Nik suggested we go fix some lunch, and I agreed, needing something to distract me from the heaviness of our conversation. He mentioned he could use a glass of vodka, which didn't surprise me.

As we moved around the kitchen, prepping for a salad, Nik reached into the refrigerator for a bottle of Beluga Gold, then poured himself a generous glass. His movements were mechanical, the tension in his shoulders speaking volumes. He took a deep swig before putting a couple of pieces of chicken onto the pan to grill; the sizzle filling the silence between us.

"You ever hear the story about how you ended up in America, Ana?" Nik asked finally, his eyes not meeting mine as he pointed to a cucumber for me to slice.

I picked it up and shook my head, focusing on chopping. "Not really. Just bits and pieces."

Nik washed and dried his hands before leaning against the counter, then took another slug of the vodka. "Viktor wanted to infiltrate the American Genovese family, because of their ties to the world's most powerful politicians, and form an alliance they couldn't deny. Valentina's sister Elena secured a marriage to Luca Genovese and built his trust over the years. When Elena found out she couldn't have kids, she and our mother came up with the idea of bringing you to America. You were put in an American boarding school, adopted by the Geneveses, and given a new name and an American passport. From the beginning, the plan was for you to marry into one of the other powerful American mafia families and establish a formidable alliance."

"The marriage contract. That's what it all comes down to," I guessed, already dreading the answer.

"Exactly." Nik nodded grimly. "Last year, Frankie Moretti surfaced as their ideal candidate. He isn't exactly Mr. Popular, given his...let's just say, less-than-attractive attributes. As you know, he's not exactly sought after by the ladies, given his looks and personality. But he's valuable as the Moretti's bean counter. Plus, the Morettis are muscle, not masterminds."

He poured more vodka, his hands steadier now. "With foreign mafias squeezing into New York, the big families felt the heat. Antonio Genovese, Luca's brother and the boss of the family, agreed an alliance with the Morettis was necessary. A blood alliance between all the families would guarantee support from the powerful Volkov family, keeping other Russians from encroaching on New York turf. Your marriage to Frankie—merging Volkov blood with a Genovese name and potentially Moretti offspring—it's like a damn mobster match made in heaven to them."

My hand was trembling slightly. I put down the knife and looked at Nik. "So, I'm just a piece in their game. My life is completely inconsequential?" I asked, the bitterness in my voice sharper than the blade I had been using.

Nik met my gaze, his eyes somber. "No, hun. You're the damn jackpot. I'm sorry, Ana. I tried to keep you out of it as much as I could. But yeah, that's the grim truth. They've been planning this since we were kids."

I glanced down, and my lip quivered. "And...a baby?"

The injustice of my situation was suffocating.

Nik took a sip of his vodka. "That's the plan. To create the most powerful mafia organization ever."

The thought of bringing a child into this life was horrifying. "I can't do it, Nik. I won't."

With that declaration, I sliced through a fresh tomato with more force than necessary. He set down his glass and pulled on my arm so I was facing him.

"Ana, there's something you need to understand about Viktor. He's not just planning to use this marriage to bind the families. I overheard him a while back; he might be planning something...more drastic to eliminate the other bosses once you're married to Frankie."

I gasped, my heart racing. "What do you mean? He wants to kill the other bosses?"

Nik nodded. "I don't know all the details, but it's possible. Regardless, you're the key to his plans. For now, it's best if you just grin and bear the marriage to Frankie. Play along and keep your head down."

The very idea made my stomach churn. "Why do I have to be at the center of his plot?" I complained, sounding like the kind of whiny brat I'd always hated.

Nik knocked back the rest of his vodka and poured us each a glass, his way of dealing with tough conversations. "Because you're the perfect link between the Russian and American families, a tool he's crafted since our childhood. But listen..." He leaned in closer, dropping his voice to a whisper. "I'm working on an exit strategy. Not just for me, but for you too."

I perked up, hope flickering. "An exit? How?"

Nik glanced around before continuing. "I've picked up... certain skills over the years. I've been setting up some companies under the radar that Viktor and the others don't know about. It's risky, but it might just work to get us out."

"But Viktor's still powerful, Nik," I argued, my voice trembling. "I'm done with the mafia. I can't keep living this lie, becoming a monster like them."

He reached out, grabbing my hand tightly. "I know, Ana. And I won't let you live that life. I'm close to securing a safe house and a new identity for you. But for now, you need to do as they say and not cause any trouble. If you bolt, the families will hunt you down."

"Fuck the arranged marriage," I spat out, my spirit rebelling against the very idea of being traded like some whore.

Nik's face hardened, a protective fierceness overcoming his features. "I'd rather die than see you hurt. But if you try to run, you'll have the most powerful Russian and American mafia families after you. You won't live a day. Just trust me a little longer. I won't let anything happen to you."

I was sure he meant his words to be comforting, but all they did was remind me of the cage I was in. I wanted to believe him, but the stakes were too high. I couldn't let Nik get killed trying to protect me. And I couldn't ignore the danger Conan, Atticus, Braxton, and Samantha were in because of me either. I decided I would contact Samantha because I had her email address on the laptop. I would write to her and explain who I really was and tell her everything. Then she could pass on the message to the others. They needed to know the truth.

For the next couple of hours, Nik and I spent some time catching up. After we had eaten and cleaned up from lunch, he showed me around the estate, pointing out all the recent changes, especially the new security measures. "No one can get in or out without my say-so," he said proudly.

As I listened, my mind raced with plans of my own. Nik never mentioned his side work again, but I held onto the hope that he was building a way out for us. In the meantime, I had to make sure the people I cared about were safe, both here and in New York.

I spent the afternoon in a haze, half-listening to Nik while I plotted my next move and helped him board up the window I'd broken. I was more determined than ever to take control of my fate. It was time to tell the Thorins everything and figure out a way to protect us all. Even though Nik insisted I stay with him and let him handle things, I wasn't going to be able to do that.

I needed to warn Conan, Atticus, Braxton, and Samantha, and get back to the city.

When we were sitting once again in the living room, Nik's phone buzzed. His eyes narrowed slightly as he listened to the caller on the other end. "Business," he mouthed at me before stepping aside to talk.

"I have to head out for a few hours," he announced after he hung up, the urgency in his voice poorly masked. "The house is secure, and if you need anything, just call me."

"I lost my phone in the garage the day of the wreck. I'll follow you down there on your way out and see if I can find it."

Nik chuckled, shaking his head. "That's right. I almost forgot. One of my guys found it. Let me get it for you."

He disappeared for a moment and returned with my phone and the duffle bag I had brought from New York. I sighed in relief as I took the phone and bag, grateful to have some of my things back now that my memories were intact.

"You okay?" Nik asked. "You look really shaken up." He pulled me into a hug, and I wrapped my arms tightly around him, trying to hold back my tears. I was about to leave, and I might never see him again. He noticed how emotional I was getting and gave me a protective squeeze.

"Don't worry, Ana. We'll figure this out." Although his words were full of confidence, his voice held a note of doubt.

"I'm just tired, Nik," I lied, pulling back slightly. "And still reeling from everything."

"I'll be back soon. Why don't you chill? I'm sure you have a lot of catching up to do." He pressed a kiss to my forehead. "See you in a few hours, little sis." With that, he was out the door. He armed the security system on his way out, and I made sure to register the keypad code.

Once I was certain Nik had driven far enough away that he wouldn't catch me leaving, I grabbed my duffle bag, backpack, and phone, then headed to the garage. Smugly, I punched in the security code on the door's keypad. The thought that Viktor had transferred all the assets into my name lingered in my mind. The fact that I was the beneficiary of the trust he'd set up was a lot to process. But then again, his attorney was the trustee, so I knew he was really the one in control. Still, though, it made me feel better about taking one of the cars this time. Technically, I wasn't stealing anything.

I climbed into the first vehicle I came to, once again finding the key in the glove box. As I drove out and shut the garage door with a push of a button, I contemplated my next move.

I grappled with my next steps. I couldn't stay here in Tacoma, not with the danger looming over everyone I cared about.

At the end of the driveway, I paused, taking a minute to pull up the flight schedules on my newly reclaimed phone. I found one last flight from SEA to JFK that I could just make if I hurried.

At the airport, I parked in the garage, then ran inside and rushed through security, making it to my gate just in time. The gate agent was preparing to close the door to the jet bridge as I ran up but thankfully let me on anyway. I hurriedly made my way to my first-class cabin, welcoming the privacy it offered.

Once seated, I went to work drafting an email to Samantha. Hers was the only contact I had used on the laptop she'd given me. I considered giving Conan a quick call but hesitated, unsure if I could talk to him about everything just yet. There was so much I hadn't processed or fully understood, and I didn't want to make things worse. I didn't want to pull Conan and the others further into the treacherous mafia world I belonged to. Hurting them was the last thing I wanted to do, but I needed a little time to figure out what to say and how best to protect them. Besides, after finding out who I really was, none of them should have anything to do with me—it was too dangerous. The truth of my identity was going to be a gut punch to all of them, and whatever was happening between Conan and me had been completely derailed. There was absolutely no chance that he would have any romantic interest in me once he discovered I was Viktor's daughter, and I couldn't bring myself to lie to him. He was too good of a guy, and he was the only person I'd ever had an honest connection with—no lies, no hidden agendas, no looming mafia obligations. The thought of Conan getting killed because of me made my blood run cold. It was best for him if I walked out of his life; he didn't need all the baggage that came along with mine. Cutting ties was the safest option.

My fingers trembled as I typed. I poured out my heart, explaining the return of my memories, my true identity, and the imminent danger facing them all. I expressed my hatred for the mafia's violent ways and my desperation to protect them. I told Samantha how I was bound by an arranged marriage—a mafia contract that could only be broken by death. It was the hardest thing I'd ever written, and my words were clumsy at best. How could you describe the ways of the mafia to a sane, rational outsider? To a woman who'd been kidnapped and nearly raped by my father! Leaving the people who had literally saved my life and who had liked and accepted me for who I was ripped my heart out. This was one of the worst days of my life, surpassed only by the day I was torn from Nikolai and everything I knew and sent to America.

With the email sent, I leaned back, letting out a shaky breath swatting away the tears I hadn't realized were rolling down my cheeks. I tried to relax, but my mind was a chaotic mess of memories and worries. My thoughts wandered back to last night, one of the best nights of my life...the way Conan had touched me, how he drank in my every response, how he knew exactly how to set me at ease or ablaze. He was the best person who had ever walked into my life and the hardest to walk away from.

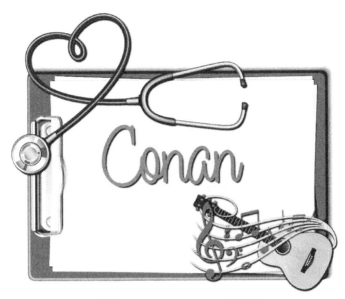

Chapter Twenty-Nine

6/25

After my shift, my body was still buzzing from last night's high. I strolled into Atticus and Samantha's kitchen from the garage, whistling a tune. Angel and I had spent one hell of a night together, and I figured she'd be just as amped to see me as I was to see her. But instead of finding Angel hanging out in the kitchen, I found Atticus and Samantha sitting at the island, staring down at a laptop with the kind of grim expressions that could freeze a room. Samantha's mouth was a tight line, and Atticus, usually the more reserved of the two, had a deep furrow in his brow. His fingers were drumming on the countertop—a sure sign he was deep in thought, even worried. I hadn't seen him looking this grave since Samantha was kidnapped.

"What's with the funeral faces?" I asked, tossing my keys on the counter. "Looks like you two just saw a ghost." I scanned the kitchen. "Where's Angel?"

No laughs, no smart comebacks. Just heavy air and tense shoulders.

Samantha glanced up from the laptop, her eyes full of something that screamed bad news. "Conan, you need to sit down. We have something shocking to share with you."

"You're scaring me, Sam. Just spit it out."

She took a deep breath, her gaze flicking to Atticus before settling back on me. "When we got home from work, we found Angel gone. At first, we thought she might be out taking a walk, but then Atticus checked the security cameras and saw that she left in a car, carrying a bag of some of her stuff. We assumed it was an Uber since she got into the backseat."

"What's the big deal? Maybe she needed to run some errands," I said, irritation creeping into my tone.

Samantha shook her head, pushing a strand of hair behind her ear. "That wouldn't make sense since she had a backpack with her. Besides, there's more."

I crossed my arms, trying to wrap my head around what they were saying. "All right, so what's going on?"

"We didn't know what to think. But after we settled into the kitchen, I opened my laptop to take a closer look at the security feed. That's when I realized I had just received an email from Angel."

I frowned, crossing the kitchen in three strides, and leaned over the island to peer at the screen. "What did the email say?"

Samantha chewed on the inside of her cheek as she clicked open the email, her eyes scanning the screen. "It's...it's a lot, Conan."

She turned the laptop toward me, and I stepped closer, catching sight of the body of the email—a long dissertation. I pulled a bar stool up under me. "How about you give me the Cliff Notes version?"

Samantha took a deep breath and gave me a sympathetic look. "Angel tried to explain everything in her email, starting with how the bloody boots from the ED triggered all her memories to return in a massive rush. Sounds like it hit her hard. She went on to write that she was sending me this email because I was the only contact she had and wanted a chance to explain everything before she left. She also asked that I make sure to share this with you."

"Before she left?" I muttered under my breath.

"Conan, brace yourself—her real name is Anastasia Genovese. But she was born Anastasia Volkov. She's Viktor Volkov's daughter."

The room spun for a second as if her words had punched me in the face. The Russian boss of the Volkovi Notchi, the ruthless bastard who had kidnapped Samantha and tried to kill us all last December, was none other than...Angel's...Anastasia's...father?

I slammed a fist on the counter, needing something to absorb the shock and fury building up inside me.

Samantha flinched, tapping her fingers nervously on the keyboard. She sighed, steeling herself to come up with the right words. "Angel...wrote about how much she hates the mafia life. She didn't even know about my kidnapping until we told her about it. It seems she's been kept in the dark about most of the Volkovi Notchi's activities. Evidently, she's just a pawn in Viktor's plan to ally with the American mob in New York. She sounded scared and warned us not to come after her because these mafia families would kill us. They're wealthy and extremely dangerous."

"Kept in the dark, huh?" I asked myself more than Sam, struggling to reconcile the woman I knew with the underworld princess Angel apparently was.

Samantha nodded solemnly. "She apologized over and over. She said if she'd had any idea who she was, she never would have let you get close to her or stayed at our house."

My gut twisted at the thought of Angel apologizing for something she had no control over.

Atticus spoke for the first time since I'd entered the kitchen. "She's been under the control of her aunt since she was a little girl and raised to be a perfect little American mafia wife—seen but not heard."

I jumped up and paced the kitchen, anger boiling in my chest. My fists clenched in front of me as I pictured Angel trapped in that life. "This is fucking insane. Angel—Anastasia—whatever the hell name we're calling her, she's so deep in this mafia shit that she can't escape their grip."

Samantha held up a hand. "There's more. She's been forced into an arranged marriage with a man she despises. And according to her, the only way out of a mafia marriage contract is death. She's in real danger, and she says that we are too—Viktor has ordered a hit on all of us."

The words hung heavy in the air. Death. It wasn't an option. Not for her—not for us. "Like hell she'll marry some mafia thug," I snapped, slamming my hand down again, making the cups in the sink rattle. "I'll go get her myself and bring her back here if I have to. She can't go back to her old life. Those assholes better understand that I'm not easily intimidated."

Samantha's eyes filled with worry. "Conan, you can't just rush in there."

"You just watch me!" I shouted.

"Goddamn it, Conan!" Atticus yelled. "Calm the fuck down. We need to think this through. We can't just storm in after a bunch of mafiosi. It's not just about rescuing her. We have to protect her and potentially fight off two powerful mafia families. I just don't know..." He joined me in pacing around the kitchen, wrapping his hand around the back of his neck and shaking his head in frustration.

"Calm down? How the fuck am I supposed to calm down? They're treating her like property. Arranged marriages are just human trafficking and rape with a different name. I can't let her suffer that kind of fate. No one—not her goddamn father nor any mafia thug—will force her into something she doesn't want. I'm going to get her and bring her back here."

By this point, I was shaking with rage, and I balled up a dish towel in my fist in an effort to contain my anger before I did some actual damage. It was difficult to fathom that Angel had such a deep, dark past.

Atticus grabbed my arm, his grip firm. "Conan, think about this. We need to be smart. We can't lose you too."

Samantha's breathing quickened, her face going pale. "You can't put yourself in that kind of danger and get yourself killed."

"If I don't go after her, who will?!" I yelled. "She's my girl to protect. I'll go to New York and bring her back while you guys stay here and figure out how to protect us all from Viktor."

Atticus whirled around and walked around the island toward the living room. He whipped out his phone to make a call. "Colton, we need protection. Viktor Volkov has put a hit on us. Yeah, the Russian mafia. Get your best team over here. Viktor's back—"

As I listened, I continued pacing.

Samantha joined me in pacing the kitchen. None of us could sit still. "Conan, she was very specific in her email. Don't try to play the hero and do something stupid. She was born into that world and doesn't want anyone else dragged into it. She's doing everything she can to protect us."

She was right of course, but every fiber of my being screamed to go to Angel. To protect her. "Then we make a plan. Fast," I said. "She's not facing this alone, not while I breathe. Not a chance."

Atticus's phone conversation continued, his tone clipped. "Yes, now. We need eyes on us twenty-four seven."

Bulldozing around the kitchen, I fumed, losing my shit. "We have to do something now. We can't just let Viktor feed her to the wolves! A sacrificial lamb!" I shouted.

Atticus wrapped up his call and joined us in the kitchen. "Colton's on it. We'll have a security detail here within the hour."

I pulled out my phone, desperately searching for flights. "Dammit! All the flights to New York have already left for the day. I'll have to wait until morning."

Samantha placed a hand on my arm. "Conan, Angel warned us. We need to stay safe and plan our next move carefully. Rushing in won't help her or us."

Her words hit hard, but my anger and my worry for Angel were overwhelming. "We can't just sit here and do nothing!"

I stormed around the kitchen like a raging bull, swinging my arm and knocking a glass off the counter. It shattered, pieces scattering across the floor.

Samantha clutched her chest. "Conan, stop. Don't be so reckless."

"Dammit, Sam. I have to do this. She's more than just some girl. Since the day she came into the ED, I knew she was mine. I can't breathe without her. She's my destiny. I'll move heaven and earth to protect her."

Everyone was shouting, voices overlapping in a chaotic mess. Samantha's breathing grew rapid, her face flushing as she gripped the edge of the counter. Atticus noticed, and his expression darkened.

His face turned red with anger. "Goddamn it, Conan! Look what you've done! You've pushed her too far. Sit down and shut the fuck up."

I watched in horror as Samantha went into a full-blown panic attack. Her breaths came in ragged gasps, and she couldn't seem to get enough air. Atticus gently guided her to a chair and had her bend over. Then he scurried around the kitchen and found a paper bag for her to breathe into. He rubbed soothing circles on her back as he whispered to her gently.

"Samantha, you're okay. Breathe with me. In and out, slowly," he coaxed, his voice calm and steady.

Feeling like a complete asshole, I slumped into a chair, watching helplessly as Atticus took care of Samantha. "Sam, I'm sorry. I didn't mean to upset you."

When Samantha finally calmed down, Atticus shot me a glare that could melt steel. "We need to think rationally. No more yelling. We need a plan to figure out how to protect the house and Samantha."

Braxton had walked in during the commotion and now stood next to the island, a look of shock on his face. "What the hell is going on?"

Quickly, Atticus filled him in while I rubbed my temples, trying to calm my racing thoughts.

Atticus looked at me. "No rash decisions, Conan."

I nodded reluctantly. "Fine. But we can't leave Angel to fend for herself." I took a deep breath, trying to get my thoughts in order. "There's got to be a reason she ended up in our emergency department the very day we were all working. Of all the hospitals in all the towns in all the world, she ended up in ours. I have to go save her. She's mine to protect."

I clenched and unclenched my fists, seething but trying to rein it in. I told them, "After we lock this place down, I'm still going to New York. I'm getting Angel back, and I'm not taking no for an answer. I don't care about the risks. She's worth it. I'll put my life on the line for her just like I would for any of you."

Samantha shook her head. "Conan, you can't just up and leave. You need to think about this. Think about your job... You're already on probation."

"Don't worry about me. I'll take some time off from the hospital. I've got tons of sick leave and vacation. And if they refuse to let me go, I'll quit. I don't give a fuck. No job is more important than saving Angel from those mobsters."

Atticus and Samantha exchanged a look, clearly taken aback by my determination. I pushed on, my voice unwavering. "I can't describe it, but since the day she came into the ED, I knew she was mine. No woman has ever affected me like this."

Samantha said cautiously, "Conan, now that she has her memories back, she may see things differently. You might get your heart broken. She's not the same person we've gotten to know since the wreck. She seems resigned to her arranged marriage."

"I got to know the true person she is," I argued firmly. "Not the one manipulated and controlled by mafia dynamics. I have to go to her and do all that I can. I would never forgive myself if I didn't. My mind is made up. What is life worth if you can't protect and provide for the people you care about? I don't have many people I'm close to, but for those I am, I'm a hundred percent loyal."

Braxton, who had been listening quietly, stepped forward, grasping my shoulder. "You can't go alone. Atticus needs to stay here with Sam to keep her safe, so I'll fly to New York with you. You'll need someone to watch your back."

"Braxton, you should stay. I'll be fine," I said.

But he shook his head. "I'm going with you, brother. This isn't up for debate. You're not doing this alone."

Braxton may have been the quietest of us brothers, but he was also the most empathetic. He was the one who always kept us tied together with his levelheadedness. I honestly could never recall him getting angry or losing control of his emotions. I guess that was what made him such a good EMT. No matter the scene, he would calmly assess the situation and deal with it. Nothing could fluster him, and he handled even the worst accidents with kindness and professionalism.

A tense silence settled over the kitchen. Samantha finally broke the quiet. "I've never seen you so enthralled about a woman before."

I shrugged. "There's something about this entire situation. It's fate. She's mine to protect and care for. What more is there to say?"

Atticus gave me a knowing look and chuckled softly before returning his attention to Sam, brushing his knuckles along her cheek and then pulling her to her feet. She melted into his chest and hugged him fiercely. My knees felt like jelly as I watched them. God, how I wished I could hold Angel in my arms right now.

We all sat down at the table and began to plan the best strategy, determined to bring Angel back and keep everyone safe.

Chapter Thirty

6/26

After stepping off the plane at JFK, I dragged myself through the terminal, my body aching from the long flight. I barely managed to hail a cab, slump into the backseat, and murmur my Chelsea address as exhaustion seeped into my bones. As we drove through the streets, I watched the city's neon lights flicker brightly against the backdrop of the setting sun. After a month away, the lights seemed more colorful, the smells more pungent, and the bustle of the city more chaotic. It was like seeing an old movie in high definition.

My memories of the past month flooded back, intermingling with memories I thought I'd lost forever. The sudden return of my past, things I'd experienced with Conan—from the way he'd played his guitar to the way he'd played my body—was all too much. I just needed to get home and collapse. When the car finally pulled up in front of my brownstone, I paid the driver, stumbled out, and stood for a moment, gazing up at the familiar building. It felt like a dream, like I was watching someone else's life. I punched in the security code, grateful my mind had retained that detail.

When I stepped inside, a pile of mail that had accumulated during my absence greeted me. I barely glanced at the mountain of envelopes and flyers; all I wanted were comfy clothes and my bed. Coming home after a month of being away was surreal. There was a layer of dust on everything. The place I'd called my own for the last six years didn't feel like mine any more. The memories of my life here were mine, but I was no longer connected to them—to my old life.

God, it had been a long day. I was spent, ready to collapse into bed and drift off to blackness. I prayed there would be no dreams tonight. I just needed some peace.

I headed to the kitchen to grab a bottle of water from the fridge. When I opened the door, the stench of spoiled food hit me hard. The fridge was full of rank, moldy leftovers, a testament to how long I'd been gone. Wrinkling my nose, I grabbed the water and quickly shut the door. That was a problem for tomorrow.

Once upstairs, I changed into an old T-shirt and shorts and sank onto the bed, pulling out my cell phone to check my messages. Nik had left a bunch, each one more anxious than the last. I sighed and sent him a quick text, letting him know I was safe and back home. I told him I needed to return to my life and get my head wrapped around what I wanted to do next and that I was too exhausted to talk about it tonight. Promising to touch base in the morning, I silenced my phone and crawled into bed.

Sleep took me quickly, weariness pulling me under.

After a good, hard, restful sleep, I woke up and my head was clear, clearer than it had been since the wreck. I was determined to figure out a way to get out from under the marriage contract and protect everyone I cared about. My best bet was to visit my Uncle Luca and ask for help. Nik had given me a lot to think about regarding Viktor's plot to take out the leaders of the American mafia families. Maybe I could use that piece of information to convince Uncle Luca to help me.

As my uncle, godfather, and the underboss of the Genovese family, Luca had always provided for me like a real father. If anyone could help me, it would be him.

First things first, though. My house was a mess after I'd been gone for so long, and I needed to eat. I placed a big grocery order online, choosing all my favorite foods that I hadn't had since the wreck. While I waited for the delivery, I tackled the house. I cleaned up, went through the mountain of mail, and tossed out the dead flowers I'd bought just before racing out to find Nik a month ago.

Just as I finished up, the groceries arrived. The place was feeling more like home again. I put everything away, made a quick omelet, and brewed a strong cup of coffee. The simple act of cooking and cleaning had given me a sense of accomplishment. After finishing breakfast, I headed upstairs to shower, letting the hot water wash away the grime and lingering exhaustion.

There was no time to waste. I would make an unannounced visit to Uncle Luca today. He was the only person who might be able to get me out of the marriage contract and protect those in Tacoma I'd grown to care so much about. I selected my clothing carefully. Luca was old-school and demanded respect in all things. I chose a fashionable yet professional blue dress that would bring out the color of my eyes. To complete my professional look, I picked out some high-heeled shoes, styled my hair down in waves because I knew he liked it that way, and put on just a touch of makeup. Then I grabbed my black Armani bag, slid my laptop and phone inside it and, with a quick glance in the mirror, headed downstairs.

I ordered an Uber and directed the driver to an office building in the Wall Street district. As I stepped out of the car, I marveled at the opulence of the building. Luca's wealth was evident in every detail. The security guard recognized me and thankfully didn't bother to stop me when I made my way to the elevator. I punched in the code for the top floor, where Luca had his office. The ride was fast, and soon I was stepping into the well-appointed reception area.

I walked past his assistant without stopping, hoping if I appeared confident enough no one would stop me.

A couple of bodyguards were stationed outside his office. Without slowing down, I barreled right past them and into the office without knocking. This wasn't standard protocol, but I had to show my uncle I meant business. And I didn't want to get turned away. My heart pounded, all my nerves firing off like a thousand tiny alarms. I just hoped my smile would keep me from getting shot.

Luca looked up, shock flashing across his face. This expression was rapidly replaced by a hint of amusement. I rushed over, kissing him on the cheek and giving him a sweet hug. The bodyguards stormed in behind me, guns drawn.

"Lower them," Luca ordered, waving them off. "Respect my goddaughter."

All he had to do was glare at them with his dark eyes to intimidate them. "Impressive security you provide, letting a petite thing like her waltz right in. Go, and shut the door behind you."

The men, offering apologies, lowered their guns and left. Luca turned his attention back to me, his brows drawing together in annoyance. "What do you want?" he asked bluntly.

"Uncle Luca," I said firmly yet respectfully, "we need to talk about a security matter."

He glanced over his shoulder at me. His mouth twitched with mild concern before his features relaxed. "Anastasia," he said, motioning for me to sit. "What brings you here so wound up and unannounced?"

"I need your help," I said as I moved to the other side of his desk.

"I'm a busy man. Make it quick."

Feigning offense, I sat in the chair opposite him and perched on the edge with my back straight as an arrow. "You're not happy to see me after a month of me being gone?" I asked with a hint of sarcasm.

He raised an eyebrow, clearly unimpressed by my theatrics. Undeterred, I continued. "Most of that time, I was confined to a hospital bed, Uncle Luca. The car wreck shattered me in so many ways. I was lucky to escape with my life."

Luca's eyes narrowed a bit, but he said nothing, waiting for me to go on.

"It wasn't just the wreck," I said, growing more serious. "I lost my memories. Complete amnesia. Imagine waking up in a hospital bed, surrounded by strangers, with no idea who you are or how you got there. Every part of my body ached. I had cuts and bruises everywhere, and oh, God, how my head constantly throbbed. I had to rely on the kindness of strangers to survive."

Uncle Luca remained stoic, but I detected a flicker of something—maybe remorse—in his eyes.

"It was hell, Uncle Luca," I continued, my tone unwavering. "Every day was a struggle—not just to heal physically but to remember who I was. To reconnect with my past, my identity. It was terrifying."

He leaned back in his chair and steepled his fingers under his chin, watching me intently.

"And while I was dealing with all of that," I said, "you were here, carrying on as if nothing had happened. As if your goddaughter wasn't lying in a hospital bed, fighting to remember her own name. I had to claw my way back to some semblance of normalcy completely alone, all the while worried that I might never get my memories back."

Luca finally spoke. "Yes, I learned about the wreck, Anastasia, but had to keep things quiet. Drawing attention to you would have brought the authorities to our doorstep. So you can knock it off with the guilt trip. We wouldn't want the authorities to figure out you were Viktor Volkov's daughter, now would we? Besides, Elena saw to all of your responsibilities here in the city, ensuring the reason for your absence remained under wraps and notifying the library you would no longer be able to work for them."

I nodded, understanding but not willing to forgive him this easily. "I get that. But it doesn't change what I went through all alone. But I'll just put that aside. For now, I need your help."

He chuckled at my bravado, leaning back in his chair. "You were rash, going to Tacoma without a plan." I wanted to argue, to remind him that I'd tried calling him, but he'd ignored me. Instead, I took a deep breath and crafted my response carefully. "I apologize for my behavior, Uncle Luca. I take full responsibility for what happened. You're right; I should have come to you first."

His expression softened, as though he approved of my acceptance of his criticism and appreciated that I wasn't getting emotional.

"I have something very important to share with you," I said, leaning in and lowering my voice. "I think your life may be in danger."

That got his attention. His eyes sharpened, focusing entirely on me.

I took a deep breath and dove in. "Uncle Luca, this isn't easy for me to say, but I've learned something that puts us all in danger."

He leaned back, scrutinizing me with those cold black eyes, saying nothing but allowing me to continue. I pressed on. "It isn't easy for me to say this, but I respect you more than I ever did my parents. You've been more of a parent to me than they ever were. First, I understand why I've been contracted to marry Frankie Moretti. Even though he's weak, whiny, and frankly, creepy. But if marrying him is what's best for the family, I'm willing to make that sacrifice."

Uncle Luca's gaze didn't waver. I cleared my throat. "But I think Viktor wants to take out the leaders of both the Genovese and Moretti families after I marry Frankie, so that he can take over everything. It's a power grab, and you're in the crosshairs."

Luca's jaw tightened subtly, his hands curling slightly around the armrests of his chair. "You're making dangerous allegations, Anastasia. Anyone else would be killed at the mere mention of something like that."

I fought to keep my composure, struggling against the urge to tremble, and maintained eye contact. "I know how serious this is. I wouldn't risk telling you if I didn't believe it to be true."

Uncle Luca's eyes bored into mine, searching for any sign of deceit. "What proof do you have?" he demanded. "I need evidence."

My mouth went dry, but I forced myself to speak. "I don't have anything concrete, just that someone very close to me overheard conversations about this plot."

He leaned forward, continuing to scrutinize me. "Who?"

I swallowed hard. I couldn't betray Nik. "I can't say. But I trust this person completely. They have no reason to lie."

Uncle Luca's eyes narrowed, and he remained silent, waiting for more. But I remained resolute and held my tongue.

He finally spoke, scrubbing his hand over his scruffy beard. "You're shrewd to come to me with this. I'll look into it."

The tension in the room eased a little, and I managed a small nod. "Thank you, Uncle Luca."

"Don't thank me yet," he replied. "This is far from over."

I nodded, understanding the gravity of the situation. "I know. But I had to tell you."

Luca stood, walking around his desk to stand in front of me. "I'm proud of you for coming to me," he said, placing a hand on my shoulder. "But be careful. You're playing a dangerous game."

I took that as my cue to leave, so I stood and gave him a respectful nod. "I understand. Thank you for listening."

But then I remembered I'd come here for another reason. Biting my lip, I plowed forward, hoping I wasn't pushing my luck. I didn't want to piss the man off.

"Uncle Luca, there's more. I need a favor," I said, my heart pounding but my voice steady.

He raised an eyebrow, waiting for me to continue. "It's about the people who took care of me in the hospital and saved my life," I said. "An EMT named Braxton Thorin rescued me from the mangled car and brought me to the hospital. His brother, an emergency department doctor, Atticus Thorin, along with their brother Conan, an ED nurse, treated me that morning. Afterward, they continued to look after me and protect me from the press. Atticus's fiancée, Samantha, who suffered a TBI too, took me under her wing and provided so much help. Together, they made sure I had everything I could possibly need, including legal help to fight all the charges. They took care of me way beyond what they were obligated to do as medical professionals. They even gave me a place to stay. I'm indebted to them."

"Get to the point, Anastasia."

I took a deep breath and continued. "Samantha is the woman Viktor tried to kidnap in December. She, along with Atticus, Conan, and Braxton, outsmarted him. They're the reason Viktor got caught for all his human trafficking, drug dealing, and everything else and had to flee back to Russia. Now, Viktor has ordered a hit on all of them. They're good people, Uncle Luca. They have no interest in the mafia. They just want to be left alone."

Luca sighed, rubbing his temples. "What are the fucking odds of that happening? Damn, this is a tough situation, but my alliance with Viktor is crucial to the family. My hands may be tied."

"But they saved me, Luca. They deserve to be protected."

He looked at me for a long moment before nodding slowly. "I'll look into it. But don't expect miracles."

Facing Luca had been a nerve-racking experience, but I had managed to hold my ground. Now, I had one more favor to ask. Asking three favors from a mafia leader would put me in his debt for a lifetime, but what choice did I have?

"One more thing... It's about the marriage to Frankie. Is there any way out of it?"

Luca's eyes hardened. "We have already agreed upon the contract. We need the Moretti family's support against the foreign crime syndicates that have been moving in and building strength in our territory. Plus, if what you say is true about your father, then we'll need them all the more. You'll just have to suck it up, buttercup," he said, patting me on the cheek. "But let me give you a piece of advice... Tomaso Moretti is a violent man. Don't trust him or speak freely in his presence. He thinks women are only good for fucking and that everyone is disposable."

"But—"

Luca pierced me with a glare. "You have no choice, Anastasia. Be a good wife to Frankie, give him a couple of babies, and then you can do whatever you want. Have yourself a couple of paramours. Run your little club." He winked. "That secret is still safe with me."

"Yes, sir." I leaned in and gave him a kiss on each cheek. "Thank you, Uncle Luca."

With that, I opened the door and stepped through, but I couldn't resist a parting shot. "Dead men have no contracts," I quipped, flouncing my hair over my shoulder.

Uncle Luca's low rumble of laughter followed me out of his office. I smiled politely at his bodyguards, my heart racing as I darted to the elevator. Once inside, I leaned against the handrail, the adrenaline coursing through my veins making my legs weak. I couldn't believe I had faced Luca and stood my ground.

I was proud of myself for standing tall but also disappointed that he wouldn't budge on the marriage contract or commit to protecting Samantha, Atticus, Conan, and Braxton. Yet I had a gut feeling he would help somehow, especially considering how he'd reacted when I told him about Viktor's plans.

Shaking off my worries, I headed to Club Xyst. I needed to confront my business partners. They had supposedly been my friends for the past six years, but none of them had looked for me when I suddenly disappeared. It was time to address that.

Chapter Thirty-One

6/26

When I stepped out of the taxi in front of Club Xyst, a thrill of excitement shot up my spine. I had fucking missed this place. Slade was hard at work on a ladder adjusting a security camera that hung off the eave of the portico. As much as I adored him and wanted to stop and chat, I was hell-bent on getting some answers from the guys, especially Lucian.

"Hi, Slade. Good to see you. I'll come say hello in a little bit." I gave him a quick nod and a wave and hurried past. His face fell a little. A small pang of regret went through me. I tugged the door open and was greeted by a whoosh of cool air.

Inside, I found Lucian and Lachlan unpacking a crate of liquor bottles next to the main bar. As I approached, they looked up, their eyes widening in disbelief. For a moment, they just stared at me, shocked, as if they couldn't quite process that I was standing there after disappearing for a month. Then, they broke into wide, astonished smiles.

"Ana! Where the hell have you been?" Lucian called out, but I didn't slow down, tossing the bag with my laptop on the bar with a thud.

Marching straight up to him, I shoved him—hard. He slammed into the bar, a bottle of whiskey slipping from his grasp and shattering on the floor.

"That's right, I'm fucking alive!" I screamed, inches from his face. In the most annoying way possible, I poked my finger in his chest with each accusing word. "Not that any of you give two shits. I nearly died and had amnesia for a month, and you never stopped to think, '*Hey, I wonder where Anastasia is? Weird. Wonder why our co-owner and business manager never showed up again?*' I thought you guys would have at least made an effort to figure out what happened to me. Good to know how little I mean to you!"

Lucian raised his hands defensively. "Whoa, whoa, whoa, Ana. Slow down. Your uncle—Luca *Genovese*—and his men paid us a visit and said you had to step away for a while for family business. His thugs made it clear that the type of business you were taking care of was none of ours. He straight up told us he'd break our knees if we went looking for you."

Lachlan added, "When Lucian said it didn't sound right to him and copped an attitude, one of the thugs beat the crap out of him. Check out the new curve to his nose. So maybe you should stop being so self-righteous, lose the damn attitude, and tell us about your fucking mafia ties."

I pulled Lucian's face toward me and took a closer look. Sure enough, his nose had been broken and still looked tender. My stomach twisted with guilt. "Oh my God. No. I'm so sorry. Fuck me, all I do is bring misery to everyone I care about." Exhaling a pent-up breath and trying to iron out the creases on my forehead with my fingertips, I stepped back a little. In a much softer voice, I asked, "How can I make this right?"

Lucian pushed off the bar, putting more distance between us. "Well, you could start by telling us the truth about your mafia connections... You're a goddamn mafia princess, for crying out loud. No wonder we were able to run a gambling room and the whole NYSLA issue just disappeared. I must be stupid because I assumed the uncle you were so close to was just politically well-connected. None of us would have ever thought the shy librarian who came in that first night for a job as a waitress was under the notorious Luca Genovese's guardianship. I think that small detail should have come out over the last few years, don't you?"

More guilt hammered at my conscience. I grabbed a towel and started cleaning up the mess from the broken bottle. "I'm sorry, Lucian. I should have told you."

"Step back, Ana," he said, waving me away. "In that fancy dress and those heels, it won't be long before you're flat on your ass."

Just then, Julian and Gabriel came out from the back.

Gabriel's eyebrows shot up as recognition hit. "Ana, I can't believe it's you! Where've you been?" His smile fell, and he cocked his head to the side. "It's good to see you, but I've got to admit, I can't believe you just checked out on us like that."

"Yeah, and what's up with mafia thugs?" Julian asked.

They both stared at me expectantly. My time of reckoning had come. I had to tell them the truth but didn't know where to begin. No more secrets. I pulled out a bar stool and hiked myself up on it. "It's complicated...especially now. For most of my life, I had no idea who my family really was. Over the years, I slowly learned they were powerful and tied to the mafia, but I had no clue what that meant until I got much older." I let out a huff.

Waiting for me to continue, Julian and Gabriel crossed their arms, while Lachlan jammed his hands in his pockets and Lucian leaned against the bar.

"I was shipped from Russia to a boarding school in upstate New York when I was twelve." I hesitated, gathering my thoughts. It was difficult to condense twenty-seven years into a brief explanation that would make sense. "They separated me from my twin brother, the only person who ever loved me. My last name was changed to that of my aunt, Elena Genovese, and she and Luca became my godparents."

My cheeks flushed with embarrassment as I tried to hurriedly recount my past. "Over time, I became the typical American girl, passport and all. After boarding school, I went to Kennedy University and earned my master's in library and information science, just as my aunt and uncle wanted me to." Nervously, I chewed on my cheek. I hated sharing all this with them.

"It wasn't easy for me as a young girl. My lack of English and my thick Russian accent made it hard to learn and make friends, not to mention I was super shy. So, I spent loads of time watching TV, carefully observing and listening to my classmates and then practicing alone in my room. I tried to speak like they did and forced any hint of my accent away. I wanted to be like all the popular girls in my school, but my aunt and uncle made it clear that my only purpose in life was to be a dutiful daughter, marry whomever they chose, and have babies. Sounds easy, I know. The problem was, I was lonely and completely miserable. I was desperate to taste freedom and live a little but didn't have a clue where to begin. Not long after I started working for the library, I came across your ad for a job at Club Xyst. Coming to work here was the best thing I've ever done for myself." I glanced around at each of them, hoping the truth of who I was hadn't ruined things between us. "I want you guys to know that I had no clue about the types of dealings my family was really involved in until after I began working here. And then...how on earth was I supposed to tell you?"

Gabriel raised an eyebrow. "No clue about the drugs and human trafficking, huh?"

I shook my head. "None. It was almost a year later that my aunt sort of told me about how mafia families work," I said, a lump forming in my throat. "She told me they were searching for the best marriage contract to benefit the family and explained I was part of one of the most powerful families in the world. She called it a privilege, saying I'd be the beneficiary of immense wealth, but didn't get into any specifics about where all that money had come from. All I had to do was stay a virgin, marry who I was told to marry, and I would be a pampered mafia wife for the rest of my life, never having to work."

Julian sat down next to me, his brows knitting in worry. "And if you didn't?"

"At first I tried to refuse, to tell her I wouldn't go along with the arranged marriage, but that didn't go over so well. She laughed right in my face and said the alternative was an untimely death." I paused, steadying myself. "She followed up later by sending me images of women's dead bodies—those who had stood up against family expectations. They were tortured and mutilated. So what choice did I have? It was then I truly realized what it meant to be part of the mafia. Before, I'd thought they were just powerful businessmen who walked the line of what was legal and illegal. I didn't understand about the violence, the drugs, the sex trade. I'd never had a reason to dig deeper. I mean, you guys have gambling in the basement, but it doesn't mean you sell women or drugs on the side."

Lucian stepped closer, raking a hand through his hair, and said softly, "Ana, I had no idea."

They all stared at me in shock.

"I did everything I could to keep the club a secret from my family and friends," I said apologetically, glancing down at my hands. "It was the one thing in my life that I'd achieved on my own, something that meant everything to me. Here, for the first time, I could be strong and independent. If I hadn't met you guys, I would have jumped off a building long ago."

Lucian released a sigh and relaxed his shoulders, coming to stand in front of me. He now wore a look of protective concern on his face. "I'm sorry, Ana. If I'd known, I would've never even considered a physical relationship with you. I never would have put you in that sort of danger."

"Oh, God, Lucian, don't say that." I hopped off the stool. "Without you, I would have never known how amazing sex could be. I just wanted a taste of normalcy before being stuck with someone I'd probably hate for the rest of my life. There was no pressure to find the perfect guy or have a perfect relationship. You made it fun and easy. Our open arrangement kept things simple for us and everyone here. Right, guys?" I asked, glancing at the others.

They all grinned and nodded.

Resting my palms on Lucian's chest, I implored him to understand. "Please don't regret being that person for me. Your friendship means everything." I turned to the guys. "You *all* mean the world to me."

"Don't you worry, hun; we've got your back," Lachlan said. "You'll always be like a sister to us—well, except for Lucian, and that's between the two of you." He chuckled.

I smiled. "You guys need to understand, everything about the club's operation is the same as it's always been. No one in

298

my family knows I'm a part owner except Uncle Luca." I took a deep breath, twisting my fingers around a strand of my hair. "He was the first person I went to see. I just got home late last night. Actually," I paused, shifting my weight from one foot to the other, "I met with him just before coming here to get answers about some information my brother told me about...our family."

I glanced around the room, making eye contact with each of them. "But I made a point of asking him about the club, and he assured me the rest of the family still didn't know about it. I don't know how he found out about it a couple of years ago, but he promised to never tell Elena or anyone else. I don't think he would ever do that. He's always respected me and seems supportive of my ownership. He's even helped us by keeping the police off our backs."

I turned to Lucian, my expression softening. "But Lucian, I can't explain why he came down here and let one of his thugs beat you up." I reached out, placing a hand on his arm. "I'm really sorry he did that to you. Please believe me."

The tension in the room eased as Lucian enveloped me in a big hug. When he released me, he gripped my face in his hands and kissed me hard. For a moment, I melted into the kiss, but then thoughts of Conan surfaced, and I realized this was nothing compared to what I felt with him.

A loud smack on the far end of the bartop rattled the glasses, making me jump.

Gabriel shouted, "Who the fuck are you? We're not open!"

I turned to find the source of what had rattled the bar, and my heart skipped a beat. There was Conan, coming in hot, his long strides eating up the distance between us. His intense gaze was locked on me. I pulled away from Lucian, wiping my mouth and flushing with embarrassment. Conan's unexpected arrival would have thrown me off balance as it was, but the radical change in his appearance truly stunned me. His gorgeous long hair, which he had often worn in a ponytail or bun, was now buzzed off, making him appear even more menacing than he had before.

"Conan? What are you doing here?" I stammered. For the life of me, I couldn't pull my attention away from him. Between the fire in his eyes and his fierce appearance, he had my insides smoldering. "And what happened to your hair? You look... different. Intimidating. Don't get me wrong—I love it—but why the drastic change?"

He stepped closer, his eyes never leaving mine. "It's not good to have long hair when you're preparing for battle, so I shaved it off. Don't you think for a minute that I will not protect you from Viktor. You're my girl, and I'll be more than happy to cut Viktor's tongue off and shove it down his throat."

His ferocious words took my breath away. "You came all the way here to fight for me?"

"No, I came here to die for you."

His declaration stunned me.

"How...how did you find me?" I asked, bridging the distance between us and reaching out for his arms. But he stepped back, his face hardening.

"Since the fucking mafia attacked Sam, Atticus has implemented extremely high security measures, including tracking all electronic devices. We followed your laptop as soon as we got off our flight from Tacoma." My mouth dropped as my breath hitched. I hadn't ever seen this aggressive side of Conan, and I was taken aback. "So, Angel, care to tell me who your little friend is?" he asked, jutting his thumb toward Lucian.

Lucian, never one to back down, shoved Conan. "None of your fucking business, mate."

The tension exploded.

Conan and Lucian started throwing punches, and Julian shouted, "Where the fuck is Slade? How did this asshole get in?"

Throwing myself between them, I tried to break them apart. "Stop it, both of you!" But in the chaos, I was knocked into the side of the bar. My arm hit a couple of bottles, sending them crashing to the ground. Between the high heels and the slick, whiskey-covered floor, I slipped and fell onto my hands and knees, a piece of glass slicing into my palm. Blood surged out and ran down my arm as I lifted it.

"Angel!" Conan's anger morphed into fear, and he rushed to my side. Lucian wasn't far behind. Both of them struggled to help me up without slipping in the mess. "Back off," Conan barked at Lucian. "Go get a first aid kit or a clean towel."

Lucian hesitated, then nodded and hurried to the other side of the bar. Conan gently lifted me onto a bar stool before examining the cut on my hand. The others hovered near, their earlier hostility fading at the sight of my cut.

Within seconds, Lucian pulled a first aid kit out and flipped it open. After unwrapping a stack of gauze pads, he gestured for Conan to take one.

Conan took the gauze and pressed it firmly against my wound, applying enough pressure to slow the bleeding. "Keep this here," he instructed, guiding my other hand to hold the gauze in place. He grabbed a small bottle of antiseptic from the kit, then gently removed the gauze. "This is going to sting," he warned. Then he poured the antiseptic over the cut.

I winced at the sharp pain, but Conan's touch remained steady. He patted the area dry before reaching for the Steri-Strips.

"Stay still," he murmured, carefully aligning the edges of the cut. He meticulously placed each strip to close the wound and ensure the skin stayed together. Once he was satisfied, he wrapped my hand with a clean bandage, securing it until it was snug but not too tight.

"There, my pretty Angel. That should take care of it." He lifted my palm to his lips and gave it a chaste kiss. Lucian's eyes darkened at the endearment, but he said nothing.

Hoping to ease the tension, I made some quick introductions. "Conan, this is Lucian. This is his brother Lachlan, and these two are Julian and Gabriel," I said, gesturing to each one.

Lucian's lips curled into a smirk. "Conan, huh? Are you thick in the head like Conan the Barbarian?"

"Stop antagonizing him, Lucian," I snapped.

Conan looked Lucian dead in the eye. "My real name is Constantine. I picked up the nickname Conan in high school because, in my senior year, I was the biggest guy. Not because it came naturally, but because I've always put in the work. Physical fitness is important to me, and I've enjoyed mixed martial arts for many years."

Conan's real name surprised me. There was so much I didn't know about him. Despite the time we'd spent together, our relationship was still new.

The guys were eyeing him suspiciously. His presence here demanded an explanation. "Conan was on duty in the ED the day I had the wreck." I looked from Conan to Lucian. "He was the one who first treated my injuries."

Conan nodded. "Her injuries were pretty severe. The trauma to her brain resulted in a form of amnesia where she couldn't remember anything from before the wreck. We feared she might never regain her memories or be able to return to her previous life."

"It was awful. I had no clue who I was for almost a month," I said. "Just a black hole where my memories should have been."

"Yeah, Ana said something about almost dying...and losing her memory," Lucian said.

Conan's face tightened with anger. "And none of you assholes thought to look for her when she disappeared out of the blue?" he spat, glaring at Lucian and then others.

Lucian raised his hands defensively. "Whoa, man. Her mob uncle had one of his thugs beat the crap out of me and threatened to kill us if we went sniffing around. He said she was away on family business. Nothing about a car wreck on the other side of the fucking country."

Just then, Braxton burst in, a little disheveled, with Slade trailing behind him. Annoyed, Gabriel quipped, "What?! This is the second guy who's burst in here. You're just allowing random dudes in when we're closed now? What the fuck?"

Slade, who was sporting a busted lip, rubbed his jaw and shrugged. "Sorry, boss. Wasn't expecting them, and this one got the better of me," he said, pointing to Braxton.

The guys eyed Conan and Braxton with a newfound respect. "Slade, you're one of the toughest guys I know," I said. "Didn't think anyone could get the better of you. Looks like today neither of us fared too well." I held up my hand and smiled.

Slade dropped his chin and shook his head.

Lucian reached behind the bar, filled a towel with ice, and handed it to Slade. "Here, take care of that jaw."

Just then, a few of the club's employees came in.

"Let's head up to the office," I suggested. "We need to talk about what's going on with me and my family. You guys deserve to know all the ugly details."

We headed toward the elevator, leaving Slade to return to his post at the entrance of the club. The tension was thick as we made our way up. I could almost taste the unease and the unspoken questions hanging in the air.

Chapter Thirty-Two

Once we were in the office, we gathered around the small, round conference table. All eyes were on me. I took a deep breath and faced the men. "Okay, I admit that I rushed off—without a solid plan—to the Volkov estate in Tacoma because my brother didn't show up on our birthday," I began. "But, for the last fourteen years, Nik has never missed coming to see me, and I panicked when he didn't respond to my messages."

Lucian crossed his arms. "That was reckless, Ana. You should've told us. You had to have known it would be dangerous to go off like that in search of a guy involved with the mafia and not tell anyone. When you called me that morning, I offered to help you in any way you needed, but you blew me off."

Conan leaned back in his chair. "What I want to know is why did you run from the police? Braxton said they clocked you doing double the speed limit, running away like you robbed a bank. What the hell were you thinking?"

Their disappointment tore at my conscience. Having them pissed off at me would have been a much better alternative. Anger I could have dealt with, but not this.

"I didn't have time to think it through," I said, meeting Conan's eyes. "I was desperate to find Nik, and when I showed up at the house and saw it covered in police tape, the yard unkempt, and the place practically ransacked, it freaked me out. I didn't know what I was walking into. I hadn't been inside but maybe twenty minutes when I heard police sirens. I ran because the fact that the Volkovs are my biological family has been a closely guarded secret since I was a young girl." I looked at each of them in turn. "I had no explanation for why I broke into that home. They would have assumed I was a thief, arrested me, and checked into my background. Keeping my identity under wraps is crucial for my father's plans. If the authorities learned who I really was, it would have blown everything up. He's obsessed with gaining a stronghold here in the states and has spent years setting me up to help make that happen."

"So, bottom line, you're a part of not one but two mafia family crime syndicates, and you didn't think we should know about it? Damn, Ana, you could get us all killed," Julian grumbled.

"She was protecting you, dumbass. You know, the whole *ignorance is bliss* sort of thing," Conan shot back.

"There's a lot you don't know," I admitted. "And for that, I'm sorry. But I did everything I could to keep the club separate from my family. It was the only thing in my life I thought I had control over."

Gabriel sighed and walked over to the office's private bar. "Anyone need a drink? Conan? Braxton?"

"Redbreast 12, if you have it," Conan said, his eyes never leaving mine. "Neat."

Braxton nodded. "Same for me."

Lachlan, who had been silent thus far, perked up. "Well, at least they have good taste in whiskey. Redbreast 12 is one of Ireland's finest. Smooth, with just the right amount of spice."

Gabriel fetched the drinks, and soon the whiskey was flowing, easing the tension a bit.

The guys stared at me, waiting for me to continue. I squared my shoulders and inhaled slowly, ready to lay it all out.

"My real father, Viktor Volkov, is a notorious Russian Pakhan—mob boss. The Russian mafia isn't just some street gang. It's a massive organization involved in human trafficking, drug dealing, and pretty much every horrific crime you can imagine."

Pausing, I took a sip of my drink. The fire burned my throat as the golden liquor descended, boosting my confidence.

"Like I said before, I was shipped to America when I was twelve and placed in Elena and Luca Genovese's custody. I knew I came from a Russian family, but I was raised as a Genovese. They mostly kept me in the dark about what that actually meant. I've met with my biological family a handful of times at their estate in Tacoma, but they never really felt like family except for Nik. I think they only had me visit because they wanted to evaluate my progress in becoming an American socialite. I feel so stupid for never looking into the Volkovs and learning about the terrible things they were involved in. It wasn't until I was in the hospital that I discovered the truth about Viktor and his disgusting empire...and what he did to Samantha."

My breath hitched, and I had to look away from Conan for a moment to gather my thoughts. What that monster had done to Samantha was hard to share. "Six months ago, Viktor kidnapped

Sam. He tried to kill her, Atticus, Conan, and Braxton."

Julian let out a low whistle.

"She was smacked around and grabbed from Atticus's house. Her hands were zip-tied, and she was thrown in the back of a van and taken to a warehouse at the port. She tried to escape and almost drowned in the frigid water of the bay. Then they dragged her back to the warehouse, where Viktor nearly raped her. If Atticus and the others hadn't arrived in the nick of time, he would have. Sam told me how he stripped her and started doing the unimaginable to her. Gunshots distracted him, and somehow Sam was able to escape the office she was locked in just to find herself in the middle of a shoot-out. Atticus threw himself in front of a bullet meant for her, knocking her off her feet, and she ended up cracking her head on the concrete floor."

I trembled, fighting back tears as I continued. "Conan, Braxton, and a bunch of private-security men fought off Viktor and his thugs. If you guys could only meet Sam. She's such an amazing person. She became my friend while in the hospital—a real friend when I needed one most. It makes me sick knowing it was my father who did that to her. And now I've made matters worse for them all."

Conan, who was sitting across from me, leaned forward. "Angel, you shouldn't blame yourself. Viktor's the monster here, not you." He chuckled darkly, shaking his head. "What are the odds that, six months later, Viktor Volkov's daughter would wind up in the emergency department under the care of all three of the Thorin brothers, suffer from amnesia, and become *close* to my family and friends?" He emphasized the word *close*, and I noticed Lucian cock an eyebrow, but I was too mad at myself to say anything.

I clenched my fists, trying to control the anger boiling inside me. "I'm so furious that I'm associated with a family capable of such horrors. I feel terrible for dragging Samantha and everyone else further into Viktor's violent world and putting their lives at risk."

I studied my hands resting in my lap. My lip quivered as I forced the next part out. "Conan...Nik told me...Viktor has put a hit out on you guys."

Conan inhaled deeply, then rose from his chair and moved behind me. He gathered my hair in his hands, placing a tender kiss behind my ear. "We'll figure out how to protect you and everyone else, my Angel," he murmured. His touch calmed me, making me feel important, wanted, cared for.

I leaned into him, savoring the warmth of his presence. "And now I've made things worse by involving you guys from the club," I said, glancing at each of them in turn.

Lucian turned his chair, and then mine, so we faced each other. He leaned forward, put his elbows on his thighs, and took my hands in his. "Ana, you have our complete loyalty. We've believed in you for the last six years. That's one of the reasons why we made you an equal partner. We all love you and will do whatever it takes to protect you."

The others nodded in agreement, and my heart melted.

Lucian's eyes darkened with that all-too-familiar smoldering gaze. He let go of my hands and ran his fingers up my thighs. "You know I'm still here any time you need a release. Nothing's changed between us." He swallowed hard. "I know your life's been turned upside down, but I hope you know I'll be there for you, no matter what you need. Fuck, I know we have shit to do, but right now, all I want to do is you."

My face blazed red hot as heat shot to my core and an inferno burst to life between my thighs. Did he really just say that in front of Conan?

There were a couple of chuckles.

My head snapped over to Conan, who was leaning against the edge of the table next to me. He crossed his ankles and rubbed his chin between his thumb and forefinger. "Angel, what exactly does Lucian mean by he's *still here any time you need a release*?" he growled.

I sat there between Lucian and Conan, tension crackling in the air. Lucian had just spilled the beans about our *special relationship*, and Conan was understandably shocked by it. The whiskey had everyone talking more freely, so there was no stopping now.

"Lucian and I have had a no-strings-attached thing for years," I explained, choosing to address Conan directly. "We enjoy each other's company without any emotional baggage or exclusivity. We're great business partners and friends, but nothing more."

Conan pressed his lips into a thin line. "So, you two just fuck and that's it?"

Someone across the table cleared their throat. But I hadn't done anything wrong, so I straightened my spine and slapped on a smile.

Lucian leaned back, crossing his arms. "Pretty much. We agreed from the start—no emotions, no complications. Just two people who like and trust each other."

Conan snorted. "Sounds like a convenient arrangement. But I didn't come all this way for a woman who's just a casual fuck."

Lucian raised an eyebrow. "Funny, it didn't sound like you were invited. Maybe she didn't want you here."

"Well, it's obvious she needs me here. If she had the kind of man she deserves in her life, she wouldn't have ended up wrapping a car around a tree, nearly killing herself. But don't worry; I'll take it from here. No need for you to add *complications* to your life now, is there?"

A smirk played on Lucian's lips. "Maybe she likes having options. Besides, there's nothing wrong with a little variety, is there, Conan?"

Conan's eyes narrowed. "No need to shop around when you've found exactly what you want."

I sighed, rolling my eyes at their macho posturing. "Both of you, cut it out." I huffed. "Conan and I had a chance to get to know each other without all the family drama casting a shadow over us. I didn't have any memories, so I didn't have a marriage contract or a fake identity hanging over my head. We had an opportunity to see each other for who we really are. But then my memories and all the ugliness of my life came back and slapped me back into reality. So I don't know where things could have gone. Now we'll probably never know." I shrugged, my mind a chaotic mess of worries about what my future held.

Conan grasped my chin and turned me to face him. His gaze locked onto mine, burning with a raw intensity. "Eyes on me, Angel," he commanded, closing the space between us, his breath brushing across my lips. "I'm going to know everything about you—your fears, your dreams, your past, the best and the worst. I want to be the one who stands by you when you're at your lowest and lifts you up higher at your best. I'll be the one who fights off anyone or anything that tries to hurt you. You're mine now, and I will know every part of you, even your darkest origins. Nothing will get in my way. Nothing."

My breath hitched, my surroundings evaporated, and then there were only the two of us. I took his face in my hands and lost myself in his kiss. A sudden movement to my right broke me out of my trance. Lucian stood there with his hand on Conan's shoulder, pulling him back.

"All right, buddy. You don't get to just waltz in here and lay claim to a woman you've just met. She might be a little caught up in her emotions for a guy who provided her care in the hospital when she was at her worst, but you don't even know her." Lucian cupped my cheek and gave me a kind smile. "Ana, you know you can always count on me. We've got years of history. And you know you can trust me. Your happiness is what matters to me."

The two men exchanged possessive glances, each trying to outdo the other. Annoyed to my limit, I shook my head. "Listen, neither one of you is the boss of me." I let out an exasperated breath. "Besides, by contract, I'm owned by the Moretti family, and in particular by that weasel Frankie."

Conan and Lucian both scowled at the mention of Frankie's name. "That marriage contract is bullshit," Conan growled. "How's it even possible in today's world?! You should be free to choose."

Lucian nodded in agreement. "You're not some commodity to be traded. We need to find a way to get you out of that situation. When is this wedding anyway?"

My lips rolled in tight, as if they were barring me from speaking the truth. I squinched my eyes closed; it killed me to say it out loud.

"Angel?" Conan prompted.

"June twenty-ninth."

There was a collective gasp.

"What the fuck? That only gives us two and a half days to figure this out!" Braxton shouted.

I opened my eyes and glanced around the room. All of their stunned expressions were gut-wrenching.

"No way, Ana," Lachlan said, shaking his head. "You've got to get out of here. Go live off the grid long enough for us to figure things out."

Their protectiveness was touching, but I needed them to understand I wasn't a damsel in distress—I was just shit out of luck. "Thanks, guys. But remember, this is an alliance between some of the world's most powerful mafia organizations. It's not like a handful of well-intentioned guys can take them on. It's my cross to bear, and I don't want you all to get involved any more than you already have."

Conan placed a firm hand on my shoulder. "We know that, Angel. But we'll be damned if we let you be forced into something you don't want."

Lucian's gaze softened, but his protective bravado was still evident by his consternated expression. "We'll figure this out, Ana. Together."

Lucian and Conan passed each other a knowing look—a truce.

Gabriel cleared his throat. "Anastasia, tell us about your brother. You haven't mentioned him until today, but it's obvious he means a lot to you, seeing as you took off across the country when you were worried about him. Is there any possibility he might be able to help?"

I nodded, rubbing my temples. "Nik means the world to me. But it's complicated. He hates the mafia business, but Viktor controls him. He's a Russian citizen, not American, which makes it harder for him to get out from under Viktor. Since childhood, he's been forced to do Viktor's bidding and prove his loyalty to the Volkovi Notchi. He wants out but doesn't think he can do anything about it yet."

Braxton frowned. "How deeply entrenched do you think he is? Maybe it's better if you don't contact him."

Anger surged through me. "Nik has always been there for me. I'll do anything to protect him like he's always protected me." With that, I stood up. "I need to go home. I'm exhausted."

Lucian and Conan both turned toward me. "I'll take you home," they said in unison, then glared at each other.

I shook my head. "No, I need to be alone."

Conan stepped closer. "We're staying at the High Line Hotel and have a rental car. We can come pick you up for dinner."

I managed a small smile. "Oh, that's really close to where I live."

Conan grinned. "Yeah, we know. The laptop gave us your overnight location. We figured as much."

I laughed. "Of course you would know. But tonight, I just want to crash. Alone time is what I need so that I can sort out some of the chaos zinging around in my head. How about I call you when I'm ready to talk more?"

He nodded and stepped away, his shoulders and arms tensing. It was obvious he didn't want to let me go alone, but he resisted the urge to say more.

Lucian stopped me as I headed for the elevator. "Come by the club in the morning. We'll update you on everything that's happened since you left."

"I'll let you know," I said over my shoulder. I walked through the reception area and pushed the elevator button.

As I stepped outside, I took a deep breath of the cool night air, trying to clear my head. I spotted Slade standing by the entrance and patted him on the side of the arm. "Take care of that jaw. Sorry for those guys forcing their way in like that. If I'd had any idea they might show up, I would've given you a heads-up."

"No worries, Ana. I'd do anything for you. Let's catch up tomorrow, yeah?"

"Sounds good." I smiled as he raised his hand.

A cab pulled forward. He opened the door, and I slid into the backseat, giving Slade a grateful nod before the cab drove off into the bustle of traffic.

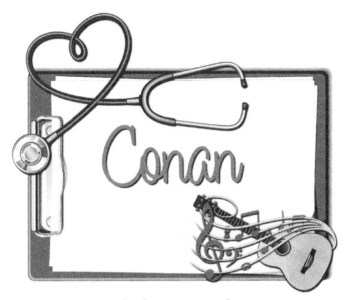

Chapter Thirty-Three

6/26

The elevator doors closed behind Angel with a dull thud. Soon the soft whir of its descent faded away. Returning to the table, I slumped back into my chair and stretched out my legs. Allowing her to leave on her own, to let her sort out her thoughts in peace, was the right decision. She needed space to calm her chaotic thoughts, and I had to respect that.

I glanced around the office at the men who'd been in Angel's life long before me, regretting making a scene downstairs earlier when I'd seen Lucian kissing her. I'd acted like a jealous high school punk. Not my finest moment. Brawling with a guy she was close to, someone she worked with, had been idiotic.

Lachlan poured me another shot, and I downed it immediately, letting the burn of the alcohol fuel my frustration. I was mad at myself for losing control and letting my emotions dictate my actions. I could only hope I hadn't ruined things with Angel and that my impulsive display hadn't pushed her away. There was no explanation for why I cared so much, but I just did.

Lost in my thoughts, I stared into the empty glass. The truth was, my feelings for Angel ran deeper than I had suspected, and I was only now able to admit that to myself. She was Pandora's box, and I was the one forbidden to open it, tempted by what I couldn't resist. She was an enchantment, calling to me, whispering promises that would unlock my heart and hand over the power to break me. There was danger involved, yes, but being prudent and safe was for the cautious. And I was a reckless man.

I ran my hand over my freshly buzzed hair, the stubble prickly under my palm. Angel was different from anyone I'd ever met. She wasn't just a woman I needed to protect; she was a woman who stirred something profound inside of me, something I couldn't ignore even if I wanted to. And God, did I want her.

Rising from the table, I walked over to Lucian, who was staring out at the bar below. I extended my hand. "Look, man, I'm sorry for being a dick earlier. I guess I'm on edge and short-fused. I just want to keep Angel safe, and I have no idea how to protect her from the fucking mafia."

Lucian grasped my hand tightly and shook it. "Think nothing of it, man. I wouldn't have respected you if you'd been a pussy and not stood up for Ana. She's important to all of us." He turned to the others. "All right, guys, we need to get back to work. The club doesn't run itself."

Lachlan, Julian, and Gabriel nodded, heading off to their tasks.

I turned to Braxton. "Time to leave."

We left the club and headed to our hotel. After we'd checked in and settled into our room, I decided to take a shower to relax.

The hot water didn't do much to ease my restlessness though. My mind kept drifting back to Angel.

As I toweled off, I paced the room. I had nothing better to do than let my mind gnaw on everything I'd learned today. Finally, I turned to Braxton. "I'm going to take Angel some food. She's probably too wound up to eat."

Braxton nodded. I decided I would look up the little Italian place Angel had told me she liked to order from. I would order some carbonara since that was her favorite. I grabbed my phone, searched the area, and found what had to be the restaurant. Pocketing my phone, I headed out of the hotel. Instead of getting a cab, I decided to walk; I needed the fresh air and the time to think.

As I strolled through the Chelsea neighborhood, I thought about Angel's life before the wreck. New York City was a far cry from Tacoma. Would she ever consider moving? Probably not, with her family ties and her job at the club keeping her bound here.

Soon, I entered the cozy Italian restaurant and approached the back counter, where a teenage boy stood. He glanced up at me, eyes widening, and leaned his head back as I neared the counter, clearly intimidated by my size.

"Hey, by chance, do you know Anastasia Genovese?" I asked, trying to sound friendly.

The kid hesitated. "Uh, yeah, I know her. Why?"

"I'm bringing her dinner and wanted to ensure I had the right place. She loves the carbonara here, right?"

"I haven't seen her in a while," he said. The boy was all kinds of flustered. This had to be the one Anastasia had told me about.

I smiled. "Yeah, she's been out of town and just got back late last night. I thought I'd surprise her and bring her favorite dinner. I want to make sure she gets what she loves. She mentioned how there was this nice guy—Elliot, I think his name was—who would deliver it to her and how he always gave her a little something extra. Is that you?"

The kid blushed. "Yeah, it's me. I know exactly how she likes it. Would you want anything else?"

"Everything looks good. Surprise me."

Elliot grinned. "She also loves our shrimp Alfredo."

"Perfect. I'll take that. Thanks, kid."

When the food was paid for and packed up, I headed out. On my way to her place, I stopped at a nearby liquor store and picked up a couple of bottles of Chianti Classico, a perfect match for the Italian feast.

I was standing at Angel's doorstep with the bags of food and wine in one hand, ringing the intercom with the other, when I heard footsteps behind me. Curious, I turned around. Lucian was coming up the steps, carrying a bottle of whiskey and a couple of carryout bags.

"No surprise to find you on her doorstep like a lost puppy," he said, smirking.

"Yeah, well, great minds must think alike. I see you've got dinner too. Good thing I know her favorite," I replied, holding up my bags.

Lucian shrugged. "I've got a bottle of Skrewball Peanut Butter Whiskey, her favorite. It'll make for a nice dessert."

Anastasia opened the door barefoot. She was wearing a cute pair of pink-and-white sleep shorts and a pink tank top. She rolled her eyes dramatically. "You two are like twins. I swear."

"Stop rolling your eyes," Lucian and I said in unison, then exchanged a brief glare.

She sighed. "Come on in, you guys. We'll make it a smorgasbord."

Angel went about getting plates and glasses while we organized the food on a little round table by the window.

I handed Lucian a glass of wine and took a generous sip from mine.

"Conan, first time in New York?" he asked, passing a dish over.

"Yeah, the city's a beast. Nothing like Tacoma."

Angel handed me a forkful of carbonara. "It's not so bad once you get used to it. There's always something to do, and we are, after all, a cultural and entertainment mecca, with all the theaters, museums, and galleries. Not to mention the culinary diversity. Everything from Michelin-starred fine dining to the food carts at the Queens night market. There's something for everyone all the time. You know, the city that never sleeps."

Lucian laughed. "Yeah, hot and crowded in the summer and cold and windy in the winter. But the nightlife makes up for it."

"And Club Xyst is a whole other world," Angel said. "Speaking of... Lucian, why did you leave early tonight? Last call isn't until three."

Lucian shrugged. "Wanted to make sure you were okay. I know how stressful everything's been for you."

"Oh, that's sweet. I appreciate it, but I'm good, considering... well, the circumstances," she said, her tone softening as her eyes fell to her plate.

Lucian raised a brow. "So, what exactly happened with the wreck? Why were you in the hospital for so long?"

I jumped in. "She had to be cut out of the car using the jaws of life. The wreck was horrific. She's lucky to be alive."

Lucian's eyes widened. "Damn, that must have been some impact."

"She was unconscious for days, covered in bruises and burns from the seatbelt and airbags, and she got a big ole gash on her forehead," I explained.

Lucian nodded. "I noticed the scar earlier at the club."

Frowning, Angel reached up quickly to touch her forehead, her fingers tracing the thin, raised line as her chin dropped to her shoulder.

Talking about the wreck had upset her, and she was obviously self-conscious about the scar. I cursed myself for bringing it up. Rising from my chair and moving behind her, I gathered her hair in my hand. God, how I loved her thick, long chestnut locks. Taking her chin in my fingers, I turned her face gently and kissed the scar on her forehead, trailing kisses down the side of her face and along her neck. She sighed softly and leaned into it, her body relaxing.

Lucian watched our every move. Angel licked her lips and gave me a come-hither look. Smirking, I pulled back and returned to my seat.

"Damn, Ana, if you keep looking at him like that, we might have to skip dessert," Lucian said. Although he seemed amused, his words held the hint of a challenge.

"Who says we can't have both?" Angel shot back, her tone playful but dripping with innuendo.

We all laughed, but her words had opened a door. Was it one I was willing to walk through? I leaned back in my chair, noting how they looked at each other. Choosing not to fan the flames of where I guessed her comment was meant to go, I drained the last of my wine. From there, the conversation flowed easily as we shared the rest of the food, talking about everything from the club to summertime in the city. Once the second bottle of wine was polished off, the lingering tension had eased, and the air buzzed with an underlying prickle of possibilities.

While we were clearing the dishes, Lucian nudged me with his elbow and handed me a stack of plates. "Think you can handle washing the dishes, or are you too distracted by our lovely hostess?"

"Just trying to figure out if there's anything she can't make look good. It's awfully hard to ignore that tank top she's sporting," I shot back, carrying the plates to the sink. "But I'm more than capable of multitasking."

Lucian smirked, glancing over at Angel as she opened the whiskey. She found three shot glasses and hopped up on the counter, letting her legs and feet dangle off. She poured each of us a shot of the Skrewball Lucian had brought for dessert.

"Hope you boys are ready for this," she said with a playful grin, handing us each a glass.

I dried my hands on a towel, took the glass, and took a whiff of the sweet drink. I'd never had peanut butter flavored whiskey.

We downed the shots. The warm, smooth taste coated my throat in a pleasing way.

"Damn, that's good," I said, savoring the lingering flavor. "Smooth with a bit of a kick, just like our hostess."

Once everything was clean and put away, we made our way to the living room, drinks in hand. The whiskey was already warming my blood. Angel settled in the middle of the sofa, pulling me down on one side and Lucian on the other. She grabbed the remote and put on *Magic Mike*, a classic chick flick.

Angel curled up to my side and rested her head on my chest, giving me no other choice but to wrap my arm around her waist. She stretched her legs out toward Lucian, putting her feet in his lap. He started to massage them, and she sighed contentedly. "It's so nice to have two men who are so attentive and like pleasing me," she teased.

Lucian chuckled, his hands working on her feet. "We aim to please, don't we, Conan?"

I took another sip of my drink, letting the burn slide all the way down my throat before setting the glass onto the end table. "Yeah, it's like she's got us both wrapped around her finger. Not that I'm complaining."

She giggled. It was obvious she was enjoying every second of the attention. I watched her, the way her eyes lit up, the way she responded to both of us. Her flirtations were drawing both of us in.

It hit me hard—this wasn't about making her choose between Lucian and me. I wanted to please her, make her happy, not tear her apart, make her choose between her present and past. Dark thoughts crept in. How awful it must be for her to be locked in a not-so-gilded cage she couldn't escape from. Her life had been controlled, sheltered, and filled with expectations and restrictions. She deserved to experience everything life had to offer.

I had been in threesomes before, where sex was casual and fun. But now, with Angel, everything was different. So many new and unexplained emotions swirled inside me—possessiveness, protectiveness, worry for her well-being. The idea of sharing her with another man twisted something deep inside me, but I also knew it might be good for her.

I wouldn't stand in her way if she was interested in something more adventurous tonight. In fact, I'd encourage it. Maybe it would help her feel more liberated, more in control of her own choices. I didn't want her to feel like she had missed out on any life experience. She shouldn't be controlled by her family, shouldn't be controlled by me. She deserved to experience everything she'd been denied. Maybe this could be a step toward her feeling whole. Watching her with another man was a risk, but if it helped her, it would be worth it.

Why force her to choose now, when our relationship was still so new? The night we'd spent together in Tacoma before she fled had been incredible, but she hadn't had her memories then. Expecting her to commit to me exclusively was unfair.

No matter how much it tore my heart out to watch her with Lucian, at least it would be better if it was part of a shared experience. I could be there with her, for her, making sure she felt safe and cared for. It could be a bonding experience rather than something that drove a wedge between us. And maybe, if I was good enough, she would end up choosing me one day.

I glanced over at Lucian, who was watching Angel intently, and then down at her, nestled against me. I was determined to be whatever she needed me to be tonight.

Gently, I swiped her hair off her neck, exposing the smooth skin there so I could trail kisses along it. Savoring her taste, I nipped my way down to her collarbone. Her pulse quickened beneath my lips. I glanced up at Lucian and cocked a brow, giving him a questioning glance as if to ask, *You in?* Even though I already knew the answer by his hooded eyes and the way his jaw clenched.

He licked his lips and smiled, his green eyes gleaming with lust. "I'd love nothing more than for the three of us to be together tonight," he said, his deep Irish accent thickening with desire. His lips turned up into a mischievous grin. He was clearly excited by the idea of sharing Angel with me.

Now only thin rims of blue surrounded her blown-wide pupils. Her eyes, irresistibly captivating, darted between us. Arousal flickered within them before she angled her head toward mine. She reached up with one hand and pulled me down for a demanding kiss. I could taste the whiskey on her tongue, mingling with her unique sweetness. She pressed her lips against mine with a fiery passion while at the same time running her feet teasingly along Lucian's thighs. Her touch ignited a hunger in me, a hunger that demanded satisfaction.

"Have you ever been with two men before, Angel?" I asked her.

"Never," she admitted, her cheeks flushing with excitement. "You are the only men I've ever been with. But something about you two makes me want to try it."

"Would you be willing to do this, Angel?" I asked. "We're here to make you feel good, nothing more. No strings, no jealousy. Just you, us, and a whole lot of pleasure."

I wanted to make sure she was comfortable with our intentions. Even though she'd never been with two men at once, I could tell she was intrigued by the idea. I was half lit by the wine and whiskey, but my protective instincts needed to be pacified—I needed to know this was what she wanted and that I wasn't taking advantage of her.

"Show me what it's like," she whispered, glancing back and forth between me and Lucian.

"Are you sure about this?" I asked, giving her the chance to back out. But she nodded, a sexy smile playing on her lips as she pushed her body closer to mine.

"Fuck, you're irresistible," I muttered, capturing her lips with mine. Our tongues tangled together, and we explored every inch of each other's mouths. Her taste was intoxicating, making me crave her even more. Lucian watched us intently, his breathing growing heavy. My hands roamed over Angel's curves, sliding up under her top. I was desperate to feel her soft skin beneath my fingertips. I wanted to fuck her so badly, to have every inch of her body pressed against mine.

"Let's get this off," I said, leaning her forward just enough to slide her top off and over her head. The fabric fell away, revealing her perfect breasts. They were round and pert, more than a handful, her nipples already formed tight peaks. Lucian growled with lust.

Angel nervously curled her fingers around a necklace I'd never seen her wearing before. I gently placed my fingers around hers, seeing that the pendant was a wolf. I wanted to ask her about it, but decided that was a story for another time. Instead, I let it fall between her breasts before drawing a lazy circle around one with my finger.

"Damn," Lucian breathed, his eyes locked on her exposed flesh.

As I continued to explore her body, I watched Lucian's hands trace up her legs while he planted soft kisses on her inner thighs. His fingers roamed up under her shorts, grazing over her pussy. His touch sent shivers through her body.

"Ana, I need complete access to you," he grunted, yanking her shorts off in a rough move. He dropped them onto the floor next to the sofa, pushing her legs apart to reveal her core. "You're so fucking beautiful...and so wet for us."

I moaned at the sight, cupping one breast in my hand while I licked and nipped at the other. My mouth closed around her hard nipple, sucking and biting gently as I continued to watch Lucian.

He shifted, positioning his mouth at her entrance, tantalizingly close but not yet touching her. "God, you're beautiful," he murmured before diving in for a taste. I could only stare, utterly enthralled, as his tongue flicked over her clit. Then he buried his face in her folds and devoured her.

Pulling back, he glanced from me to her, his lips coated with her juices. He groaned, "You have the most delicious pussy I've ever tasted."

Angel's eyes fluttered closed, an invitation for us to continue.

Together, we feasted on her, our tongues and hands working in tandem to bring her to the edge. She was caught between us, her breath coming in short, sharp gasps, and it only made me want her more. And as she trembled and moaned beneath us, I felt a surge of pride in giving my Angel such an indulgence.

I mimicked the rhythm of Lucian's licks, my tongue taking care of one nipple while my fingers pinched and teased the other. She squirmed, her breathy moans filling the room as Lucian plunged his tongue deep into her center. The scent of her arousal was intoxicating; I wanted nothing more than to taste her for myself.

Lucian grasped her ass cheeks, holding her in place as he continued his exploration. He slipped a finger inside her, and I couldn't tear my eyes away from the sight of him finger-fucking our beautiful girl.

"Mmm, fuck," I muttered, unable to resist touching her pussy any longer. My hand slid down her belly and over her mound to her swollen clit. I swirled my finger over the sensitive nub in tight circles.

"Fuck, don't stop," she begged, her breath coming in ragged gasps. It was intoxicating to see her like this, so uninhibited and craving more, her body writhing against our fingers and mouths.

It was clear she was close to the edge of orgasm, and I felt the urge to take control. My finger dove into her wet heat alongside Lucian's. We moved in unison within her tight channel, plunging deep within her as she rolled her hips against us.

Her body trembled with need as I curled my finger just right, brushing against that sensitive spot inside her. That was all it took for her to shatter, her body convulsing while she came undone.

Reflexively, I captured her lips in a passionate kiss, swallowing her cries as she rode out her climax on our fingers. When I finally pulled back, her eyelids were heavy with gratification. A satisfied smile spread across her face.

"Nice dessert," Lucian commented with a grin.

"Absolutely," I agreed, trailing my fingers up her belly, over her curves, and pausing between her breasts. "But we both know you need more, Angel."

Giggling, Anastasia replied, "You two play my body like a finely tuned instrument."

I lifted her up in my arms and headed toward the stairs. I glanced back at Lucian, raising a brow in question. He dropped his head to the side, smirking at me but making no move to follow. Frowning, I called over my shoulder, "Lucian, get your ass up here. Angel deserves to be properly worshiped."

"Right behind you," he replied, finally rising to join us in what promised to be an unforgettable night.

Chapter Thirty-Four

6/26

It was astonishing to think that these two guys, who had been so close to tearing each other apart earlier, were now teaming up to provide me with unimaginable pleasure—the kind I'd never dared to dream of. As Conan carried me up the stairs, I could only wonder what they had in store for me.

"Which way?" he asked when we reached the top.

Lucian, who had been here before, caught up to us and headed to the right. He walked straight to my king-size bed and ripped off his shirt without hesitation while toeing off his shoes. Conan continued to cradle me in his arms as we watched Lucian uninhibitedly shove his trousers off and roll onto the bed with his head facing up at the bottom edge. He was handsome and so well-endowed, but there was something about the power and charisma that Conan exuded that held me captive. I wanted to prove to him I was a lover willing to meet his needs no matter where they led.

Lucian's brows bounced, and he smirked at Conan as if they were sharing a secret message. The sight of him sprawled out on my bed, ready and waiting, sent a thrill through me. I tightened my arms around Conan's neck and leaned in closer, reveling in his strong, solid presence.

Conan playfully nibbled my neck just behind my ear, making me squirm. When he pulled back, his expression grew serious.

He leaned his forehead against mine. "Angel, what do you think about getting fucked by two men at the same time?" His question hung in the air, charged with raw intensity. My pulse jumped. Could it be that bad? So far, what they had done was fabulous. I'd seen my share of porn and read enough romance books to know that women loved being with two men. But obviously, there was the potential for things to go wrong, or else Conan wouldn't be so worried, which made me all the more nervous.

I hesitated, the idea both thrilling and intimidating. "As I said downstairs, I've never done it before, but the thought of doing it...with you and Lucian is a temptation I can't resist," I admitted.

Lucian chimed in, a smug grin on his face, "I took her v-card, but she would never let me pop her ass's cherry."

Conan's brow furrowed, his eyes darkening with concern. "What do you think about trying to take two dicks at one time?" he asked bluntly. The thought of me experiencing any discomfort set off such an intense protectiveness about him.

At this point, I was about to jump and run, but the night had been amazing so far, and I wanted to give these two men something special to remember me by. And the impending wedding hung over me like a dark cloud, so I wanted to make the most of my remaining days.

The lump in my throat made it hard to speak. "Do I have to?" I managed, my nerves twisting inside me.

Conan shook his head, a dark chuckle escaping him. "Of course not. There are plenty of ways we can fuck you until you don't remember your name," he said, glancing down at Lucian, who lay there with a cocky grin on his face.

I forced myself to relax, trusting that neither of them would push me past my limits. At least, I hoped that was the case.

Lucian's eyes sparkled with mischief. "Hand her over, Conan. Let's get her warmed back up."

Conan carried me over to the bed, keeping his eyes on Lucian. As he started to position me over him, there was a fire in his gaze, a raw hunger that made my breath catch.

"Looks like we're in for quite the adventure, Angel," Conan murmured.

He turned me around so I faced the headboard, then lowered me over Lucian until my legs were straddling his head, my knees were pressing against his shoulders, and my pussy was hovering just above his face. Lucian helped position me, his hands rough but tender as they skimmed over my legs, sending shivers through me. Conan's massive hand traveled from the base of my spine up between my shoulder blades, pushing me forward until my hands landed on either side of Lucian's hips.

The sight of Lucian's cock, so close and hard, made my mouth water. A surge of heat flared between my thighs, making me ache with anticipation.

Conan moved to the side of the bed, his gaze roaming over my body. "Fuck, you're beautiful like this," he said, his voice a rough growl. "Ass in the air and that hungry look in your eyes."

He reached over and trailed his fingers from the seam of my bottom to the nape of my neck, pulling my mouth to his for a quick kiss.

Fiery tingles shot from my lips to the apex of my thighs. Lucian's hands gripped my hips, guiding me down, and the next thing I knew, his tongue was flicking against my clit. My gasp was met with Conan's approving nod.

"Enjoying yourself, Angel?" he asked, his eyes locked on mine.

Biting my lip, I moaned in response, the sensation of Lucian's mouth on me driving me wild. My hands trembled as I reached for Lucian's cock. I wrapped my fingers around him and gave a firm stroke. Lucian groaned into me, his hips lifting slightly in encouragement.

Conan watched us with darkened eyes, his arousal evident against his jeans. "Take your time," he instructed, his tone low and commanding. "We've got all night."

"You like that he's watching you," Lucian said. "Now be a good girl and show him how fucking desperate you are for my dick," he demanded against my folds.

I slid my tongue up, across the bulging veins of his shaft. Then I flicked it across his sensitive frenulum before leaning forward and taking the tip into my mouth, the pre-cum leaving a salty taste. Just then, Lucian's thumb entered me as he nipped hard on my swollen nub with his teeth, causing me to throw my head back and gasp.

Conan growled, "God dammit, I need to get out of these fucking clothes."

By the time I glanced over at him, he was already shirtless and working his jeans off. The sight of his powerful body made my pulse race. I couldn't believe I was actually considering this—having two men I cared about fuck me at the same time. I'd never imagined this would turn me on so much, but here I was, practically shaking with eagerness.

A sigh slipped from my lips, and my whole body burned. I was on the edge of an orgasm from the mere thought of having both of them. Lucian noticed immediately. "Oi, what's got you so worked up suddenly, love? Your walls just clenched so fucking tight around my thumb. What are you thinking about?" he asked, his voice vibrating against my clit.

Conan chuckled, stepping closer. "Don't worry, Lucian. She'll be showing us exactly what she's thinking soon enough. Right, Angel?"

Before I could respond, Lucian hauled me tighter to his face, and his mouth went to work as if I were his ultimate feast. He devoured me, nipping at my clit and drawing it into his mouth with such intensity that my legs trembled. His tongue worked its magic on me, each movement precise and demanding.

"Mmm, fuck," I moaned, one hand gripping the sheets while the other held his cock between my lips. His mouth was relentless as he pushed me closer and closer to the edge.

Conan came up behind me, his hands warm and firm on my hips. "That's it, Angel," he murmured. "Show us how good this feels, how much you want this. Come all over his mouth."

I could barely think, lost in the pleasure Lucian was giving me. My moans turned into desperate cries, and I bucked against his mouth and hand, chasing the climax that was building so fast.

Conan's hands moved up my sides, brushing my breasts and tweaking my nipples. The combination of their touches sent me spiraling. I let out a muffled cry around Lucian's cock, my body convulsing with the force of my climax.

Lucian didn't let up, his tongue and lips drawing out every last shudder of satisfaction from my body. Conan pressed his chest against my back and wrapped his arm around my middle, grounding me, keeping me from completely losing myself in the sensations.

His breath brushed against my ear as I came down from the high. "That's my girl," he whispered. "But we're not nearly done yet."

Lucian's thumb slid out of me, and he moved his hands to my hip bones to help support my unsteady legs. "That's right, we're just getting started, Anastasia. Now it's our turn."

My breath hitched, the heat between us igniting all over again. This night was far from over. I was more than willing for them to do whatever they wanted with me.

I wanted to return the pleasure Lucian was giving me, so I stroked him firmly as I gently circled his crown with my teeth. When his cock jerked, a soft laugh escaped me. I was driving him just as crazy as he was making me.

Conan's hands and fingers circled over my lower back and ass as Lucian's tongue dove deep into my pussy once more, eliciting a whine from me. Conan slid his thumb between my cheeks, whispering, "I want to be the first to fuck this tight little ass of yours. But we'll need to ensure you're ready for it first."

He dragged the tip of his cock around the curve of my ass and downward, sending jolts of anticipation through me. Lucian grabbed hold of my cheeks, pulling me closer to his mouth while Conan pressed hard on the center of my back, forcing me to arch even more.

As I moved my lips further down Lucian's shaft, he inhaled sharply. At that, Conan drove himself inside my needy pussy, and I let out a loud groan against Lucian's cock, making him jerk against my throat.

"Fuck, Angel, you're so tight," Conan grunted as he slowly began pumping his cock inside me. My walls gripped him, making it difficult for him to move. He caressed my back tenderly and whispered, "Relax, baby."

I listened, focusing on my breathing and letting my body loosen up. As I did, Conan's pace gradually became more steady. "Good girl. That's the way," he praised me. "Even relaxed, you're still so fucking tight. Thank God you're dripping wet."

Every thrust from Conan pushed me further down onto Lucian, until my mouth was filled with his hardness and it bounced against my throat. Lucian's tongue made wet noises as he flicked and sucked, heightening my arousal. Conan gripped my hips, his fingers digging into my flesh as he moved with a powerful rhythm. The boundaries between us seemed to blur as we explored one another's bodies, driven by an insatiable hunger for connection.

Lucian's hands moved to my breasts, squeezing and kneading them as I bobbed my head up and down while sucking his cock. Our groans of satisfaction, the noises of our mouths licking and sucking, and the smacking of flesh on flesh created a symphony of lust that filled the room.

I was desperate to hold off my impending orgasm, wanting to come with both of them. So I took Lucian's dick into my throat, moving at a quicker pace. The curve of my throat started to catch against the ridge of his cock's crown. One of Lucian's hands slipped around to the back of my leg. "Ahh," Conan hissed out, and I knew Lucian had to be rolling Conan's balls in his hand by the sudden increase in tension inside me.

As soon as I realized what Lucian was doing, the first wave of my climax crashed through me, and I spiraled out of control. At the same moment, Lucian's hips drew up, and he shoved his dick into my mouth to the hilt. Hot cum shot down my throat. I swallowed hard a couple of times, pulling back, panting, and desperate for air as Lucian dropped his hips down.

"Fuck, yes!" Conan roared as his climax burst through. He dropped one hand on the bed next to me, pulling my hips against him with the other. His release filled me, and we rode out the last waves of rapture together.

The room was filled with our ragged breaths, the scent of sex thick in the air. After a minute of recovery, Conan growled, pulled out of me, and stepped back. "Fuck, it's sexy as hell watching my cum drip out of your pussy," he said.

Lucian, never one to miss an opportunity, pulled me forward a little. He leaned in, catching Conan's cum in his mouth, and then gave my folds a slow lick with the flat of his tongue.

"That's the hottest move I've ever seen," Conan admitted, his voice rough.

Lucian and I collapsed in a heap of tangled limbs, our bodies spent but deeply satisfied. This was a new level of intimacy, something I had never imagined but would never forget. I would file it away for future fantasies.

Lucian chuckled, then flipped me onto my side. The room spun as I tried to regain my senses, still swimming in orgasmic bliss. Conan walked over to my side of the bed, leaned one knee onto the mattress, dragged me up to rest against the pillows at the top, and slid into bed beside me. Lucian repositioned himself against the headboard on the other side.

Sandwiched between these two massive men, I couldn't have felt more secure. My king-size bed, which usually seemed too big for one, now barely accommodated the three of us. Conan's and Lucian's muscular frames took up most of the space, their warmth and presence enveloping me completely. I relished being so close to them.

Conan's fingers traced lazy patterns over my arm, his touch both gentle and possessive. "You're incredible, Angel," he murmured, eyes full of unspoken promises.

Lucian, always the playful one, leaned in and nipped at my ear. "Yeah, she is. And she's ours all night."

The implication of his words hung in the air, full of possibility. My heart raced, but it wasn't just from the physical sensuality. It was because of this connection we'd made, raw and untamed, and the realization that I was exactly where I wanted to be at this moment.

I giggled to myself. Lucian looked at me, curiosity lighting up his eyes. "What's so funny?"

I glanced from him to Conan. "Never in a million years did I imagine having sex with two men at once," I admitted, "especially not with two alpha types who wanted to tear each other apart just a few hours ago."

Lucian grinned, resting his hand casually on my hip. "Life's full of surprises, isn't it?"

Conan shifted beside me. "What happens if the mafia finds out you're not a virgin, especially the dude you're supposed to marry?"

I rolled my eyes. "It'll be too late. Knowing him, he wouldn't notice. He's probably only had sex with women he's paid, if that. The guy is a total loser. Even if he did realize I wasn't a virgin, he wouldn't say anything to save face. He likes playing with spreadsheets all day more than he likes sex, I'm guessing."

Conan's eyes darkened. "You're not marrying that guy."

I waved my hand. "I don't want to talk about it right now."

Conan tilted his head, a thoughtful expression crossing his face. "You were lost in thought when you first started going down on Lucian. What were you thinking about?"

I growled softly, my cheeks heating up. "I was thinking about your question, about what it would be like to have two men's dicks inside me at once." I paused, embarrassed. "I can't believe I just said that out loud. It was just some wild fantasy that popped into my mind."

"Really now?" Conan rose on his elbows slightly, looking over at Lucian. "What do you think, Lucian? Interested in helping our girl test her limits?"

Lucian chuckled. "The best sex is when you take your time and experiment with boundaries—no expectations, only *not-so-clean* fun."

Conan turned to me, his eyes filled with amusement and heat. "Angel, do you have any toys or lube?"

Lucian grinned, leaning over to the bottom drawer of my nightstand. "I know the answer to that." He started pulling out various vibrators and a tube of lube.

Mortified, I covered my face with my hands. "How did you know I had those?"

He shrugged, his smile widening. "I'm a snoop. I've known about them for a long time, but I didn't bring it up because I figured you'd say something if you wanted to play with them. Besides, we hardly ever come to your place for sex. It's usually in the office." He laughed, his fingers toying with a sleek vibrator.

I just shook my head, the embarrassment fading. Lucian slid his hand up my thigh, a wicked grin on his face. "Let's see what kind of fun we can have with these."

"Well, what are we waiting for?" Conan said, rolling off the bed. "How about you get on all fours," he instructed me, his tone leaving no room for hesitation.

I moved into position, sliding my shins along the cool sheets, and grabbed a pillow to hold under my chest. Conan set out the various toys on the bed, lining up the colorful, oddly shaped implements of pleasure like surgical tools, reminding me that he was a nurse.

"Do you believe that your men will take care of you? Do you trust us?"

"I do," I whispered, my voice steady despite the flutter of nerves in my stomach.

The vulnerability of being laid bare sent my pulse into overdrive. Being naked and on display, with my ass in the air, exposed me in a way that made me self-conscious. "I feel ridiculous," I admitted, a shaky laugh escaping my lips.

Conan moved closer, running his hand down my spine in a soothing gesture. "Relax," he said. "You look perfect. Let us show you how good this can be. Now, shut your eyes and focus on how your body responds—from your breathing to the tingles in your belly and the direct sensations from what we do to you."

I took a long, deep breath, then let it out slowly, trying to center myself. "I trust you both completely," I whispered. "I'm ready."

Conan's touch was reassuring, and Lucian's presence on the other side affirmed that the only two men who'd ever given me sexual pleasure were solely focused on me tonight.

Conan glanced at the toys spread out and smirked. "These are pretty basic, Angel. Ever thought about spicing things up?"

I shot him a look. "I wouldn't need toys if I had the right man."

He chuckled. Leaning in, he bit me playfully on the ass. "Point taken."

Lucian stretched out beside me, trailing his finger over my back and arm, gently nibbling on my shoulder. His hand slid up under me, fingers finding my clit, making me squirm.

Conan picked up the Air-Pulse Satisfyer and handed it to Lucian. "No lube needed for this one."

Lucian switched it on and moved it down to my clit, fiddling with it. I laughed at the awkward positioning, but then he adjusted it to where it hit the right spot, and I gasped.

Conan watched with a satisfied grin. "All right, Angel," he said, picking up the bullet vibrator and rubbing his thumb over the smooth surface. "This might be a bit big for your little asshole to start with, so I'll use plenty of lube. Let me know if anything hurts in a bad way."

I nodded, focusing on the softness of his fingers as he traced the curve of my ass cheeks. The cool lube made me shiver. Conan slid his fingers into my seam, brushing against my tight muscles. "Relax," he reminded me.

Lucian pulled the Satisfyer away and began toying with my nipple while pulling my butt cheek aside to give Conan better access. As Conan's fingers circled the tight ring, I took a deep breath, letting it out slowly. Lucian's touches, combined with the anticipation, had me panting.

Conan's finger pressed against my tight ring, and I willed myself to relax. Sliding under me, Lucian took my nipple into his mouth, and the combination of sensations drove me wild.

"Good girl," Conan praised as he eased his finger in. "You love this, don't you? Our dirty girl's thinking about getting her ass fucked."

"Tell us if it's too much," Lucian murmured against my skin.

I managed a nod, getting lost in the bliss. Conan added another finger, stretching me slowly. The pressure was intense, but the pleasure far outweighed any discomfort.

"Ready for more?" Conan asked.

"Yes," I breathed, craving everything they had to give.

Conan's fingers moved in a steady rhythm, opening me up while Lucian's tongue flicked over my nipple, his other hand gripping my hip.

Conan's other hand rested on my back, holding me in place. "You're incredible, Angel. So tight, so perfect," he said, sliding his fingers out.

"Just imagine your perfect pussy and tight hole wrapped around our cocks," Lucian whispered, his breath tickling my skin. He positioned the Satisfyer against me, quickly finding the right spot.

I relaxed into their touches, knowing I was exactly where I was meant to be.

Conan bent down and kissed the middle of my lower back. "Focus on the toy," he reminded me softly.

The cool point of the bullet pressed against my entrance. Conan nudged it in, pulled it out a little, then pushed deeper. "How are you doing?" he asked.

"Good, very good," I mumbled, barely able to form words.

"I'm going to slide it in. Relax and press out a little," Conan instructed. Lucian increased the speed of the Satisfyer. Electricity coiled within my core.

Slowly, Conan pushed the larger part of the bullet in, his fingers touching my outer ring. I was on the edge of my orgasm, loving this new dual sensation. This was naughty, wicked, and absolutely divine.

Then Conan clicked the bullet's vibrator on. It was like rocket fuel, igniting a mind-bending orgasm. My thigh muscles tightened. My entire body pulsed. Conan and Lucian held me in place until every shudder and whimper was over.

Conan removed the bullet, and Lucian slid out from under me, allowing me to collapse on the bed.

Conan chuckled. "I see you enjoyed that. Maybe I'll be able to pop that cherry tonight after all."

I curled up on my side, savoring the afterglow of the best orgasm I'd ever had. Conan sat on the bed next to me, trailing his fingers down my side, along my waist and hip, then back up, drawing small circles over my belly. I glanced at Lucian, biting my lip, nervous about asking for both men to take me at the same time.

Lucian caught my wanton look and suggested, "How about we take this to the shower? I'd love to slide my cock inside your tight pussy surrounded by the hot steam."

Conan groaned softly and kissed my shoulder. "Would you like to try taking both of us, Angel?" he asked.

"Mmm, that sounds divine," I responded, my heart racing with excitement and a hint of nervousness.

Lucian smirked at Conan. "I'll hold her, and then you can see what you can do about taking that tight little hole." He scooped me up, turning me so I straddled his waist. I laughed, the sound echoing off the walls as he carried me to the bathroom. He nipped my neck hard enough to make me squeal.

Conan followed, grabbing the lube. He turned on the shower to heat it up and set the lube in the niche. He then found some large bath towels and laid them out beside the shower.

Lucian carried me in, laving kisses along my neck. Conan followed, dipping his head under the spray and scrubbing his hand over his freshly cut hair before turning and leaning his back against the wall. A smirk curved his lips as his chin dropped toward his shoulder. He crossed his arms, watching, waiting. The lust radiating off him told me he was enjoying watching every caress Lucian made and my reaction to him too. He was an incredible man to allow me this indulgence when I knew good and well he wanted me only to himself.

Lucian held me by my thighs and lifted me up, situating me so that his already rock-hard cock was pressing against my entrance. Then he slid in, inch by gloriously thick inch, allowing me a moment to adjust to his size. My breath hitched at the fullness. With the spray of the warm water falling in rivulets down my skin, I began losing myself in the sheer ecstasy. I draped my arms over Lucian's neck and melted into his chest.

His heart hammered under my breast.

Conan grinned, his eyes gleaming with hunger. "Ready to pop that tight little ass's cherry?" he teased as he lubed up his dick. "The lube and steam will make me very slippery. You're gonna love how it feels."

Conan watched as Lucian started to pump inside me, his thrusts slow and deliberate. I slowly nodded to Conan and turned to Lucian, pulling his lips to mine and giving him a demanding kiss. I wanted to be lost in the ministrations of his mouth when Conan took charge of what was to come.

Conan's voice was husky with arousal. "I'm super fucking hard just thinking about this, Angel."

A tremble ran through me. Lucian pulled back slightly, despite my protests, and locked his eyes onto mine. "Eyes on me, Angel." He paused. "Remember, it's okay to stop at any point." Hearing the name Conan used for me fall from Lucian's lips stole my breath away. God, how I loved that term of endearment.

Positioning himself behind me, Conan wrapped his arm around my waist and slid his hand between us, down my belly and to my folds that were being stretched wide by Lucian. His fingers rimmed Lucians dick as his palm brushed across my clit, making us both groan. He moved his fingers and began stroking my clit, sending jolts of electricity through my body as he began to push his cock inside my tight hole. The initial pressure made me tighten instinctively.

"You've got to relax, Angel," Conan instructed. "Push out a little, just like with the bullet. If you can't, I won't enter you."

I wanted to give this to Conan, to show him how much I appreciated his acceptance of my flaws and his willingness to share me with Lucian. Taking a deep breath, I tried to relax, to push out as he suggested. Lucian stood still, holding his breath in silent anticipation. "Keep those eyes on me," he brusquely demanded. "I want to connect with everything you feel through those silvery blue pools."

Conan's fingers were gentle but insistent, stroking me, coaxing my body to respond. Gradually, I began to relax, allowing him to push a little deeper. The sensation was intense, a mix of pain and pleasure that made my bottom lip tremble.

"That's it, Angel," Conan murmured. "You're doing so good."

Lucian's eyes never left mine. "You're incredible, Angel. So fucking tight. I feel Conan through your wall."

As Conan pushed further inside me, my heart hammered in excitement. Being filled in both holes was intoxicating, unlike anything I'd ever dreamed. My body shuddered, a moan escaping my lips as the decadence built to an unbearable peak.

"Fuck, you're amazing," Conan groaned, his hands gripping my hips.

My breathing started coming in short, panicky gasps, and Lucian responded by kissing me hard. Desperate for a distraction from the overwhelming burning and stretching, but not wanting to give up or break this moment, I entwined my fingers in Lucian's hair and pulled him closer to me. His kiss was unrelenting as his tongue explored my mouth. What Lucian and Conan were doing was mind-blowing. Every nerve in my body was lit up.

"Just let go, Angel, and embrace the stretch," Lucian whispered against my lips. "We've got you."

And with that, I surrendered completely, giving myself to the two men who held me transfixed.

As Lucian took my mouth, I forced myself to fully relax. I let my mind drift to how good it had felt when the bullet entered me. Conan praised, "Now that's my good girl." Then he pulled out partway, added more lube, and finally pushed inside me, all the way to the hilt. A whimper escaped me, followed by a whining sound I didn't recognize.

My head fell back against Conan's chest, and I gasped for breath. "Oh my God, this is...this is so much."

Lucian started to pump in and out of me while Conan held still.

"I'm going to stay still while you adjust to my size," Conan whispered, keeping his hands steady on my hips. "Focus on Lucian's dick rocking in and out of you, sweet girl."

The fullness from both of them was intense, almost overpowering. Lucian's thrusts were steady, his eyes never leaving mine. Each movement sent waves of pleasure through me, making it hard to concentrate on anything else.

Lucian groaned, his fingers digging into my thighs as he increased his pace slightly.

"That's it," Conan whispered, once again sliding a hand between me and Lucian and swirling his finger over my clit. "You're taking us so well."

I tried to focus on Lucian's rhythm, letting his movements guide me.

Lucian's thrusts grew more urgent. "You're so fucking perfect."

"Let go, Angel. We've got you," Conan grunted.

Their combined efforts drove me toward my climax. My body tensed, a moan escaping my lips as the pleasure built to an unbearable peak. Lucian's thrusts grew erratic as he chased his own release.

"Come for us, Angel," Conan urged, his fingers working my clit with expert precision as his hips began to rock and his shaft pumped within me.

The coiled electricity in my belly spread through my body, and my cries echoed off the shower walls. Conan, sensing how close I was, matched his rhythm to Lucian's, both of them thrusting in and out of me feverishly.

Conan growled and bit down on my shoulder.

Lucian groaned. "Man, I've never experienced anything this good before. Her tight heat is so fucking delicious, and I can feel your dick stroking against mine."

The burning fullness was too much. Tears ran down my cheeks, but I refused to tell them to stop. The exquisite pain blended with my longing to please them, making it impossible to deny them—or myself.

Suddenly, my orgasm crashed over me, and stars flashed behind my lids as my inner muscles clenched and my thighs squeezed, setting off both Conan's and Lucian's releases. The force of their orgasms made me worry they might tear me apart or drop me, but they held me securely, pounding into me in perfect sync as we rode out our climaxes together.

And then all was quiet. We stood there, breathing raggedly, while the water sprayed down onto our spent bodies. Conan rested his forehead on my back while Lucian pressed his forehead against mine. Bit by bit, our breathing returned to normal. Conan pulled out first, and then Lucian withdrew, still holding me in his hands. A sudden sadness hit me at the loss of the physical connection to them. I wrapped my arms around Lucian's neck, burying my face in his neck.

He sat down on the bench, keeping me in his lap. Together, the guys carefully and gently began to wash every crook and crevice of my body. Lost in the euphoria, I remained quiet and smiled softly as I watched them tenderly take care of me.

Conan turned off the shower and handed Lucian a towel while grabbing another for himself. Together, they took their time drying me, their hands moving over my skin with loving care. Once they were done, they dried themselves off quickly.

Conan scooped me up in his strong arms and carried me to the bed, laying me down gently and stamping a kiss on my forehead. I didn't even care about my damp hair. Lucian slid in on one side, and Conan joined us on the other.

"How are you feeling, my sweet Angel?" Conan asked, pulling my back against his chest and draping his arm around my waist.

"I don't really have words for it. But good...very good," I whispered, snuggling deeper into him.

Lucian chuckled softly as he turned to face me, brushing a strand of hair from my forehead. "Guess we did our job right then."

Their bodies were solid and comfortable. I smiled, a wave of contentment washing over me. Being snuggled here between them made me feel special—loved in a way I hadn't realized I craved. Conan and Lucian were like a protective barrier against the world.

Within minutes, the night's exhaustion took over, and I drifted off to sleep, secure in the warmth of their embrace.

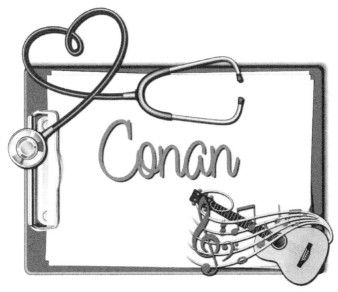

Chapter Thirty-Five

6/27

Though I was groggy from all the wine and whiskey, the rustle of movement stirred me awake. I opened my eyes to see Lucian leaving the bedroom. I realized Angel was sprawled out over my chest, her leg draped over mine. I took a couple of deep breaths, thinking about how completely satisfied and beautiful she had been in the shower, how Lucian and I had left her speechless. Her willingness and curiosity to engage in such a completely new kind of sexual connection fascinated me. Although sharing her with Lucian was an erotic encounter I'd never forget, it was a one-and-done situation for me. I'd been happy to indulge her, but I couldn't ever share her again. Angel was different. She's been given to me by an act of fate, and she was mine, even if she didn't know it yet.

I needed to talk to Lucian before he left, to get a better sense of his intentions and feelings for her. Carefully, I moved her off me. She stirred but then buried her face into the pillow, her lips slightly parted, and drifted back into a sound sleep. I got up quietly, leaving her wrapped in the sheets, her breathing soft and even. She looked so peaceful, but my mind was anything but. I hunted for my clothes, found my boxer briefs on the other side of the bed, and slid them on. Making my way downstairs, I found Lucian pouring himself a cup of coffee.

"Smells nice and strong," I said.

"Isn't that the only way to drink it? Here, have a cup," he said, handing one to me. He leaned against the counter, a smirk playing on his lips. "Last night was great, huh? I'm glad we worked through any issues between us and focused on what was important...giving our girl some pleasure."

Taking a sip, I hesitated before responding. I didn't want to cause a rift between us. I would need his help with this whole arranged marriage mess. Any conflict between us would put Angel in the middle. So I chose my words carefully. "Yeah, I'd do just about anything for her."

Lucian shook his head as his smirk broadened into a smile. "You're too obvious, dude. Your feelings for her are written all over your face."

Unsure of what to say but wanting to get right to the point, I dropped my chin toward my shoulder and eyed Lucian skeptically for a minute. "Tell me what your plans are for her. Do you just want to fuck her, or is there more between you? I know you've been in her life for a long time. How can you not have feelings for the woman?"

He set his cup on the counter, and his brows drew together as he rubbed the scruff on his chin. "Here's where you're mistaken, my friend. Ana and I have carefully maintained a sex-only, no-commitment arrangement. She is as close a friend as I have, much like the other men at the club, but that's all it will ever be between us."

"So do you see the two of you continuing to be fuck buddies?" I asked, unable to keep my tone from being caustic as the jealousy raged in my gut.

Lucian laughed darkly. "Buddy, you've got it so bad for the girl. And you know what? I think it's great that she's got someone like you now. I see the way you look at her. You worship her. She's lucky to have found a guy who would hop on a plane at a moment's notice and fly across the country to make sure she's safe. She's a good girl just trying to make her way in life under shit circumstances. Don't worry, you won't have any issues with me. If Ana wants to have an exclusive relationship with you, then I'll support it one hundred percent. No weirdness between us. You think you can manage that?"

"I can't share her," I said. "So all I can do is hope that's what she wants. If not, I don't know what I'll do."

Lucian gave me an understanding look. "First, we've got to help her deal with the fucking arranged marriage bullshit. It's hard to believe something that archaic is still happening."

"Agreed," I said quickly. "We need to figure out a plan for dealing with the mafia, even if it means I have to take Angel and live off grid or go to some other drastic measures to protect her."

Lucian nodded. "Let's meet at the club in a couple of hours to come up with a strategy. Going against the New York mafia isn't going to be easy. Not something I'd ever envisioned dealing with, but here we are."

"Sounds good."

Lucian glanced at his phone. "All right, I've gotta get out of here. Ana won't be surprised I left. I always keep things simple and leave before she wakes so there are no awkward conversations." He gulped down his remaining coffee and then headed out.

I stood there for a moment, absorbing everything he had said. I thought more about the nightmare ahead and how we'd protect Angel. The way he'd talked about her rubbed me wrong. It wasn't that I wanted him to have feelings for her or pursue a deeper relationship with her, but his detached coolness bothered me. He treated her with no more care than a drive-through pickup, knowing full well he'd been her first. And she accepted that as if she didn't deserve better. She was so resigned to the fact that she would marry some mafia goon that everything else was a privilege to her.

Witnessing this from a different perspective made me hate myself for doing the very same thing to so many other women. Sure, I had my fucked-up excuses, but that was all they were— excuses. No woman was just a vessel for men's gratification. Every single one was worth more. Dammit, I'd never do it again, regardless of what happened with my Angel. She'd changed me.

I decided to bring Angel breakfast in bed, hoping to ease her into the morning. Looking through her kitchen, I found an assortment of breakfast foods that I hoped would hit the spot.

I grabbed the bag of coffee beans and ground some for a fresh pot, taking a second to inhale the rich aroma before setting it to brew. As the machine hissed and gurgled, I grabbed a glass and poured some orange juice. She could definitely use some vitamin C. My mind kept circling back to last night. It had been intense, more intense than anything I'd ever experienced. I'd shared her willingly with Lucian to ensure she never felt like she had missed out on anything, and it was a decision I was at peace with, but it was clear to me now—I couldn't do that again.

Pausing, I wondered how Angel would feel about the threesome. She'd had a lot to drink. Maybe she had done things she wouldn't have otherwise. Would she regret it? Did she see me differently now that she had all her memories back? I scooped some strawberry yogurt into a bowl and sprinkled granola on top, trying to push those worries aside.

The way I cared for Angel was unlike anything I'd experienced before. It was risky, powerful, almost overwhelming. It had seemed like she was catching feelings for me too, right before she'd left Tacoma. But she was confronting more than anyone should ever have to—recovering from the wreck, the shock of regaining her memories, dealing with her father and the arranged marriage—which meant her emotions were all tangled up.

I didn't want to pressure her about what was happening between us, but I wasn't going to walk away either. She'd been through so much. My goal now was to protect her, both physically and emotionally, but I also wanted her to know that she wasn't obligated to be with me and that she could take her time to sort through everything. But damn, I had fallen hard for her, and I wanted to make her mine.

Once the coffee finished brewing, I poured a cup, savoring the strong, robust scent. I knew what I needed to do. Be patient. Be understanding.

I found a tray in the cabinet, arranged everything on it, and headed upstairs. I had to talk to her, to figure out where she stood with Lucian. Just because he wanted nothing more than sex didn't mean she felt the same way.

When I got to the door of the bedroom, I peeked in. The sight of her sprawled out on the bed, still lost in sleep, made my heart squeeze. She was mine, and I was going to protect her from everything, even if it meant taking on the whole damn mafia.

Balancing the tray, I nudged the door open wider with my foot and walked to the edge of the bed. Her stillness reminded me of the days she had spent unconscious. It occurred to me that she'd spent most of her life emotionally closed off, unconscious in a sense, without ever hoping to find love—much like I had been until she landed in my ED.

I placed the tray on the bedside table and sat on the edge of the bed. Gently, I brushed a strand of hair from her face, watching as she stirred.

She groaned softly, stretching before rubbing her eyes. "Morning, sleepyhead," I greeted her, unable to suppress a grin.

Opening her eyes, she blinked at me. "Morning," she croaked, her voice still heavy with sleep. She shifted and winced, moving a hand to her lower abdomen as she sat up.

"How are you feeling?" I asked, handing her the mug. "Thought you might like some good, strong coffee after last night."

Angel sat up, dragging the covers around her waist and taking the coffee with a grateful nod. "God, my head is killing me. I thought getting my memories back was the worst stabbing pain, but this might just be more dreadful." She blew on the coffee before taking a sip. "And...I'm sore in places I didn't even know could be sore."

I chuckled. "Yeah, wine and whiskey aren't the best combination if you want to avoid a hangover. And, well, taking two men for the first time...you'd have to expect to be a little sore."

She laughed weakly, then winced again. "No kidding. Yeah, I suppose that comes with the territory. But honestly, I don't mind. Last night was...something else. I'm so glad I trusted you."

She handed me the cup, threw the covers off, and darted into the bathroom.

"You okay?"

"Fine. Just gotta go," she said over her shoulder before shutting the bathroom door. After a little while, she walked out wearing an old, oversized T-shirt that barely reached her thighs. Her face was flushed and still damp from washing it, and her hair was tied up in a messy bun. A breathtaking smile was spread across her face, lighting up those icy blue eyes as she closed the distance between us. God, she was the most gorgeous creature. My cock rose to attention. There was no way I'd ever get enough of her.

I shifted from the middle of the bed, scooting down to the lower part so she could climb back in. With one foot resting on the floor and the other leg bent, I positioned myself so I could face her as she flopped back against the headboard. Her shirt rode up, giving me a glance of her pretty pussy. All I wanted to do was throw her down on the bed and worship every inch of her. I wished we could stay here all day and fuck until we both passed out, but I needed to get some clarity on how she felt first. Damn, it was hard to focus. I leaned forward, reached for the glass of orange juice, and handed it to her, trying to shake off my desire.

"Oh, you have no idea how good that looks," she said. "My head is pounding. You're right—the wine and whiskey combo did a number on me." She laughed, taking the cold glass and pressing it against her forehead. "But it was worth it. Last night was fabulous. More than I could have imagined. I trusted you and Lucian completely, and you both made me feel...cherished."

She giggled. The sound made my heart race and distracted me further. "I may not be able to sit much today," she continued, "but it will be a nice reminder of how incredible it was to have you inside me like that." She reached out, taking my hand and pulling me to her for a quick kiss. "Aren't you sweet, bringing me breakfast in bed? That's a first."

My brows bounced in surprise. "What, no man has ever done that? What a shame."

"Well, you know Lucian is the only other man I've ever been with, and he's not the type to do anything the least bit romantic. The few times he stayed the night here, he was up and gone before the crack of dawn. He likes to fuck and move on. No time for cuddles or chitchat."

I nodded, watching her take another sip of her juice. I wanted to know if she saw her relationship with him any differently now. "Hmm, that surprises me, knowing you've had a thing for years. You two seem pretty close to me. More than just fuck buddies."

"Oh God, don't call it that... Even though, I guess, bottom line, that's what we are. Lucian and I are friends and coworkers, and we're both in a place where we can't have or don't want any sort of emotional relationship. From the beginning, we were up front about it and have always respected that boundary. We made sure the other guys at the club understood what was going on so no one would be uncomfortable and we could all acknowledge it out in the open. Lucian and I enjoy each other physically, and that's it. No dinner dates or meeting up with friends and family outside of the club. He and I see each other the same as any of the other guys at Xyst. It's never been a big deal."

I studied her face, trying to gauge her emotions. "So, Lucian's still not a big deal?"

Angel took a sip of her juice, set the glass on the nightstand, and picked up the bowl of yogurt. After taking a bite, she chewed slowly as she contemplated my words. Then she looked at me and asked, "What I think you really want to know is *not* how I feel about Lucian...but how I feel about you?"

I hesitated, then nodded. "You're right. But I don't want to stress you out."

She huffed out a breath. "Just say what's on your mind."

"Okay, okay. So, now that you have your past and an entire life's worth of memories, I'm curious about your thoughts on what's happened between us these last few weeks. Especially our night together just before you left so abruptly."

Angel bit her lip. She took another bite of yogurt, then set the bowl down and scooted over to me, draping her legs over my lap. She curled around me, snuggling up to my chest, and I wrapped my arms around her tightly.

"You're different, Conan," she said. "You're the first person in my life that I've gotten to know in the light. Before waking up with amnesia, I lived every moment in the dark shadow of my family. I never knew what I was missing because I'd never known life any other way. The last month has irrevocably changed me. For the first time, I've tasted what life has to offer."

She paused, squeezing my hand. "Getting to know you was an unbelievable opportunity, one I'd never even imagined. You've been so good to me—better than I deserved, actually. You made me feel alive in ways I never thought possible. It wasn't just the sex—though God, that was amazing. It was everything about you. Your possessiveness made me feel like I mattered. The way you visited me in the hospital every day, playing your guitar and singing so passionately; your laid-back, easygoing manner that made you so approachable; and your willingness to help and accept me under such bizarre circumstances are all reasons I'll never forget you. It seemed like there was a world of future possibilities for us to share...until there wasn't."

I squeezed her, brushing a kiss over her temple before leaning back and taking a minute to soak in her warmth. "Why do you say all of that as if it's in the past tense?"

She raised her face until she met my eye, placing her hand on my cheek. A single tear rolled down her face. "Because I have an expiration date. In less than two days, my life will pretty much be over."

Then she leaned against my chest, her silent tears leaving wet trails.

Wrapping my hand around her head, I dropped my chin to the top of her hair and rocked her back and forth in my arms.

When she began to tremble, I tightened my hold on her. "My Angel...listen to me," I said, my voice low and raspy. "If it's the last thing I ever do, I will get you out of here—away from this toxic mafia life, away from that scumbag Frankie, and away from your abusive family. You're not marrying him. I swear to you, I'll take you away from all of this."

She jerked away from my embrace, turning to face me with wide eyes. Sniffing, she wiped her tears away and stared at me. "Conan, you can't fight this battle for me," she insisted in desperation. "You can't take on three mafia family syndicates. I can't stand the thought of you putting yourself in danger for me. The Volkovs have already caused enough pain in your life and your family's lives. Besides, how bad can marrying Frankie Moretti be?"

She gripped my shoulders tightly. "Promise me you won't fight for me." Her voice cracked. "The time we shared—even though it was short—was the best of my life. I'm grateful for having at least tasted the freedom to love and be loved."

Tears streamed down her face, and she clung to me. "Please, just make love to me, Conan. Don't think about anything else. I want to know what it feels like to have an emotional connection, not just a physical one. I want to know what it's like to have a man make love to me at least once in my life."

Her words cut through me like a knife. I cupped her face, wiping away her tears with my thumbs. "Angel, I..."

"Please, Conan," she begged. "Don't speak of the future or anything outside of the here and now. Let's just focus on what we have, because none of us are promised a tomorrow."

I tugged her to me, my lips finding hers in a desperate kiss. She cupped the back of my head, pulling me closer as if she could meld us together. Her mouth was warm and soft, tasting faintly of strawberry yogurt. My lips found hers. Our breaths mingled, creating an intoxicating mix that made me want to lose myself in her.

I lifted Angel in my arms and pivoted, placing her gently on the bed. Then I leaned over on one knee. Starting at her hips and tracing the curves of her body, I slid my hands up her sides, taking the T-shirt with me. I pulled it off over her head and tossed it to the floor. Then I shoved down the boxer briefs I was wearing and climbed into the bed next to her.

Lovingly I kissed away her tears, trailing my lips down her neck, along her collarbone, then between the swell of her breasts, breathing in her scent. She smelled like vanilla and something uniquely her, something that drove me wild. She arched her back as I kissed and nibbled. While my fingers glided over her skin, I lavished attention on her breasts.

Her hands roamed over my back, tracing the lines of my muscles. She sighed softly and melted into my touch. I wanted to give her everything, to make this moment something she'd never forget.

I brushed kisses down her center and over her mound, finally settling between the apex of her legs. There I took my time, savoring the way she tasted and the way she responded to me. Slowly, I licked and explored her folds as she gripped the back of my head.

"I miss your long hair and being able to twist my fingers in it," she whined, searching for a way to get the friction she craved. I slipped a hand under her leg and grasped her hip, tugging her closer to me, giving her what she begged for.

Her body shuddered, and she let out a moan. "Oh God, Conan...yes..."

I licked and swirled my tongue over her clit, diving a finger into her wet channel. "God, you're so wet and tight, my Angel," I praised, increasing the speed of my finger and the flicking of my tongue against her clit in a coordinated rhythm. Under my ministrations, she writhed and moaned, spurring me on.

Her breathing became erratic, and she started bucking her hips against my mouth. Needing to give her more friction to reach climax, I sucked her clit into my mouth, flicking my tongue quickly and more firmly. At the same time I curled my finger within her, brushing over her sensitive spot. She cried out, her body tensing as she tumbled over the edge. Her inner muscles clenched around my finger while she exploded.

I loved the way she came all over my face, the way her body trembled with pleasure. Satisfied, I continued my strokes, prolonging her orgasm until she was spent and her body collapsed back onto the bed. This was only the beginning of what I wanted to do to her.

I moved up her body, kissing her hip bone, tracing circles over her skin with my tongue, and positioning my hips between her legs. Her chest heaved with each breath she took, and her eyes were glazed with satisfaction. My lips traveled along her ribs, between her breasts, and up her throat before capturing her mouth in a passionate, loving kiss. It wasn't hard or demanding; I wanted her to feel loved and cherished. I savored the thought that she could taste herself on my lips. Playfully, I bit her lower lip and sucked it into my mouth. Her breath hitched, and I smiled against her skin.

"I love making you feel this way," I whispered, brushing a strand of hair from her face. "You're so beautiful."

I kissed her deeply. This was more than just physical. This was something that made me want to protect her, cherish her, and never let her go.

Sliding my arms up under hers, I cradled her head in my hands, tangling my fingers in her luscious brown locks. This time, I would be careful and tender with her—it was all about her pleasure. The head of my cock pressed against her entrance, and I gradually slid inside her, inch by tantalizing inch. My kiss turned more fervent, and I groaned. "Your tight heat feels so good wrapped around my cock."

Pausing for a moment, I allowed just enough of my weight to rest on her body to make her feel surrounded and protected without discomfort. Then I began to rock my hips, pumping in and out of her in a slow, sensual rhythm. She tried to moan, but I refused to let go of her mouth, swallowing all her delectable sounds as my hands pulled her close to me in a claiming embrace.

We moved together, lost in the moment, lost in each other. Every touch, every kiss, was filled with a passion that went beyond words. I sensed her need for this connection, and I gave everything I had.

When my climax surfaced, I held back, knowing she needed more time and more contact from me to reach her peak. I refused to come until she did, so I adjusted my hips until my pubic bone was rubbing against her clit, then increased my pace.

I kissed her, and feelings I'd never allowed myself to acknowledge welled up. My heart was so full it was breaking. Struggling to keep my composure, I rocked my hips deliberately, rubbing against her nub as she built toward another orgasm. Our breathing grew erratic. I trailed kisses along her cheek and behind her ear, finally burying my face in her neck.

A flood of raw, unrestrained love and vulnerability surged through me and suddenly, emotions that I had never been brave enough to face before bombarded me. I refused to pull back, desperately trying to hide the tears I didn't dare let her see. "Let go and come," I whispered against her skin. "I want to feel your muscles squeeze my cock and milk the cum from me." She was close but still held back. "On three," I growled. "One... two...three."

Like a good girl, she did exactly what she was told. Her knees pulled up, her thighs tightened, and she came hard, screaming my name and begging that I come too. My balls pulled tight, and I exploded inside her. Our bodies convulsed together, riding out the waves of our climax, and then I collapsed on top of her, my face still buried in her neck. I was so choked up I could barely breathe.

"I'll never share you again," I whispered so softly I didn't know if she heard me.

We lay there together, the world outside forgotten. In that moment, nothing else mattered.

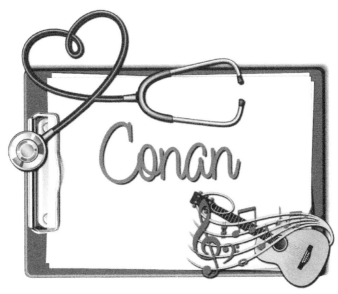

Chapter Thirty-Six

6/27

I buried my face in Angel's neck, fighting back the turmoil that raged inside me. This girl was wrecking me, and she didn't even know it. I had to fucking get myself together. If Angel saw me upset, it would hurt her confidence in me. She might worry that I wouldn't be able to protect her from the mafia's arranged marriage and those who would harm her if she didn't comply.

She traced her fingers along my sides and back. "You always make me Jell-O in your arms. I seriously don't know if I'm going to be able to walk," she said, breathing heavily. "You all good?" she asked, sensing my angst.

"Yeah, more than good." I sniffed, cleared my throat, and turned my face from her neck to kiss her cheek. Pulling out of her, I rolled onto my back and heaved her onto my chest, giving me the chance to regain my composure.

"Angel," I said, giving her a playful squeeze. "I'd love nothing more than to stay in bed and fuck you six ways to Sunday, but we've got to get up and face reality. Lucian told me earlier that he and the other guys would meet us at the club, and they're probably already waiting."

She focused on me, her icy blue eyes full of sadness and hope and regret and a world of other emotions. "I never want this moment to end," she whispered. "Conan, you make me feel... safe. More than that, you make me feel valued. You're the first person who has ever made me feel truly alive. Before I met you, my life was on a course dictated by others. You've shown me what it means to be cherished, to matter. Every moment with you is a gift I never thought I'd get. I don't have the words to express how much you mean to me, but know this: you are my strength and my courage. I trust you with my life—with my heart. I've never experienced anything like this, and I never will again. You're everything I never knew I needed."

Her words ignited a fire within me, a burn that would forever mark my soul. I pulled her closer, tenderly capturing her lips. Holding her face in my hands, I poured all of myself into that one kiss—my promise to protect her, my desire to worship her body forever, my unwavering commitment to her until the end of our days.

When we finally pulled apart, I pressed my forehead to hers. "I promise you eternity, Angel. I will protect you, no matter what. You're mine, and I won't let anyone take you away from me."

Her eyes shimmered with unshed tears. She took my face in her hands, planting kisses all over my face. "We may only have today and tomorrow, but I will forever hold you in my heart. You've given me a lifetime's worth of love, and no matter what happens next, I have no regrets."

After giving me a final, chaste kiss, she slipped out of bed, leaving me breathless and more determined than ever.

With that, we rushed to shower and dress. As I tugged on my clothes from the previous day, Angel laughed.

"Looks like you could use something clean to wear," she teased, slipping into a pair of leggings and a flowy yellow top.

"Guess I'll have to make do."

"Why don't you and Braxton stay here? I have an extra bedroom. Don't you think it'll be easier for all of us to be together right now?"

"I was just about to tell you I wasn't going to let you out of my sight," I said, a smirk tugging at my lips. "I'm glad you suggested it."

I found my phone lying on the floor and called Braxton. He answered on the first ring.

"Everything okay?" he asked.

"For the moment, yes. Angel has invited us both to stay with her while we try to figure things out. Think you could get on over here with all our stuff? I could use a change of clothes."

"Sure, no problem," he said before hanging up, not making any effort to linger on the call.

While we waited for him to arrive, we started cleaning up from the night before. A few minutes later, the intercom buzzed repeatedly, interrupting us. Angel buzzed the person in and found a local courier in the vestibule, holding a large box. "Sign here," the man said, handing Angel a tablet and stylus.

She signed for it and then brought the box into the living room. After dropping it onto the center of the sofa, she untied the strings and opened the lid. Inside was a beautiful wedding gown and a fancy black dress. Angel sat down, pulling the wedding dress partially out of the box, fingering the intricate lace. A sad expression overtook her features.

"What a waste for such an incredible dress," she lamented. "This whole wedding is such a farce."

I walked over and stood beside the sofa, lifting her chin with my fingers. "Don't be sad, my Angel. It's just a dress. Focus on what your life will be like once you're out from under your family and the marriage contract."

She sighed, nodding. "You're right. I was hardly involved with any of the wedding planning anyway. My aunt Elena took care of everything. I was supposed to help with the arrangements this past month, but instead, I was lost in Tacoma. I'm sure she's handled it all without me, exactly as she wanted it. Frankie's family hasn't even met me yet. Can you believe that? Considering he's forty-six, his older sisters haven't been eager to connect with his twenty-seven-year-old contract bride. We were all supposed to have dinner the Thursday after I left for Tacoma. I wonder what Frankie thinks about my disappearance. I bet Aunt Elena has made up a bunch of lies."

"Who knows and, honestly, who cares?" I said. "One way or another, I'm going to get you out of this mess."

I moved to sit on the other side of the sofa, where I'd sat last night, the dress box between us. When I stretched my arms out along the back edge, our shenanigans replayed in my mind. Food, wine, and whiskey had opened up possibilities I'd never imagined.

"What are you smirking about over there?" she asked, reading my face. I bet she knew full well what was running through my mind.

I didn't answer her. I needed to change the subject before I acted on my impulses.

Making a U-turn, I asked, "So, why did you just up and leave Tacoma without saying a word?"

She sat there, speechless, as though she hadn't expected me to ask that question. She obviously still didn't know me that well. I wasn't one to mince words. I'd always been the type to just say what I was thinking.

"I didn't want to put you in any more danger than I already had," she finally answered. "I never dreamed you'd be so bold and follow me here, much less find me in the middle of Manhattan, for Christ's sake. But you did, and here we are. Now, you pretty much know all my deep, dark, ugly secrets, and you're still hanging around." She let out a cleansing breath. "Besides, I did send an email explaining everything."

"Yeah, to Sam."

"I had no clue how to contact you. I don't have access to any souped-up Atticus-fueled tech measures like you do."

"Well, it had better never happen again." I said this in jest, but it came out with a sharper edge than I'd intended.

"Oh, my God, don't be so butthurt. We're obviously past that already." She moved the box with the dresses to the coffee table, walked over to the kitchen counter, and grabbed her phone. When she returned to the sofa, she tossed me her phone and sat next to me. "How about you enter your contact info and anyone else's you can think of?"

Glancing down at the unlocked phone, I hesitated. "Do you think this thing could be hijacked by your uncle...what was his name, Luca?"

Angel's eyebrows scrunched as she cocked her head. "Hmm, I doubt it. But Nik, on the other hand, he'd definitely be the type to do something like that."

"Then maybe I shouldn't put my information into it?"

"Honestly, Conan, knowing Nik, if he wanted to know your number, he'd find it. He's a born-and-bred Volkovi Notchi. I just wish I knew what he was thinking."

She was right. If these mafia types wanted someone's number, they had their ways to find it. I entered my number, as well as Atticus's and Braxton's, and handed it back to her. She stared at the phone and frowned.

"I should have already called Aunt Elena. I'm sure Uncle Luca told her I stopped by his office yesterday, and she'd expect that I would call her right away. I just don't want to talk to her. Ugh."

"I wouldn't worry about your aunt," I said. "She knows how to reach you. Where's Luca's office again? And why did you go there first thing?"

"It's in Tribeca," Angel replied. "It's a beautiful building. You'd be surprised by how many ventures Uncle Luca's involved in. Most of them are legitimate and make good covers for the illegal stuff. Not that I know much about the details. As a girl, I spent most of my time at boarding school, and then, when I was off at college, I lived in a dorm. I was never close to my family except for my brother Nik, and I only saw him once or twice a year. During holidays, I would see my aunt and uncle, but my family would always send me away to camps or summer internships when I got older."

"That must have been hard on a twelve-year-old girl," I said. Shaking my head, I tried to piece together what I'd learned about her past. "So, Luca is an intimidating underboss who signed a contract basically selling you to a man, yet he was always warm to you? That's nuts."

She chewed on the corner of her mouth, taking a minute before she replied. "It's hard to explain my relationship with Luca. He's always good to me, but in a more formal way. He likes the fact that I look him in the eye and speak to him without pretenses though. As a kid, I used to ask him a lot of questions and talk his ear off every holiday. I had no idea he was a stone-cold killer. It wasn't until after college that I started connecting the dots about who the Genovese family really was."

Angel explained how she'd uncovered details about the Genoveses and other New York mafia families after she started working at one of the Kennedy University libraries. She'd learned a lot about their history but not much about the modern-day family.

"You see, arranged marriages are very common among mafia families, dating back to the beginning of the organization's history, when Italian immigrants, especially from Sicily, arrived in the United States. They brought their traditions and criminal organizations with them."

"But marriage contracts aren't legal in our country," I said. "Why would anyone go along with something that's practically human trafficking? I don't get it." I still couldn't believe she lived in a world where this kind of thing seemed so commonplace.

"They may not be legal, but they are definitely enforceable by mob justice. You see, mafia contracts and disputes are governed by the Commission, which formed after the Castellammarese War consolidated power among the American families." She paused to gather her thoughts. "I was always raised to live as a daughter of the mafia. I never questioned it, because it was all I'd ever known. That is, until I wrapped a car around a tree and had some sense knocked into me."

I frowned. "Don't joke about that. You could have died. But I'm glad you were brought to me for care, because you changed my life."

Angel's eyes softened, and she reached for my hand. "You've changed mine too, Conan. Thank you. You'll never know how grateful I am for everything you've done for me. You've been my rock through all of this."

I leaned over and kissed the top of her head. The more I learned about her, the more impressed I was by her toughness.

Just then, the intercom rang again. Angel pushed off the sofa and went to answer it.

It was Braxton with all our luggage.

"Great timing," Angel said. "Welcome to my place. Let's get you settled and then head to the club."

Braxton nodded, taking in his surroundings as he walked in. "Good to see you, Angel. Thanks for letting me crash at your place."

"No problem. Sorry for the awful circumstances. I never imagined you two would come after me. It's good to have you here though, even if it kills me knowing it's putting you in danger."

"Don't worry about it, hun," he said. "We did the same for Samantha. If you can't stand up for what matters, then you're not much of a man. It's always been just us. We might give each other hell, but if anyone comes after one of us, they're taking on all of us."

"You Thorin brothers are something else. You've got your own brotherhood. Kind of like a mafia family without all the... illegal shit." Angel smiled and showed Braxton to his room as I took my bag to her room and changed clothes.

When I came back downstairs, they were chatting in the kitchen. I joined them and leaned against the counter next to Angel. "You ready to get to the club and figure out how to deal with all this crazy-ass bullshit?"

She smirked. "I'm sure all my guys will figure it out."

I mimicked her, "*All your guys*, huh? You need more girlfriends and fewer men in your life."

She rolled her eyes dramatically, shooting back, "Jealous much?"

I pulled her in for a rough kiss, stroking her throat with my thumb. "When this is all over, I'll show you just what effect rolling your eyes has on me, my Angel."

She laughed, but I just shook my head. She really didn't have a clue about the things I wanted to do to her. "Let's go," I said, giving her a playful smack on the ass as we headed for the door.

We took the subway, which wasn't very busy at this time of day. Once we arrived at Club Xyst, we immediately met up with Lucian, Lachlan, Julian, and Gabriel and went up to the office.

When we were all seated around the conference table, Lachlan leaned forward, his eyes on Angel. "How about we start by you explaining more about how you fit into the Genovese crime family, especially since you have a biological Russian mafia family too. It's so hard to believe you're some mafia princess."

Angel opened her mouth to speak, but her phone rang. She glanced at the screen, groaning. "It's my aunt Elena. I should have called her yesterday. She's going to be raging mad."

She answered the call, putting it on speaker and setting it on the table. "Hello, Aunt Elena."

Elena's voice came through, sharp and scathing. "Anastasia, your disrespect is wholly uncalled for. You should have called me the moment you were back in town. Is your memory as bad as your driving? If I didn't know better, I'd think you were intentionally provoking me. Showing up unannounced at Luca's office and ignoring me for an entire day! Forcing me to shoulder the burden of *your* entire wedding! Have you forgotten that you are to be wed on Saturday?"

Frowning, Angel reached up to trace the scar on her forehead. "My memories came back in a rush, and I flew to New York that same day from fucking Tacoma, Washington. I met with Uncle Luca first thing the next morning, and I assumed he'd tell you I was back. If you wanted to talk to me, you could have called anytime."

"Watch your mouth and remember your place," Elena snapped.

Angel took a deep breath. "I'm sorry, Aunt Elena. I've had a lot to deal with since I got back."

"Is that so? And do you think that excuses you from your responsibilities? The wedding is in less than two days, Anastasia! Tonight is the rehearsal dinner. Everyone will be coming over to our house following the rehearsal at the church, even Father Russo."

Angel glanced around the table. All of us watched her intently. "I know. I'm just trying to figure things out."

"Figure things out?" Elena snapped. "There's nothing to figure out. You will get yourself properly dressed and meet us at the church at three p.m. Keep in mind you have a duty to this family." She let out a huff. "At least you're no longer a vapid idiot traipsing around Tacoma with a pack of fools that Viktor is out to kill. I see you had enough sense to get yourself home."

My fists clenched as I started to rise from my seat. Elena's treatment of Angel was intolerable.

Lucian, ever the diplomat, stretched out his hands and waved for everyone to stay calm. He mouthed to Angel, "*Keep her talking. Let's get as much information as we can.*"

Angel's jaw tightened. "How did you know I had amnesia?"

"We've all known, Anastasia—Luca, Viktor, Valentina, Nik, and I—since the day you so carelessly drove into a tree."

"Why didn't you come to help me in the hospital?"

Elena cackled. "Silly girl, why would I risk linking myself to the Volkov matters in Tacoma by going to the hospital? Now, focus. All the wedding arrangements have been made. As you know, the plan is for a small traditional wedding mass, mostly for the families. Tonight, at the rehearsal, just go along with whatever Father Russo directs you to do. I've met with Frankie over the last few weeks, explaining your situation and that we had someone ready to retrieve you. He knows you've been in Tacoma recovering from a car crash but has no idea you had a brain injury. We didn't want him to think you might end up being a burden to him. We were just about to remove you from Dr. Thorin's home when we realized you'd left. We lost track of you for a few hours but then picked back up on your whereabouts when you bought an airline ticket on your credit card. So thank you for taking care of that yourself and not putting us through the unnecessary stress of having to take you by force. I guess I should be thankful for that much at least." Elena let out an irritated breath. "So I assume you received the dress and will be on time, hmm?"

Angel's head dropped, and she massaged her temples in frustration. "Yes, ma'am. I received the dress this morning." Her voice was strained, and the way she kowtowed to her aunt made my skin crawl. It was obvious she'd been browbeaten her entire life, and it took all the self-control I could muster not to react.

Elena continued, "This is an important social event, so be on your best behavior. You'll meet Frankie's sisters and his groomsmen this afternoon. Look your best, skip the gaudy makeup, and act like a proper young woman. Remember, only speak when spoken to. I am relieved you're not a babbling idiot after your little accident. Don't disappoint us, Anastasia."

With that, she hung up.

The room was filled with a charged silence as we all fumed. Lucian finally broke the tension and spoke first. "What a fucking piece of work!"

Braxton added, "I've never heard someone so arrogant and uncaring."

Gabriel crossed his arms. "We need a plan, and we need it now. This isn't just a wedding—it's a death trap."

Lachlan nodded. "Agreed. But we're going to have to be careful to figure out how to get Ana away from all this without setting off a war."

"Lucky me. I got to go to Tacoma for my bachelorette trip, and slamming into a tree was the highlight of my pre-wedding plans," Angel joked darkly.

"Hey, at least you got to meet me," I said, giving her an apologetic grin. Rising to my feet, I went to lean against the table next to her. She looked up at me through her eyelashes and half smiled.

We debated whether Angel could skip the rehearsal dinner, but it quickly became clear that this would tip Elena and the others off. Her family was eager to see her married off, so we figured she was in no immediate danger being around them. Julian, who apparently had experience surveilling people, offered to watch Elena's house during dinner and keep an eye on Angel. He would be careful to stay just close enough to help her if she needed it. I didn't like the idea of her going alone, but I wanted some time to investigate a few things on my own, so I went along with it.

As we discussed the rehearsal at the church, tonight's dinner, and the wedding, Angel grew more anxious, her foot bouncing up and down. She'd been too quiet, so I reached out to her, pulling her to her feet and wrapping her in a big bear hug. She buried her face in my chest. "I'm so grateful to have you in my life," she whispered.

The guys exchanged looks, and Lucian gave me an approving smile.

Angel pulled away and sighed. "I need to call Nik. I didn't tell him I was leaving, and I want to know where he stands.

His mixed messages have left me unsure if he's on Viktor's side or mine."

Picking up her phone, she scrolled through her contacts and called him, but there was no answer. Her shoulders slumped, and she looked deflated. She shrugged. "I guess I'll try again later."

It was after one o'clock, and she needed to go home, get dressed, and head to the church. We agreed to reconvene tomorrow morning. Hopefully, we could make a solid plan after she learned how the wedding was set to go down. There was so much we didn't know about these people. One thing was clear though—they were all violent assholes who didn't care about killing people, so we needed to proceed with caution.

Chapter Thirty-Seven

6/27

Conan stood on the stoop in front of my house, arms crossed, with an expression that could freeze hell.

"Thank you, Julian. I'll see you tomorrow," I said as I exited his car.

I was so thankful that Julian had been true to his word and had kept watch outside Aunt Elena's house. When I'd bolted from the rehearsal dinner, he had taken me straight home.

Before I had even crossed the sidewalk, Conan was there, hoisting me up by the waist. I jumped into his arms, wrapping my legs around him. My dress bunched up around my hips, giving whoever was near a free peep show. He kissed me ferociously, like he hadn't seen me in forever. Then he turned and carried me straight into the kitchen, plopping me down on the counter without breaking our kiss.

373

As he devoured my mouth, a loud clearing of a throat interrupted us, and we wrenched ourselves from each other. Conan took my face in his giant hands and pulled me in for a sweet kiss on the forehead, inhaling slowly through his nose, his jaw clenched, clearly annoyed by the interruption.

"Well then, looks like you're unscathed," Braxton said with a chuckle. "When Julian texted us you'd requested a fast exit, we didn't know what to expect."

Conan and I turned and faced him. Here I was, precariously perched on the counter with my dress hiked up, flushed from his passionate kiss. Meanwhile, Conan had an obvious pocket rocket.

"You would be right," I said, motioning for Conan to step back so I could hop off the counter. "What a suffocating night. From the moment I arrived at the church until just a few minutes ago, I was held hostage to my aunt's fuckery."

My blood boiled, and I stormed around the apartment, replaying the awful encounter in my mind. I paced back and forth, flailing my hands around as I began ranting to Conan and Braxton.

"I'm telling you guys, from the minute I stepped into St. Peter's Church, it was like I'd been transported back to childhood—everyone treating me like I was still twelve. From the get-go, Bianca and Carlotta, Frankie's older sisters, stared at me like I was a stray dog that had wandered into their precious garden. They barely spoke to me, just enough to get the introductions over with," I all but shouted.

"Then there were his parents, whom I was directed to address as Mr. and Mrs. Moretti only. Now let me just say, I've known intimidating people—my parents are no saints—but these two exuded menace as if it was second nature to them—a legacy of their mafia family roots, I'm sure. The way they watched me, it was like they were sizing up a lamb for slaughter. And those groomsmen, Frankie's friends, leered at me the entire time. Disgusting, lecherous pigs, eyeing me like a piece of meat. I can't even remember their names, but his best man leaned in close and said, *'Can't wait to have my turn with you after Frankie's done. Hope you're ready for a real man.'*"

Conan's face went crimson, fury radiating from him. He clenched his teeth until his jaw started twitching, but I didn't stop. I needed to get it all out.

"Aunt Elena orchestrated everything like it was her big Broadway debut. Everyone marched to her orders, even Father Russo, who I used to think was unshakable. He just went along with whatever she said. And me? I barely got a word in. Frankie's sisters complained nonstop, especially about the dressing room at the back of the church. Too small. Too old. They even griped to Father Russo about everything."

I paused for a breath, thinking about St. Peter's.

"I love that church. It has always been my safe haven, a place where peace and kindness thrived amidst the cold indifference I endured from my family during visits to the city. But Frankie's family, they were so irreverent and bitchy. The stained glass, the tabernacle, the altars—they respected none of it. Can you believe that?"

I stopped pacing and turned to face Conan and Braxton, who were both now leaning against the counter, listening intently. "After the rehearsal, I was shoved into a town car with Frankie and his family. That ride to Elena and Luca's home was the longest, most uncomfortable hour of my life. No one said a word. We just sat there in this oppressive silence. It was horrendous.

"When we got to the house, it was as cold and formal as ever. I felt like a stranger. The food was pretentious and gross too. They served some weird caviar dish that smelled like rotten fish and a foie gras that looked like a science experiment gone wrong."

Conan and Braxton's expressions hardened as they listened. "I kept trying to get a private word with Luca, but Elena clung to him like a leech. The one moment I got with him when I first arrived, Luca hugged me, kissed my cheeks, and whispered, *'Trust me, I'm taking care of everything.'* Cryptic as hell. I had no idea what he meant, and I wanted to talk further, but my aunt wouldn't leave his side."

I started to pace again.

"As the dinner wore on and the alcohol flowed, my aunt made a couple of remarks about how I should just stay with them until after the wedding so I wouldn't cause any more trouble. That put me on edge. Then I overheard her telling Bianca and Carlotta that my appearance was atrocious and that she was going to have a couple of personal stylists come and *whip me into shape.* She suggested I stay the night so they could start on my *reformation* first thing in the morning. They cackled, and Bianca made a nasty remark about the scar on my forehead." I traced it with my fingers, reminding myself how Conan had called it a badge of courage.

"Those two make Cinderella's stepsisters look like Goody Two-shoes," I muttered.

Conan looked ready to break something.

"Settle down, brother," Braxton warned, glancing at Conan's clenched fists. But it was too late. Conan picked up a glass and hurled it against the wall, shattering it into pieces.

"Your family is sick, Angel. I want to kill those motherfuckers for treating you like that and thinking they can marry you off to that bastard Frankie..."

Braxton placed a hand on his shoulder. "Breaking stuff won't help."

Seeing Conan so angry, I tried to wrap up my rant. "So, anyway, I panicked, thinking Elena might hold me against my will, and texted Julian to pick me up at the end of the driveway. Then I bolted out the back patio door, around the house, down the driveway, and there he was, thank God. The only reason I got away without being noticed was because no one would ever expect me to do something that audacious."

I flopped down on the sofa, crossing my arms. Conan joined me, wrapping his arm around my shoulders, but I shrugged him off. "Now is not the time to baby me. We need to figure out a way for me to get away from all this. Fast."

Braxton nodded. "We'll come up with something, Angel. We're not letting them take you without a fight."

Conan grasped my chin between his fingers, turning my face toward him. "You know I will burn down the world to keep you safe. Never doubt that."

I frowned and nodded against his hold. But what could be done in a situation like this?

Braxton joined us in the living room, sitting down in a chair next to us. Together, they filled me in about how Atticus's friend Colton had connections with the owner of a security firm. They'd been discussing the possibility of sending a team to infiltrate the church to ensure my safety.

I couldn't help but joke darkly, "With all the security people and the mafia families I've never met, I won't know who anyone at my wedding is or who wants to kill whom."

Conan fumed. "We should just run right now. Go somewhere and live off the grid for a while."

"Between the three families, they'd find us and kill us both," I said. "The mafia doesn't like public embarrassment or defiance. You can't cross the ruling families. Viktor already wants all the Thorin brothers dead."

The room was thick with tension, and my body was buzzing from feeling pissed off and helpless.

Finally, Braxton sighed, looking at his watch. "It's late. We need to get some sleep. The guys from the club want to meet early tomorrow to decide what to do. There's not much time, and we need a plan now. I'll update the guys and share with them everything Angel just told us so they can be thinking it through."

"There's no way I can sleep," I said, rubbing my forehead in frustration.

Conan swept me up in his arms, giving Braxton a look. "This one is all wound up," he said with a smirk. "But I know exactly what she needs. She needs to have the angst fucked right out of her."

Braxton just shook his head.

Conan carried me upstairs to my bedroom, tossing me face down over the end of the bed. In one rough motion, he yanked my dress up and off. He didn't bother removing his pants, just jerked them open enough to unleash his dick and impale me from behind. I was instantly wet by the way he dominated me. He wasn't afraid of taking exactly what he wanted—me. I gasped, clutching the sheets as he roughly fucked me.

Our breaths were ragged as he reached around, his fingers finding my clit. With all my built-up tension, I came quickly, shuddering against him. But he didn't stop there. He took me in every position imaginable until I lost count of how many orgasms I'd had.

This man had just walked into my life, and now I was wondering how I had ever lived without him. He grounded me with every touch, every kiss. His raw passion made me realize how deeply I craved him—not just his body, but his strength, his protectiveness, his unwavering presence. It wasn't just about the physical pleasure; it was about the way he made me feel whole, cherished, and safe in a world that was anything but. Every thrust, every whispered promise against my skin solidified the bond we shared, a bond I had never known could exist.

Some hours later, we were spent and sticky with sweat and cum. I was completely undone by this man, addicted to him. It was clear to me now that I would never be able to live without him again. The warmth of his body and the steady rhythm of his breathing lulled me into a sense of security I had longed for my entire life. I was so exhausted that I barely remembered Conan coming one last time before I slipped into a deep, satisfying sleep.

Chapter Thirty-Eight

6/28

Since we needed to be up and out early, we only had time for a quick cup of coffee before heading to the club. Conan and Braxton were both tense, making me all the more nervous. I had forgotten that I had silenced my phone last night, so I looked at my messages during our cab drive over. Aunt Elena had left a message demanding that I return right away. What I'm sure she didn't know was that Uncle Luca had texted me, saying to ignore anything Elena was demanding. He told me to plan on returning to their house by noon, staying the night, and going to the wedding straight from their house.

I showed the messages to Conan and then Braxton. Conan pinched the bridge of his nose in frustration.

Leaning into him, I teasingly asked, "Are you always this uptight?"

Braxton let out a laugh. "Ha, you have no idea who you're sitting next to. Since he met you, he's gone from the laid-back party boy with no fucks to give to Mr. Touch Her and Die. Not that long ago, we both were giving Atticus hell for his dramatic personality change over Sam. Damn, if this is what falling in love with a woman does to a man, I don't want any part of it."

"Shut the fuck up. This is different," Conan shot back, rolling his eyes at Braxton.

"Oh, sure. Different. You keep telling yourself that." Braxton grinned, clearly knowing he was getting under Conan's skin.

"Rolling your eyes?" I asked. "Hmm, seems like I may have to deal with that once this is over..." I poked Conan in the ribs, mimicking his earlier threat. He gave me the side-eye and that half grin that always made me tingle.

The cab soon stopped out front of the club. We bailed out and walked into the main floor of the bar, where we were met by all the guys. They looked as tired as we did.

"Ana, you hanging in there?" Lucian asked, his brow furrowed.

"Yeah, just want to be done and move on from all this," I said, trying to muster a smile.

Gabriel motioned to the bar. "Got doughnuts and espressos. Figured we could all use a sugar and caffeine boost with all the crazy shit going on."

"Thanks, Gabriel," Julian said, grabbing a doughnut. "You and your sugar addiction keeping us wired."

Gabriel smirked. "You're welcome. Just don't complain when you're bouncing off the walls."

We all grabbed doughnuts and espressos and headed upstairs to the office.

Once we were gathered around the conference table, Lachlan set up a whiteboard, explaining how he'd spent the last few days diving deep into the tangled mess that was the New York mafia.

He stood by the board with a marker in hand, his eyes scanning his notes. "All right, here's what I've managed to figure out so far," he said. "I've dug into everything you told me, cross-referenced it with what I know about the families, and filled in the gaps with some good old-fashioned common sense. I don't have all the specifics, and I can't be sure about every detail, but based on what we've got, this is the most logical conclusion I see. I've tried to look at all the angles and haven't been able to come up with any other plausible explanations for what's happening."

He drew three circles and labeled them *Volkov*, *Genovese*, and *Moretti*, overlapping them in the center, where he wrote the word *wedding*. "Here's how I see it: Viktor Volkov, your biological father, is playing the long game. He sent you to America to be adopted by Elena and Luca Genovese. The plan was to raise you as an American socialite, then marry you into the Moretti or some other influential mafia family to create a powerful alliance... which is where Frankie Moretti comes into the picture. From what you've told us, Viktor's always been about dominance, control, and expanding his empire. He's never been one to let family ties get in the way of his ambitions. I think the plan to have you adopted by Luca and Elena was just the beginning. Viktor's been setting this up for years, with the ultimate goal of taking over the New York mafia territory."

Lachlan frowned slightly, his gaze intense as he studied each of us. "I don't have all the facts, but it seems clear that Viktor wants to merge the Volkov, Genovese, and Moretti families under his rule. He needs you, Ana, to solidify the alliance with the Moretti family through this marriage to Frankie. But here's where it gets tricky: I think that Viktor doesn't just want to marry you off. He wants to eliminate the current leaders of both the Genovese and Moretti families. And by eliminate, I mean he wants to kill them and install himself as the kingpin of New York's mafia scene. He's already put a contract out on Conan and his brothers because they pushed him out of Tacoma and bit into his US operations."

Conan's jaw tightened, and I could tell anger was simmering just below the surface.

"So, Viktor's plan," Lachlan went on, "is to marry you to Frankie, use that alliance to kill Tomaso Moretti, the current Moretti boss, and then kill Frankie once he's in charge. This way, he takes over the Moretti family. Frankie Moretti thinks he's in league with Viktor to become the new boss of the Moretti family while Viktor takes over the Genovese organization. He doesn't know that Viktor's planning to take him out too. Frankie's just a pawn in Viktor's game, and he's too blinded by his ambition to see it."

I shook my head, breaking out into a cold sweat. "And what about Luca?"

Lachlan then turned to the circle that represented the Genovese family. "Luca's in a tight spot. He's been playing along with Viktor and Elena's plan, but he's not blind, and he seems to be considering Ana's warning, based on what he told her at the rehearsal dinner. My guess is, he's catching on to Viktor's real intentions. Luca agreed years ago with the marriage idea to secure alliances against other crime families and foreign threats," Lachlan said, taking a breath. "My guess is, he didn't realize Viktor's full intentions or Elena's part in this. He wants to protect his family and his territory, and luckily, he's also fond of you, Ana. Even though he might not be looking to start a war, he'll still do whatever it takes to secure his position. While he might not want to take out Viktor outright, he must be getting wary."

Braxton chimed in, "So let me make sure I've got this straight. Frankie thinks he's working with Viktor to take out the

Genovese family, not realizing Viktor plans to kill him too, and Luca is getting wise to it all."

"Exactly." Lachlan nodded. "Frankie is a greedy bastard. He wants to take over the Moretti family but doesn't know Viktor plans to use him and then dispose of him. Viktor obviously wants the Moretti and Genovese territories for himself. And Frankie, who is just a tool, doesn't realize he's already marked for death. It's the only conclusion that makes sense to me."

"And what about the wedding?" I asked, dreading the answer.

Lachlan circled the word on the board. "The wedding is a tinderbox waiting for a spark. All the key players will be there— Tomaso Moretti, Luca, Viktor—and all the highest leaders. It's a setup for a bloodbath. I suspect Viktor's planning to make his move then."

Conan clenched a fist on the table. "We need to get Angel out of here, but she says running isn't an option; they'd find us and kill us."

"Agreed," Lachlan said. "But we need some sort of plan. Maybe we can use this against them. If we can get to Luca and make him see the full picture, he might help us take down Viktor and Frankie."

"I already tried warning him, like I told you," I said, "but he said I still had to marry Frankie. That he couldn't disrespect the Moretti family by reneging on the contract. I don't think he's going to change his mind about that. But at the rehearsal dinner, he did tell me in confidence that he was going to take care of everything, and that I should trust him. But that was it. Nothing specific, so who knows? And last night, he sent me a text instructing me to be at his house by noon today, where I'm to stay until we leave for the wedding tomorrow." Leaning back in my chair, I sighed. This was hopeless. I just wanted to live life on my terms, but that didn't seem possible at this point.

Conan, staring a hole into the bottom of his cup, drew slow circles around its edge, frowning hard but not saying anything. At this point, I knew him well enough to surmise that he was contemplating doing something but didn't want to share it with me because he figured I would object.

Lachlan placed his fists on the table and leaned in, meeting my eyes. "I don't have all the answers, but based on everything you've told me and what I've found, this thing is going down at the wedding. We need a plan, and we need it now. Let's figure out how to turn their scheming against them and get you out of this, Ana."

I turned to Conan. "What are you thinking?"

"I don't trust Luca. He's an arrogant asshole that only does what's in his own best interests." Conan said this in such a grim way that it made me wonder if he'd met the man.

"They're all that way," I said. "We just have to work around them the best we can."

I wished I hadn't brought this nightmare into Conan's life. What Braxton had said about him always being laid back and carefree haunted me. I wondered if I'd ever get to know that side of him.

Braxton leaned back in his chair, a grin spreading across his face. "Lachlan, you must have some Irish mobster blood in you to figure all this out."

I stood up and started pacing around the office, biting my thumbnail. Suddenly, an idea struck me. "I know the layout of St. Peter's Church well. Catholic weddings follow the same routine because they rely on tradition and rote memorization. We need to go along with the wedding plans like we don't suspect anything."

The guys watched me as I paced. "The bridal party uses one of the rooms in the back of the church to get dressed. It even has

a large full-length mirror and a vanity for doing your makeup."
I pulled out my phone, showing them some pictures I'd taken at
a friend's wedding there last summer. "I'll wear biker shorts, a
white tank top, and white sneakers while I'm getting ready and
keep them on under my dress so I can quickly take it off and be
ready to run. Frankie is short and hates when I wear anything
but flats, so no one will think twice about it."

I paused while showing them some more pictures from inside
the church. "I'll be ready to walk down the aisle with Uncle
Luca. Just as the bridesmaids start their way to the front of the
church from the side hallway, I'll fake that I need to throw up
from nerves. I'll tell the girls I'll be there in a minute, but instead,
I'll bolt to the back door, throw off the dress, and run out. You
need to have a car waiting for me and subdue anyone at the back.
We'll leave the church and let the families figure out who wants
to kill whom without me in the middle."

The guys exchanged uneasy looks.

"You can't be seen, and you have to stay undercover, no
matter what happens," I said. "I can't do this if I think any of
you will play the hero and come charging into the church."

Although the guys objected at first and made their attempts
to come up with a better strategy, nothing seemed as feasible.
With no other options, they finally agreed on my plan, promising
to keep watch and never let me out of their sight.

Conan nodded, but I could tell he wasn't happy about the
idea of me being in the church with those people. "I'm meeting
with the security firm this afternoon. They'll have a team ready
to help as well," he said.

I shared my location on my phone with everyone, ensuring
they'd know where I was at all times. "I need to go home, pack,
and get to Elena and Luca's house. I can't be late and make Luca

mad. We need him on our good side."

As I grabbed my things, Conan and Lucian discussed their next steps. Then Conan turned to me, his expression softening. "Ready?"

"Let's go," I said, taking a deep breath. This had to work. It was our only shot. We left the club with a plan in place and a sliver of hope in our hearts.

Chapter Thirty-Nine

6/29

I stood in front of the full-length mirror and hardly recognized the woman staring back. This was surreal, like I was looking at a stranger. The past twenty-four hours had been a whirlwind. My hair, now a cascade of soft waves highlighted with golden streaks, framed a face meticulously made up to perfection. My fingernails and toenails gleamed with a delicate French manicure, and my skin glowed from a spray tan. I'd been plucked, shaved, and buffed to an almost unreal version of myself.

When Conan had dropped me off at Aunt Elena and Uncle Luca's ostentatious mansion yesterday, I'd plastered on a confident smile to keep him from worrying. Luca had insisted I arrive at noon sharp, and the moment I'd stepped through the door, a swarm of people had whisked me away to one of the guest rooms. They'd handled me as if I were a makeover challenge they were determined to win.

An entire team of stylists had descended on me, stripping me of my belongings and violating my personal space without a second thought. It was as though I were a prisoner being processed at a jail—no, it was worse than that. My one experience with being taken into custody back in Tacoma hadn't been pleasant, but it was nowhere near as awful as this had been.

They'd scrubbed me clean, waxed everything—even places I'd never imagined—plucked my eyebrows, given me a spray tan, and even highlighted my hair. I'd endured manicures, pedicures, and an endless array of treatments. It had been exhausting and invasive. They'd left no part of me untouched. They didn't care about my feelings or comfort.

My cell phone was the first thing Elena had taken from me, cutting off any chance of contacting Conan.

Standing here now, I clutched my rumbling stomach. Dinner the night before had been a joke. I'd barely eaten because I was so upset, but even if I had been hungry, the bland, steamed vegetables and plain grilled chicken wouldn't have done much to fill me up. The idea was to keep me from getting bloated, I was sure, but it was also about control, about making sure I knew my place.

At the crack of dawn, the stylists had woken me for a hot bath to wash off any spray tan residue, and then they'd started on my hair and makeup. Breakfast had been a single piece of toast, to avoid a *food baby* in my wedding dress as they'd so charmingly put it. Elena forbade me from wearing the tank top, shorts, and sneakers I'd planned for my escape, instead forcing me into sexy lingerie and ballet slippers. At least they were flat and I would still be able to run in them.

Late in the morning, Elena had burst into my room with a new plan: the bridesmaids were coming to the house to get ready together. Fully dressed, we would take a limo straight to the church, walk up the front steps, and march down the aisle without delay.

Panic was setting in. My plan had been to dress at the church and fake being sick so I could escape out the back door. Now, I had no idea how I was going to get away.

My mind whirled with these thoughts as I continued to stare at myself in the mirror. The woman in the reflection was stunning, the complete opposite of the nervous, tormented mess I was inside. My waist was cinched tight, and I could barely breathe, but I had to admit the dress was beautiful. Glancing over my shoulder at the deep *V* of the back, I admired how it showed off my spine in an elegant way.

My thoughts were interrupted when the door swung open and Frankie's two sisters strode in.

"Oh, it must've taken an army to make you presentable," Bianca said with a sneer, her eyes scanning me from head to toe.

Carlotta chimed in, "Long hair at your age? Seriously? And wearing it down at a wedding? How inappropriate. It should be up in a conservative bun or chignon. And those bangs...smoothed back and held in place with hairspray would be so much classier."

I tried to ignore their cutting remarks, instead turning back to the mirror to focus on the beautiful dress I wore. It was perfect, like something out of a fairy tale. I felt like Cinderella, but this was no ball. This was a nightmare dressed up as a wedding. Their criticisms faded into the background as I ran my hands down the gown. The intricate lace, the delicate beading—everything about it was exquisite. It was such a waste for this beautiful dress to be part of a sham. I sighed. What a shame that this day— meant to be one of the happiest in a woman's life—was so utterly miserable for me.

Elena burst into the room, already dressed. "Let's go, ladies," she snapped brusquely. "Time to head out."

"Finally," Bianca said. "Let's get this over with so Frankie can have his little plaything, the Moretti and Genovese families can cement their alliance, and we can get on with our lives." She muttered this to Carlotta under her breath as if I were invisible.

I turned to Elena, annoyed. "Aunt Elena, may I have my cell phone back?"

She dismissed me with a cold "No."

I chewed on the inside of my cheek, nerves gnawing at me.

"Stop that nasty habit," she snapped.

With a frustrated huff, I headed to the door. Two stylists trailed behind, gathering the train of my dress and guiding me down the stairs. My mind raced with each step I took. When we got outside, they helped me into the waiting limo.

The drive to the church was a form of slow torture, giving me plenty of time to worry about everything that might happen. I wished I could tell Conan about the change of plans—that we wouldn't be dressing at the church but heading straight inside. Our strategy hadn't been great to begin with, and now it was completely shot. My only hope was to escape from Elena's clutches by sprinting to the other end of the church and out the back door. But now, that would create a big scene, and I'd most likely be stopped. I worried that one of the guys would charge in after me and get gunned down.

Panic bubbled inside me as the limo rolled along, but I tried desperately not to let it show. From under my dress, I pulled out the necklace Nik had given me and fidgeted with it. When the stylists and Elena had tried to take it, I'd threatened to ruin my appearance and told Elena she should be grateful I was going along with this farce. I even said I'd rather be dead than go through with the wedding. Elena had laughed, telling me that death could

391

be arranged, but in the end, she'd relented and allowed me to wear the necklace. I wondered if Nik would show up, if he even knew what was going to happen today.

At least Elena had gone in a separate car with Uncle Luca.

One other thing I was grateful for: Elena had decided not to allow any children in the ceremony. The thought of a child being caught in the middle of a possible shoot-out was unbearable to me. Even if it meant I would be harmed, I would never risk a child's safety.

After the long, torturous drive, the limo pulled up to the front steps of the church. I continued to twist the necklace around my finger, staring out the window. There was nothing I wanted less than to walk down that aisle. This was like a bad dream.

Bianca snapped at me, "Stop fiddling around with that thing." After I had tucked it back inside my dress, she added, "Make sure to watch your step and not trip on your way down the aisle."

Carlotta laughed. "Wouldn't that be humiliating?"

I scanned the front of the church, hoping I would see one of the guys and perhaps at least be able to say something to one of them, but none of them were there. Without my phone, I had no way of knowing what was going on with them. Anything could have happened overnight. What if they had been taken somehow or were hurt? My thoughts were interrupted when the car door opened and a big guy I didn't recognize offered me his hand to help me out.

Getting out of the car in that massive wedding gown was like trying to wrangle a wild beast. Eventually, I managed to stand on the sidewalk with the chapel-length train billowing around me. Bianca and Carlotta were quick to exit the vehicle behind me. The two stylists were right behind them. They fussed over my dress, shaking out the train and pulling the veil over my head, making sure everything was perfectly situated. Bianca and

Carlotta wasted no time heading up the stairs of St. Peter's.

I glanced around, wondering if I should take off running now. At this point, improvisation was my only option. I hated Elena, Viktor, and Valentina. None of them had ever shown me an ounce of kindness. My entire life had been a lie, and I was nothing more than a poker chip in Viktor's game. Just as I was about to bolt, Luca stepped up beside me, taking me by the elbow.

"You're not having thoughts of running, are you?" he asked. "The church is full of some of New York's most powerful people. You wouldn't want to disappoint them now, would you?"

I turned to face him, forcing a weak smile onto my face. "No, Uncle Luca. Of course not. This was my sole purpose for being born, right?" He squinted and frowned, nodding his head slightly. A rare reaction to my sarcasm.

Luca was the one walking me down the aisle because most people didn't know that Viktor Volkov was my father. Despite everything, I was happy Luca was here. For some reason, I trusted him—at least a little—to keep me safe. I glanced up the stairs, wondering if my legs would even carry me. They were shaking like jelly.

My uncle placed one hand around my waist and took my arm. Then we slowly made our way up the stairs, the wind catching my veil and sending a chill down my spine. As we walked, Luca had to support my weight. His expression was as impassive as usual while he kept us moving forward.

We reached the top of the stairs and then the doors leading to the narthex. Bianca and Carlotta had already entered and should be heading down the aisle. Two men stood on either side of the doors, ready to open them. The string quartet started playing the "Bridal Chorus" by Wagner. Just before I stepped forward, a soft whistle caught my attention. I snapped my head to the left and spotted Lucian standing at the corner of the portico. He gave me a barely noticeable nod before disappearing to the side of the building.

Luca made a gesture to the men at the doors, and they opened them in unison.

All the guests stood, fixing their eyes on me. Heat rose to my cheeks, spreading through my whole body. Luca turned and pretended to fix my veil, smiling at me. "Pay attention," he said. Then he tucked my arm over his, and we crossed into the narthex.

I started to ask him what he meant, but he only enigmatically whispered, "You will know." The tension in the church was palpable, and other than the music, it was deadly silent. We slowly made our way across the narthex.

No, no, no—I couldn't marry Frankie Moretti.

My eyes scanned for an escape, and I tried to pull away, but Luca had a firm hold and was all but dragging me down the aisle. My mind raced as I frantically tried to find a way out. I visualized how the rooms on either side of the sanctuary were laid out. To my left was the sacristy and the vestry, and to the right was a cloakroom, with a door leading out to the side of the building. That was my only hope for escaping, but I would have to dart past Frankie and his groomsmen to get there.

When we crossed from the narthex into the sanctuary, my breath caught. There were so many faces I didn't recognize, and I assumed most of the men were carrying guns. I had no idea who among them would care if I were murdered in broad daylight, but I guessed most of them wouldn't blink an eye. It was up to me to save myself.

My eyes darted from side to side, while my feet dragged, desperate to find a way out. Then I saw Frankie, and bile rose in my throat. This couldn't be happening. Not him, not now. I swallowed hard. A few more steps, and we were in front of the priest and next to Frankie. Luca lifted my veil over my head and kissed my cheeks. My feet felt like they were made of concrete as he turned and placed my hand into Frankie's sweaty palm. My future husband's hand seared into mine, and tears threatened to spill over.

Frankie turned toward the priest, towing me along with him.

Father Russo began with the sign of the cross and a greeting. I glanced over my shoulder as he started the opening prayer and saw Viktor, Valentina, and Elena sitting stoically, as if they didn't know me, only a few feet away. Painful childhood memories flashed through my mind. Then I caught sight of Nik behind them, on the end of the pew, and froze.

Frankie tugged on my hand, trying to bring my attention back to the priest, but my eyes were locked on Nik. I could always read his features like a book. Something bad was about to go down. He was nervous, worried even. Nik never got nervous. My bottom lip quivered. Terror surged through me.

Just as I turned back toward Father Russo, a gunshot echoed through the sanctuary.

Time stopped. Everything slowed down, each second seeming to last an eternity. Father Russo's throat burst open in a gruesome spray of blood. I recoiled, rotating in time to watch Frankie's face disintegrate from the impact of the bullet. Blood and bits of flesh spewed everywhere. The priest's body crumpled forward, colliding with Frankie. Both men fell onto me, their combined weight knocking me to the floor.

Warm, sticky blood sprayed over me, soaking into my dress. The air was filled with the metallic scent of it, as well as a faint smell of Frankie's cologne, gagging me. The once pristine white lace of my gown had become a grotesque canvas of dark crimson streaked with Father Russo's and Frankie's blood, bone, and flesh, creating a macabre painting of life and death.

Screams erupted in the sanctuary. I turned my head, every movement sluggish, to see Nik diving out from the pew. His body seemed to be moving through water, slow and deliberate, as he reached for me. Finally, he grabbed me under my arms and yanked, but I couldn't move. Frankie's body was pinning the train of my dress to the floor.

Nik kicked Frankie's corpse off me, and it flopped over like a dead fish. My almost-groom's head was twisted at a bizarre angle, and one of his eyes was missing, replaced by a gaping, bloody socket. More shots rang out, ricocheting off the stone columns, creating a deafening cacophony. The sanctuary descended into bedlam. All around me, guns were being drawn and safeties clicked off. Those caught in the crossfire continued screaming and running for cover.

Blood dripped from my face and ran down my neck as I tried to comprehend the scene surrounding me. I lay there, immobilized by the horror of the moment, while Nik struggled to pull me up amidst the layers of my gown. The church, a place of supposed sanctity and peace, had become a grisly battleground.

Nik screamed something, snapping me out of my slow-motion nightmare and thrusting me into a fast-speed reality. "We have to go!" he shouted. He lunged toward the door to the sacristy, but I remembered the gunshot had come from there and tugged him to the right, toward the cloakroom. Together, we made a run for it as more shots rang out.

Just as we reached the door, it flew open. Conan stood there, his expression radiating rage and fear. His eyes were wide, his jaw was clenched, and his nostrils flared with each breath. Nik shoved me into Conan's arms, gathered up my train, and pushed us both into the cloakroom before joining us, slamming the door shut, and locking it.

Chapter Forty

6/29

Conan lunged at Nik, but I grabbed his arm. "He's my brother, Conan! Don't! He's helping me! Come on. Let's go! Let's get out of here, now!"

Conan didn't hesitate. He turned, dragging me with him, Nik following closely behind. We scampered through the small cloakroom, dodging piles of boxes and clutter. The sounds of the chaos in the sanctuary echoed through the walls, urging us to move faster.

When we reached the door on the other side, Conan pushed it open, and we stumbled down the short flight of steps leading to the outside.

When we reached the bottom of the steps, I fought my way through the outer door, battling my voluminous dress. I burst through the door and glanced over my shoulder. An unconscious man lay slumped against the wall.

We were met by Lucian and Braxton as they ran toward us.

"This way!" Lucian shouted, turning back and waving us toward a black SUV parked down the street.

We ran toward them, the sounds of gunfire making my heart pound in my chest as fear and adrenaline coursed through my veins.

"What the fuck is going on?" Lucian shouted as we neared him.

There was no time for an explanation. Conan barked, "Let's go! Move! Move! Move!"

The SUV was waiting with its doors open at the curb. We ran toward it as shots rang out. Lucian sprinted to the front-passenger side while Braxton dove into the open side door. Lachlan was at the wheel.

I struggled to run down the sidewalk, my wedding dress billowing around me like a storm of white silk. The veil caught in the wind, twisting and snapping free, whipping away like a ghostly specter. The train of my gown dragged behind, a cumbersome, fluttering reminder of my captivity. I tripped, the fabric catching underfoot, but Conan was there. He snagged the train, gathering it in his hands. "Keep running!" he shouted, and I surged forward, my breath coming in gasps.

The moment we reached the open side door of the SUV, Conan grabbed me by the waist and tossed me inside before jumping in after me. Nik, who was a few steps behind us, screamed in pain just as he reached the open door. The guys dragged him inside, his feet bouncing off the pavement and leaving streaks of blood, while Lachlan threw the vehicle into drive and started to speed away.

Blood was everywhere. Braxton quickly switched places with Conan and me, moving us to the third row so he could take care of Nik's leg. Conan checked me for wounds, his hands moving rapidly over my arms and torso.

"Are you okay?" he asked, scrutinizing every inch of me.

"I'm fine. Just help my brother," I begged, pushing his hands away. I turned my attention to Nik, who was bleeding heavily. Braxton had already pulled off his shirt and was pressing it against the wound.

Conan's eyes softened for a moment before he rotated in the seat to help Braxton with Nik. "We'll take care of him," he assured me.

Nik groaned in pain, his face pale and sweaty.

"We've got you, Nik," Braxton said calmly.

The SUV roared down the block, speeding away from the bloodbath we'd left behind in the church.

Nik was slumped in the backseat, blood pooling beneath his leg. "We've got to get this bleeding under control," Conan said, leaning over to press his hand firmly against the shirt that was covering Nik's injury. Blood oozed between his fingers, but Nik didn't flinch.

"We need a tourniquet," Braxton said. He began searching the backseats.

Lucian tore off his belt and tossed it to Braxton, who immediately wrapped it around Nik's upper thigh and tightened it.

Nik's face contorted in agony.

"Hang in there, Nik," I whispered in a shaky voice. I reached over the backseat and took his hand, needing to be connected to him somehow.

"I've had worse. Just...don't let me bleed out."

Conan wrapped his massive hand tightly around Nik's thigh, clamping down on the wound. "Pressure's key," he said to Braxton. "We need to slow the bleeding until we can get him somewhere safe."

Braxton nodded, his eyes focused on Nik's leg. "Keep talking to him, Angel. Keep him conscious."

Swallowing hard, I nodded. "Nik, remember when we were kids, and you dared me to jump when we were out on the frozen lake behind the house? You had to break through the ice downstream to pull me out, remember?"

Nik managed a weak chuckle. "Yeah, you always did crazy stuff and never backed down from a dare."

Conan glanced over at me, cocking a brow. I rolled my eyes in return.

Forcing a smile, I leaned closer to Nik. "You were supposed to be the sensible one. The nanny always said you had to look out for me because I had more guts than brains."

Nik's breathing was ragged, but he glanced over at me, his eyes glassy and unfocused. "You scared the hell out of me that day, Ana. I thought I'd lost you."

I squeezed his hand, which was sticky with blood. "But you didn't. You always kept me safe. You pulled me out, wrapped me in your coat, and ran all the way back to the house. What were we—ten, maybe?"

His eyes fluttered, and I tightened my grip on his hand. "Stay with me, Nik. Remember how mad the nanny was? She couldn't decide whether to beat us or hug us."

Nik's lips twitched into a faint smile. "She did both and then grounded us for a month."

"That's right, and every day you managed to sneak me snacks and books so I wouldn't get bored."

Braxton looked up. "Good, Angel. Keep him talking."

My throat was tight as I chewed on my cheek, trying to think of something else. "Remember how we used to sneak out at night, just to look at the stars? You said you wanted to be a cosmonaut so you could get away from all the craziness down here."

Nik's eyes sparkled with a distant memory. "Yeah, and you wanted to be a pop star."

I laughed softly. "You told me I'd have to travel the world, and we'd never get to see each other... I thought I wanted nothing more than to leave the boring confinement of the estate in Russia. God, how I complained all the time. Little did I know, a couple of years later, I'd get more than I bargained for."

"You were always sassy and stubborn as a kid; that's for sure."

"Still am, I suppose," I muttered, brushing a strand of hair from his forehead. "You promised we'd always look out for each other, no matter what. We made it through everything else, and we'll make it through this."

His grip on my hand tightened slightly. "You were always the strong one, Ana."

"And you were always my hero," I whispered.

The SUV hit a bump, and Nik winced. Braxton adjusted the pressure, making sure the tourniquet held firm.

"Almost there," Lachlan said, glancing at me in the rearview mirror. "Twenty minutes, tops."

Nik's grip on my hand loosened, but I held tight. "Ana... sorry about...everything," he said on an exhale.

"Shut up, Nik. Just stay awake," I demanded. "You don't get to check out on me now."

"Hey, guys, look what I found in the glove box!" Lucian called. "It's not a lot, but maybe something in here could help." He handed back what appeared to be a homemade first aid kit.

Conan took it and opened it. "Hmm, these aren't your typical emergency supplies. There's combat gauze, a suture kit, and some other items—as if whoever owns this car expected that someone might get shot." He showed it to Braxton, who lit up with a smile.

"Damn, that's some good stuff. Combat gauze is impregnated with kaolin, which promotes clotting," he said, shifting in the seat to take it from Conan. "Here, hold the tourniquet."

Conan let go of Nik's thigh and took over holding the belt. Nik swiftly opened a package of the gauze.

"I'm warning you, buddy, this isn't gonna feel good," Braxton said.

"Just do it," Nik growled.

With a nod, Braxton expertly packed the combat gauze into the exit wound on the top of Nik's thigh. We watched the gauze rapidly absorb blood while Braxton explained that it would expand to apply pressure internally and help with clotting. He then moved to the back of the thigh, carefully packing more gauze into the entry wound. Nik winced, squeezing my hand. His knuckles were white as his face twisted in pain.

Braxton held the gauze firmly in place on the entry wound. Once it was secure, he checked the tourniquet, adjusting it to ensure it was tight but not excessively so. He met my eyes briefly and gave me a reassuring nod.

Conan leaned toward me, giving me that half grin I loved so much. "He's tough. He'll be fine."

The metallic tang of blood was suffocating in the cramped conditions of the SUV. Nik was sweating but much more alert now. I guessed that's what acute pain did to a person. Clutching his thigh, he sat up straighter and shook his head as if to clear away his misery. He pulled himself forward and, through gritted teeth, called out an address, demanding to be taken there.

"Nik, my brother's friend has already set up a safe house for us," Conan said. "We're heading there now. He's the guy who provided the SUV."

"Huh, somehow you both are correct," Lachlan shot out in surprise.

Nik let out a sarcastic laugh, wincing. "Oh, I didn't know that my buddy, Colton Davidson, had already given it to you. I hired him a long time ago to work for my company, DarkMatter, and eventually we became partners. He's the good guy to my bad guy. He focuses on security and client relations while I handle...other things."

My heart raced as I listened. "Nik, what are you saying?"

He hesitated, catching his breath. "After I came back to the estate and found out that Ana had taken off, I tracked her phone and saw her last location was at the airport and assumed she was flying back to New York. I called Colton right away because I knew I'd need to get a team together to protect her. He runs everything for the security side of DarkMatter; I've been hands-off for several years. We've never needed to discuss details of the firm's client needs here in the US. When I told him my sister was in trouble and Viktor had put a hit on three brothers with the last name of Thorin, Colton was stunned by the connection. And, coincidently, he had just gotten a panicked call from Atticus Thorin, telling him about Jane Doe's true identity."

Nik paused, grimacing as the car took a sharp turn. "Colton had already sent a security detail to Atticus's house by the time I spoke with him. He had never talked to me about what happened back in December. Viktor, wanting to keep a lid on the losses he'd suffered, had only informed me of the basics and how it had impacted his operations. Since I've spent so much of my time in the UK and Kyiv these past couple of years, I haven't kept up with Volkovi Notchi business. I've been trying to separate myself from it as much as possible. Russian mafia dealings have never been my thing. Colton hadn't mentioned anything to me about what happened in Tacoma because he had no idea I was connected to the kidnapping nightmare Viktor unleashed on Samantha and Atticus. He's always known I had underworld ties but didn't know my real last name, much less that I was Viktor Volkov's son. So, yeah, we had a lot to discuss."

"What? I can't believe this is all so connected!" I gasped.

Nik took a long, deep breath and then continued, "We've been working together for the last two days, trying to come up with a plan. As soon as Ana landed at JFK, I knew where she was because I had installed a tracer on her phone. By the time we got security on her, you and Braxton had already left for New York." He turned to look at Conan, whose brows were pinched tight. "When Ana showed up at Club Xyst the morning after getting back to the city, we discovered Luca was closely watching her too. My guys spotted his thugs and another crew, which we assumed was from the Moretti organization, tailing her. We chose to lie low, and we've kept eyes on her ever since so we could figure out who all the players were."

Conan growled, "Why the hell didn't you communicate with us, Nik?"

"Because," Nik said through gritted teeth, "as soon as you showed up at Club Xyst, everyone knew who you were. And since then, Luca's been watching you—*all* of you. My guess is that Ana's apartment is a hot mess of bugs and video surveillance. You guys didn't even try to be discreet—busy enjoying yourselves with my sister. So get the fuck off my back."

My breath caught. "What?! That's so fucking wrong! You should have told me, Nik. I feel so degraded—dirty. That's such an invasion of my privacy. How could you not tell me?"

Nik licked his lips, shaking his head. "Ana, it was the only way I could help you. With that many eyes on you, there was no way I could extract you. None of them suspected me of being involved with anything outside the Volkovi Notchi. To them, I'm just Viktor's lackey, so they all assumed I was in town for the wedding. I thought it was best to just let things play out, to get them all in one place so my guys could take them out. The plan was for me to whisk you away immediately after the ceremony ended as you moved into the narthex. Then, as all the kingpins headed out, they'd be sitting ducks. There are only two ways out of that church—the front or the side entrance—and we had them both more than covered. I never imagined someone would take Frankie out in the most loaded room in the city."

Conan's eyes burned with anger. "I get it. You used Angel as bait, you goddamn motherfucker! If you weren't already shot, I'd put a bullet in you."

Nik groaned, pain etched in his face. "It's not like I had much time to deal with what was going down—a three-family mafia war. Once Ana's hot-headed self up and left Tacoma without giving it two thoughts or letting anyone know, it was too late. Damn, Ana, that's twice now your impulsiveness has almost gotten you killed."

Conan and Nik looked like they wanted to murder each other.

I threw up my hands. "All right, all right, I get it. Now's not the time to bitch about things. People fucking died in that church, for Christ's sake."

At this point, I'd begun shaking from shock, anger, and guilt. This whole mess was my fault. "I didn't want anyone to get killed. Poor Father Russo," I said, my heart sinking.

Nik sighed. "Ana, I hate to tell you this, but I'm sure Frankie and the priest aren't the only ones who lost their lives back there. Luca found out about my suspicions that Viktor wanted to take over all of New York, which escalated this mafia showdown."

"Oh my God," I whispered. "It was me. I'm the one who went to Luca. He's always been good to me, and I wanted to warn him."

Nik winced again. "Well, that explains why he and his men started taking so many defensive measures all over the city. I'm sure he's been searching for Viktor and his goons, just like we have. Viktor's been slippery. If we'd known where he was or what kind of men and guns he had in the city, we would've gotten you out before the wedding. But we needed access to him. I hated to use you as bait, but we had to get all the players into one room. Too many loose ends otherwise."

"Fucking bait," Conan snarled, jerking on the belt, causing Nik to yelp.

"Watch it, brother," Braxton warned.

Nik's face tightened. "The big question now is, what side is Luca on? He might take out Viktor and the Morettis who were involved in Frankie's plans with Viktor, but who knows, with him married to Elena. I've never met the man, but I've studied him. He's smart. He'll do whatever's best for the Genovese family."

I stared at Nik, my mind a whirlpool of fear. "So, what now?"

Conan snatched Nik by his hair, yanking his head back. "I'll tell you what's now. You're going to stay the fuck away from my girl."

"No, no!" I cried. "You guys can't hate each other. None of this is your fault. It's mine! Nik's right. I was an idiot flying off to Tacoma without a thought and then foolishly thinking Uncle Luca would help me... I was wrong. I was the one who stirred up the hornet's nest." My breaths started coming shallow and fast as my vision blurred. Conan saw my reaction, leaned back, and pulled me close with one arm.

My hands started to shake uncontrollably. Everything hit me at once—guilt, anger, and sadness all swirling together. The blame sat heavy on my shoulders, and I could hardly breathe. My chest tightened, and a panic attack hit me hard.

Conan's face softened. "Hey, I'm sorry, my sweet Angel. Breathe, slow and steady, to the count of three. We'll figure this out." His voice was firm yet soothing as he pulled me against his chest. His touch was grounding, but my mind still raced, unable to process everything I'd just been through.

As Lachlan sped out of the city toward the safe house, the car grew silent. The tension in the SUV was thick, and my thoughts were a jumbled mess. The images of the blood, the screams, and the violence at the church replayed in my mind like a nightmare I couldn't wake up from. Conan's arms were the only thing keeping me tethered to reality. I clung to him, desperate for the small comfort amidst the madness.

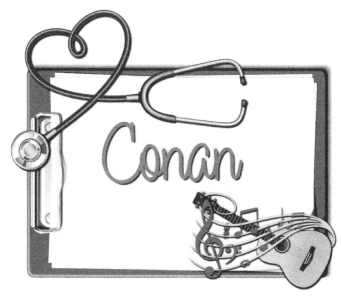

Chapter Forty-One

6/29

Angel sat in silence for the rest of the drive to the safe house. Her eyes were empty, and I feared she had gone into shock. The sight of her draped over the backseat, clutching Nik's blood-covered hand, made my blood boil. I was furious at him for using her as bait, but I had to push that aside. I worried about what might happen once she snapped out of her numbness and realized the extent of the horror she'd just lived through. When the shock wore off, Angel would likely experience a torrent of emotions—fear, anger, confusion, and who knew what else. I worried she might freak out and struggle with flashbacks, leaving her grappling with the terror long after all this had passed. So as much as I wanted to confront Nik, right now, I needed to focus on her.

We arrived at a small house nestled in an unassuming neighborhood. It was surrounded by a fence and some thick hedges. Braxton and Lucian jumped out of the SUV first, moving to carry Nik inside. I slid from the vehicle as Angel dragged herself out of the third row and to the open door. She was about to hop down when I swept her up in my arms and carried her inside. She didn't protest, just stared blankly ahead.

Nik had lost a lot of blood and was only semiconscious now. As much as I wanted to sit here and hold Angel, I needed to go help Braxton tend to his gunshot wound. I glanced around the small living room before gently placing her on a sofa. Her silence scared me more than anything. Braxton and Lucian disappeared into the back with Nik. I headed to the kitchen, rummaging around until I found a candy bar and a bottle of water. Returning to Angel, I offered them to her.

"Eat this," I said firmly. "Something sweet will help with the shock."

Her eyes barely flickered in response as I set them next to her on the table. I spotted a blanket and covered her with it, both for warmth and to cover the blood and guts on her dress. "Stay here with Lach," I said, nodding toward him. "Keep a close watch on her and let me know if she needs anything."

"Will do," he said, his forehead wrinkling with worry.

When I went down the hallway in search of the others, I noticed that this wasn't just any house. It was a sophisticated hideout. One room had a high-tech computer system and a lot of other expensive-looking equipment. Continuing down the hallway, I came to a room with the door open. Braxton was just telling Lucian to find some scissors. Once inside, I realized it was set up like a mini emergency department. Lucian and Braxton had already laid Nik on a gurney and were in the process of cutting his pants off.

"Holy shit," I muttered. "What the hell is this place?"

Lucian shook his head, eyes wide. "Never seen anything like it."

Braxton worked quickly to remove Nik's shirt and then began prepping him for treatment, removing the gauze we'd wrapped around his thigh in the van.

Lucian's eyes went wide. "Okay, I'm out of here. I'll leave you two to take care of Nik, and I'll go check on Ana."

"Let's get him cleaned up before infection sets in," Braxton said. "Looks like we've got what we need here. You ready to play doctor?"

"I guess there's no other choice," I said, chuckling darkly and stepping up to help.

I looked around at the room again. This place was beyond anything I'd imagined, and we were lucky to have access to it. The supplies on hand would be crucial. I'd never expected such a place to exist, but then again, I wasn't part of Nik's world.

I rolled up my sleeves, washed my hands, and prepared to help. As I took stock of the myriad supplies available to us here, I wondered how often this place was used. Braxton and I gathered everything we could think of and placed it on a rolling table next to Nik or on the counter behind us.

Just as we donned gloves, Nik's body went limp, and his eyes closed as he slipped into unconsciousness. Braxton and I sprang into action. I switched on the medical monitors, surprised to find them in top-notch condition. The equipment was state of the art, probably better than what we had at the hospital. I hooked up the pulse ox to Nik's finger to monitor his oxygen saturation, watching the numbers stabilize around ninety-five percent. That was a good sign; at least his breathing wasn't compromised.

"Braxton, hand me the BP cuff and the ECG leads." He reached behind him and passed me the kit. After I wrapped the cuff around Nik's upper arm, and attached it to the vital signs display unit, the automated monitor kicked in, inflating and then slowly deflating. The reading came back at 85/55. Not great, but not catastrophic. We needed to get it up at some point, but we had other things to focus on right now.

"His BP's low but holding. Let's keep an eye on it," I said, glancing at Braxton, who was attaching the ECG leads to Nik's chest. The machine started beeping softly, displaying the heart's electrical activity. Nik's heart rate was elevated, around a hundred twenty beats per minute.

I nodded to Braxton. "Let's get an IV line in. We need to replace the fluids he's lost."

Braxton prepped the IV line while I located a suitable vein and then inserted the catheter and secured it with tape. We started a saline drip to help stabilize his blood pressure and replenish some of the volume he'd lost.

"Before we go any further," I said, "we need to ensure he stays unconscious and doesn't move during the procedure." Reaching for a syringe, I filled it with the most conservative amount of propofol I thought would do the job, then injected it into his IV line, watching the medication flow in. "This will keep him sedated and ensure he doesn't wake up suddenly."

As I administered the drug, I couldn't help but wonder how Nik's company could acquire and have propofol on hand, considering it was a highly protected drug.

While Braxton kept an eye on the monitors, I checked Nik's injury. The entrance wound on the back of his thigh was small and clean, but the exit wound on the front was larger, with jagged edges.

"Braxton, he's getting paler. We need to check his hemoglobin levels," I said, reaching for the portable hemoglobinometer I'd seen while gathering supplies from the cabinet behind me.

Braxton wiped Nik's finger with an antiseptic pad and then pricked it, drawing a small drop of blood. The machine beeped, displaying a reading far below the normal range.

"He really needs a transfusion," I muttered. "Do we have any bags of blood in the supplies?"

"Yes, there's some in the refrigerator. But we need to confirm his blood type."

He grabbed a blood-typing kit, took another blood sample, and mixed it with the reagents. The results indicated he was O positive—a relief since it was a common type and we had a bag of it in the refrigerator.

"All right, let's get this warmed up," I said, pulling out the portable blood warmer. "This place is made for working on a person with a gunshot wound." I was still amazed by all the gear.

Braxton handed me the bag of blood, and I placed it in the warmer, setting the device to bring it up to normal body temperature.

While the blood warmed, we monitored Nik's vitals closely. His heart rate was still elevated, and his blood pressure remained low. "The blood transfusion should help stabilize him if he can just hold on," I said, watching the monitors. After a few minutes, the blood was at the right temperature.

I set up the transfusion kit, connecting the line to Nik's IV catheter. The rich, red liquid began to flow into his veins. After a few minutes, the blood pressure cuff cycled again, showing a slight improvement. His heart rate started to come down, and color began to return to his face.

Braxton monitored the flow of blood, ensuring there were no air bubbles in the line. "He's looking better already," he commented, adjusting the flow rate slightly.

Then he maneuvered Nik's leg so that I could clean both the front and back of his thigh. Now it was time to deal with the wound itself. It appeared that the combat gauze had done its job, but now we had to do ours.

I focused back on the wound. "We need to remove the combat gauze carefully. Hand me the saline," I said. Braxton passed me the bottle, and I began to gently irrigate the wound, the saline washing away the dried blood and helping to loosen the gauze. The pink-tinged liquid flowed over his skin, pooling on the sterile pads Braxton had placed beneath his leg.

"Easy does it," I muttered to myself, peeling back the gauze slowly. The edges of the wound were raw and inflamed, but the bleeding had slowed significantly. "We've got to clean this thoroughly before we do anything else."

Once the gauze was fully removed, I inspected the wound again and used more saline to flush it. This cleared out any debris but also caused some bleeding to resume. "No major vessels were torn, and he's lucky the bullet didn't hit the bone, but even so, he's lost a lot of blood," I said to Braxton, who stood across from me.

"Cauterization next," I said, reaching for the cautery pen he had readied. Once the device had hummed to life, I applied it to the areas of the wound that required it. The sizzling sound of burning tissue was accompanied by a distinctly acrid odor that I had never been completely able to ignore. "Hold him steady," I instructed Braxton, who kept a firm grip on Nik's leg.

After the cauterization was complete, I checked for any residual bleeding. Satisfied, I began suturing the wound. "We need to close this in layers," I explained as I began to work. "First the deeper tissues, then the outer layers." As the needle moved in and out of his flesh, the texture of the tissue beneath my fingers was a reminder of the damage the bullet had caused.

With the wound sutured, I cleaned the area again, applying a layer of antibiotic ointment to prevent infection. "Let's get him bandaged up," I said. Braxton handed me the sterile bandages, and together we wrapped his thigh carefully, securing the dressing in place.

Braxton nudged my elbow. "You did well, Conan. Atticus would be proud."

"Thanks," I said, heaving a sigh of relief. "I've spent years in the ED with him. Maybe I learned a few things. But damn, I'm glad I don't have to do this every day. It's stressful as hell."

I glanced at the blood bag. "The transfusion seems to have worked. His color is so much better." The monitors showed a steady heart rate and stable blood pressure. The bag of blood was nearly empty, and it had done its job. Once it had drained all the way, Braxton replaced the blood with a saline drip.

"We'll need to keep the IV line in for fluids," he said, adjusting the drip rate. "And we should give him something for the pain as soon as he shows signs of waking up."

As he rested, Braxton and I cleaned up the area. Soon, Nik stirred, his eyes fluttering open. He mumbled something incoherent, his gaze unfocused. Braxton leaned in, speaking softly and brushing a strand of his hair off his forehead.

"Everything's fine, Nik. You're going to be okay. Just rest and get some sleep."

Nik gave him a half smirk and closed his eyes again, his breathing even and deep. Braxton and I exchanged a relieved look.

"I'll give him some antibiotics through his IV," Braxton said. "Infection will be our biggest worry now. He's responsive and stable, so that's good. I'll keep monitoring him. You should go check on Angel."

I nodded, grateful for his support. "Thanks, Brax—especially for having my back on all this. I know it's been a lot." I gave Nik one last glance, ensuring he was resting easy before washing up and heading back to the living room to take care of Angel. "Let me know if you need anything," I said on my way out.

She was still sitting on the sofa, wrapped in the blanket, staring off into space. Her eyes were distant. I kneeled in front of her, taking her hand gently. "Nik's fine, my sweet Angel. He's a tough guy. Good thing, too, because when this is over, I'm going to kick his ass." I gave her a wry grin, trying to lighten the mood.

But she scarcely acknowledged me. I decided against telling her any of the details about Nik's procedure. She'd had enough for one day. First thing I needed to do was get her out of that bloody dress. "Come on, let's get you cleaned up," I said gently. She nodded, but her blank stare didn't waver.

I lifted her into my arms, and her body went limp against me. The scent of blood was overpowering.

I remembered seeing a staircase earlier that led downstairs, so I headed in that direction. I hoped it would take us to a quiet place where she could get a shower, lie down, and rest. After carrying her down and turning to the right, I found a large bedroom. It was dark and quiet, which would help her sleep.

The room was posh. "Nice to see mobsters like living the good life and taking care of their safe houses," I joked, but she didn't react. Her gaze was fixed on her bloodstained dress.

I took her straight to the en suite bathroom and made sure she faced away from the mirrors. Just outside of the shower, I placed her on her feet and turned her around. The dress was a nightmare of fabric and fastenings. As I worked through the layers, she stood there, passive. Finally, I was able to remove the complicated gown, revealing the sexy lingerie underneath. A grateful thought crossed my mind—thank God she hadn't ended up with Frankie tonight. This day could've ended in so many worse ways.

With sensitive hands, I removed the frilly pieces, doing my best to be respectful. I worked to focus on her well-being, not her gorgeous body. She was covered in dried blood and who knew what else. "Don't look in the mirror," I ordered gently, lifting her in my arms. She buried her face in my chest, and I cradled her while the water heated up. "Everything's going to be okay," I said, trying to reassure her, but I knew that no matter what I said, it wouldn't make a difference at the moment.

I kicked off my shoes, shoving them aside, and stood her in the shower. The water cascaded over her, washing away the grime and blood. She stood there, with her head lolled forward, staring at the red rivulets swirling down the drain. The pungent metallic smell mixed with the steam filling the room, creating a dank odor of death. Angel stood there watching the water turn pink as I kept a steady hand on her, making sure she didn't fall.

Without warning, she gagged, her body shuddering under the shower's spray.

I didn't hesitate to step into the shower with her. Still fully dressed, I soaped up my hands and began to clean her, ignoring the water soaking my clothes. I was desperate to rid her of all the bad things capturing her attention. Her skin was clammy, the grime clinging to her.

"Angel, focus on me," I said, rubbing the soap into her skin. Tenderly, I washed her face, moving the soft cloth over her closed eyes, down her cheeks, and across her forehead. Each swipe revealed more of her natural beauty beneath the bloody crud. "There you are," I murmured, rinsing the cloth and moving down her body.

I washed every part of her, my touch light and reverent, until no trace of the nightmare from the church remained on her skin. Her hair was a tangled mess though, sticky with dried blood. I reached for the shampoo and massaged it onto her scalp, the floral scent mixing with the steam, ridding her of the last remnants of the shootout. She closed her eyes and leaned into me. I worked the conditioner through her hair, my fingers detangling the knots. "You're doing great, my Angel. Almost done." I tilted her head back to rinse her hair, careful to avoid getting soap in her eyes.

When I was finished, I stepped out of the shower. My clothes were soaked, so I grabbed a towel and dried off as best I could. Then I drew her a hot bath, hoping that it might help her relax. Lifting her out of the shower, I placed her into the piping hot water. She sank into the tub with a sigh, eyes closing as the heat enveloped her.

While she soaked, I took the wedding dress and everything else she had been wearing out to the trash. Then I went to the SUV to retrieve the suitcase Ana had packed before heading to her Aunt Elena's house. I grabbed it and returned to the bedroom. Placing it on the dresser, I opened it and rummaged through its contents, finding an old T-shirt with the Club Xyst logo and some fuzzy socks. Hopefully she would like these. I returned to the bathroom and set them on the counter.

When she was ready, I helped her out of the tub, then wrapped a towel around her and dried her off. I slipped the T-shirt over her head, guiding her arms into the sleeves. She sat on the padded stool as I slid the socks onto her feet. I massaged them for a minute, wanting to take my time with her.

She let me use the blow-dryer on her hair, and the mundane hum of it was a comforting sound. Angel sweetly smiled up at me. When her hair was dry, I lifted her up again and placed her in bed, tucking the blankets around her.

While she rested, I took a quick shower, the hot water washing away the grime but not the worry. There were so many unknowns. What would the fallout of this be? Where was Luca now? Viktor? I couldn't stop thinking about how all this would affect Angel.

Once I was clean, I slid into bed, spooning up against her. She was awake, but I didn't press for information. I just held her for a long time in silence. Then she started to cry. The sheer sorrow in it broke my heart. I pulled her tighter against my chest, brushing my hand along her skin in soothing strokes.

Slowly, quietly, she told me everything that had happened, from the time she arrived at her aunt's home to the moment when the priest and Frankie were killed. Over and over, she repeated the word "killed," her whispers turning to sobs.

I held her, rocking her back and forth against my chest, saying nothing, just letting her get it all out. Finally, exhausted, she fell into a fitful sleep. I watched her for a long time, tracing the lines of her body and the contours of her face, thinking about how beautiful and strong she was.

Leaning close, I whispered, "I love you, Angel. I'll never let you go. For the rest of our days, I promise to protect and love you. Nothing will come between us—nothing."

Eventually, I drifted off to sleep, holding her close.

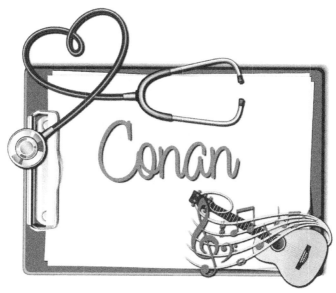

Chapter Forty-Two

6/30

Early in the morning, I woke up and carefully slipped out of bed, making sure not to wake Angel. I threw on some clothes and headed upstairs to the kitchen. Lucian, Lachlan, and Braxton were already there, quietly sipping coffee and chatting about our situation.

"Think anyone followed us to the safe house?" Lucian asked.

Lachlan shook his head. "Doesn't seem like it. We were careful. If we'd been tailed, we would know it by now."

"Good," I said as I entered. Stepping up to the counter, I grabbed a cup of coffee. "We need to keep it that way." I leaned against the counter and blew across the hot liquid before taking a sip. "How's Nik doing this morning?"

Braxton looked up from his phone. "He's stable and healing well. I crashed on the cot in the medical room to keep an eye on him all night. He was out the whole time and didn't move much, which is a good sign. I changed his dressing a couple of times. The wound was clean, and there were no signs of infection. We'll keep him on a broad-spectrum antibiotic and pain meds if he needs them for the next week, and then he should be good to go as long as he doesn't do anything to rip it open."

"Thanks, Brax," I said. "It gave me the chance to be with Angel. She's tougher than she looks, but it was a hell of a lot for anyone to go through." I took a deep breath, remembering the chaos of the previous day. "She's seen nothing like that before. She may have been born into a mafia family, but she's never seen a person shot or a gory injury like that. The priest and Frankie... it was brutal. She was right there, holding Frankie's hand when it happened. A scene like that changes a person."

I paused, glancing at the guys. "Trauma can affect people in so many ways. It can mess with your head, give you nightmares— you know, make you jump at shadows. It sticks with you, sometimes for the rest of your life."

Lucian nodded. "She's got you though. That counts for a lot."

"Yeah, not sure if she's the type of person to want help," I said, "but I know she's gonna need some. The worst thing she could do is isolate herself. Now I get how Atticus felt after everything Sam went through. It's hard, feeling helpless, hell-bent on retribution with no one to take it out on, determined to put back together all the broken pieces, knowing full well the scars will always be there."

Angel's resilience amazed me, but I worried about the long-term impact of what she'd witnessed. Trauma like that didn't just fade away.

I looked around at them. "Keep an eye on her and Nik for me. I'm gonna go grab us some food."

I drove to a nearby fast-food joint, picked up a variety of breakfast items, and headed back to the house, taking a few minutes to call Atticus and let him know the basics. When I returned, Angel was sitting in the kitchen, sipping coffee with all the guys. I set the bags of food on the table in front of her and kissed her on the cheek. She smiled a little but said nothing, which worried me.

"Any sign of Nik?" I asked.

"Not yet," Braxton replied. "He needs lots of rest and will be out of commission while he heals from the gunshot wound. But you know I'll keep my eyes on him."

I walked behind Angel, taking her hair in my hands and moving it to the side before brushing soft kisses along her neck. She leaned into my touch and whispered, "Thanks for last night. I think everything just hit me all at once. Don't worry, I'll be okay; I just need some time."

I kissed her forehead gently. "Take all the time you need," I said, then shifted to unpack the bags. In the center of the table, I laid out a spread of bacon, egg, and cheese sandwiches, breakfast burritos, bagels, yogurt, and some other things. The guys dove in.

"Thanks, man," Lucian said through a mouthful of biscuit. "This is just what we needed."

Braxton leaned back in his chair. "You always come in clutch. Thanks for taking care of us. I didn't realize how hungry I was. Man, I'm starving."

As we ate, I kept an eye on Angel. She was still too quiet.

She didn't take anything to eat, just stared at the food. I leaned over, saying firmly but gently, "You need to eat if you're going to be able to deal with everything that comes next. You're no good to anyone if you're running on empty. Who knows what we're facing at this point?"

She sighed, then begrudgingly grabbed a yogurt, took a spoonful, and started nibbling on it.

Braxton spoke up. "Nik's doing well, Angel, if that's what's worrying you. So well, in fact, that I removed the IV this morning. He hasn't needed any more pain meds either. All he'll need now is a round of antibiotics and some ibuprofen."

Just then, Nik shuffled into the kitchen, wearing only shorts and the bandage around his thigh. Angel jumped up and threw her arms around his neck, hugging him tight. "I've been worried sick about you," she said.

Nik grunted in pain, and Braxton was there in an instant, pulling her back. "Careful, Angel. He was just shot, remember?"

She stepped back, looking apologetic. "I'm sorry, Nik. I was just so worried."

Nik waved it off. "I'm fine. Stop worrying about me."

Braxton gestured to the chair he had been sitting in. "Nik, sit down and get some food. You lost a lot of blood and need to refuel to heal."

Nik grinned. "All right, all right. Quit fussing, you old mother hen."

"Shut up. Just sit down and eat," Braxton shot back.

Nik laughed. He reached for a biscuit, then winced. Braxton noticed immediately. "You okay?"

"Yeah, I'm fine," Nik insisted, though his face betrayed the pain.

Braxton moved closer, inspecting the bandage. "You've bled through a little. You may have torn a suture. I'll look at it after you eat something and clean it back up. You're gonna have to stay off your feet, you know." He poured Nik a cup of coffee and then handed him a bottle of water. "You need lots of fluids too."

Angel visibly relaxed as she watched the exchange, and she sat back down. Now that Nik was here and she could see he was okay, being taken care of, she seemed more like herself.

I reached over her to grab a container with gravy biscuits. Lucian snorted. "Watch it, Conan. You're going to get fat."

"Takes a lot of calories to keep up with my workouts, especially at my size," I replied, grinning.

Angel managed a small smile and continued eating her yogurt—a small victory.

With everyone in the kitchen, safe and sound, the tension dissipated somewhat. The atmosphere eased, and the chatter became more relaxed as we ate.

Angel's phone, which was lying on the table, started to ring, and the mood in the kitchen shifted instantly. She flipped it over and stared at the screen, then at us, her eyes wide with fear.

"It's Luca," she said, her voice barely above a whisper. Everyone froze. "I'm too terrified to answer."

I placed a hand on her shoulder, giving it a reassuring squeeze. "Hey, you've got a kitchen full of adoring fans right here. We're not going anywhere. Just try to get as much info out of him as you can."

She nodded, taking a deep breath. With a shaky hand, she put the phone on speaker and cautiously answered. "Hello, Uncle Luca."

"Hello, Anastasia," Luca said, his cold voice filling the room. "You're a lucky young woman to still be breathing this morning. That was one hell of a scene at the church. My crew spent all night cleaning up, and I can tell you now, our story to cover Father Russo's disappearance is thin at best."

Everyone exchanged uneasy glances. Angel's lip quivered, and I rested my hands on her shoulders, grounding her.

With no more introduction, Luca launched into a blunt rundown. "Your parents are in my basement. They're going to suffer for all their treachery, but I need to keep them alive for now."

Angel flashed a concerned look at Nik, then asked, "What are you going to do with them?"

Luca's tone was icy. "I'll hold Viktor and Valentina so I can learn more about their organization, the Volkvoi Notchi. They're going to be useful to me. I aim to take control of their syndicate, both in the US and Russia, as payback for their betrayal."

We all remained silent as he continued, "There are a lot of foreign crime syndicates trying to take over New York, and I must use these resources wisely. For now, Viktor and Valentina are no longer your worry, Anastasia."

Angel took a deep breath, processing the information. The room was quiet, the tension palpable. I squeezed her shoulders affectionately, letting her know we were all here for her.

Luca's next words were sharp, cutting through the silence. "Your aunt Elena is dead, along with Frankie, Frankie's parents, sisters, groomsmen, and a couple of our Genovese family members. In total, ten dead and several others injured."

Angel gasped, her hand shooting up to cover her mouth. Tears welled up as she spoke, her voice trembling. "It's my fault. Innocent people died because of me. I don't know how I'll live with this."

Luca laughed, a harsh sound that made the rest of us tense up. "Innocent? They were mafia, Anastasia. It's part of the lifestyle. Elena understood the risks very well. Even though I married her ages ago, I came to realize that Elena only cared about Elena. She was trouble. I hadn't trusted her in a long time, which is why I made sure she never found out about your ownership of the club."

I cocked my head. Angel owned part of the club? I had assumed she merely worked there. But I kept my mouth shut, letting the conversation play out.

"I've watched you grow up, and I never understood how Viktor and Valentina could ship you off without caring about what happened to you," Luca said. "Elena's callous treatment toward you over the years pissed me off. I watched how hard you worked and what a good person you became, despite having no one to rely on."

Luca's tone softened slightly. "You will always be a Genovese, Anastasia. You, the club, and the guys from the club are now under the protection of the Genovese family."

He paused, letting his words sink in. Then his voice took on a calculating edge. "I still want to develop an alliance with the Morettis against foreign interlopers, but I'm not sure where I stand with them now. We'll have to see how all this plays out."

Braxton and I frowned at each other. Lucian and Lachlan leaned back in their chairs, crossing their arms, while Nik stared impassively down at the phone. Angel glanced up at me, her eyes full of conflicting emotions. God, how I hated all of this for her.

Nik piped up, "Luca, you're on speaker. How about you tell us why everything went down at the church as it did. Were Frankie and his family representing all the Morettis, or did they go rogue?"

Luca laughed. "Welcome to the family, boy. You saved your sister from an untimely death. I saw your guy rush the original shooter, who ended up taking out Frankie and Father Russo from the sacristy. We found the guy with a broken neck once things calmed down and our cleanup crew got to work."

Everyone in the kitchen was taken aback. Lucian and I exchanged a shocked glance. The reality of how close Angel had come to getting shot hit me hard.

Angel started to freak out, her breaths coming fast and shallow. Lachlan stood up, giving me his seat. I wrapped my arm around Angel, holding her tightly.

Nik, his voice low and dangerous, said, "Most of my guys were placed on the outside, but a couple were inside, hidden and patrolling. One was in the passageway behind the sanctuary, another locked inside the confessional, peeking through the slats. The one in the back must have seen the guy enter the sacristy. The only reason my guy would have taken action is if he saw a gun raised at my sister. His sole purpose was to protect Ana. So, tell me, who the fuck would have done that? And how the hell do you expect me to believe you knew nothing about it?"

Braxton, noticing Nik's agitation, rested a hand on his shoulder to keep him from straining his wounded leg. Luca's tone turned colder. "Don't push my generosity too far, Nikolai. The only reason you're protected by the Genovese family is because you're Anastasia's brother and because I've always liked her. We haven't identified the original shooter yet though, so I can't tell you if he was sent by Viktor, Frankie or one of the Morettis. Regardless, we know someone wanted to kill Anastasia." Luca's voice carried a warning.

"After your guy caused the shooter to kill Frankie and Father Russo, all hell broke loose. The Morettis' men shot at Elena and me, which then caused my men to take them out. We had planned our positions within the church just in case something like that happened."

He paused before adding, "Even though it had only been a couple of days since Anastasia warned me about Viktor's plot, I got word that others suspected the same. The Morettis may have found out that Anastasia was not only Russian but Viktor Volkov's daughter. The Morettis hate the Russians. A source told me the marriage contract between Frankie and Anastasia was the idea of Frankie's immediate family. I suspect they wanted to take over the Moretti organization, kill the leaders, and install Frankie as the boss. Frankie's position as CFO meant he had all the secret financial details about every member of the Moretti family and their fortunes. I already knew that Frankie was greedy, but I just found out that he'd been using his knowledge to manipulate some of the people in the organization to feed his gambling habit."

The kitchen fell silent. Angel's hand trembled in mine, but she stiffened her back, bracing herself against Luca's words. I tightened my hold on her, silently vowing to protect her from whatever came next.

Luca's voice crackled through the speaker. "Frankie was likely turned by Viktor, lured into betraying his own family. Elena herself might have found Frankie and thought he would be an easy patsy for Viktor. Perhaps I didn't know my wife as well as i thought. She might have had higher ambitions all along. Maybe it happened after she had miscarriage after miscarriage and we grew apart. I don't know."

Nik whistled, shaking his head. "Well, damn. I had doubts about Frankie's loyalties but didn't have any proof. When you agreed to the marriage contract for Ana, I assumed you'd vetted Frankie and were on board with the plan. I guess we all make mistakes."

"You'd better watch your smart mouth, Nikolai," Luca spat, his anger flaring. "I'd be glad to put you in the ground alongside your aunt."

Angel jumped in. "Luca, Nik, didn't mean any disrespect. He's in pain from the gunshot wound and is just being protective of me."

Nik scowled. "Apologies, Luca. Ana is all that matters to me. What's your plan for Viktor, Valentina, and the Volkovi Notchi?"

"They're no longer your concern." Luca's voice was icy cold.

Nik pressed on. "As long as they're a danger to Anastasia, they are my concern."

Luca chuckled. "I have to give it to you, boy. You don't frighten easily, and your loyalty to your sister is commendable. Bottom line, you both need to get out of town and stay far away for a while. As long as I control Viktor and Valentina, and you don't try to take over the reins of the Volkovi Notchi, there shouldn't be any trouble for you and your sister. If your people see that you're loyal to me, and Viktor does what I tell him, then an alliance can be worked out, even if it's at gunpoint. If I kill Viktor, there will be a power vacuum you'd have to be strong enough to fill. But from what I've learned about you, you're not interested in your father's syndicate. You don't have the stomach for human trafficking and some of his other proclivities. Not that I do either, but I can control that sort of thing in my region. It's one reason our family wants to rid the city of all the outside scum."

Nik sighed in relief. "That's good to hear, and you're right. I don't want any part of my father's business."

"Then we have a gentleman's agreement," Luca said. "I'll make sure my brother Antonio knows you'll be a loyal soldier as long as Anastasia is safe. As for the Morettis, I can't speak for them. Right now, they have to be pretty sore about someone taking out Frankie and causing the death of an entire family within their organization. You know how this game works. I can take one of my own out at any time, but if someone else causes harm to any of my family, then there will be consequences."

The room was heavy with the implications of Luca's words. Nik and Luca continued their exchange, but my mind was already spinning, strategizing the next steps we needed to take to ensure Angel's safety.

Finally, Luca let out a heavy breath. "You two need to lie low for a while until I see how this is all going to shake out."

"I understand fully," Nik said. "You leave me alone and I leave you alone. And by lying low, how low do you mean?"

"Stay out of the Northeast and, of course, Russia," Luca said, as if it should be obvious.

Angel, who'd been quietly listening, jumped up and shouted, "But what about the club? I own a big chunk of it, and I'm the business manager. I can't just walk away. I don't *want* to walk away."

Luca's voice hardened. "It's your risk to take. I can put a security detail on you, but you'll be putting yourself in danger."

Nik shot back, "Don't worry, she'll leave town. I'll see to it."

Angel bristled. "Don't you dare speak for me. I'm a grown-ass woman, and I will make this decision for myself."

Nik glared at her. "Ana, sit down."

I couldn't hold back any longer. "Buddy, you'd better back the fuck up. Angel will make up her own damn mind. You're not her keeper."

Nik stood up, knocking his chair over. "It's not your place to speak."

Baring my teeth, I shoved my chair out of the way, drawing back a fist. Angel grabbed my bicep, digging her fingers in. Braxton placed a hand on Nik's shoulder.

Nik sneered. "You're just a nurse from Tacoma. You're in way over your head."

I stepped closer and stared him down. "I'm not afraid to take on any challenge. If I hadn't just spent hours repairing your gunshot wound, I'd beat your ass right now." With that, I reached across the table, grabbed Nik by the throat, and growled, "I don't give a fuck if you're mafia or Jesus Christ himself. You'd best not disrespect me or mine."

Nik slapped away my hand, giving me a menacing glare. "She's not yours to protect."

Angel shouted, "Both of you, enough! Stop this idiocy."

Luca chuckled. "Anastasia, maybe you'll rise to be a mafia boss one day. There's something about you that inspires unquestioned loyalty. It's a rare trait, but necessary if you're going to live long in this family. But you need to learn how to put them on a short leash. Just so you know, your tattooed mountain man is lucky to be alive after the stunt he pulled yesterday. He jumped in front of me when I first arrived at the church for the wedding. He had some balls, demanding to speak to me, and he didn't even back down when my guys pulled guns on him. He's lucky he didn't take a swim in the harbor."

Angel's eyes widened. "What?"

Luca chuckled again. "Yeah, just before you arrived, he got in my face about you marrying Frankie and how Viktor was out to take over our operations. He told me to let him take you away and disappear, as if that was a possibility. I told him I was taking care of the matter and to back the fuck off. He wasn't happy about it, but he had no choice. I'll admit, I respected the fact that he had the mettle to stand and face me. Like I said, that's a type of loyalty you can't buy."

Angel whipped her head around to me, her eyes filled with disbelief. "Thank you, Uncle Luca, for calling me. I'll consider your words and determine my path forward. I want to discuss this with you further another day. Thank you for having my back. You're the closest man to a father I've ever had. Now, if you'll excuse me, I need to manage these boys."

Luca's laugh boomed through the speaker. "She's the only one with any common sense," he said just before the call disconnected.

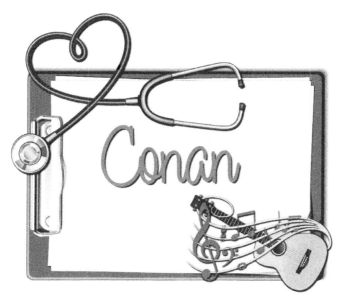

Chapter Forty-Three

6/30

A ngel paced the length of the kitchen, chewing on her thumbnail. Every time one of us tried to speak, she cut us off with a raised hand and a scowl. Nik sat back down, and I joined him and the others at the table.

Finally Angel stopped. "I'm going home. Alone. I don't want to hear any of your opinions. I don't care if you, your security firm, and a hundred of Luca's men follow me around and stand outside my house. I need to be alone. And I mean totally alone."

She glanced back and forth from Nik to me, shaking her head in frustration. "I love every single person in this room, but I'm not going to be told what to do like a child anymore. I've lived twenty-seven years as an obedient daughter of the mafia. I was never given a chance to live life on my own terms, and that stops today."

With a few quick strides, she stepped up to the table and leaned in toward her brother. "Nik, you've always treated me like the twelve-year-old lost and afraid little girl that was dumped at that boarding school so many years ago. Well, I have news for you. I'm an intelligent, hardworking, capable woman. And it's high time I start acting like it. I can't do that if you're always there to take care of everything for me."

Crossing her arms, she moved her attention to Lucian, who was leaning against the counter. "Lucian, don't you think for a minute that what happened between us was just a fun roll in the hay. I know you care about me and that it was your idea to let me buy into the club. From day one, you made it clear to the other guys that I was your responsibility, yours to protect. Your past, my situation, and the timing of things may not have allowed us to think of possibilities beyond a physical relationship, but you've always had my back and made sure I had what I needed, made sure I was safe. But I'm not that naïve little wallflower you interviewed and hired. I'm your business partner who needs to pull her own weight or get the hell out."

Relaxing her arms, Angel pulled a chair out from the table and sat down beside me, taking a minute to gather her thoughts. Then she turned in her chair to face me, rested an elbow on the edge of the table, and leaned in. We all waited silently for her to speak again.

"And as far as you go, Conan," she said, "you treat me like I'm some kind of perfect. You always think that *I* know what's best for me. Like *I* have all the answers. You treat me as if I'm worth something more than I am."

She leaned forward, gripping my thighs with her hands, getting up close to my face. "You've been better to me than I deserved. You put me on a fucking pedestal, for Christ's sake. No one can live up to some goddamn ideal—especially not me. I wish

I could be that girl for you, but I don't even know who I am."

Her eyes blinked rapidly, a hundred different emotions playing out in them. Heaving a deep sigh, she stood up, walked away from the table, and turned back to us while we all sat in stunned silence. "And as for the rest of you, you get my point. I need to figure out who the fuck I am before I can be the person any of you deserve."

Wrapping her arms around herself, she demanded, "I need to go home."

The kitchen was quiet. No one said anything, but we all nodded.

After a moment, I glared at Nik and told him, "I'll drive Angel home. Make arrangements with the guys from your security firm to watch over her." I hated the thought of letting Angel out of my sight, but she had to choose to want me in her life or at least feel like it was her choice. "Nik, you'll need to stay put for a few days to heal. This house has everything Braxton and I need to care for your wound, so I'll be back."

I turned to the group. "This is a good opportunity for us all to get to know one another." I glanced at Angel. "She's smart and knows what she needs. Right now, she doesn't need us telling her what to do. Looks like the men in her life will have to get on the same page and let our little mafia princess ascend to queen."

Angel rolled her eyes, and I growled, breaking the tension and making her chuckle. Then she turned and marched out of the kitchen, saying, "Good. Glad that's decided. I'm going to pack my things. I'm ready to blow this popsicle stand."

After she left the room, I lowered my voice. "Listen up, guys. Angel is smarter and tougher than any of us give her credit for. We need to fall in line, or we risk losing her forever."

The guys hemmed and hawed, trying to argue but unable

to find any valid reasons why we should stop her from going off alone. They finally nodded in agreement.

"All right," I said, "might as well finish eating and clean up." We all finished off what was left, sitting back and enjoying some freshly brewed coffee.

The tension in the room eased, and we began chatting. Nik focused his attention on Lucian and Lachlan. "You guys and the others from the club should be safe to resume your normal lives. But don't talk about anything that happened or even mention knowing any Genovese, Moretti, or Volkov. Luca will keep you under his wing because of Ana, but don't push your luck."

Lucian nodded. "Got it."

"Regardless of what Ana thinks or wants, she can't stay in the area," Nik continued. "The Morettis are more muscle than brains. For her whole life, she's been sheltered from the realities of mafia politics and violence, so she doesn't understand how much danger she's truly in. You should make arrangements for the club to be without her indefinitely."

Lucian sighed. "I know you're right, Nik, but I really hate it. Still, I understand the circumstances. Whenever the time is right, Ana's always welcome back at the club." He eyed Nik curiously. "So, where are you going to go? Seems to me you're in more danger than Ana is. You probably can't return to Russia unless the Volkovi Notchi accepts Luca as their new leader."

Nik shrugged. "I've been working on a plan to get out from under my father for a long time. That's why I've spent every waking hour over the last decade building a consortium of businesses all over the world. Some are legitimate, like DarkMatter, but others...let's just say, are not out in the daylight. I've got a place in Kyiv where I often work."

Braxton, intrigued, piped up, "I've never been out of the country."

434

Nik raised an eyebrow. "You're more sheltered than my sister. How's that possible?"

Everyone laughed, and Nik grinned.

"Tell you what, Braxton," he said. "Get yourself a passport, and I'll take you to Kyiv as repayment for your 'free medical care.'"

Braxton leaned back and smiled but didn't respond. He was always the quiet, cautious one of us brothers. Being the middle child, he'd always played referee between Atticus and me. He was a good guy who never took risks or challenged the status quo. But surely he wasn't considering the possibility of going off with a guy like Nik. I'd have to approach him about it later. Now wasn't the time.

Soon after, Angel returned to the kitchen, ready to leave.

I drove her home in the SUV, cranking up the radio and singing along to every song that played. I wanted to give her some space, so I avoided any conversations that might press her too much. When we arrived, I walked her to the front door of her building. As she opened it, I stayed outside, respecting her boundaries and need for solitude.

"Taking some time to think is a smart move," I reassured her. "If you need anything, I'm just a phone call away. Braxton and I are going to stay long enough to make sure Nik's wound is safe for him to take care of on his own."

She gave me a small smile. "Make sure to tell Atticus and Samantha I'm sorry for all the trouble my family has caused and that I'll pay them back for everything."

"Sam and Atticus don't hold grudges. They understand you were caught up in all this mafia mess," I replied.

With a sad sigh, she said, "I hope they forgive me."

"They already have. It's the type of people they are. I called them while I was out this morning and told them everything.

They were happy to hear that Viktor had been taken care of and that no one will bother them again."

Saying no more, I took her face in my hands, my thumbs brushing the delicate skin of her cheeks, and kissed her with a desperation that came from knowing this might be our last. Her lips were warm and soft, melding with mine in a way that made the world around us vanish.

For a fleeting moment, it was just us, lost in the depths of each other. She wrapped her hand around the back of my neck, pulling me closer, her heart hammering against my chest in a rhythm that matched my own. The kiss was evocative—a blend of love, pain, and longing—making it almost impossible to pull away. But as much as I didn't want it to end, I knew it had to.

I bit her lower lip gently, dragging my teeth slowly across the flesh, ruing the bittersweet taste of our parting. It tore at me, leaving a hollow ache as we reluctantly pulled apart. Our breaths mingled for a final second. I didn't know if we would ever find our way back to each other.

I rested my forehead against hers, catching my breath before letting her go. Angel dropped her head and haltingly stepped inside, closing the door behind her. The ache in my chest was sharp, but leaving her alone was the right call, even though it hurt.

As I walked away, I pulled out my phone and called Nik. "You got eyes on Angel's place?"

"Yeah, we're all set," he replied.

I stopped short and glanced around, knowing there was an army of men out there blending into the shadows and keeping watch over her.

Loneliness hit me hard. Fuck, did I want to turn around and force my way in—make her understand all the reasons we should be together. Instead, I got back into the SUV and drove away, comforted by the thought that she was in safe hands for now.

Chapter Forty-Four

7/4

The days after the wedding dragged on like a slow-moving storm. Staying mainly at home, I spent hour after hour mulling over everything that had happened. Working at Club Xyst in the evenings was impossible due to the army of bodyguards that followed me everywhere. When I attempted to go in and work, their presence made the club's atmosphere tense and uncomfortable, driving away the elite patrons who required a certain degree of anonymity. Even mundane tasks like grocery shopping became missions. So I chose to remain home instead of dealing with all of that, leaving me with too much time to sit and think.

Today, I found myself on the sofa, arm draped over the back, staring out the window of my Chelsea brownstone. I watched neighbors come and go, their lives unfolding in a peaceful rhythm that contrasted sharply with my own chaotic existence. A couple of young boys had just scootered by, tossing firecrackers out as they went. My TV hummed softly in the background, but my focus stayed on the world outside my window.

A large bouquet of fragrant summer flowers—stargazer lilies, roses, and peonies—sat on the table between the kitchen and the living room, their scent a gentle reminder of Conan's thoughtful nature.

Lost in my feels, I became aware of the fact that nearly dying had turned out to be the best thing that ever happened to me. Waking up as a blank slate without a past and with only a future to consider had given me a newfound hope for tomorrow. There were no worries, no obligations, no insecurities—just endless possibilities. Sure, it had been terrifying to have no clue who I was or where I came from, but I was also the luckiest girl alive. Fate had landed me in the care of a man who wanted to be with me for who I truly was—not because of my family, not for what I could give him, not out of obligation—because I was just *me*. The wreck had been a once-in-a-lifetime reset button, a chance to explore what life had to offer.

I'd spent the last few days going through my options. On every path forward, I saw myself with Conan. I'd never met a man who was as big and badass as they come yet so willing to give me his heart, a heart he'd always protected from the pain that had cut him so deeply as a boy. He'd carefully made his way through life, enjoying all it had to offer...except true love. He'd had plenty of women willing to give him his every desire, but he'd rejected them. Then I'd fallen into his life, and unexplainably, he'd handed me his heart. No strings, no pressure, no questions asked—mine for the taking.

But was I the best for him? Could I possibly give him the love he deserved? I came with lots of baggage and had no idea how to be a warm, nurturing life partner. Every relationship I'd known had been transactional—well, except for Nik. Nik was the only person who'd ever cared about me. His was the only semblance of love I'd ever experienced, and our relationship was a far cry from normal. Because he was my twin, we were tied together in a unique way, and his protective affection meant the world to me, but it wasn't the same as having someone choose to be with you.

No one got to pick their parents or the family they were born into, but we did have the power to choose who we loved. Entrusting someone with your heart was a terrifying proposition. I wasn't sure I could do it now...or ever.

Earlier, I'd promised Lucian I'd go down to the club before it opened today to meet with him and the guys about the midyear financials. Although I was restless and lonely, I didn't plan to stay long. The bodyguards were making everyone uncomfortable, driving away our exclusive clientele. I knew I should tell the guys I needed to take a break from the club, but the thought of walking away was devastating. Club Xyst had been my refuge for years. There, I was confident, powerful, and even adored. But it had become an unbearable situation. The guys would never ask me to stay away, but it was probably for the best if I did.

I arrived at the club a little before 8:00 p.m., and the line outside was already long. People were eager to participate in our special Fourth of July festivities. Slade stood at his post, towering and vigilant.

"Hey, Slade," I said, nearing the entrance.

He grinned. "Good to see you tonight, Ana. The last few days have been better with you around."

"Thanks, Slade. But tonight might be my last. I can't deal with the army of men that follows me everywhere. It's making everyone nervous and hurting the club. Our best patrons don't want attention drawn to their, let's say, extracurricular activities."

Slade nodded. "Don't worry about the club. People will get over it soon. And no matter what you decide, you know I'll always be here for you."

On the first night I'd attempted to come back to work, I had told Slade everything that happened—from leaving New York for Tacoma to the chaos of my fake wedding. He had always been a good listener, understanding and supportive, and I'd owed him that much. We'd always been close, and I wanted to make sure he heard everything straight from me. His support meant the world to me, but I didn't want to do anything that might hurt the club.

Slade glanced at the four bodyguards hovering nearby. "Yeah, I get it. It does look like the place is surrounded by FBI agents or something."

I laughed. "Exactly. It might be good for me and the club if I took some time away. Maybe I should think of it as a long-overdue vacation. I'd love to go somewhere tropical with piña coladas."

Slade chuckled and gave me a side-hug as he escorted me inside. "That sounds nice. Remember, there will always be a place for you here. Besides, you own a chunk of it. What can the guys say? It's not like they can fire you."

I hugged him tightly. "Thanks, Slade. You're the best."

While I moved toward the main floor of the bar, the familiar ambiance of Club Xyst enveloped me. This was my world. But as I glanced around, I realized it was time to make some tough decisions.

The bar was quiet, the kind of quiet that always settled in just before the bustle of the night's chaos unfolded. I walked to the end of the bar, inhaling the familiar scent of polished wood and the faint musk of spilled drinks. Out of habit, my hand reached for the receipts box beneath the counter, but before I could grab it, a throat cleared over the loudspeakers.

I turned toward the stage, my heart skipping a beat. There, in the center, sat Conan, alone on a stool with a guitar in his hands and a mic in front of him. His grin was as big as ever. He began strumming a soft ballad, and the air seemed to hum with magic. Goose bumps spread over my arms.

I was drawn to him like a magnet, my feet carrying me closer to the stage, my eyes never leaving his. The first notes hummed through the speakers, and Conan's voice filled the room, smooth and tender.

Will you live your life with me?
Wherever that may be?
Let me take you away from here,
To a place where love is free.

The melody wrapped around me, pulling me in, and as he sang, he kept his eyes locked onto mine. His lyrics painted a picture of a new life. It was a plea for me to come away with him. Every word sank deep into my soul, resonating with possibilities I hadn't dared to dream. I was mesmerized. The rest of the world faded away until it was just the two of us and the music.

I found myself walking around to the side of the stage, moving as if in a daze, climbing the stairs one by one and making my way toward Conan, the song guiding my every step until I was standing right in front of him. His gaze was filled with a depth of emotion that left me breathless.

The song ended, but he continued to play softly.

"I love you, my Angel," he said, his voice reverberating around the massive, empty space of the bar. The power of those words hit me with a force that made my knees buckle. I fell to the floor between his legs, my hand clutching his knee for support. Tears streamed down my face, words failing me as I was overcome.

Conan gently set the guitar on the floor and pulled me onto his lap, wrapping his strong arms around me. I buried my face in his neck. The warmth of his skin and the steady rhythm of his heartbeat grounded me in the moment.

"I love you so much," he whispered into my ear, his breath skittering across my skin. "It's time for us to start our new life together, anywhere you want. If you'll have me."

My words came tumbling out. "I love you too. With all that I have and all that I am."

I held onto him tightly, knowing that wherever we went, as long as we were together, it would be home. In that moment, nothing else mattered. It was just us, in our bubble of love and promise, ready to face whatever came next together.

After catching my breath, I pulled away and gazed up at him. He took my face in his big ole gentle hands, wiping my tears away with his thumbs. His touch anchored me, giving me the courage to say what had been bottled up inside.

With a shaky breath, I confessed, "I'm sorry it took me this long to swallow my pride and admit my feelings... You've been better to me than I ever deserved," I choked out. "I can't live if it means living without you. My life only makes sense when I'm with you." My voice trembled. "I want you with every fiber of my being, and to call you mine forever."

Conan's eyes softened, and I continued, "From the moment fate brought me into your emergency department, you became the best example of what a man should be. Honest, even when I couldn't be truthful about my past. Kind, when no one else was. Giving, to a complete stranger without hesitation. Funny, when things were at their worst. You protected my heart, my soul, and my body. You understood me even when I didn't understand myself."

Tears streamed down my face again as my breath hitched. "I've never experienced someone loving me just for who I am. I didn't even consider it an option. But you showed me it was possible. I'll go to the ends of the earth to be with you. I promise, Conan, I will be the woman you deserve. I will be worthy of your love."

Conan's eyes glistened as he leaned in to kiss me tenderly.

The kiss deepened, filled with all the promises we'd made to each other. As the kiss grew more passionate, a loud round of applause erupted around us. Startled, we broke apart and realized the bar was crowded with people. They clapped and cheered, and I couldn't help but laugh through my tears. Conan tightened his arms around me, a smile spreading across his face.

Heat surged to my cheeks. I was sweetly embarrassed by the applause. Conan scooped me up and carried me off the stage. As we moved through the crowd, he kissed me gently and whispered how much he loved me and how he would protect me forever. He took me up the staircase to the elevator, his lips never far from mine.

When we entered the office, Lucian, Lachlan, Julian, and Gabriel were there, clapping their hands. "Did everything we said on stage get played over the speaker system?" I asked, half-laughing.

"Absolutely," Lucian said with a teasing grin. "Loud and clear. And it was recorded on the multiple video cameras around the main floor too. I'll make sure to save you a copy."

Conan set me down, and Lucian pulled me into a big hug. "I'm so happy for you, Ana," he said with genuine affection.

"You're not mad at me for ruining our...arrangement?" I asked, worried about the impact it might have on our friendship and the club.

"Hell no," he said, shaking his head and laughing. "I always knew I wasn't the man you would spend a lifetime with. Go take some time to be a real person, not just some mafia princess. We'll hold down the fort here at Club Xyst. And besides, we can always video chat."

I kissed him on the cheek, grateful for his understanding. "You're the best, Lucian," I said, stepping back.

He extended his hand to Conan, who grasped it firmly. Then he wrapped an arm around Conan's back and tugged him into a tight embrace. He gave Conan a couple of strong pats on the back. "I couldn't be happier for both of you," he said. "Ana, you couldn't have found a better man."

Conan grinned. "Thank you, man."

Lachlan walked over to the office bar and reached underneath it, hauling out a small wooden box. Inside was a bottle of whiskey. "I've been waiting for just the right special occasion to crack open this bottle of J.J. Corry's The Chosen whiskey for years," he announced dramatically. He opened the bottle, savoring its fragrance for a moment before pouring everyone a shot.

"Before we drink, here's an old Irish toast," Lachlan said, raising his glass. "May love and laughter light your days and warm your heart and home. May good and faithful friends be yours wherever you may roam. May peace and plenty bless your world with joy that long endures. May all life's passing seasons bring the best to you and yours."

We all threw back our shots, the rich, smoky flavor of the whiskey warming us from the inside. I walked over to Lachlan and kissed him on the cheek. "I'm lucky to have so many good men—no, brothers—in my life," I said.

Just then, Braxton and Nik walked into the office. "What's the celebration?" Braxton asked, looking around. "What did we miss?"

Everyone laughed, and Lucian couldn't resist teasing. "I'll show you the video later, but let's just say the happy couple professed their love for each other in front of at least a hundred people."

"Lucian, hush," I said, rolling my eyes.

Braxton turned to me. "So does that mean you're coming back to Tacoma, Angel, or is Conan moving to the Big Apple?"

"No decisions have been made yet," I said, glancing at Conan with a smile. "It doesn't matter as long as we're together. But I could really use a break from the army that watches my every move."

Nik chuckled. "Since Angel owns the estate in Tacoma, it would only be fitting for a Thorin brother to move in. I'm sure that bit of news would piss the hell outta my father. Luca would take sport in rubbing Viktor's nose in it as he rots in his basement."

The room filled with laughter.

I looked around at my friends—my family—and felt a warmth that had nothing to do with the whiskey. For the first time in a long while, I saw a future filled with hope.

Conan stared at me, his eyes wide with shock. "You own the big Volkov estate too? Damn, every time I turn around, I find out you own another piece of luxury real estate. First the club, and now one of the largest estates in Tacoma? Did I find the right girl or what?" he teased, shaking his head.

I laughed, trying to explain. "I don't own the estate or any of Viktor's assets. I'm just the beneficiary of a trust he used to hide his American assets."

Nik smirked. "Oh, how wrong you are, dear sister. I helped draw up that agreement. It should be easy enough to take Harrison Tate to court and have him removed as the trustee. You could be installed in his place, giving you full control over all the American assets."

I frowned, skeptical about the possibility. "Tate would fight it and probably win. He's a crooked mafia attorney after all."

Nik waved a dismissive hand. "Ye of little faith. Trustees can be replaced for breach of fiduciary duty, incompetence, or conflict of interest. All of which apply in spades here. The fact that he works for our father is a clear conflict of interest in and of itself. Plus, the facts surrounding all of Viktor's illegal dealings and the warrants out for his arrest will easily provide evidence that it's in the best interest of the beneficiary and the trust assets for the shady attorney to be removed. Washington State law allows for trustees to be removed for these reasons, and there's a provision in the trust for it."

Nik's confidence was contagious, and I was starting to see a glimmer of hope. "You really think it's that simple?"

He nodded. "I'll take care of it. You and Conan could use the change of scenery in Tacoma."

Conan scrubbed his hand over his chin. "Tacoma is on the other side of the country, about as far away from Genovese and Moretti territory as we can get. Besides, you already have a bunch of friends there—Samantha, Bethany, Atticus, Braxton, and, of course, me."

The thought of starting fresh in Tacoma sounded more appealing by the second. Expectantly, I searched Conan's face, and his reassuring smile gave me the courage I needed.

"All right, let's do it," I said.

Nik clapped his hands together. "Perfect. I'll get started on the legal stuff right away."

Conan pulled me close, whispering in my ear, "We've got this, Angel. New beginnings, remember that."

I nodded, resting my head against his chest. The future

suddenly didn't seem so daunting. We had a plan, and more importantly, we had each other.

Braxton cleared his throat, looking like he had something important to say. "Conan, I might not be returning to Tacoma with you guys just yet."

We all turned to him. Nik leaned back, folding his arms, while Lucian tilted his head, waiting for an explanation.

Braxton glanced at Nik and then back at Conan and me. "Nik has invited me to work for him, and I want to have the chance to travel the world."

Conan's brows drew together, and his jaw tightened. "Are you sure about that, Brax?" He glared at Nik. "Nik's a Russian mobster in hot water with the Volkovi Notchi until and unless they accept working for Luca. No offense, but you're into a lot of shady, illegal shit all over the fucking world. What business does an EMT have traveling and working with someone like you?"

Braxton held up a hand in frustration. "Conan, back off. I know you mean well, but I want to live my life a little. I've always done the right thing, had the right job, and been there for everyone in need. It's time I take a chance and live a little."

Nik turned to Conan, a slight furrow forming between his brows. "I promise I'll take care of Braxton and see that nothing bad happens to him."

Sensing Conan's tension, I put my arm around him. "Don't be so overprotective that you smother him," I said softly.

Conan relaxed slightly into my hug, but before he could respond, loud popping sounds echoed through the room. Conan's head snapped up. "What the fuck? Is someone shooting downstairs?"

We all froze for a moment, and then Lucian burst into laughter. "Nah, it's the fireworks on the Hudson River. They're shooting them off from the barges in the middle of the river again this year."

Gabriel's eyes lit up. "Oh shit, that's fabulous. With all the big news tonight, I had forgotten about the fireworks display. Hurry, let's run up to the roof and watch."

Lachlan grabbed some keys from the desk drawer and sprinted to a door next to the elevator, all of us following. He unlocked the door to the roof and shouted for Aria to join us.

We all ran up the stairs—well, except for Nik, who limped up—and exited out onto the rooftop.

The top of our building was the perfect spot to watch the fireworks. We walked over to the edge, the warm night air enveloping us. The sky was clear, and the incredible display of fireworks lit up the night against the backdrop of the bright stars above. Bursts of color and light reflected off the Hudson River. The scent of gunpowder wafted through the air, mixing with the slight breeze from the river as the synchronized music playing from the speakers around the area added to the magic of the moment.

Conan wrapped his arms around me, pulling me close. We stood mesmerized by the stunning show. "Angel," he whispered, his breath tickling my ear. "As long as we're together, I don't care where we live. If you let me love you, my life will be complete."

He kissed me sweetly on the temple, rocking me in time to the music. I turned in his arms, looking up at him and clasping my hands behind his neck. "I love you, Conan. Living in Tacoma sounds like the fresh start I need. If you're willing to take me there, I'm ready for our new life together."

He smiled, his eyes reflecting the colorful bursts of light above us. "This is the perfect ending to the perfect night," he murmured before capturing my lips in a passionate kiss.

The fireworks flashed and boomed around us, but we weren't paying them any attention anymore. Our bodies were pressed together, the heat between us growing with every passing second. Conan's hands roamed my back, pulling me even closer as our kiss deepened.

Every touch, every caress, sent electric sparks through my body. He threaded his fingers through my hair, tilting my head to deepen the kiss even more. My hands clung to his shoulders, his muscles tensing under my touch. The taste of him was intoxicating, leaving me breathless.

When we finally pulled apart, our breaths were ragged and our hearts pounded in sync. Conan's eyes were dark with desire as he studied my face, his thumb gently brushing my swollen lips. "I can't wait to get you home, my Angel." His voice was a husky whisper filled with promise. "I want to show you how much I love you, hear you screaming my name over and over."

His words sent a thrill through me, and my body reacted immediately. Heat pooled in my core, my hunger for him growing stronger. "Take me home, Conan," I whispered back, my voice trembling with need.

He kissed me again, this time with a fierce urgency that made my knees weak. Roughly, he gripped my hips, pressing me against him, making it clear just how much he wanted me. The fireworks continued to explode above us, but the real show was the passion igniting between us.

After Conan placed one last kiss on my lips, his powerful hand enveloped mine with a protective strength, and he led me away. The electric current between us crackled, driving our steps faster in anticipation of what was to come. As we walked through the night, the future stretched out before us. This was the beginning of our forever.

If you're curious to find out about the other
Thorin brothers as they battle their own inner demons,
look for them in their respective books,
"Night Shift" and "Swing Shift," as the
"Broken Heroes" stand-alone series continues.

Enjoy the read?

Take a couple of minutes to leave a review!

Reviews are everything to an Indie Author, and we would
greatly appreciate it if you would take the time to leave one or
click on the star rating. All you need to do is leave a few words.

Thank you!

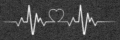

Books in the Broken Heroes stand-alone series:

Night Shift

Day Shift

Swing Shift (Coming in 2024)

Acknowledgments

I'm filled with immense gratitude. Writing "Day Shift" has been a journey of the heart and soul, and none of it would mean as much without you, the readers. Your decision to pick up this book, to spend your precious time within its pages, is a gift I do not take lightly. In a world teeming with countless stories and distractions, your choice to immerse yourself in this one is incredibly humbling. Your enthusiasm and support, whether through thoughtful reviews, kind messages, or simply enjoying the story, fuel my passion and drive me to continue crafting these tales. It's your connection to these characters and their journeys that turn my solitary hours of writing into something worthwhile.

Every time you dive into a chapter, feel for a character, or get lost in the plot, you breathe life into this work. Your investment in these fictional lives makes all the late nights, rewrites, and moments of doubt worth it. Knowing that these words resonate with you, that they find a place in your heart, is the greatest reward an author could ask for.

Thank you for being part of this journey, for believing in the story, and for allowing "Day Shift" to be a part of your world. Your presence is felt in every line, and I am endlessly grateful for each and every one of you.

Emily Cargile, your contribution to "Day Shift" was invaluable. Your careful attention to detail, your willingness to be flexible, and your deep knowledge have been vital in bringing this manuscript to its full potential. The dedication and professionalism you've demonstrated, especially under tight deadlines, have far exceeded my expectations. Your edits didn't just enhance my work; they transformed it, ensuring that every sentence was imbued with

Acknowledgments

clarity and purpose. For your tireless efforts, insightful feedback, and the countless late nights spent perfecting this manuscript, I am profoundly grateful. Thank you, Emily, for being more than just an editor. Your impact on this book is indelible, and for that, I cannot thank you enough.

Jourdan Gandy, from the very beginning, your support and guidance for my author career has made a real difference. Your wealth of knowledge, coupled with your willingness to share it, has been priceless. You've guided me through every aspect of my career, from reaching out on Instagram to find readers who will cherish my books, to selecting the perfect cover model, to planning strategies for connecting with readers at conventions, through newsletters, and via my Street Team. Your clear, actionable advice has shaped my approach at every step, and your professionalism and insight have far exceeded my expectations. You've always approached my concerns with kindness and a level head, offering solutions that are both practical and effective. Your commitment, patience, and genuine enthusiasm for my work have been a constant source of encouragement. I'm so grateful for your unwavering support and belief in me from day one. Thank you, Jourdan, for being an integral part of this adventure and for helping me navigate this path with such grace and wisdom.

Vanessa Medina, your creativity and graphic arts skills have been instrumental in helping me communicate effectively with my readers and build meaningful connections. As a PA, your contributions go far beyond mere assistance; you bring a vibrant energy and exceptional talent to everything you do. Your sense of humor and endless patience as we brainstorm posts, reels, and captions for social media have made the process not only

Acknowledgments

productive but also incredibly enjoyable. Your calm and positive demeanor creates a wonderful working environment, and your ability to make "Day Shift" shine through engaging and cohesive content has had a tremendous impact on its success. Thank you, Vanessa, for your unwavering support, your innovative ideas, and for making this journey so much fun. You are truly a joy to work with, and I am deeply grateful for all that you do.

Katie, I'm forever grateful for your contribution to "Day Shift." Your thorough review of the book's details surrounding New York City brought an authenticity that only a longtime resident could provide. Your keen insights and willingness to help me set the scene and the world for my characters made the story come alive with realism and vibrancy. Your knowledge not only made the narrative more believable but also offered me a deeper understanding of the city's unique essence. Thank you for your dedication and for sharing your expertise so generously.

Craig Richards, co-authoring "Night Shift" with you was an unforgettable experience. Your creativity, humor, and charisma brought so much life to the first book in the Broken Heroes series, and I am deeply grateful for your contributions. While life's circumstances have taken you in a different direction and you weren't able to join me for "Day Shift," your influence and our collaborative work on "Night Shift" have paved the way for this book. I wish you all the best in your new ventures and continued success with your podcasts and other creative projects.

About Evie

Evie James is a music industry business manager turned proud romance writer. When she's not busy crafting her saucy plots, she's most likely got a camera or brush in her hand. She enjoys living vicariously through the adventures of her husband and daughter, who are international airline pilots, traveling the world and bringing back stories from their journeys.

Evie lives with her family, four dogs, and a cantankerous old cat in Nashville, TN.

Where to Find Me

Website: eviejames.com

Instagram: @evie.james.author

Facebook: @evie.james.author

TikTok: @evie_james_author

Made in the USA
Las Vegas, NV
27 July 2024

93002354R00256